The Prime Minister
Volume II

by

Anthony Trollope

Double 9
BOOKS

The prime minister
Volume II
by Anthony Trollope

ISBN: 978-93-64286-02-2

Published by

DOUBLE 9 BOOKS

2/13-B, Ansari Road
Daryaganj, New Delhi – 110002
info@double9books.com
www.double9books.com
Tel. 011-40042856

ABOUT THE AUTHOR

Anthony Trollope (1815-1882) was a renowned English novelist of the Victorian era, best known for his insightful and richly detailed portrayals of 19th-century English society. His prolific writing career produced a vast array of novels, many of which have become classics of English literature. First Novels: Trollope's debut novel, "The Macdermots of Ballycloran", was published in 1847. However, it was not until the publication of "The Warden" in 1855 that he gained significant recognition. Trollope's writing is known for its realism, detailed character development, and exploration of social issues. His characters are often complex and multifaceted, reflecting the diverse nature of human experiences. He employed a straightforward narrative style, often interjecting his own commentary and opinions, which adds a distinctive voice to his works. Trollope's works remain significant in the study of Victorian literature. His keen observations of society, human relationships, and institutional behaviors continue to be appreciated for their depth and insight. Many of his novels have been adapted for television, radio, and stage, keeping his stories and characters alive for new generations. Anthony Trollope's contribution to literature is marked by his ability to combine detailed social critique with engaging storytelling, making him one of the enduring figures of English literature.

CONTENTS

Chapter XLI
The Value of a Thick Skin

Sir Orlando Drought must have felt bitterly the quiescence with which he sank into obscurity on the second bench on the opposite side of the House. One great occasion he had on which it was his privilege to explain to four or five hundred gentlemen the insuperable reasons which caused him to break away from those right honourable friends to act with whom had been his comfort and his duty, his great joy and his unalloyed satisfaction. Then he occupied the best part of an hour in abusing those friends and all their measures. This no doubt had been a pleasure, as practice had made the manipulation of words easy to him, — and he was able to revel in that absence of responsibility which must be as a fresh perfumed bath to a minister just freed from the trammels of office. But the pleasure was surely followed by much suffering when Mr. Monk, — Mr. Monk who was to assume his place as Leader of the House, — only took five minutes to answer him, saying that he and his colleagues regretted much the loss of the Right Honourable Baronet's services, but that it would hardly be necessary for him to defend the Ministry on all those points on which it had been attacked, as, were he to do so, he would have to repeat the arguments by which every measure brought forward by the present Ministry had been supported. Then Mr. Monk sat down, and the business of the House went on just as if Sir Orlando Drought had not moved his seat at all.

"What makes everybody and everything so dead?" said Sir Orlando to his old friend Mr. Boffin as they walked home together from the House that night. They had in former days been staunch friends, sitting night after night close together, united in opposition, and sometimes, for a few halcyon months, in the happier bonds of office. But when Sir Orlando had joined the Coalition, and when the sterner spirit of Mr. Boffin had preferred principles to place, — to use the language in which he was wont to speak to himself and to his wife and family of his own abnegation, — there had come a coolness between them. Mr. Boffin, who was not a rich man, nor by any means indifferent to the comforts of office, had felt keenly the injury done to him when he was left hopelessly in the cold by the desertion of his old friends. It had come to pass that there had been no salt left in the opposition. Mr. Boffin in all his parliamentary experience had known nothing like it. Mr. Boffin had been sure that British honour was going to the dogs and that British greatness was at an end. But the secession of Sir Orlando gave a little fillip to his life. At any rate he could walk home with his old friend and talk of the horrors of the present day.

"Well, Drought, if you ask me, you know, I can only speak as I feel. Everything must be dead when men holding different opinions on every subject under the sun come together in order that they may carry on a government as they would a trade business. The work may be done, but it must be done without spirit."

"But it may be all important that the work should be done," said the Baronet, apologising for his past misconduct.

"No doubt;—and I am very far from judging those who make the attempt. It has been made more than once before, and has, I think, always failed. I don't believe in it myself, and I think that the death-like torpor of which you speak is one of its worst consequences." After that Mr. Boffin admitted Sir Orlando back into his heart of hearts.

Then the end of the Session came, very quietly and very early. By the end of July there was nothing left to be done, and the world of London was allowed to go down into the country almost a fortnight before its usual time.

With many men, both in and out of Parliament, it became a question whether all this was for good or evil. The Boffinites had of course much to say for themselves. Everything was torpid. There was no interest in the newspapers,—except when Mr. Slide took the tomahawk into his hands. A member of Parliament this Session had not been by half so much bigger than another man as in times of hot political warfare. One of the most moving sources of our national excitement seemed to have vanished from life. We all know what happens to stagnant waters. So said the Boffinites, and so also now said Sir Orlando. But the Government was carried on and the country was prosperous. A few useful measures had been passed by unambitious men, and the Duke of St. Bungay declared that he had never known a Session of Parliament more thoroughly satisfactory to the ministers.

But the old Duke in so saying had spoken as it were his public opinion,— giving, truly enough, to a few of his colleagues, such as Lord Drummond, Sir Gregory Grogram and others, the results of his general experience; but in his own bosom and with a private friend he was compelled to confess that there was a cloud in the heavens. The Prime Minister had become so moody, so irritable, and so unhappy, that the old Duke was forced to doubt whether things could go on much longer as they were. He was wont to talk of these things to his friend Lord Cantrip, who was not a member of the Government, but who had been a colleague of both the Dukes, and whom the old Duke regarded with peculiar confidence. "I cannot explain it to you," he said to Lord Cantrip. "There is nothing that ought to give him a moment's uneasiness. Since he took office there hasn't once been a majority against him in either House on any question that the Government has made its own. I don't remember such a state of things,—so easy for the Prime Minister,—since the days of Lord Liverpool. He had one thorn in his side, our friend who was at the Admiralty, and that thorn like other thorns has worked itself out. Yet at this moment it is impossible to get him to consent to the nomination of a successor to Sir Orlando." This was said a week before the Session had closed.

"I suppose it is his health," said Lord Cantrip.

"He's well enough as far as I can see;—though he will be ill unless he can relieve himself from the strain on his nerves."

"Do you mean by resigning?"

"Not necessarily. The fault is that he takes things too seriously. If he could be got to believe that he might eat, and sleep, and go to bed, and amuse himself like other men, he might be a very good Prime Minister. He is over troubled by his conscience. I have seen a good many Prime Ministers, Cantrip, and I've taught myself to think that they are not very different from other men. One wants in a Prime Minister a good many things, but not very great things. He should be clever but need not be a genius; he should be conscientious but by no means strait-laced; he should be cautious but never timid, bold but never venturesome; he should have a good digestion, genial manners, and, above all, a thick skin. These are the gifts we want, but we can't always get them, and have to do without them. For my own part, I find that though Smith be a very good Minister, the best perhaps to be had at the time, when he breaks down Jones does nearly as well."

"There will be a Jones, then, if your Smith does break down?"

"No doubt. England wouldn't come to an end because the Duke of Omnium shut himself up at Matching. But I love the man, and, with some few exceptions, am contented with the party. We can't do better, and it cuts me to the heart when I see him suffering, knowing how much I did myself to make him undertake the work."

"Is he going to Gatherum Castle?"

"No;—to Matching. There is some discomfort about that."

"I suppose," said Lord Cantrip,—speaking almost in a whisper, although they were closeted together,—"I suppose the Duchess is a little troublesome."

"She's the dearest woman in the world," said the Duke of St. Bungay. "I love her almost as I do my own daughter. And she is most zealous to serve him."

"I fancy she overdoes it."

"No doubt."

"And that he suffers from perceiving it," said Lord Cantrip.

"But a man hasn't a right to suppose that he shall have no annoyances. The best horse in the world has some fault. He pulls, or he shies, or is slow at his fences, or doesn't like heavy ground. He has no right to expect that his wife shall know everything and do everything without a mistake. And then he has such faults of his own! His skin is so thin. Do you remember dear old Brock? By heavens;—there was a covering, a hide impervious to fire or steel! He wouldn't have gone into tantrums because his wife asked too many people to the house. Nevertheless, I won't give up all hope."

"A man's skin may be thickened, I suppose."

"No doubt;—as a blacksmith's arm."

But the Duke of St. Bungay, though he declared that he wouldn't give up hope, was very uneasy on the matter. "Why won't you let me go?" the other Duke had said to him.

"What;—because such a man as Sir Orlando Drought throws up his office?"

But in truth the Duke of Omnium had not been instigated to ask the question by the resignation of Sir Orlando. At that very moment the "People's Banner" had been put out of sight at the bottom of a heap of other newspapers behind the Prime Minister's chair, and his present misery had been produced by Mr. Quintus Slide. To have a festering wound and to be able to show the wound to no surgeon, is wretchedness indeed! "It's not Sir Orlando, but a sense of general failure," said the Prime Minister. Then his old friend had made use of that argument of the ever-recurring majorities to prove that there had been no failure. "There seems to have come a lethargy upon the country," said the poor victim. Then the Duke of St. Bungay knew that his friend had read that pernicious article in the "People's Banner," for the Duke had also read it and remembered that phrase of a "lethargy on the country," and understood at once how the poison had rankled.

It was a week before he would consent to ask any man to fill the vacancy made by Sir Orlando. He would not allow suggestions to be made to him and yet would name no one himself. The old Duke, indeed, did make a suggestion, and anything coming from him was of course borne with patience. Barrington Erle, he thought, would do for the Admiralty. But the Prime Minister shook his head. "In the first place he would refuse, and that would be a great blow to me."

"I could sound him," said the old Duke. But the Prime Minister again shook his head and turned the subject. With all his timidity he was becoming autocratic and peevishly imperious. Then he went to Lord Cantrip, and when Lord Cantrip, with all the kindness which he could throw into his words, stated the reasons which induced him at present to decline office, he was again in despair. At last he asked Phineas Finn to move to the Admiralty, and, when our old friend somewhat reluctantly obeyed, of course he had the same difficulty in filling the office Finn had held. Other changes and other complications became necessary, and Mr. Quintus Slide, who hated Phineas Finn even worse than the poor Duke, found ample scope for his patriotic indignation.

This all took place in the closing week of the Session, filling our poor Prime Minister with trouble and dismay, just when other people were complaining that there was nothing to think of and nothing to do. Men do not really like leaving London before the grouse calls them,—the grouse, or rather the fashion of the grouse. And some ladies were very angry at being separated so soon from their swains in the city. The tradesmen too were displeased,—so that there were voices to re-echo the abuse of the "People's Banner." The Duchess had done her best to prolong the Session by another week, telling her husband of the evil consequences above suggested, but he had thrown wide his arms and asked her with affected dismay whether he was to keep Parliament sitting in order that more ribbons might be sold! "There is nothing to be done," said the Duke almost angrily.

"Then you should make something to be done," said the Duchess, mimicking him.

Chapter XLII
Retribution

The Duchess had been at work with her husband for the last two months in the hope of renewing her autumnal festivities, but had been lamentably unsuccessful. The Duke had declared that there should be no more rural crowds, no repetition of what he called London turned loose on his own grounds. He could not forget the necessity which had been imposed upon him of turning Major Pountney out of his house, or the change that had been made in his gardens, or his wife's attempt to conquer him at Silverbridge. "Do you mean," she said, "that we are to have nobody?" He replied that he thought it would be best to go to Matching. "And live a Darby and Joan life?" said the Duchess.

"I said nothing of Darby and Joan. Whatever may be my feelings I hardly think that you are fitted for that kind of thing. Matching is not so big as Gatherum, but it is not a cottage. Of course you can ask your own friends."

"I don't know what you mean by my own friends. I endeavour always to ask yours."

"I don't know that Major Pountney, and Captain Gunner, and Mr. Lopez were ever among the number of my friends."

"I suppose you mean Lady Rosina?" said the Duchess. "I shall be happy to have her at Matching if you wish it."

"I should like to see Lady Rosina De Courcy at Matching very much."

"And is there to be nobody else? I'm afraid I should find it rather dull while you two were opening your hearts to each other." Here he looked at her angrily. "Can you think of anybody besides Lady Rosina?"

"I suppose you will wish to have Mrs. Finn?"

"What an arrangement! Lady Rosina for you to flirt with, and Mrs. Finn for me to grumble to."

"That is an odious word," said the Prime Minister.

"What;—flirting? I don't see anything bad about the word. The thing is dangerous. But you are quite at liberty if you don't go beyond Lady Rosina. I should like to know whether you would wish anybody else to come?" Of course he made no becoming answer to this question, and of course no becoming answer was expected. He knew that she was trying to provoke him because he would not let her do this year as she had done last. The house, he had no doubt, would be full to overflowing when he got there. He could not help that. But as compared with Gatherum Castle the house at Matching was small, and his domestic authority sufficed at any rate for shutting up Gatherum for the time.

I do not know whether at times her sufferings were not as acute as his own. He, at any rate, was Prime Minister, and it seemed to her that she was to be reduced to nothing. At the beginning of it all he had, with unwonted tenderness, asked her for her sympathy in his undertaking, and, according to her powers, she had given it to him with her whole heart. She had thought that she had seen a way by which she might assist him in his great employment, and she had worked at it like a slave. Every day she told herself that she did not, herself, love the Captain Gunners and Major Pountneys, nor the Sir Orlandos, nor, indeed, the Lady Rosinas. She had not followed the bent of her own inclination when she had descended to sheets and towels, and busied herself to establish an archery-ground. She had not shot an arrow during the whole season, nor had she cared who had won and who had lost. It had not been for her own personal delight that she had kept open house for forty persons throughout four months of the year, in doing which he had never taken an ounce of the labour off her shoulders by any single word or deed! It had all been done for his sake,—that his reign might be long and triumphant, that the world might say that his hospitality was noble and full, that his name might be in men's mouths, and that he might prosper as a British Minister. Such, at least, were the assertions which she made to herself, when she thought of her own grievances and her own troubles. And now she was angry with her husband. It was very well for him to ask for her sympathy, but he had none to give her in return! He could not pity her failures,—even though he had himself caused them! If he had a grain of intelligence about him he must, she thought, understand well enough how sore it must be for her to descend from her princely entertainments to solitude at Matching, and thus to own before all the world that she was beaten. Then when she asked him for advice, when she was really anxious to know how far she might go in filling her house without offending him, he told her to ask Lady Rosina De Courcy! If he chose to be ridiculous he might. She would ask Lady Rosina De Courcy. In her active anger she did write to Lady Rosina De Courcy a formal letter, in which she said that the Duke hoped to have the pleasure of her ladyship's company at Matching Park on the 1st of August. It was an absurd letter, somewhat long, written very much in the Duke's name, with overwhelming expressions of affection, instigated in the writer's mind partly by the fun of the supposition that such a man as her husband should flirt with such a woman as Lady Rosina. There was something too of anger in what she wrote, some touch of revenge. She sent off this invitation, and she sent no other. Lady Rosina took it all in good part, and replied saying that she should have the greatest pleasure in going to Matching. She had declared to herself that she would ask none but those he had named, and in accordance with her resolution she sent out no other written invitations.

He had also told her to ask Mrs. Finn. Now this had become almost a matter of course. There had grown up from accidental circumstances so strong a bond between these two women, that it was taken for granted by both their husbands that they should be nearly always within reach of one another. And the two husbands were also on kindly, if not affectionate, terms with each other. The nature of the Duke's character was such that, with a most loving heart, he was hardly capable of that opening out of himself to another which is necessary for positive friendship. There was a stiff reserve about him, of which he was himself only too conscious, which almost prohibited friendship. But he liked Mr. Finn both as a man and a member of his party, and was always satisfied to have him as a guest. The Duchess, therefore, had taken it for granted that Mrs. Finn would come to her, — and that Mr. Finn would come also during any time that he might be able to escape from Ireland. But, when the invitation was verbally conveyed, Mr. Finn had gone to the Admiralty, and had already made his arrangements for going to sea, as a gallant sailor should. "We are going away in the 'Black Watch' for a couple of months," said Mrs. Finn. Now the "Black Watch" was the Admiralty yacht.

"Heavens and earth!" ejaculated the Duchess.

"It is always done. The First Lord would have his epaulets stripped if he didn't go to sea in August."

"And must you go with him?"

"I have promised."

"I think it very unkind,—very hard upon me. Of course you knew that I should want you."

"But if my husband wants me too?"

"Bother your husband! I wish with all my heart I had never helped to make up the match."

"It would have been made up just the same, Lady Glen."

"You know that I cannot get on without you. And he ought to know it too. There isn't another person in the world that I can really say a thing to."

"Why don't you have Mrs. Grey?"

"She's going to Persia after her husband. And then she is not wicked enough. She always lectured me, and she does it still. What do you think is going to happen?"

"Nothing terrible, I hope," said Mrs. Finn, mindful of her husband's new honours at the Admiralty, and hoping that the Duke might not have repeated his threat of resigning.

"We are going to Matching."

"So I supposed."

"And whom do you think we are going to have?"

"Not Major Pountney?"

"No;—not at my asking."

"Nor Mr. Lopez?"

"Nor yet Mr. Lopez. Guess again."

"I suppose there will be a dozen to guess."

"No," shrieked the Duchess. "There will only be one. I have asked one,—at his special desire,—and as you won't come I shall ask nobody else. When I pressed him to name a second he named you. I'll obey him to the letter. Now, my dear, who do you think is the chosen one,—the one person who is to solace the perturbed spirit of the Prime Minister for the three months of the autumn?"

"Mr. Warburton, I should say."

"Oh, Mr. Warburton! No doubt Mr. Warburton will come as a part of his luggage, and possibly half-a-dozen Treasury clerks. He declares, however, that there is nothing to do, and therefore Mr. Warburton's strength may alone suffice to help him to do it. There is to be one unnecessary guest,—unnecessary, that is, for official purpose; though,—oh,—so much needed for his social happiness. Guess once more."

"Knowing the spirit of mischief that is in you,—perhaps it is Lady Rosina."

"Of course it is Lady Rosina," said the Duchess, clapping her hands together. "And I should like to know what you mean by a spirit of mischief! I asked him, and he himself said that he particularly wished to have Lady Rosina at Matching. Now, I'm not a jealous woman,—am I?"

"Not of Lady Rosina."

"I don't think they'll do any harm together, but it is particular, you know. However, she is to come. And nobody else is to come. I did count upon you." Then Mrs. Finn counselled her very seriously as to the bad taste of such a joke, explaining to her that the Duke had certainly not intended that her invitations should be confined to Lady Rosina. But it was not all joke with the Duchess. She had been driven almost to despair, and was very angry with her husband. He had brought the thing upon himself, and must now make the best of it. She would ask nobody else. She declared that there was nobody whom she could ask with propriety. She was tired of asking. Let her ask whom she would, he was dissatisfied. The only two people he cared to see were Lady Rosina and the old Duke. She had asked Lady Rosina for his sake. Let him ask his old friend himself if he pleased.

The Duke and Duchess with all the family went down together, and Mr. Warburton went with them. The Duchess had said not a word more to her husband about his guests, nor had he alluded to the subject. But each was labouring under a conviction that the other was misbehaving, and with that feeling it was impossible that there should be confidence between them. He busied himself with books and papers,—always turning over those piles of newspapers to see what evil was said of himself,—and speaking only now and again to his private Secretary. She engaged herself with the children or pretended to read a novel. Her heart was sore within her. She had wished to punish him, but in truth she was punishing herself.

On the day of their arrival, the father and mother, with Lord Silverbridge, the eldest son, who was home from Eton, and the private Secretary dined together. As the Duke sat at table, he began to think how long it was since such a state of things had happened to him before, and his heart softened towards her. Instead of being made angry by the strangeness of her proceeding, he took delight in it, and in the course of the evening spoke a word to signify his satisfaction. "I'm afraid it won't last long," she said, "for Lady Rosina comes to-morrow."

"Oh, indeed."

"You bid me ask her yourself."

Then he perceived it all;—how she had taken advantage of his former answer to her and had acted upon it in a spirit of contradictory petulance. But he resolved that he would forgive it and endeavour to bring her back to him. "I thought we were both joking," he said good-humouredly.

"Oh, no! I never suspected you of a joke. At any rate she is coming."

"She will do neither of us any harm. And Mrs. Finn?"

"You have sent her to sea."

"She may be at sea,—and he too; but it is without my sending. The First Lord, I believe, usually does go a cruise. Is there nobody else?"

"Nobody else,—unless you have asked any one."

"Not a creature. Well;—so much the better. I dare say Lady Rosina will get on very well."

"You will have to talk to her," said the Duchess.

"I will do my best," said the Duke.

Lady Rosina came and no doubt did think it odd. But she did not say so, and it really did seem to the Duchess as though all her vengeance had been blown away by the winds. And she too laughed at the matter—to herself, and began to feel less cross and less perverse. The world did not come to an end because she and her husband with Lady Rosina and her boy and the private Secretary sat down to dinner every day together. The parish clergyman with the neighbouring squire and his wife and daughter did come one day,—to the relief of M. Millepois, who had begun to feel that the world had collapsed. And every day at a certain hour the Duke and Lady Rosina walked together for an hour and a half in the park. The Duchess would have enjoyed it, instead of suffering, could she only have had her friend, Mrs. Finn, to hear her jokes. "Now, Plantagenet," she said, "do tell me one thing. What does she talk about?"

"The troubles of her family generally, I think."

"That can't last for ever."

"She wears cork soles to her boots and she thinks a good deal about them."

"And you listen to her?"

"Why not? I can talk about cork soles as well as anything else. Anything that may do material good to the world at large, or even to yourself privately, is a fit subject for conversation to rational people."

"I suppose I never was one of them."

"But I can talk upon anything," continued the Duke, "as long as the talker talks in good faith and does not say things that should not be said, or deal with matters that are offensive. I could talk for an hour about bankers' accounts, but I should not expect a stranger to ask me the state of my own. She has almost persuaded me to send to Mr. Sprout of Silverbridge and get some cork soles myself."

"Don't do anything of the kind," said the Duchess with animation;—as though she had secret knowledge that cork soles were specially fatal to the family of the Pallisers.

"Why not, my dear?"

"He was the man who especially, above all others, threw me over at Silverbridge." Then again there came upon his brow that angry frown which during the last few days had been dissipated by the innocence of Lady Rosina's conversation. "Of course I don't mean to ask you to take any interest in the borough again. You have said that you wouldn't, and you are always as good as your word."

"I hope so."

"But I certainly would not employ a tradesman just at your elbow who has directly opposed what was generally understood in the town to be your interests."

"What did Mr. Sprout do? This is the first I have heard of it."

"He got Mr. Du Boung to stand against Mr. Lopez."

"I am very glad for the sake of the borough that Mr. Lopez did not get in."

"So am I. But that is nothing to do with it. Mr. Sprout knew at any rate what my wishes were, and went directly against them."

"You were not entitled to have wishes in the matter, Glencora."

"That's all very well;—but I had, and he knew it. As for the future, of course, the thing is over. But you have done everything for the borough."

"You mean that the borough has done much for me."

"I know what I mean very well;—and I shall take it very ill if a shilling out of the Castle ever goes into Mr. Sprout's pocket again."

It is needless to trouble the reader at length with the sermon which he preached her on the occasion,—showing the utter corruption which must come from the mixing up of politics with trade, or with the scorn which she threw into the few words with which she interrupted him from time to time. "Whether a man makes good shoes, and at a reasonable price, and charges for them honestly,—that is what you have to consider," said the Duke impressively.

"I'd rather pay double for bad shoes to a man who did not thwart me."

"You should not condescend to be thwarted in such a matter. You lower yourself by admitting such a feeling." And yet he writhed himself under the lashes of Mr. Slide!

"I know an enemy when I see him," said the Duchess, "and as long as I live I'll treat an enemy as an enemy."

There was ever so much of it, in the course of which the Duke declared his purpose of sending at once to Mr. Sprout for ever so many cork soles, and the Duchess,—most imprudently,—declared her purpose of ruining Mr. Sprout. There was something in this threat which grated terribly against the Duke's sense of honour;—that his wife should threaten to ruin a poor tradesman, that she should do so in reference to the political affairs of the borough which he all but owned,—that she should do so in declared opposition to him! Of course he ought to have known that her sin consisted simply in her determination to vex him at the moment. A more good-natured woman did not live;—or one less prone to ruin any one. But any reference to the Silverbridge election brought back upon him the remembrance of the cruel attacks which had been made upon him, and rendered him for the time moody, morose, and wretched. So they again parted ill friends, and hardly spoke when they met at dinner.

The next morning there reached Matching a letter which greatly added to his bitterness of spirit against the world in general and against her in particular. The letter, though marked "private," had been opened, as were all his letters, by Mr. Warburton, but the private Secretary thought it necessary to show the letter to the Prime Minister. He, when he had read it, told Warburton that it did not signify, and maintained for half-an-hour an attitude of quiescence. Then he walked forth, having the letter hidden in his hand, and finding his wife alone, gave it her to read. "See what you have brought upon me," he said, "by your interference and disobedience." The letter was as follows:—

Manchester Square, August 3, 187—.

My Lord Duke,

I consider myself entitled to complain to your Grace of the conduct with which I was treated at the last election at Silverbridge, whereby I was led into very heavy expenditure without the least chance of being returned for the borough. I am aware that I had no direct conversation with your Grace on the subject, and that your Grace can plead that, as between man and man, I had no authority from yourself for supposing that I should receive your Grace's support. But I was distinctly asked by the Duchess to stand, and was assured by her that if I did so I should have all the assistance that your Grace's influence could procure for me;—and it was also explained to me that your Grace's official position made it inexpedient that your Grace on this special occasion should have any personal conference with your own candidate. Under these circumstances I submit to your Grace that I am entitled to complain of the hardship I have suffered.

I had not been long in the borough before I found that my position was hopeless. Influential men in the town who had been represented to me as being altogether devoted to your Grace's interests started a third candidate,—a Liberal as myself,—and the natural consequence was that neither of us succeeded, though my return as your Grace's candidate would have been certain had not this been done. That all this was preconcerted there can be no doubt, but, before the mine was sprung on me,—immediately, indeed, on my arrival, if I remember rightly,—an application was made to me for £500, so that the money might be exacted before the truth was known to me. Of course I should not have paid the £500 had I known that your Grace's usual agents in the town,—I may name Mr. Sprout especially,—were prepared to act against me. But I did pay the money, and I think your Grace will agree with me that a very opprobrious term might be applied without injustice to the transaction.

My Lord Duke, I am a poor man;—ambitious I will own, whether that be a sin or a virtue,—and willing, perhaps, to incur expenditure which can hardly be justified in pursuit of certain public objects. But I must say, with the most lively respect for your Grace personally, that I do not feel inclined to sit down tamely under such a loss as this. I should not have dreamed of interfering in the election at Silverbridge had not the Duchess exhorted me to do so. I would not even have run the risk of a doubtful contest. But I came forward at the suggestion of the Duchess, backed by her personal assurance that the seat was certain as being in your Grace's hands. It was no doubt understood that your Grace would not yourself interfere, but it was equally well understood that your Grace's influence was for the time deputed to the Duchess. The Duchess herself will, I am sure, confirm my statement that I had her direct authority for regarding myself as your Grace's candidate.

I can of course bring an action against Mr. Wise, the gentleman to whom I paid the money, but I feel that as a gentleman I should not do so without reference to your Grace, as circumstances might possibly be brought out in evidence,—I will not say prejudicial to your Grace,—but which would be unbecoming. I cannot, however, think that your Grace will be willing that a poor man like myself, in his search for an entrance into public life, should be mulcted to so heavy an extent in consequence of an error on the part of the Duchess. Should your Grace be able to assist me in my view of getting into Parliament for any other seat I shall be willing to abide the loss I have incurred. I hardly, however, dare to hope for such assistance. In this case I think your Grace ought to see that I am reimbursed.

I have the honour to be,
My Lord Duke,
Your Grace's very faithful Servant,

Ferdinand Lopez.

The Duke stood over her in her own room upstairs, with his back to the fireplace and his eyes fixed upon her while she was reading this letter. He gave her ample time, and she did not read it very quickly. Much of it indeed she perused twice, turning very red in the face as she did so. She was thus studious partly because the letter astounded even her, and partly because she wanted time to consider how she would meet his wrath. "Well," said he, "what do you say to that?"

"The man is a blackguard,—of course."

"He is so;—though I do not know that I wish to hear him called such a name by your lips. Let him be what he may he was your friend."

"He was my acquaintance."

"He was the man whom you selected to be your candidate for the borough in opposition to my wishes, and whom you continued to support in direct disobedience to my orders."

"Surely, Plantagenet, we have had all that about disobedience out before."

"You cannot have such things 'out,'—as you call it. Evil-doing will not bury itself out of the way and be done with. Do you feel no shame at having your name mentioned a score of times with reprobation as that man mentions it;—at being written about by such a man as that?"

"Do you want to make me roll in the gutter because I mistook him for a gentleman?"

"That was not all,—nor half. In your eagerness to serve such a miserable creature as this you forgot my entreaties, my commands, my position! I explained to you why I, of all men, and you, of all women, as a part of me, should not do this thing; and yet you did it, mistaking such a cur as that for a man! What am I to do? How am I to free myself from the impediments which you make for me? My enemies I can overcome,—but I cannot escape the pitfalls which are made for me by my own wife. I can only retire into private life and hope to console myself with my children and my books."

There was a reality of tragedy about him which for the moment overcame her. She had no joke ready, no sarcasm, no feminine counter-grumble. Little as she agreed with him when he spoke of the necessity of retiring into private life because a man had written to him such a letter as this, incapable as she was of understanding fully the nature of the irritation which tormented him, still she knew that he was suffering, and acknowledged to herself that she had been the cause of the agony. "I am sorry," she ejaculated at last. "What more can I say?"

"What am I to do? What can be said to the man? Warburton read the letter, and gave it me in silence. He could see the terrible difficulty."

"Tear it in pieces, and then let there be an end of it."

"I do not feel sure but that he has right on his side. He is, as you say, certainly a blackguard, or he would not make such a claim. He is taking advantage of the mistake made by a good-natured woman through her folly and her vanity;"—as he said this the Duchess gave an absurd little pout, but luckily he did not see it,—"and he knows very well that he is doing so. But still he has a show of justice on his side. There was, I suppose, no chance for him at Silverbridge after I had made myself fully understood. The money was absolutely wasted. It was your persuasion and then your continued encouragement that led him on to spend the money."

"Pay it then. The loss will not hurt you."

"Ah;—if we could but get out of our difficulties by paying! Suppose that I do pay it. I begin to think that I must pay it;—that after all I cannot allow such a plea to remain unanswered. But when it is paid;—what then? Do you think such a payment made by the Queen's Minister will not be known to all the newspapers, and that I shall escape the charge of having bribed the man to hold his tongue?"

"It will be no bribe if you pay him because you think you ought."

"But how shall I excuse it? There are things done which are holy as the heavens,—which are clear before God as the light of the sun, which leave no stain on the conscience, and which yet the malignity of man can invest with the very blackness of hell! I shall know why I pay this £500. Because she who of all the world is the nearest and the dearest to me,"—she looked up into his face with amazement, as he stood stretching out both his arms in his energy,—"has in her impetuous folly committed a grievous blunder, from which she would not allow her husband to save her, this sum must be paid to the wretched craven. But I cannot tell the world that. I cannot say abroad that this small sacrifice of money was the justest means of retrieving the injury which you had done."

"Say it abroad. Say it everywhere."

"No, Glencora."

"Do you think that I would have you spare me if it was my fault? And how would it hurt me? Will it be new to any one that I have done a foolish thing? Will the newspapers disturb my peace? I sometimes think, Plantagenet, that I should have been the man, my skin is so thick; and that you should have been the woman, yours is so tender."

"But it is not so."

"Take the advantage, nevertheless, of my toughness. Send him the £500 without a word,—or make Warburton do so, or Mr. Moreton. Make no secret of it. Then if the papers talk about it—"

"A question might be asked about it in the House."

"Or if questioned in any way,—say that I did it. Tell the exact truth. You are always saying that nothing but truth ever serves. Let the truth serve now. I shall not blench. Your saying it all in the House of Lords won't wound me half so much as your looking at me as you did just now."

"Did I wound you? God knows I would not hurt you willingly."

"Never mind. Go on. I know you think that I have brought it all on myself by my own wickedness. Pay this man the money, and then if anything be said about it, explain that it was my fault, and say that you paid the money because I had done wrong."

When he came in she had been seated on a sofa, which she constantly used herself, and he had stood over her, masterful, imperious, and almost tyrannical. She had felt his tyranny, but had resented it less than usual,—or rather had been less determined in holding her own against him and asserting herself as his equal,—because she confessed to herself that she had injured him. She had, she thought, done but little, but that which she had done had produced this injury. So she had sat and endured the oppression of his standing posture. But now he sat down by her, very close to her, and put his hand upon her shoulder,—almost round her waist.

"Cora," he said, "you do not quite understand it."

"I never understand anything, I think," she answered.

"Not in this case,—perhaps never,—what it is that a husband feels about his wife. Do you think that I could say a word against you, even to a friend?"

"Why not?"

"I never did. I never could. If my anger were at the hottest I would not confess to a human being that you were not perfect,—except to yourself."

"Oh, thank you! If you were to scold me vicariously I should feel it less."

"Do not joke with me now, for I am so much in earnest! And if I could not consent that your conduct should be called in question even by a friend, do you suppose it possible that I could contrive an escape from public censure by laying the blame publicly on you?"

"Stick to the truth;—that's what you always say."

"I certainly shall stick to the truth. A man and his wife are one. For what she does he is responsible."

"They couldn't hang you, you know, because I committed a murder."

"I should be willing that they should do so. No;—if I pay this money I shall take the consequences. I shall not do it in any way under the rose. But I wish you would remember—"

"Remember what? I know I shall never forget all this trouble about that dirty little town, which I never will enter again as long as I live."

"I wish you would think that in all that you do you are dealing with my feelings, with my heartstrings, with my reputation. You cannot divide yourself from me; nor, for the value of it all, would I wish that such division were possible. You say that I am thin-skinned."

"Certainly you are. What people call a delicate organisation,—whereas I am rough and thick and monstrously commonplace."

"Then should you too be thin-skinned for my sake."

"I wish I could make you thick-skinned for your own. It's the only way to be decently comfortable in such a coarse, rough-and-tumble world as this is."

"Let us both do our best," he said, now putting his arm round her and kissing her. "I think I shall send the man his money at once. It is the least of two evils. And now let there never be a word more about it between us."

Then he left her and went back,—not to the study in which he was wont, when at Matching, to work with his private Secretary,—but to a small inner closet of his own, in which many a bitter moment was spent while he thought over that abortive system of decimal coinage by which he had once hoped to make himself one of the great benefactors of his nation, revolving in his mind the troubles which his wife brought upon him, and regretting the golden inanity of the coronet which in the very prime of life had expelled him from the House of Commons. Here he seated himself, and for an hour neither stirred from his seat, nor touched a pen, nor opened a book. He was trying to calculate in his mind what might be the consequences of paying the money to Mr. Lopez. But when the calculation slipped from him,—as it did,—then he demanded of himself whether strict high-minded justice did not call upon him to pay the money let the consequences be what they might. And here his mind was truer to him, and he was able to fix himself to a purpose,—though the resolution to which he came was not, perhaps, wise.

When the hour was over he went to his desk, drew a cheque for £500 in favour of Ferdinand Lopez, and then caused his Secretary to send it in the following note:—

Matching, August 4, 187—.

Sir,—

The Duke of Omnium has read the letter you have addressed to him, dated the 3rd instant. The Duke of Omnium, feeling that you may have been induced to undertake the late contest at Silverbridge by misrepresentations made to you at Gatherum Castle, directs me to enclose a cheque for £500, that being the sum stated by you to have been expended in carrying on the contest at Silverbridge.

I am, sir,
Your obedient servant,

Arthur Warburton.

Ferdinand Lopez, Esq.

Chapter XLIII
Kauri Gum

The reader will no doubt think that Ferdinand Lopez must have been very hardly driven indeed by circumstances before he would have made such an appeal to the Duke as that given in the last chapter. But it was not want of money only that had brought it about. It may be remembered that the £500 had already been once repaid him by his father-in-law,—that special sum having been given to him for that special purpose. And Lopez, when he wrote to the Duke, assured himself that if, by any miracle, his letter should produce pecuniary results in the shape of a payment from the Duke, he would refund the money so obtained to Mr. Wharton. But when he wrote the letter he did not expect to get money,—nor, indeed, did he expect that aid towards another seat, to which he alluded at the close of his letter. He expected probably nothing but to vex the Duke, and to drive the Duke into a correspondence with him.

Though this man had lived nearly all his life in England, he had not quite acquired that knowledge of the way in which things are done which is so general among men of a certain class, and so rare among those beneath them. He had not understood that the Duchess's promise of her assistance at Silverbridge might be taken by him for what it was worth, and that her aid might be used as far as it went,—but, that in the event of its failing him, he was bound in honour to take the result without complaining, whatever that result might be. He felt that a grievous injury had been done him, and that it behoved him to resent that injury,—even though it were against a woman. He just knew that he could not very well write to the Duchess herself,—though there was sometimes present to his mind a plan for attacking her in public, and telling her what evil she had done him. He had half resolved that he would do so in her own garden at the Horns;—but on that occasion the apparition of Arthur Fletcher had disturbed him, and he had vented his anger in another direction. But still his wrath against the Duke and Duchess remained, and he was wont to indulge it with very violent language as he sat upon one of the chairs in Sexty Parker's office, talking somewhat loudly of his own position, of the things that he would do, and of the injury done him.

Sexty Parker sympathised with him to the full,—especially as that first £500, which he had received from Mr. Wharton, had gone into Sexty's coffers. At that time Lopez and Sexty were together committed to large speculations in the guano trade, and Sexty's mind was by no means easy in the early periods of the day. As he went into town by his train, he would think of his wife and family and of the terrible things that might happen to them. But yet, up to this period, money had always been forthcoming from Lopez when absolutely wanted, and Sexty was quite alive to the fact that he was living with a freedom of expenditure in his own household that he had never known before, and that without apparent damage. Whenever, therefore, at some critical moment, a much-needed sum of money was produced, Sexty would become light-hearted, triumphant, and very sympathetic. "Well;—I never heard such a story," he had said when Lopez was insisting on his wrongs. "That's what the Dukes and Duchesses call honour among thieves! Well, Ferdy, my boy, if you stand that you'll stand anything." In these latter days Sexty had become very intimate indeed with his partner.

"I don't mean to stand it," Lopez had replied, and then on the spot had written the letter which he had dated from Manchester Square. He had certainly contrived to make that letter as oppressive as possible. He had been clever enough to put into it words which were sure to wound the poor Duke and to confound the Duchess. And having written it he was very careful to keep the first draft, so that if occasion came he might use it again and push his vengeance farther. But he certainly had not expected such a result as it produced.

When he received the private Secretary's letter with the money he was sitting opposite to his father-in-law at breakfast, while his wife was making the tea. Not many of his letters came to Manchester Square. Sexty Parker's office or his club were more convenient addresses; but in this case he had thought that Manchester Square would have a better sound and appearance. When he opened the letter the cheque of course appeared bearing the Duke's own signature. He had seen that and the amount before he had read the letter, and as he saw it his eye travelled quickly across the table to his father-in-law's face. Mr. Wharton might certainly have seen the cheque and even the amount, probably also the signature, without the slightest suspicion as to the nature of the payment made. As it was, he was eating his toast, and had thought nothing about the letter. Lopez, having concealed the cheque, read the few words which the private Secretary had written, and then put the document with its contents into his pocket. "So you think, sir, of going down to Herefordshire on the 15th," he said in a very cheery voice. The cheery voice was still pleasant to the old man, but the young wife had already come to distrust it. She had learned, though she was hardly conscious how the lesson had come to her, that a certain tone of cheeriness indicated, if not deceit, at any rate the concealment of something. It grated against her spirit; and when this tone reached her ears a frown or look of sorrow would cross her brow. And her husband also had perceived that it was so, and knew at such times that he was rebuked. He was hardly aware what doings, and especially what feelings, were imputed to him as faults,—not understanding the lines which separated right from wrong; but he knew that he was often condemned by his wife, and he lived in fear that he should also be condemned by his wife's father. Had it been his wife only, he thought that he could soon have quenched her condemnation. He would soon have made her tired of showing her disapproval. But he had put himself into the old man's house, where the old man could see not only him but his treatment of his wife, and the old man's good-will and good opinion were essential to him. Yet he could not restrain one glance of anger at her when he saw that look upon her face.

"I suppose I shall," said the barrister. "I must go somewhere. My going need not disturb you."

"I think we have made up our mind," said Lopez, "to take a cottage at Dovercourt. It is not a very lively place, nor yet fashionable. But it is very healthy, and I can run up to town easily. Unfortunately my business won't let me be altogether away this autumn."

"I wish my business would keep me," said the barrister.

"I did not understand that you had made up your mind to go to Dovercourt," said Emily. He had spoken to Mr. Wharton of their joint action in the matter, and as the place had only once been named by him to her, she resented what seemed to be a falsehood. She knew that she was to be taken or left as it suited him. If he had said boldly,—"We'll go to Dovercourt. That's what I've settled on. That's what will suit me," she would have been contented. She quite understood that he meant to have his own way in such things. But it seemed to her that he wanted to be a tyrant without having the courage necessary for tyranny.

"I thought you seemed to like it," he said.

"I don't dislike it at all."

"Then, as it suits my business, we might as well consider it settled."
So saying, he left the room and went off to the city. The old man was still
sipping his tea and lingering over his breakfast in a way that was not
usual with him. He was generally anxious to get away to Lincoln's Inn,
and on most mornings had left the house before his son-in-law. Emily of
course remained with him, sitting silent in her place opposite to the teapot,
meditating perhaps on her prospects of happiness at Dovercourt,—a place
of which she had never heard even the name two days ago, and in which it
was hardly possible that she should find even an acquaintance. In former
years these autumn months, passed in Herefordshire, had been the delight
of her life.

Mr. Wharton also had seen the cloud on his daughter's face, and had
understood the nature of the little dialogue about Dovercourt. And he was
aware,—had been aware since they had both come into his house,—that
the young wife's manner and tone to her husband was not that of perfect
conjugal sympathy. He had already said to himself more than once that she
had made her bed for herself, and must lie upon it. She was the man's wife,
and must take her husband as he was. If she suffered under this man's mode
and manner of life, he, as her father, could not assist her,—could do nothing
for her, unless the man should become absolutely cruel. He had settled that
within his own mind already; but yet his heart yearned towards her, and
when he thought that she was unhappy he longed to comfort her and tell
her that she still had a father. But the time had not come as yet in which he
could comfort her by sympathising with her against her husband. There
had never fallen from her lips a syllable of complaint. When she had spoken
to him a chance word respecting her husband, it had always carried with
it some tone of affection. But still he longed to say to her something which
might tell her that his heart was soft towards her. "Do you like the idea of
going to this place?" he said.

"I don't at all know what it will be like. Ferdinand says it will be cheap."

"Is that of such vital consequence?"

"Ah;—yes; I fear it is."

This was very sad to him. Lopez had already had from him a considerable
sum of money, having not yet been married twelve months, and was now
living in London almost free of expense. Before his marriage he had always
spoken of himself, and had contrived to be spoken of, as a wealthy man, and
now he was obliged to choose some small English seaside place to which to

retreat, because thus he might live at a low rate! Had they married as poor people there would have been nothing to regret in this;—there would be nothing that might not be done with entire satisfaction. But, as it was, it told a bad tale for the future! "Do you understand his money matters, Emily?"

"Not at all, papa."

"I do not in the least mean to make inquiry. Perhaps I should have asked before;—but if I did make inquiry now it would be of him. But I think a wife should know."

"I know nothing."

"What is his business?"

"I have no idea. I used to think he was connected with Mr. Mills Happerton and with Messrs. Hunky and Sons."

"Is he not connected with Hunky's house?"

"I think not. He has a partner of the name of Parker, who is,—who is not, I think, quite—quite a gentleman. I never saw him."

"What does he do with Mr. Parker?"

"I believe they buy guano."

"Ah;—that, I fancy, was only one affair."

"I'm afraid he lost money, papa, by that election at Silverbridge."

"I paid that," said Mr. Wharton sternly. Surely he should have told his wife that he had received that money from her family!

"Did you? That was very kind. I am afraid, papa, we are a great burden on you."

"I should not mind it, my dear, if there were confidence and happiness. What matter would it be to me whether you had your money now or hereafter, so that you might have it in the manner that would be most beneficial to you? I wish he would be open with me, and tell me everything."

"Shall I let him know that you say so?"

He thought for a minute or two before he answered her. Perhaps the man would be more impressed if the message came to him through his wife. "If you think that he will not be annoyed with you, you may do so."

"I don't know why he should,—but if it be right, that must be borne. I am not afraid to say anything to him."

"Then tell him so. Tell him that it will be better that he should let me know the whole condition of his affairs. God bless you, dear." Then he stooped over her, and kissed her, and went his way to Stone Buildings.

It was not as he sat at the breakfast table that Ferdinand Lopez made up his mind to pocket the Duke's money and to say nothing about it to Mr. Wharton. He had been careful to conceal the cheque, but he had done so with the feeling that the matter was one to be considered in his own mind before he took any step. As he left the house, already considering it, he was inclined to think that the money must be surrendered. Mr. Wharton had very generously paid his electioneering expenses, but had not done so simply with the view of making him a present of money. He wished the Duke had not taken him at his word. In handing this cheque over to Mr. Wharton he would be forced to tell the story of his letter to the Duke, and he was sure that Mr. Wharton would not approve of his having written such a letter. How could any one approve of his having applied for a sum of money which had already been paid to him? How could such a one as Mr. Wharton,—an old-fashioned English gentleman,—approve of such an application being made under any circumstances? Mr. Wharton would very probably insist on having the cheque sent back to the Duke,—which would be a sorry end to the triumph as at present achieved. And the more he thought of it the more sure he was that it would be imprudent to mention to Mr. Wharton his application to the Duke. The old men of the present day were, he said to himself, such fools that they understood nothing. And then the money was very convenient to him. He was intent on obtaining Sexty Parker's consent to a large speculation, and knew that he could not do so without a show of funds. By the time, therefore, that he had reached the city he had resolved that at any rate for the present he would use the money and say nothing about it to Mr. Wharton. Was it not spoil got from the enemy by his own courage and cleverness? When he was writing his acknowledgement for the money to Warburton he had taught himself to look upon the sum extracted from the Duke as a matter quite distinct from the payment made to him by his father-in-law.

It was evident on that day to Sexty Parker that his partner was a man of great resources. Though things sometimes looked very bad, yet money always "turned up." Some of their buyings and sellings had answered pretty well. Some had been great failures. No great stroke had been made as yet, but then the great stroke was always being expected. Sexty's fears were greatly exaggerated by the feeling that the coffee and guano were not always real coffee and guano. His partner, indeed, was of opinion that in such a trade as this they were following there was no need at all of real coffee and real guano, and explained his theory with considerable eloquence. "If I buy a ton of coffee and keep it six weeks, why do I buy it and keep it, and why does the seller sell it instead of keeping it? The seller sells it because he thinks he can do best by parting with it now at a certain price. I buy it because I think I can make money by keeping it. It is just the same as though we were to back our opinions. He backs the fall. I back the rise. You needn't have coffee and you needn't have guano to do this. Indeed the possession of the coffee or the guano is only a very clumsy addition to the trouble of your profession. I make it my study to watch the markets;—but I needn't buy everything I see in order to make money by my labour and intelligence." Sexty Parker before his lunch always thought that his partner was wrong, but after that ceremony he almost daily became a convert to the great doctrine. Coffee and guano still had to be bought because the world was dull and would not learn the tricks of trade as taught by Ferdinand Lopez,—also possibly because somebody might want such articles,—but our enterprising hero looked for a time in which no such dull burden should be imposed on him.

On this day, when the Duke's £500 was turned into the business, Sexty yielded in a large matter which his partner had been pressing upon him for the last week. They bought a cargo of Kauri gum, coming from New Zealand. Lopez had reasons for thinking that Kauri gum must have a great rise. There was an immense demand for amber, and Kauri gum might be used as a substitute, and in six months' time would be double its present value. This unfortunately was a real cargo. He could not find an individual so enterprising as to venture to deal in a cargo of Kauri gum after his fashion. But the next best thing was done. The real cargo was bought, and his name and Sexty's name were on the bills given for the goods. On that day he returned home in high spirits, for he did believe in his own intelligence and good fortune.

Chapter XLIV
Mr. Wharton Intends to Make a New Will

On that afternoon, immediately on the husband's return to the house, his wife spoke to him as her father had desired. On that evening Mr. Wharton was dining at his club, and therefore there was the whole evening before them; but the thing to be done was disagreeable, and therefore she did it at once,—rushing into the matter almost before he had seated himself in the arm-chair which he had appropriated to his use in the drawing-room. "Papa was talking about our affairs after you left this morning, and he thinks that it would be so much better if you would tell him all about them."

"What made him talk of that to-day?" he said, turning at her almost angrily and thinking at once of the Duke's cheque.

"I suppose it is natural that he should be anxious about us, Ferdinand;— and the more natural as he has money to give if he chooses to give it."

"I have asked him for nothing lately;—though, by George, I intend to ask him and that very roundly. Three thousand pounds isn't much of a sum of money for your father to have given you."

"And he paid the election bill;—didn't he?"

"He has been complaining of that behind my back,—has he? I didn't ask him for it. He offered it. I wasn't such a fool as to refuse, but he needn't bring that up as a grievance to you."

"It wasn't brought up as a grievance. I was saying that your standing had been a heavy expenditure—"

"Why did you say so? What made you talk about it at all? Why should you be discussing my affairs behind my back?"

"To my own father! And that too when you are telling me every day that I am to induce him to help you!"

"Not by complaining that I am poor. But how did it all begin?" She had to think for a moment before she could recollect how it did begin. "There has been something," he said, "which you are ashamed to tell me."

"There is nothing that I am ashamed to tell you. There never has been and never will be anything." And she stood up as she spoke, with open eyes and extended nostrils. "Whatever may come, however wretched it may be, I shall not be ashamed of myself."

"But of me!"

"Why do you say so? Why do you try to make unhappiness between us?"

"You have been talking of—my poverty."

"My father asked why you should go to Dovercourt,—and whether it was because it would save expense."

"You want to go somewhere?"

"Not at all. I am contented to stay in London. But I said that I thought the expense had a good deal to do with it. Of course it has."

"Where do you want to be taken? I suppose Dovercourt is not fashionable."

"I want nothing."

"If you are thinking of travelling abroad, I can't spare the time. It isn't an affair of money, and you had no business to say so. I thought of the place because it is quiet and because I can get up and down easily. I am sorry that I ever came to live in this house."

"Why do you say that, Ferdinand?"

"Because you and your father make cabals behind my back. If there is anything I hate it is that kind of thing."

"You are very unjust," she said to him sobbing. "I have never caballed. I have never done anything against you. Of course papa ought to know."

"Why ought he to know? Why is your father to have the right of inquiry into all my private affairs?"

"Because you want his assistance. It is only natural. You always tell me to get him to assist you. He spoke most kindly, saying that he would like to know how the things are."

"Then he won't know. As for wanting his assistance, of course I want the fortune which he ought to give you. He is man of the world enough to know that as I am in business capital must be useful to me. I should have thought that you would understand as much as that yourself."

"I do understand it, I suppose."

"Then why don't you act as my friend rather than his? Why don't you take my part? It seems to me that you are much more his daughter than my wife."

"That is most unfair."

"If you had any pluck you would make him understand that for your sake he ought to say what he means to do, so that I might have the advantage of the fortune which I suppose he means to give you some day. If you had the slightest anxiety to help me you could influence him. Instead of that you talk to him about my poverty. I don't want him to think that I am a pauper. That's not the way to get round a man like your father, who is rich himself and who thinks it a disgrace in other men not to be rich too."

"I can't tell him in the same breath that you are rich and that you want money."

"Money is the means by which men make money. If he was confident of my business he'd shell out his cash quick enough! It is because he has been taught to think that I am in a small way. He'll find his mistake some day."

"You won't speak to him then?"

"I don't say that at all. If I find that it will answer my own purpose I shall speak to him. But it would be very much easier to me if I could get you to be cordial in helping me."

Emily by this time quite knew what such cordiality meant. He had been so free in his words to her that there could be no mistake. He had instructed her to "get round" her father. And now again he spoke of her influence over her father. Although her illusions were all melting away,—oh, so quickly vanishing,—still she knew that it was her duty to be true to her husband, and to be his wife rather than her father's daughter. But what could she say on his behalf, knowing nothing of his affairs? She had no idea what was his business, what was his income, what amount of money she ought to spend as his wife. As far as she could see,—and her common sense in seeing such things was good,—he had no regular income, and was justified in no expenditure. On her own account she would ask for no information. She was too proud to request that from him which should be given to her without any request. But in her own defence she must tell him that she could use no influence with her father as she knew none of the circumstances by which her father would be guided. "I cannot help you in the manner you mean," she said, "because I know nothing myself."

"You know that you can trust me to do the best with your money if I could get hold of it, I suppose?" She certainly did not know this, and held her tongue. "You could assure him of that?"

"I could only tell him to judge for himself."

"What you mean is that you'd see me d——d before you would open your mouth for me to the old man!"

He had never sworn at her before, and now she burst out into a flood of tears. It was to her a terrible outrage. I do not know that a woman is very much the worse because her husband may forget himself on an occasion and "rap out an oath at her," as he would call it when making the best of his own sin. Such an offence is compatible with uniform kindness and most affectionate consideration. I have known ladies who would think little or nothing about it,—who would go no farther than the mildest protest,—"Do remember where you are!" or, "My dear John!"—if no stranger were present. But then a wife should be initiated into it by degrees; and there are different tones of bad language, of which by far the most general is the good-humoured tone. We all of us know men who never damn their servants, or any inferiors, or strangers, or women,—who in fact keep it all for their bosom friends; and if a little does sometimes flow over in the freedom of domestic life, the wife is apt to remember that she is the bosomest of her husband's friends, and so to pardon the transgression. But here the word had been uttered with all its foulest violence, with virulence and vulgarity. It seemed to the victim to be the sign of a terrible crisis in her early married life,—as though the man who had so spoken to her could never again love her, never again be kind to her, never again be sweetly gentle and like a lover. And as he spoke it he looked at her as though he would like to tear her limbs asunder. She was frightened as well as horrified and astounded. She had not a word to say to him. She did not know in what language to make her complaint of such treatment. She burst into tears, and throwing herself on the sofa hid her face in her hands. "You provoke me to be violent," he said. But still she could not speak to him. "I come away from the city, tired with work and troubled with a thousand things, and you have not a kind word to say to me." Then there was a pause, during which she still sobbed. "If your father has anything to say to me, let him say it. I shall not run away. But as to going to him of my own accord with a story as long as my arm about my own affairs, I don't mean to do it." Then he paused a moment again. "Come, old girl, cheer up! Don't pretend to be broken-hearted because I used a hard word. There are worse things than that to be borne in the world."

"I—I—I was so startled, Ferdinand."

"A man can't always remember that he isn't with another man. Don't think anything more about it; but do bear this in mind,—that, situated as we are, your influence with your father may be the making or the marring of me." And so he left the room.

She sat for the next ten minutes thinking of it all. The words which he had spoken were so horrible that she could not get them out of her mind,— could not bring herself to look upon them as a trifle. The darkness of his countenance still dwelt with her,—and that absence of all tenderness, that coarse un-marital and yet marital roughness, which should not at any rate have come to him so soon. The whole man too was so different from what she had thought him to be. Before their marriage no word as to money had ever reached her ears from his lips. He had talked to her of books,—and especially of poetry. Shakespeare and Moliere, Dante and Goethe, had been or had seemed to be dear to him. And he had been full of fine ideas about women, and about men in their intercourse with women. For his sake she had separated herself from all her old friends. For his sake she had hurried into a marriage altogether distasteful to her father. For his sake she had closed her heart against that other lover. Trusting altogether in him she had ventured to think that she had known what was good for her better than all those who had been her counsellors, and had given herself to him utterly. Now she was awake; her dream was over, and the natural language of the man was still ringing in her ears!

They met together at dinner and passed the evening without a further allusion to the scene which had been acted. He sat with a magazine in his hand, every now and then making some remark intended to be pleasant but which grated on her ears as being fictitious. She would answer him,— because it was her duty to do so, and because she would not condescend to sulk; but she could not bring herself even to say to herself that all should be with her as though that horrid word had not been spoken. She sat over her work till ten, answering him when he spoke in a voice which was also fictitious, and then took herself off to her bed that she might weep alone. It would, she knew, be late before he would come to her.

On the next morning there came a message to him as he was dressing. Mr. Wharton wished to speak to him. Would he come down before breakfast, or would he call on Mr. Wharton in Stone Buildings? He sent down word that he would do the latter at an hour he fixed, and then did not show himself in the breakfast-room till Mr. Wharton was gone. "I've got to go to your father to-day," he said to his wife, "and I thought it best not to begin till we come to the regular business. I hope he does not mean to be unreasonable." To this she made no answer. "Of course you think the want of reason will be all on my side."

"I don't know why you should say so."

. "Because I can read your mind. You do think so. You've been in the same boat with your father all your life, and you can't get out of that boat and get into mine. I was wrong to come and live here. Of course it was not the way to withdraw you from his influence." She had nothing to say that would not anger him, and was therefore silent. "Well; I must do the best I can by myself, I suppose. Good-bye," and so he was off.

"I want to know," said Mr. Wharton, on whom was thrown by premeditation on the part of Lopez the task of beginning the conversation,— "I want to know what is the nature of your operation. I have never been quite able to understand it."

"I do not know that I quite understand it myself," said Lopez, laughing.

"No man alive," continued the old barrister almost solemnly, "has a greater objection to thrust himself into another man's affairs than I have. And as I didn't ask the question before your marriage,—as perhaps I ought to have done,—I should not do so now, were it not that the disposition of some part of the earnings of my life must depend on the condition of your affairs." Lopez immediately perceived that it behoved him to be very much on the alert. It might be that if he showed himself to be very poor, his father-in-law would see the necessity of assisting him at once; or, it might be, that unless he could show himself to be in prosperous circumstances, his father-in-law would not assist him at all. "To tell you the plain truth, I am minded to make a new will. I had of course made arrangements as to my property before Emily's marriage. Those arrangements I think I shall now alter. I am greatly distressed with Everett; and from what I see and from a few words which have dropped from Emily, I am not, to tell you the truth, quite happy as to your position. If I understand rightly you are a general merchant, buying and selling goods in the market?"

"That's about it, sir."

"What capital have you in the business?"

"What capital?"

"Yes;—how much did you put into it at starting?"

Lopez paused a moment. He had got his wife. The marriage could not be undone. Mr. Wharton had money enough for them all, and would not certainly discard his daughter. Mr. Wharton could place him on a really firm footing, and might not improbably do so if he could be made to feel some confidence in his son-in-law. At this moment there was much doubt with the son-in-law whether he had better not tell the simple truth. "It has gone in by degrees," he said. "Altogether I have had about £8000 in it." In truth he had never been possessed of a shilling.

"Does that include the £3000 you had from me?"

"Yes; it does."

"Then you have married my girl and started into the world with a business based on £5000, and which had so far miscarried that within a month or two after your marriage you were driven to apply to me for funds!"

"I wanted money for a certain purpose."

"Have you any partner, Mr. Lopez?" This address was felt to be very ominous.

"Yes. I have a partner who is possessed of capital. His name is Parker."

"Then his capital is your capital."

"Well;—I can't explain it, but it is not so."

"What is the name of your firm?"

"We haven't a registered name."

"Have you a place of business?"

"Parker has a place of business in Little Tankard Yard."

Mr. Wharton turned to a directory and found out Parker's name. "Mr. Parker is a stockbroker. Are you also a stockbroker?"

"No,—I am not."

"Then, sir, it seems to me that you are a commercial adventurer."

"I am not at all ashamed of the name, Mr. Wharton. According to your manner of reckoning, half the business in the City of London is done by commercial adventurers. I watch the markets and buy goods,—and sell them at a profit. Mr. Parker is a moneyed man, who happens also to be a stockbroker. We can very easily call ourselves merchants, and put up the names of Lopez and Parker over the door."

"Do you sign bills together?"

"Yes."

"As Lopez and Parker?"

"No. I sign them and he signs them. I trade also by myself, and so, I believe, does he."

"One other question, Mr. Lopez. On what income have you paid income-tax for the last three years?"

"On £2000 a-year," said Lopez. This was a direct lie.

"Can you make out any schedule showing your exact assets and liabilities at the present time?"

"Certainly I can."

"Then do so, and send it to me before I go into Herefordshire. My will as it stands at present would not be to your advantage. But I cannot change it till I know more of your circumstances than I do now." And so the interview was over.

Chapter XLV
Mrs. Sexty Parker

Though Mr. Wharton and Lopez met every day for the next week, nothing more was said about the schedule. The old man was thinking about it every day, and so also was Lopez. But Mr. Wharton had made his demand, and, as he thought, nothing more was to be said on the subject. He could not continue the subject as he would have done with his son. But as day after day passed by he became more and more convinced that his son-in-law's affairs were not in a state which could bear to see the light. He had declared his purpose of altering his will in the man's favour, if the man would satisfy him. And yet nothing was done and nothing was said.

Lopez had come among them and robbed him of his daughter. Since the man had become intimate in his house he had not known an hour's happiness. The man had destroyed all the plans of his life, broken through into his castle, and violated his very hearth. No doubt he himself had vacillated. He was aware of that, and in his present mood was severe enough in judging himself. In his desolation he had tried to take the man to his heart,—had been kind to him, and had even opened his house to him. He had told himself that as the man was the husband of his daughter he had better make the best of it. He had endeavoured to make the best of it, but between him and the man there were such differences that they were poles asunder. And now it became clear to him that the man was, as he had declared to the man's face, no better than an adventurer!

By his will as it at present stood he had left two-thirds of his property to Everett, and one-third to his daughter, with arrangements for settling her share on her children, should she be married and have children at the time of his death. This will had been made many years ago, and he had long since determined to alter it, in order that he might divide his property equally between his children;—but he had postponed the matter, intending to give a large portion of Emily's share to her directly on her marriage with Arthur Fletcher. She had not married Arthur Fletcher;—but still it was necessary that a new will should be made.

When he left town for Herefordshire he had not yet made up his mind how this should be done. He had at one time thought that he would give some considerable sum to Lopez at once, knowing that to a man in business such assistance would be useful. And he had not altogether abandoned that idea, even when he had asked for the schedule. He did not relish the thought of giving his hard-earned money to Lopez, but, still, the man's wife was his daughter, and he must do the best that he could for her. Her taste in marrying the man was inexplicable to him. But that was done;—and now how might he best arrange his affairs so as to serve her interests?

About the middle of August he went to Herefordshire and she to the seaside in Essex,—to the little place which Lopez had selected. Before the end of the month the father-in-law wrote a line to his son-in-law.

> Dear Lopez, [not without premeditation had he departed from the sternness of that "Mr. Lopez," which in his anger he had used at his chambers]—
>
> When we were discussing your affairs I asked you for a schedule of your assets and liabilities. I can make no new arrangement of my property till I receive this. Should I die leaving my present will as the instrument under which my property would be conveyed to my heirs, Emily's share would go into the hands of trustees for the use of herself and her possible children. I tell you this that you may understand that it is for your own interest to comply with my requisition.
>
> Yours,
>
> A. Wharton.

Of course questions were asked him as to how the newly married couple were getting on. At Wharton these questions were mild and easily put off. Sir Alured was contented with a slight shake of his head, and Lady Wharton only remarked for the fifth or sixth time that "it was a pity." But when they all went to Longbarns, the difficulty became greater. Arthur was not there, and old Mrs. Fletcher was in full strength. "So the Lopezes have come to live with you in Manchester Square?" Mr. Wharton acknowledged that it was so with an affirmative grunt. "I hope he's a pleasant inmate." There was a scorn in the old woman's voice as she said this, which ought to have provoked any man.

"More so than most men would be," said Mr. Wharton.

"Oh, indeed!"

"He is courteous and forbearing, and does not think that everything around him should be suited to his own peculiar fancies."

"I am glad that you are contented with the marriage, Mr. Wharton."

"Who has said that I am contented with it? No one ought to understand or to share my discontent so cordially as yourself, Mrs. Fletcher;—and no one ought to be more chary of speaking of it. You and I had hoped other things, and old people do not like to be disappointed. But I needn't paint the devil blacker than he is."

"I'm afraid that, as usual, he is rather black."

"Mother," said John Fletcher, "the thing has been done and you might as well let it be. We are all sorry that Emily has not come nearer to us; but she has had a right to choose for herself, and I for one wish,—as does my brother also,—that she may be happy in the lot she has chosen."

"His conduct to Arthur at Silverbridge was so nice!" said the pertinacious old woman.

"Never mind his conduct, mother. What is it to us?"

"That's all very well, John; but according to that nobody is to talk about anybody."

"I would much prefer, at any rate," said Mr. Wharton, "that you would not talk about Mr. Lopez in my hearing."

"Oh; if that is to be so, let it be so. And now I understand where I am." Then the old woman shook herself, and endeavoured to look as though Mr. Wharton's soreness on the subject were an injury to her as robbing her of a useful topic.

"I don't like Lopez, you know," Mr. Wharton said to John Fletcher afterwards. "How would it be possible that I should like such a man? But there can be no good got by complaints. It is not what your mother suffers, or what even I may suffer,—or worse again, what Arthur may suffer, that makes the sadness of all this. What will be her life? That is the question. And it is too near me, too important to me, for the endurance either of scorn or pity. I was glad that you asked your mother to be silent."

"I can understand it," said John. "I do not think that she will trouble you again."

In the mean time Lopez received Mr. Wharton's letter at Dovercourt, and had to consider what answer he should give to it. No answer could be satisfactory,—unless he could impose a false answer on his father-in-law so as to make it credible. The more he thought of it, the more he believed that this would be impossible. The cautious old lawyer would not accept unverified statements. A certain sum of money,—by no means illiberal as a present,—he had already extracted from the old man. What he wanted was a further and a much larger grant. Though Mr. Wharton was old he did not want to have to wait for the death even of an old man. The next two or three years,—probably the very next year,—might be the turning-point of his life. He had married the girl, and ought to have the girl's fortune,—down on the nail! That was his idea; and the old man was robbing him in not acting up to it. As he thought of this he cursed his ill luck. The husbands of other girls had their fortunes conveyed to them immediately on their marriage. What would not £20,000 do for him, if he could get it into his hand? And so he taught himself to regard the old man as a robber and himself as a victim. Who among us is there that does not teach himself the same lesson? And then too how cruelly, how damnably he had been used by the Duchess of Omnium! And now Sexty Parker, whose fortune he was making for him, whose fortune he at any rate intended to make, was troubling him in various ways. "We're in a boat together," Sexty had said. "You've had the use of my money, and by heavens you have it still. I don't see why you should be so stiff. Do you bring your missus to Dovercourt, and I'll take mine, and let 'em know each other." There was a little argument on the subject, but Sexty Parker had the best of it, and in this way the trip to Dovercourt was arranged.

Lopez was in a very good humour when he took his wife down, and he walked her round the terraces and esplanades of that not sufficiently well-known marine paradise, now bidding her admire the sea and now laughing at the finery of the people, till she became gradually filled with an idea that as he was making himself pleasant, she also ought to do the same. Of course she was not happy. The gilding had so completely and so rapidly been washed off her idol that she could not be very happy. But she also could be good-humoured. "And now," said he, smiling, "I have got something for you to do for me,—something that you will find very disagreeable."

"What is it? It won't be very bad, I'm sure."

"It will be very bad, I'm afraid. My excellent but horribly vulgar partner, Mr. Sextus Parker, when he found that I was coming here, insisted on bringing his wife and children here also. I want you to know them."

"Is that all? She must be very bad indeed if I can't put up with that."

"In one sense she isn't bad at all. I believe her to be an excellent woman, intent on spoiling her children and giving her husband a good dinner every day. But I think you'll find that she is,—well,—not quite what you call a lady."

"I shan't mind that in the least. I'll help her to spoil the children."

"You can get a lesson there, you know," he said, looking into her face. The little joke was one which a young wife might take with pleasure from her husband, but her life had already been too much embittered for any such delight. Yes; the time was coming when that trouble also would be added to her. She dreaded she knew not what, and had often told herself that it would be better that she should be childless.

"Do you like him?" she said.

"Like him. No;—I can't say I like him. He is useful, and in one sense honest."

"Is he not honest in all senses?"

"That's a large order. To tell you the truth, I don't know any man who is."

"Everett is honest."

"He loses money at play which he can't pay without assistance from his father. If his father had refused, where would then have been his honesty? Sexty is as honest as others, I dare say, but I shouldn't like to trust him much farther than I can see him. I shan't go up to town to-morrow, and we'll both look in on them after luncheon."

In the afternoon the call was made. The Parkers, having children, had dined early, and he was sitting out in a little porch smoking his pipe, drinking whisky and water, and looking at the sea. His eldest girl was standing between his legs, and his wife, with the other three children round her, was sitting on the doorstep. "I've brought my wife to see you," said Lopez, holding out his hand to Mrs. Parker, as she rose from the ground.

"I told her that you'd be coming," said Sexty, "and she wanted me to put off my pipe and little drop of drink; but I said that if Mrs. Lopez was the lady I took her to be she wouldn't begrudge a hard-working fellow his pipe and glass on a holiday."

There was a soundness of sense in this which mollified any feeling of disgust which Emily might have felt at the man's vulgarity. "I think you are quite right, Mr. Parker. I should be very sorry if,—if—"

"If I was to put my pipe out. Well, I won't. You'll take a glass of sherry, Lopez? Though I'm drinking spirits myself, I brought down a hamper of sherry wine. Oh, nonsense;—you must take something. That's right, Jane. Let us have the stuff and the glasses, and then they can do as they like." Lopez lit a cigar, and allowed his host to pour out for him a glass of "sherry wine," while Mrs. Lopez went into the house with Mrs. Parker and the children.

Mrs. Parker opened herself out to her new friend immediately. She hoped that they two might see "a deal of each other;—that is, if you don't think me too pushing." Sextus, she said, was so much away, coming down to Dovercourt only every other day! And then, within the half hour which was consumed by Lopez with his cigar, the poor woman got upon the general troubles of her life. Did Mrs. Lopez think that "all this speckelation was just the right thing?"

"I don't think that I know anything about it, Mrs. Parker."

"But you ought;—oughtn't you, now? Don't you think that a wife ought to know what it is that her husband is after;—specially if there's children? A good bit of the money was mine, Mrs. Lopez; and though I don't begrudge it, not one bit, if any good is to come out of it to him or them, a woman doesn't like what her father has given her should be made ducks and drakes of."

"But are they making ducks and drakes?"

"When he don't tell me I'm always afeard. And I'll tell you what I know just as well as two and two. When he comes home a little flustered, and then takes more than his regular allowance, he's been at something as don't quite satisfy him. He's never that way when he's done a good day's work at his regular business. He takes to the children then, and has one glass after his dinner, and tells me all about it,—down to the shillings and pence. But it's very seldom he's that way now."

"You may think it very odd, Mrs. Parker, but I don't in the least know what my husband is—in business."

"And you never ask?"

"I haven't been very long married, you know;—only about ten months."

"I'd had my fust by that time."

"Only nine months, I think, indeed."

"Well; I wasn't very long after that. But I took care to know what it was he was a-doing of in the city long before that time. And I did use to know everything, till—" She was going to say, till Lopez had come upon the scene. But she did not wish, at any rate as yet, to be harsh to her new friend.

"I hope it is all right," said Emily.

"Sometimes he's as though the Bank of England was all his own. And there's been more money come into the house;—that I must say. And there isn't an open-handeder one than Sexty anywhere. He'd like to see me in a silk gown every day of my life;—and as for the children, there's nothing smart enough for them. Only I'd sooner have a little and safe, than anything ever so fine, and never be sure whether it wasn't going to come to an end."

"There I agree with you, quite."

"I don't suppose men feels it as we do; but, oh, Mrs. Lopez, give me a little, safe, so that I may know that I shan't see my children want. When I thinks what it would be to have them darlings' little bellies empty, and nothing in the cupboard, I get that low that I'm nigh fit for Bedlam."

In the mean time the two men outside the porch were discussing their affairs in somewhat the same spirit. At last Lopez showed his friend Wharton's letter, and told him of the expected schedule. "Schedule be d——d, you know," said Lopez. "How am I to put down a rise of 12s. 6d. a ton on Kauri gum in a schedule? But when you come to 2000 tons it's £1250."

"He's very old;—isn't he?"

"But as strong as a horse."

"He's got the money?"

"Yes;—he has got it safe enough. There's no doubt about the money."

"What he talks about is only a will. Now you want the money at once."

"Of course I do;—and he talks to me as if I were some old fogy with an estate of my own. I must concoct a letter and explain my views; and the more I can make him understand how things really are the better. I don't suppose he wants to see his daughter come to grief."

"Then the sooner you write it the better," said Mr. Parker.

Chapter XLVI
"He Wants to Get Rich Too Quick"

As they strolled home Lopez told his wife that he had accepted an invitation to dine the next day at the Parkers' cottage. In doing this his manner was not quite so gentle as when he had asked her to call on them. He had been a little ruffled by what had been said, and now exhibited his temper. "I don't suppose it will be very nice," he said, "but we may have to put up with worse things than that."

"I have made no objection."

"But you don't seem to take to it very cordially."

"I had thought that I got on very well with Mrs. Parker. If you can eat your dinner with them, I'm sure that I can. You do not seem to like him altogether, and I wish you had got a partner more to your taste."

"Taste, indeed! When you come to this kind of thing it isn't a matter of taste. The fact is that I am in that fellow's hands to an extent I don't like to think of, and don't see my way out of it unless your father will do as he ought to do. You altogether refuse to help me with your father, and you must, therefore, put up with Sexty Parker and his wife. It is quite on the cards that worse things may come even than Sexty Parker." To this she made no immediate answer, but walked on, increasing her pace, not only unhappy, but also very angry. It was becoming a matter of doubt to her whether she could continue to bear these repeated attacks about her father's money. "I see how it is," he continued. "You think that a husband should bear all the troubles of life, and that a wife should never be made to hear of them."

"Ferdinand," she said, "I declare I did not think that any man could be so unfair to a woman as you are to me."

"Of course! Because I haven't got thousands a year to spend on you I am unfair."

"I am content to live in any way that you may direct. If you are poor, I am satisfied to be poor. If you are even ruined, I am content to be ruined."

"Who is talking about ruin?"

"If you are in want of everything, I also will be in want and will never complain. Whatever our joint lot may bring to us I will endure, and will endeavour to endure with cheerfulness. But I will not ask my father for money, either for you or for myself. He knows what he ought to do. I trust him implicitly."

"And me not at all."

"He is, I know, in communication with you about what should be done. I can only say,—tell him everything."

"My dear, that is a matter in which it may be possible that I understand my own interest best."

"Very likely. I certainly understand nothing, for I do not even know the nature of your business. How can I tell him that he ought to give you money?"

"You might ask him for your own."

"I have got nothing. Did I ever tell you that I had?"

"You ought to have known."

"Do you mean that when you asked me to marry you I should have refused you because I did not know what money papa would give me? Why did you not ask papa?"

"Had I known him then as well as I do now you may be quite sure that I should have done so."

"Ferdinand, it will be better that we should not speak about my father. I will in all things strive to do as you would have me, but I cannot hear him abused. If you have anything to say, go to Everett."

"Yes;—when he is such a gambler that your father won't even speak to him. Your father will be found dead in his bed some day, and all his money will have been left to some cursed hospital." They were at their own door when this was said, and she, without further answer, went up to her bedroom.

All these bitter things had been said, not because Lopez had thought that he could further his own views by saying them;—he knew indeed that he was injuring himself by every display of ill-temper;—but she was in his power, and Sexty Parker was rebelling. He thought a good deal that day on the delight he would have in "kicking that ill-conditioned cur," if only he could afford to kick him. But his wife was his own, and she must be taught to endure his will, and must be made to know that though she was not to be kicked, yet she was to be tormented and ill-used. And it might be possible that he should so cow her spirit as to bring her to act as he should direct. Still, as he walked alone along the sea-shore, he knew that it would be better for him to control his temper.

On that evening he did write to Mr. Wharton, — as follows, — and he dated his letter from Little Tankard Yard, so that Mr. Wharton might suppose that that was really his own place of business, and that he was there, at his work: —

My dear Sir,

You have asked for a schedule of my affairs, and I have found it quite impossible to give it. As it was with the merchants whom Shakespeare and the other dramatists described, — so it is with me. My caravels are out at sea, and will not always come home in time. My property at this moment consists of certain shares of cargoes of jute, Kauri gum, guano, and sulphur, worth altogether at the present moment something over £26,000, of which Mr. Parker possesses the half; — but then of this property only a portion is paid for, — perhaps something more than a half. For the other half our bills are in the market. But in February next these articles will probably be sold for considerably more than £30,000. If I had £5000 placed to my credit now, I should be worth about £15,000 by the end of next February. I am engaged in sundry other smaller ventures, all returning profits; — but in such a condition of things it is impossible that I should make a schedule.

I am undoubtedly in the condition of a man trading beyond his capital. I have been tempted by fair offers, and what I think I may call something beyond an average understanding of such matters, to go into ventures beyond my means. I have stretched my arm out too far. In such a position it is not perhaps unnatural that I should ask a wealthy father-in-law to assist me. It is certainly not unnatural that I should wish him to do so.

I do not think that I am a mercenary man. When I married your daughter I raised no question as to her fortune. Being embarked in trade I no doubt thought that her means,— whatever they might be,—would be joined to my own. I know that a sum of £20,000, with my experience in the use of money, would give us a noble income. But I would not condescend to ask a question which might lead to a supposition that I was marrying her for her money and not because I loved her.

You now know, I think, all that I can tell you. If there be any other questions I would willingly answer them. It is certainly the case that Emily's fortune, whatever you may choose to give her, would be of infinitely greater use to me now,—and consequently to her,—than at a future date which I sincerely pray may be very long deferred.

Believe me to be,
Your affectionate son-in-law,

Ferdinand Lopez.

A. Wharton, Esq.

This letter he himself took up to town on the following day, and there posted, addressing it to Wharton Hall. He did not expect very great results from it. As he read it over, he was painfully aware that all his trash about caravels and cargoes of sulphur would not go far with Mr. Wharton. But it might go farther than nothing. He was bound not to neglect Mr. Wharton's letter to him. When a man is in difficulty about money, even a lie,—even a lie that is sure to be found out to be a lie,—will serve his immediate turn better than silence. There is nothing that the courts hate so much as contempt;— not even perjury. And Lopez felt that Mr. Wharton was the judge before whom he was bound to plead.

He returned to Dovercourt on that day, and he and his wife dined with the Parkers. No woman of her age had known better what were the manners of ladies and gentlemen than Emily Wharton. She had thoroughly understood that when in Herefordshire she was surrounded by people of that class, and that when she was with her aunt, Mrs. Roby, she was not quite so happily placed. No doubt she had been terribly deceived by her husband,—but the deceit had come from the fact that his manners gave no indication of his character. When she found herself in Mrs. Parker's little sitting-room, with Mr. Parker making florid speeches to her, she knew that she had fallen among people for whose society she had not been intended. But this was a part, and only a very trifling part, of the punishment which she felt that she deserved. If that, and things like that, were all, she would bear them without a murmur.

"Now I call Dovercourt a dooced nice little place," said Mr. Parker, as he helped her to the "bit of fish," which he told her he had brought down with him from London.

"It is very healthy, I should think."

"Just the thing for the children, ma'am. You've none of your own, Mrs. Lopez, but there's a good time coming. You were up to-day, weren't you, Lopez? Any news?"

"Things seemed to be very quiet in the city."

"Too quiet, I'm afraid. I hate having 'em quiet. You must come and see me in Little Tankard Yard some of these days, Mrs. Lopez. We can give you a glass of cham. and the wing of a chicken;—can't we, Lopez?"

"I don't know. It's more than you ever gave me," said Lopez, trying to look good-humoured.

"But you ain't a lady."

"Or me," said Mrs. Parker.

"You're only a wife. If Mrs. Lopez will make a day of it we'll treat her well in the city;—won't we, Ferdinand?" A black cloud came across "Ferdinand's" face, but he said nothing. Emily of a sudden drew herself up, unconsciously,—and then at once relaxed her features and smiled. If her husband chose that it should be so, she would make no objection.

"Upon my honour, Sexty, you are very familiar," said Mrs. Parker.

"It's a way we have in the city," said Sexty. Sexty knew what he was about. His partner called him Sexty, and why shouldn't he call his partner Ferdinand?

"He'll call you Emily before long," said Lopez.

"When you call my wife Jane, I shall,—and I've no objection in life. I don't see why people ain't to call each other by their Christian names. Take a glass of champagne, Mrs. Lopez. I brought down half-a-dozen to-day so that we might be jolly. Care killed a cat. Whatever we call each other, I'm very glad to see you here, Mrs. Lopez, and I hope it's the first of a great many. Here's your health."

It was all his ordering, and if he bade her dine with a crossing-sweeper she would do it. But she could not but remember that not long since he had told her that his partner was not a person with whom she could fitly associate; and she did not fail to perceive that he must be going down in the world to admit such association for her after he had so spoken. And as she sipped the mixture which Sexty called champagne, she thought of Herefordshire and the banks of the Wye, and,—alas, alas,—she thought of Arthur Fletcher. Nevertheless, come what might, she would do her duty, even though it might call upon her to sit at dinner with Mr. Parker three days in the week. Lopez was her husband, and would be the father of her child, and she would make herself one with him. It mattered not what people might call him,—or even her. She had acted on her own judgment in marrying him, and had been a fool; and now she would bear the punishment without complaint.

When dinner was over Mrs. Parker helped the servant to remove the dinner things from the single sitting-room, and the two men went out to smoke their cigars in the covered porch. Mrs. Parker herself took out the whisky and hot water, and sugar and lemons, and then returned to have a little matronly discourse with her guest. "Does Mr. Lopez ever take a drop too much?" she asked.

"Never," said Mrs. Lopez.

"Perhaps it don't affect him as it do Sexty. He ain't a drinker;—certainly not. And he's one that works hard every day of his life. But he's getting fond of it these last twelve months, and though he don't take very much it hurries him and flurries him. If I speaks at night he gets cross;—and in the morning when he gets up, which he always do regular, though it's ever so bad with him, then I haven't the heart to scold him. It's very hard sometimes for a wife to know what to do, Mrs. Lopez."

"Yes, indeed." Emily could not but think how soon she herself had learned that lesson.

"Of course I'd do anything for Sexty,—the father of my bairns, and has always been a good husband to me. You don't know him, of course, but I do. A right good man at bottom;—but so weak!"

"If he,—if he,—injures his health, shouldn't you talk to him quietly about it?"

"It isn't the drink as is the evil, Mrs. Lopez, but that which makes him drink. He's not one as goes a mucker merely for the pleasure. When things are going right he'll sit out in our arbour at home, and smoke pipe after pipe, playing with the children, and one glass of gin and water cold will see him to bed. Tobacco, dry, do agree with him, I think. But when he comes to three or four goes of hot toddy, I know it's not as it should be."

"You should restrain him, Mrs. Parker."

"Of course I should;—but how? Am I to walk off with the bottle and disgrace him before the servant girl? Or am I to let the children know as their father takes too much? If I was as much as to make one fight of it, it'd be all over Ponder's End that he's a drunkard;—which he ain't. Restrain him;—oh, yes! If I could restrain that gambling instead of regular business! That's what I'd like to restrain."

"Does he gamble?"

"What is it but gambling that he and Mr. Lopez is a-doing together? Of course, ma'am, I don't know you, and you are different from me. I ain't foolish enough not to know all that. My father stood in Smithfield and sold hay, and your father is a gentleman as has been high up in the Courts all his life. But it's your husband is a-doing this."

"Oh, Mrs. Parker!"

"He is then. And if he brings Sexty and my little ones to the workhouse, what'll be the good then of his guano and his gum?"

"Is it not all in the fair way of commerce?"

"I'm sure I don't know about commerce, Mrs. Lopez, because I'm only a woman; but it can't be fair. They goes and buys things that they haven't got the money to pay for, and then waits to see if they'll turn up trumps. Isn't that gambling?"

"I cannot say. I do not know." She felt now that her husband had been accused, and that part of the accusation had been levelled at herself. There was something in her manner of saying these few words which the poor complaining woman perceived, feeling immediately that she had been inhospitable and perhaps unjust. She put out her hand softly, touching the other woman's arm, and looking up into her guest's face. "If this is so, it is terrible," said Emily.

"Perhaps I oughtn't to speak so free."

"Oh, yes;—for your children, and yourself, and your husband."

"It's them,—and him. Of course it's not your doing, and Mr. Lopez, I'm sure, is a very fine gentleman. And if he gets wrong one way, he'll get himself right in another." Upon hearing this Emily shook her head. "Your papa is a rich man, and won't see you and yours come to want. There's nothing more to come to me or Sexty let it be ever so."

"Why does he do it?"

"Why does who do it?"

"Your husband. Why don't you speak to him as you do to me, and tell him to mind only his proper business?"

"Now you are angry with me."

"Angry! No;—indeed I am not angry. Every word that you say is good, and true, and just what you ought to say. I am not angry, but I am terrified. I know nothing of my husband's business. I cannot tell you that you should trust to it. He is very clever, but—"

"But—what, ma'am?"

"Perhaps I should say that he is ambitious."

"You mean he wants to get rich too quick, ma'am."

"I'm afraid so."

"Then it's just the same with Sexty. He's ambitious too. But what's the good of being ambitious, Mrs. Lopez, if you never know whether you're on your head or your heels? And what's the good of being ambitious if you're to get into the workhouse? I know what that means. There's one or two of them sort of men gets into Parliament, and has houses as big as the Queen's palace, while hundreds of them has their wives and children in the gutter. Who ever hears of them? Nobody. It don't become any man to be ambitious who has got a wife and family. If he's a bachelor, why, of course, he can go to the Colonies. There's Mary Jane and the two little ones right down on the sea, with their feet in the salt water. Shall we put on our hats, Mrs. Lopez, and go and look after them?" To this proposition Emily assented, and the two ladies went out after the children.

"Mix yourself another glass," said Sexty to his partner.

"I'd rather not. Don't ask me again. You know I never drink, and I don't like being pressed."

"By George!—You are particular."

"What's the use of teasing a fellow to do a thing he doesn't like?"

"You won't mind me having another?"

"Fifty if you please, so that I'm not forced to join you."

"Forced! It's liberty 'all here, and you can do as you please. Only when a fellow will take a drop with me he's better company."

"Then I'm d—— bad company, and you'd better get somebody else to be jolly with. To tell you the truth, Sexty, I suit you better at business than at this sort of thing. I'm like Shylock, you know."

"I don't know about Shylock, but I'm blessed if I think you suit me very well at anything. I'm putting up with a deal of ill-usage, and when I try to be happy with you, you won't drink, and you tell me about Shylock. He was a Jew, wasn't he?"

"That is the general idea."

"Then you ain't very much like him, for they're a sort of people that always have money about 'em."

"How do you suppose he made his money to begin with? What an ass you are!"

"That's true. I am. Ever since I began putting my name on the same bit of paper with yours I've been an ass."

"You'll have to be one a bit longer yet;—unless you mean to throw up everything. At this present moment you are six or seven thousand pounds richer than you were before you first met me."

"I wish I could see the money."

"That's like you. What's the use of money you can see? How are you to make money out of money by looking at it? I like to know that my money is fructifying."

"I like to know that it's all there,—and I did know it before I ever saw you. I'm blessed if I know it now. Go down and join the ladies, will you? You ain't much of a companion up here."

Shortly after that Lopez told Mrs. Parker that he had already bade adieu to her husband, and then he took his wife to their own lodgings.

Chapter XLVII
As for Love!

The time spent by Mrs. Lopez at Dovercourt was by no means one of complete happiness. Her husband did not come down very frequently, alleging that his business kept him in town, and that the journey was too long. When he did come he annoyed her either by moroseness and tyranny, or by an affectation of loving good-humour, which was the more disagreeable alternative of the two. She knew that he had no right to be good-humoured, and she was quite able to appreciate the difference between fictitious love and love that was real. He did not while she was at Dovercourt speak to her again directly about her father's money,—but he gave her to understand that he required from her very close economy. Then again she referred to the brougham which she knew was to be in readiness on her return to London; but he told her that he was the best judge of that. The economy which he demanded was that comfortless heart-rending economy which nips the practiser at every turn, but does not betray itself to the world at large. He would have her save out of her washerwoman and linendraper, and yet have a smart gown and go in a brougham. He begrudged her postage stamps, and stopped the subscription at Mudie's, though he insisted on a front seat in the Dovercourt church, paying half a guinea more for it than he would for a place at the side. And then before their sojourn at the place had come to an end he left her for awhile absolutely penniless, so that when the butcher and baker called for their money she could not pay them. That was a dreadful calamity to her, and of which she was hardly able to measure the real worth. It had never happened to her before to have to refuse an application for money that was due. In her father's house such a thing, as far as she knew, had never happened. She had sometimes heard that Everett was impecunious, but that had simply indicated an additional call upon her father. When the butcher came the second time she wrote to her husband in an agony. Should she write to her father for a supply? She was sure that her father would not leave them in actual want. Then he sent her a cheque, enclosed in a very angry letter. Apply to her father! Had she not learned as yet that she was not to lean on her father any longer, but simply on him?

And was she such a fool as to suppose that a tradesman could not wait a month for his money?

During all this time she had no friend,—no person to whom she could speak,—except Mrs. Parker. Mrs. Parker was very open and very confidential about the business, really knowing very much more about it than did Mrs. Lopez. There was some sympathy and confidence between her and her husband, though they had latterly been much lessened by Sexty's conduct. Mrs. Parker talked daily about the business now that her mouth had been opened, and was very clearly of opinion that it was not a good business. "Sexty don't think it good himself," she said.

"Then why does he go on with it?"

"Business is a thing, Mrs. Lopez, as people can't drop out of just at a moment. A man gets hisself entangled, and must free hisself as best he can. I know he's terribly afeard;—and sometimes he does say such things of your husband!" Emily shrunk almost into herself as she heard this. "You mustn't be angry, for indeed it's better you should know all."

"I'm not angry; only very unhappy. Surely Mr. Parker could separate himself from Mr. Lopez if he pleased?"

"That's what I say to him. Give it up, though it be ever so much as you've to lose by him. Give it up, and begin again. You've always got your experience, and if it's only a crust you can earn, that's sure and safe. But then he declares that he means to pull through yet. I know what men are at when they talk of pulling through, Mrs. Lopez. There shouldn't be no need of pulling through. It should all come just of its own accord,—little and little; but safe." Then, when the days of their marine holiday were coming to an end,—in the first week in October,—the day before the return of the Parkers to Ponder's End, she made a strong appeal to her new friend. "You ain't afraid of him; are you?"

"Of my husband?" said Mrs. Lopez. "I hope not. Why should you ask?"

"Believe me, a woman should never be afraid of 'em. I never would give in to be bullied and made little of by Sexty. I'd do a'most anything to make him comfortable, I'm that soft-hearted. And why not, when he's the father of my children? But I'm not going not to say a thing if I thinks it right, because I'm afeard."

"I think I could say anything if I thought it right."

"Then tell him of me and my babes,—as how I can never have a quiet night while this is going on. It isn't that they two men are fond of one another. Nothing of the sort! Now you;—I've got to be downright fond of you, though, of course, you think me common." Mrs. Lopez would not contradict her, but stooped forward and kissed her cheek. "I'm downright fond of you, I am," continued Mrs. Parker, snuffling and sobbing, "but they two men are only together because Mr. Lopez wants to gamble, and Parker has got a little money to gamble with." This aspect of the thing was so terrible to Mrs. Lopez that she could only weep and hide her face. "Now, if you would tell him just the truth! Tell him what I say, and that I've been a-saying it! Tell him it's for my children I'm a-speaking, who won't have bread in their very mouths if their father's squeezed dry like a sponge! Sure, if you'd tell him this, he wouldn't go on!" Then she paused a moment, looking up into the other woman's face. "He'd have some bowels of compassion;—wouldn't he now?"

"I'll try," said Mrs. Lopez.

"I know you're good and kind-hearted, my dear. I saw it in your eyes from the very first. But them men, when they get on at money-making,— or money-losing, which makes 'em worse,—are like tigers clawing one another. They don't care how many they kills, so that they has the least bit for themselves. There ain't no fear of God in it, nor yet no mercy, nor ere a morsel of heart. It ain't what I call manly,—not that longing after other folks' money. When it's come by hard work, as I tell Sexty,—by the very sweat of his brow,—oh,—it's sweet as sweet. When he'd tell me that he'd made his three pound, or his five pound, or, perhaps, his ten pound in a day, and'd calculate it up, how much it'd come to if he did that every day, and where we could go to, and what we could do for the children, I loved to hear him talk about his money. But now—! why, it's altered the looks of the man altogether. It's just as though he was a-thirsting for blood."

Thirsting for blood! Yes, indeed. It was the very idea that had occurred to Mrs. Lopez herself when her husband had bade her to "get round her father." No;—it certainly was not manly. There certainly was neither fear of God in it, nor mercy. Yes;—she would try. But as for bowels of compassion in Ferdinand Lopez—; she, the young wife, had already seen enough of her husband to think that he was not to be moved by any prayers on that side. Then the two women bade each other farewell. "Parker has been talking of my going to Manchester Square," said Mrs. Parker, "but I shan't. What'd I be in Manchester Square? And, besides, there'd better be an end of it. Mr.

Lopez'd turn Sexty and me out of the house at a moment's notice if it wasn't for the money."

"It's papa's house," said Mrs. Lopez, not, however, meaning to make an attack on her husband.

"I suppose so, but I shan't come to trouble no one; and we live ever so far away, at Ponder's End,—out of your line altogether, Mrs. Lopez. But I've taken to you, and will never think ill of you any way;—only do as you said you would."

"I will try," said Mrs. Lopez.

In the meantime Lopez had received from Mr. Wharton an answer to his letter about the missing caravels, which did not please him. Here is the letter:—

> My dear Lopez,
>
> I cannot say that your statement is satisfactory, nor can I reconcile it to your assurance to me that you have made a trade income for some years past of £2000 a year. I do not know much of business, but I cannot imagine such a result from such a condition of things as you describe. Have you any books; and, if so, will you allow them to be inspected by any accountant I may name?
>
> You say that a sum of £20,000 would suit your business better now than when I'm dead. Very likely. But with such an account of the business as that you have given me, I do not know that I feel disposed to confide the savings of my life to assist so very doubtful an enterprise. Of course whatever I may do to your advantage will be done for the sake of Emily and her children, should she have any. As far as I can see at present, I shall best do my duty to her, by leaving what I may have to leave to her, to trustees, for her benefit and that of her children.
>
> Yours truly,
>
> A. Wharton.

This, of course, did not tend to mollify the spirit of the man to whom it was written, or to make him gracious towards his wife. He received the letter three weeks before the lodgings at Dovercourt were given up,—but during these three weeks he was very little at the place, and when there did not mention the letter. On these occasions he said nothing about business, but satisfied himself with giving strict injunctions as to economy. Then he took her back to town on the day after her promise to Mrs. Parker that she would "try." Mrs. Parker had told her that no woman ought to be afraid to speak to her husband, and, if necessary, to speak roundly on such subjects. Mrs. Parker was certainly not a highly educated lady, but she had impressed Emily with an admiration for her practical good sense and proper feeling. The lady who was a lady had begun to feel that in the troubles of her life she might find a much less satisfactory companion than the lady who was not a lady. She would do as Mrs. Parker had told her. She would not be afraid. Of course it was right that she should speak on such a matter. She knew herself to be an obedient wife. She had borne all her unexpected sorrows without a complaint, with a resolve that she would bear all for his sake,—not because she loved him, but because she had made herself his wife. Into whatever calamities he might fall, she would share them. Though he should bring her utterly into the dirt, she would remain in the dirt with him. It seemed probable to her that it might be so,—that they might have to go into the dirt;—and if it were so, she would still be true to him. She had chosen to marry him, and she would be his true wife. But, as such, she would not be afraid of him. Mrs. Parker had told her that "a woman should never be afraid of 'em," and she believed in Mrs. Parker. In this case, too, it was clearly her duty to speak,—for the injury being done was terrible, and might too probably become tragical. How could she endure to think of that woman and her children, should she come to know that the husband of the woman and the father of the children had been ruined by her husband?

Yes,—she would speak to him. But she did fear. It is all very well for a woman to tell herself that she will encounter some anticipated difficulty without fear,—or for a man either. The fear cannot be overcome by will. The thing, however, may be done, whether it be leading a forlorn hope, or speaking to an angry husband,—in spite of fear. She would do it; but when the moment for doing it came, her very heart trembled within her. He had been so masterful with her, so persistent in repudiating her interference, so exacting in his demands for obedience, so capable of making her miserable by his moroseness when she failed to comply with his wishes, that she could not go to her task without fear. But she did feel that she ought not to be afraid, or that her fears, at any rate, should not be allowed to restrain her. A wife, she knew, should be prepared to yield, but yet was entitled to be her husband's counsellor. And it was now the case that in this matter she was conversant with circumstances which were unknown to her husband. It was to her that Mrs. Parker's appeal had been made, and with a direct request from the poor woman that it should be repeated to her husband's partner.

She found that she could not do it on the journey home from Dovercourt, nor yet on that evening. Mrs. Dick Roby, who had come back from a sojourn at Boulogne, was with them in the Square, and brought her dear friend Mrs. Leslie with her, and also Lady Eustace. The reader may remember that Mr. Wharton had met these ladies at Mrs. Dick's house some months before his daughter's marriage, but he certainly had never asked them into his own. On this occasion Emily had given them no invitation, but had been told by her husband that her aunt would probably bring them in with her. "Mrs. Leslie and Lady Eustace!" she exclaimed with a little shudder. "I suppose your aunt may bring a couple of friends with her to see you, though it is your father's house?" he had replied. She had said no more, not daring to have a fight on that subject at present, while the other matter was pressing on her mind. The evening had passed away pleasantly enough, she thought, to all except herself. Mrs. Leslie and Lady Eustace had talked a great deal, and her husband had borne himself quite as though he had been a wealthy man and the owner of the house in Manchester Square. In the course of the evening Dick Roby came in and Major Pountney, who since the late affairs at Silverbridge had become intimate with Lopez. So that there was quite a party; and Emily was astonished to hear her husband declare that he was only watching the opportunity of another vacancy in order that he might get into the House, and expose the miserable duplicity of the Duke of Omnium. And yet this man, within the last month, had taken away her subscription at Mudie's, and told her that she shouldn't wear things that wanted washing! But he was able to say ever so many pretty little things to Lady Eustace, and had given a new fan to Mrs. Dick, and talked of taking a box for Mrs. Leslie at The Gaiety.

But on the next morning before breakfast she began. "Ferdinand," she said, "while I was at Dovercourt I saw a good deal of Mrs. Parker."

"I could not help that. Or rather you might have helped it if you pleased. It was necessary that you should meet, but I didn't tell you that you were to see a great deal of her."

"I liked her very much."

"Then I must say you've got a very odd taste. Did you like him?"

"No. I did not see so much of him, and I think that the manners of women are less objectionable than those of men. But I want to tell you what passed between her and me."

"If it is about her husband's business she ought to have held her tongue, and you had better hold yours now."

This was not a happy beginning, but still she was determined to go on. "It was I think more about your business than his."

"Then it was infernal impudence on her part, and you should not have listened to her for a moment."

"You do not want to ruin her and her children!"

"What have I to do with her and her children? I did not marry her, and I am not their father. He has got to look to that."

"She thinks that you are enticing him into risks which he cannot afford."

"Am I doing anything for him that I ain't doing for myself! If there is money made, will not he share it? If money has to be lost, of course he must do the same." Lopez in stating his case omitted to say that whatever capital was now being used belonged to his partner. "But women when they get together talk all manner of nonsense. Is it likely that I shall alter my course of action because you tell me that she tells you that he tells her that he is losing money? He is a half-hearted fellow who quails at every turn against him. And when he is crying drunk I dare say he makes a poor mouth to her."

"I think, Ferdinand, it is more than that. She says that—"

"To tell you the truth, Emily, I don't care a d—— what she says. Now give me some tea."

The roughness of this absolutely quelled her. It was not now that she was afraid of him,—not at this moment, but that she was knocked down as though by a blow. She had been altogether so unused to such language that she could not get on with her matter in hand, letting the bad word pass by her as an unmeaning expletive. She wearily poured out the cup of tea and sat herself down silent. The man was too strong for her, and would be so always. She told herself at this moment that language such as that must always absolutely silence her. Then, within a few minutes, he desired her, quite cheerfully, to ask her uncle and aunt to dinner the day but one following, and also to ask Lady Eustace and Mrs. Leslie. "I will pick up a couple of men, which will make us all right," he said.

This was in every way horrible to her. Her father had been back in town, had not been very well, and had been recommended to return to the country. He had consequently removed himself,—not to Herefordshire,— but to Brighton, and was now living at an hotel, almost within an hour of London. Had he been at home he certainly would not have invited Mrs. Leslie and Lady Eustace to his house. He had often expressed a feeling of dislike to the former lady in the hearing of his son-in-law, and had ridiculed his sister-in-law for allowing herself to be made acquainted with Lady Eustace, whose name had at one time been very common in the mouths of people. Emily also felt that she was hardly entitled to give a dinner-party in his house in his absence. And, after all that she had lately heard about her husband's poverty, she could not understand how he should wish to incur the expense. "You would not ask Mrs. Leslie here!" she said.

"Why should we not ask Mrs. Leslie?"

"Papa dislikes her."

"But 'papa,' as you call him, isn't going to meet her."

"He has said that he doesn't know what day he may be home. And he does more than dislike her. He disapproves of her."

"Nonsense! She is your aunt's friend. Because your father once heard some cock-and-bull story about her, and because he has always taken upon himself to criticise your aunt's friends, I am not to be civil to a person I like."

"But, Ferdinand, I do not like her myself. She never was in this house till the other night."

"Look here, my dear, Lady Eustace can be useful to me, and I cannot ask Lady Eustace without asking her friend. You do as I bid you,—or else I shall do it myself."

She paused for a moment, and then she positively refused. "I cannot bring myself to ask Mrs. Leslie to dine in this house. If she comes to dine with you, of course I shall sit at the table, but she will be sure to see that she is not welcome."

"It seems to me that you are determined to go against me in everything I propose."

"I don't think you would say that if you knew how miserable you made me."

"I tell you that that other woman can be very useful to me."

"In what way useful?"

"Are you jealous, my dear?"

"Certainly not of Lady Eustace,—nor of any woman. But it seems so odd that such a person's services should be required."

"Will you do as I tell you, and ask them? You can go round and tell your aunt about it. She knows that I mean to ask them. Lady Eustace is a very rich woman, and is disposed to do a little in commerce. Now do you understand?"

"Not in the least," said Emily.

"Why shouldn't a woman who has money buy coffee as well as buy shares?"

"Does she buy shares?"

"By George, Emily, I think that you're a fool."

"I dare say I am, Ferdinand. I do not in the least know what it all means. But I do know this, that you ought not, in papa's absence, to ask people to dine here whom he particularly dislikes, and whom he would not wish to have in his house."

"You think that I am to be governed by you in such a matter as that?"

"I do not want to govern you."

"You think that a wife should dictate to a husband as to the way in which he is to do his work, and the partners he may be allowed to have in his business, and the persons whom he may ask to dinner! Because you have been dictating to me on all these matters. Now, look here, my dear. As to my business, you had better never speak to me about it any more. I have endeavoured to take you into my confidence and to get you to act with me, but you have declined that, and have preferred to stick to your father. As to my partners, whether I may choose to have Sexty Parker or Lady Eustace, I am a better judge than you. And as to asking Mrs. Leslie and Lady Eustace or any other persons to dinner, as I am obliged to make even the recreations of life subservient to its work, I must claim permission to have my own way." She had listened, but when he paused she made no reply. "Do you mean to do as I bid you and ask these ladies?"

"I cannot do that. I know that it ought not to be done. This is papa's house, and we are living here as his guests."

"D—— your papa!" he said as he burst out of the room. After a quarter of an hour he put his head again into the room and saw her sitting, like a statue, exactly where he had left her. "I have written the notes both to Lady Eustace and to Mrs. Leslie," he said. "You can't think it any sin at any rate to ask your aunt."

"I will see my aunt," she said.

"And remember I am not going to be your father's guest, as you call it. I mean to pay for the dinner myself, and to send in my own wines. Your father shall have nothing to complain of on that head."

"Could you not ask them to Richmond, or to some hotel?" she said.

"What; in October! If you think that I am going to live in a house in which I can't invite a friend to dinner, you are mistaken." And with that he took his departure.

The whole thing had now become so horrible to her that she felt unable any longer to hold up her head. It seemed to her to be sacrilege that these women should come and sit in her father's room; but when she spoke of her father her husband had cursed him with scorn! Lopez was going to send food and wine into the house, which would be gall and wormwood to her father. At one time she thought she would at once write to her father and tell him of it all,—or perhaps telegraph to him; but she could not do so without letting her husband know what she had done, and then he would have justice on his side in calling her disobedient. Were she to do that, then it would indeed be necessary that she should take part against her husband.

She had brought all this misery on herself and on her father because she had been obstinate in thinking that she could with certainty read a lover's character. As for love,—that of course had died away in her heart,— imperceptibly, though, alas, so quickly! It was impossible that she could continue to love a man who from day to day was teaching her mean lessons, and who was ever doing mean things, the meanness of which was so little apparent to himself that he did not scruple to divulge them to her. How could she love a man who would make no sacrifice either to her comfort, her pride, or her conscience? But still she might obey him,—if she could feel sure that obedience to him was a duty. Could it be a duty to sin against her father's wishes, and to assist in profaning his house and abusing his hospitality after this fashion? Then her mind again went back to the troubles of Mrs. Parker, and her absolute inefficiency in that matter. It seemed to her that she had given herself over body and soul and mind to some evil genius, and that there was no escape.

"Of course we'll come," Mrs. Roby had said to her when she went round the corner into Berkeley Street early in the day. "Lopez spoke to me about it before."

"What will papa say about it, Aunt Harriet?"

"I suppose he and Lopez understand each other."

"I do not think papa will understand this."

"I am sure Mr. Wharton would not lend his house to his son-in-law, and then object to the man he had lent it to asking a friend to dine with him. And I am sure that Mr. Lopez would not consent to occupy a house on those terms. If you don't like it, of course we won't come."

"Pray don't say that. As these other women are to come, pray do not desert me. But I cannot say I think it is right." Mrs. Dick, however, only laughed at her scruples.

In the course of the evening Emily got letters addressed to herself from Lady Eustace and Mrs. Leslie, informing her that they would have very much pleasure in dining with her on the day named. And Lady Eustace went on to say, with much pleasantry, that she always regarded little parties, got up without any ceremony, as being the pleasantest, and that she should come on this occasion without any ceremonial observance. Then Emily was aware that her husband had not only written the notes in her name, but had put into her mouth some studied apology as to the shortness of the invitation. Well! She was the man's wife, and she supposed that he was entitled to put any words that he pleased into her mouth.

Chapter XLVIII
"Has He Ill-treated You?"

Lopez relieved his wife from all care as to provision for his guests. "I've been to a shop in Wigmore Street," he said, "and everything will be done. They'll send in a cook to make the things hot, and your father won't have to pay even for a crust of bread."

"Papa doesn't mind paying for anything," she said in her indignation.

"It is all very pretty for you to say so, but my experience of him goes just the other way. At any rate there will be nothing to be paid for. Stewam and Sugarscraps will send in everything, if you'll only tell the old fogies downstairs not to interfere." Then she made a little request. Might she ask Everett, who was now in town? "I've already got Major Pountney and Captain Gunner," he said. She pleaded that one more would make no difference. "But that's just what one more always does. It destroys everything, and turns a pretty little dinner into an awkward feed. We won't have him this time. Pountney'll take you, and I'll take her ladyship. Dick will take Mrs. Leslie, and Gunner will have Aunt Harriet. Dick will sit opposite to me, and the four ladies will sit at the four corners. We shall be very pleasant, but one more would spoil us."

She did speak to the "old fogies" downstairs,—the housekeeper, who had lived with her father since she was a child, and the butler, who had been there still longer, and the cook, who, having been in her place only three years, resigned impetuously within half-an-hour after the advent of Mr. Sugarscraps' head man. The "fogies" were indignant. The butler expressed his intention of locking himself up in his own peculiar pantry, and the housekeeper took upon herself to tell her young mistress that "Master wouldn't like it." Since she had known Mr. Wharton such a thing as cooked food being sent into the house from a shop had never been so much as heard of. Emily, who had hitherto been regarded in the house as a rather strong-minded young woman, could only break down and weep. Why, oh why, had she consented to bring herself and her misery into her father's house?

She could at any rate have prevented that by explaining to her father the unfitness of such an arrangement.

The "party" came. There was Major Pountney, very fine, rather loud, very intimate with the host, whom on one occasion he called "Ferdy, my boy," and very full of abuse of the Duke and Duchess of Omnium. "And yet she was a good creature when I knew her," said Lady Eustace. Pountney suggested that the Duchess had not then taken up politics. "I've got out of her way," said Lady Eustace, "since she did that." And there was Captain Gunner, who defended the Duchess, but who acknowledged that the Duke was the "most consumedly stuck-up cox-comb" then existing. "And the most dishonest," said Lopez, who had told his new friends nothing about the repayment of the election expenses. And Dick was there. He liked these little parties, in which a good deal of wine could be drunk, and at which ladies were not supposed to be very stiff. The Major and the Captain, and Mrs. Leslie and Lady Eustace, were such people as he liked,—all within the pale, but having a piquant relish of fastness and impropriety. Dick was wont to declare that he hated the world in buckram. Aunt Harriet was triumphant in a manner which disgusted Emily, and which she thought to be most disrespectful to her father;—but in truth Aunt Harriet did not now care very much for Mr. Wharton, preferring the friendship of Mr. Wharton's son-in-law. Mrs. Leslie came in gorgeous clothes, which, as she was known to be very poor, and to have attached herself lately with almost more than feminine affection to Lady Eustace, were at any rate open to suspicious cavil. In former days Mrs. Leslie had taken upon herself to say bitter things about Mr. Lopez, which Emily could now have repeated, to that lady's discomfiture, had such a mode of revenge suited her disposition. With Mrs. Leslie there was Lady Eustace, pretty as ever, and sharp and witty, with the old passion for some excitement, the old proneness to pretend to trust everybody, and the old incapacity for trusting anybody. Ferdinand Lopez had lately been at her feet, and had fired her imagination with stories of the grand things to be done in trade. Ladies do it? Yes; why not women as well as men? Any one might do it who had money in his pocket and experience to tell him, or to tell her, what to buy and what to sell. And the experience, luckily, might be vicarious. At the present moment half the jewels worn in London were,—if Ferdinand Lopez knew anything about it,—bought from the proceeds of such commerce. Of course there were misfortunes. But these came from a want of that experience which Ferdinand Lopez possessed, and which he was quite willing to place at the service of one whom he admired so thoroughly as he did Lady Eustace. Lady Eustace had been charmed, had seen her way into a new and most delightful life,—but had not yet put any of her money into the hands of Ferdinand Lopez.

I cannot say that the dinner was good. It may be a doubt whether such tradesmen as Messrs. Stewam and Sugarscraps do ever produce good food;—or whether, with all the will in the world to do so, such a result is within their power. It is certain, I think, that the humblest mutton chop is better eating than any "Supreme of chicken after martial manner,"—as I have seen the dish named in a French bill of fare, translated by a French pastrycook for the benefit of his English customers,—when sent in from Messrs. Stewam and Sugarscraps even with their best exertions. Nor can it be said that the wine was good, though Mr. Sugarscraps, when he contracted for the whole entertainment, was eager in his assurance that he procured the very best that London could produce. But the outside look of things was handsome, and there were many dishes, and enough of servants to hand them, and the wines, if not good, were various. Probably Pountney and Gunner did not know good wines. Roby did, but was contented on this occasion to drink them bad. And everything went pleasantly, with perhaps a little too much noise;—everything except the hostess, who was allowed by general consent to be sad and silent;—till there came a loud double-rap at the door.

"There's papa," said Emily, jumping up from her seat.

Mrs. Dick looked at Lopez, and saw at a glance that for a moment his courage had failed him. But he recovered himself quickly. "Hadn't you better keep your seat, my dear?" he said to his wife. "The servants will attend to Mr. Wharton, and I will go to him presently."

"Oh, no," said Emily, who by this time was almost at the door.

"You didn't expect him,—did you?" asked Dick Roby.

"Nobody knew when he was coming. I think he told Emily that he might be here any day."

"He's the most uncertain man alive," said Mrs. Dick, who was a good deal scared by the arrival, though determined to hold up her head and exhibit no fear.

"I suppose the old gentleman will come in and have some dinner," whispered Captain Gunner to his neighbour Mrs. Leslie.

"Not if he knows I'm here," replied Mrs. Leslie, tittering. "He thinks that I am,—oh, something a great deal worse than I can tell you."

"Is he given to be cross?" asked Lady Eustace, also affecting to whisper.

"Never saw him in my life," answered the Major, "but I shouldn't wonder if he was. Old gentlemen generally are cross. Gout, and that kind of thing, you know."

For a minute or two the servants stopped their ministrations, and things were very uncomfortable; but Lopez, as soon as he had recovered himself, directed Mr. Sugarscraps' men to proceed with the banquet. "We can eat our dinner, I suppose, though my father-in-law has come back," he said. "I wish my wife was not so fussy, though that is a kind of thing, Lady Eustace, that one has to expect from young wives." The banquet did go on, but the feeling was general that a misfortune had come upon them, and that something dreadful might possibly happen.

Emily, when she rushed out, met her father in the hall, and ran into his arms. "Oh, papa!" she exclaimed.

"What's all this about?" he asked, and as he spoke he passed on through the hall to his own room at the back of the house. There were of course many evidences on all sides of the party,—the strange servants, the dishes going in and out, the clatter of glasses, and the smell of viands. "You've got a dinner-party," he said. "Had you not better go back to your friends?"

"No, papa."

"What is the matter, Emily? You are unhappy."

"Oh, so unhappy!"

"What is it all about? Who are they? Whose doing is it,—yours or his? What makes you unhappy?"

He was now seated in his arm-chair, and she threw herself on her knees at his feet. "He would have them. You mustn't be angry with me. You won't be angry with me;—will you?"

He put his hand upon her head, and stroked her hair. "Why should I be angry with you because your husband has asked friends to dinner?" She was so unlike her usual self that he knew not what to make of it. It had not been her nature to kneel and to ask for pardon, or to be timid and submissive. "What is it, Emily, that makes you like this?"

"He shouldn't have had the people."

"Well;—granted. But it does not signify much. Is your aunt Harriet there?"

"Yes."

"It can't be very bad, then."

"Mrs. Leslie is there, and Lady Eustace,—and two men I don't like."

"Is Everett here?"

"No;—he wouldn't have Everett."

"Oughtn't you to go to them?"

"Don't make me go. I should only cry. I have been crying all day, and the whole of yesterday." Then she buried her face upon his knees, and sobbed as though she would break her heart.

He couldn't at all understand it. Though he distrusted his son-in-law, and certainly did not love him, he had not as yet learned to hold him in aversion. When the connection was once made he had determined to make the best of it, and had declared to himself that as far as manners went the man was well enough. He had not as yet seen the inside of the man, as it had been the sad fate of the poor wife to see him. It had never occurred to him that his daughter's love had failed her, or that she could already be repenting what she had done. And now, when she was weeping at his feet and deploring the sin of the dinner-party,—which, after all, was a trifling sin,—he could not comprehend the feelings which were actuating her. "I suppose your aunt Harriet made up the party," he said.

"He did it."

"Your husband?"

"Yes;—he did it. He wrote to the women in my name when I refused." Then Mr. Wharton began to perceive that there had been a quarrel. "I told him Mrs. Leslie oughtn't to come here."

"I don't love Mrs. Leslie,—nor, for the matter of that, Lady Eustace. But they won't hurt the house, my dear."

"And he has had the dinner sent in from a shop."

"Why couldn't he let Mrs. Williams do it?" As he said this, the tone of his voice became for the first time angry.

"Cook has gone away. She wouldn't stand it. And Mrs. Williams is very angry. And Barker wouldn't wait at table."

"What's the meaning of it all?"

"He would have it so. Oh, papa, you don't know what I've undergone. I wish,—I wish we had not come here. It would have been better anywhere else."

"What would have been better, dear?"

"Everything. Whether we lived or died, it would have been better. Why should I bring my misery to you? Oh, papa, you do not know,—you can never know."

"But I must know. Is there more than this dinner to disturb you?"

"Oh, yes;—more than that. Only I couldn't bear that it should be done in your house."

"Has he—ill-treated you?"

Then she got up, and stood before him. "I do not mean to complain. I should have said nothing only that you have found us in this way. For myself I will bear it all, whatever it may be. But, papa, I want you to tell him that we must leave this house."

"He has got no other home for you."

"He must find one. I will go anywhere. I don't care where it is. But I won't stay here. I have done it myself, but I won't bring it upon you. I could bear it all if I thought that you would never see me again."

"Emily!"

"Yes;—if you would never see me again. I know it all, and that would be best." She was now walking about the room. "Why should you see it all?"

"See what, my love?"

"See his ruin, and my unhappiness, and my baby. Oh,—oh,—oh!"

"I think so very differently, Emily, that under no circumstances will I have you taken to another home. I cannot understand much of all this yet, but I suppose I shall come to see it. If Lopez be, as you say, ruined, it is well that I have still enough for us to live on. This is a bad time just now to talk about your husband's affairs."

"I did not mean to talk about them, papa."

"What would you like best to do now,—now at once. Can you go down again to your husband's friends?"

"No;—no;—no."

"As for the dinner, never mind about that. I can't blame him for making use of my house in my absence, as far as that goes,—though I wish he could have contented himself with such a dinner as my servants could have prepared for him. I will have some tea here."

"Let me stay with you, papa, and make it for you."

"Very well, dear. I do not mean to be ashamed to enter my own dining-room. I shall, therefore, go in and make your apologies." Thereupon Mr. Wharton walked slowly forth and marched into the dining-room.

"Oh, Mr. Wharton," said Mrs. Dick, "we didn't expect you."

"Have you dined yet, sir?" asked Lopez.

"I dined early," said Mr. Wharton. "I should not now have come in to disturb you, but that I have found Mrs. Lopez unwell, and she has begged me to ask you to excuse her."

"I will go to her," said Lopez, rising.

"It is not necessary," said Wharton. "She is not ill, but hardly able to take her place at table." Then Mrs. Dick proposed to go to her dear niece; but Mr. Wharton would not allow it, and left the room, having succeeded in persuading them to go on with their dinner. Lopez certainly was not happy during the evening, but he was strong enough to hide his misgivings, and to do his duty as host with seeming cheerfulness.

Chapter XLIX
"Where Is Guatemala?"

Though his daughter's words to him had been very wild they did almost more to convince Mr. Wharton that he should not give his money to his son-in-law than even the letters which had passed between them. To Emily herself he spoke very little as to what had occurred that evening. "Papa," she said, "do not ask me anything more about it. I was very miserable,—because of the dinner." Nor did he at that time ask her any questions, contenting himself with assuring her that, at any rate at present, and till after her baby should have been born, she must remain in Manchester Square. "He won't hurt me," said Mr. Wharton, and then added with a smile, "He won't have to have any more dinner-parties while I am here."

Nor did he make any complaint to Lopez as to what had been done, or even allude to the dinner. But when he had been back about a week he announced to his son-in-law his final determination as to money. "I had better tell you, Lopez, what I mean to do, so that you may not be left in doubt. I shall not intrust any further sum of money into your hands on behalf of Emily."

"You can do as you please, sir,—of course."

"Just so. You have had what to me is a very considerable sum,—though I fear that it did not go for much in your large concerns."

"It was not very much, Mr. Wharton."

"I dare say not. Opinions on such a matter differ, you know. At any rate, there will be no more. At present I wish Emily to live here, and you, of course, are welcome here also. If things are not going well with you, this will, at any rate, relieve you from immediate expense."

"My calculations, sir, have never descended to that."

"Mine are more minute. The necessities of my life have caused me to think of these little things. When I am dead there will be provision for Emily made by my will,—the income going to trustees for her benefit, and the capital to her children after her death. I thought it only fair to you that this should be explained."

"And you will do nothing for me?"

"Nothing;—if that is nothing. I should have thought that your present maintenance and the future support of your wife and children would have been regarded as something."

"It is nothing;—nothing!"

"Then let it be nothing. Good morning."

Two days after that Lopez recurred to the subject. "You were very explicit with me the other day, sir."

"I meant to be so."

"And I will be equally so to you now. Both I and your daughter are absolutely ruined unless you reconsider your purpose."

"If you mean money by reconsideration,—present money to be given to you,—I certainly shall not reconsider it. You may take my solemn assurance that I will give you nothing that can be of any service to you in trade."

"Then, sir,—I must tell you my purpose, and give you my assurance, which is equally solemn. Under those circumstances I must leave England, and try my fortune in Central America. There is an opening for me at Guatemala, though not a very hopeful one."

"Guatemala!"

"Yes;—friends of mine have a connection there. I have not broken it to Emily yet, but under these circumstances she will have to go."

"You will not take her to Guatemala!"

"Not take my wife, sir? Indeed I shall. Do you suppose that I would go away and leave my wife a pensioner on your bounty? Do you think that she would wish to desert her husband? I don't think you know your daughter."

"I wish you had never known her."

"That is neither here nor there, sir. If I cannot succeed in this country I must go elsewhere. As I have told you before, £20,000 at the present moment would enable me to surmount all my difficulties, and make me a very wealthy man. But unless I can command some such sum by Christmas everything here must be sacrificed."

"Never in my life did I hear so base a proposition," said Mr. Wharton.

"Why is it base? I can only tell you the truth."

"So be it. You will find that I mean what I have said."

"So do I, Mr. Wharton."

"As to my daughter, she must, of course, do as she thinks fit."

"She must do as I think fit, Mr. Wharton."

"I will not argue with you. Alas, alas; poor girl!"

"Poor girl, indeed! She is likely to be a poor girl if she is treated in this way by her father. As I understand that you intend to use, or to try to use, authority over her, I shall take steps for removing her at once from your house." And so the interview was ended.

Lopez had thought the matter over, and had determined to "brazen it out," as he himself called it. Nothing further was, he thought, to be got by civility and obedience. Now he must use his power. His idea of going to Guatemala was not an invention of the moment, nor was it devoid of a certain basis of truth. Such a suggestion had been made to him some time since by Mr. Mills Happerton. There were mines in Guatemala which wanted, or at some future day might want, a resident director. The proposition had been made to Lopez before his marriage, and Mr. Happerton probably had now forgotten all about it;—but the thing was of service now. He broke the matter very suddenly to his wife. "Has your father been speaking to you of my plans?"

"Not lately;—not that I remember."

"He could not speak of them without your remembering, I should think. Has he told you that I am going to Guatemala?"

"Guatemala! Where is Guatemala, Ferdinand?"

"You can answer my question though your geography is deficient."

"He has said nothing about your going anywhere."

"You will have to go,—as soon after Christmas as you may be fit."

"But where is Guatemala;—and for how long, Ferdinand?"

"Guatemala is in Central America, and we shall probably settle there for the rest of our lives. I have got nothing to live on here."

During the next two months this plan of seeking a distant home and a strange country was constantly spoken of in Manchester Square, and did receive corroboration from Mr. Happerton himself. Lopez renewed his application and received a letter from that gentleman saying that the thing might probably be arranged if he were in earnest. "I am quite in earnest," Lopez said as he showed this letter to Mr. Wharton. "I suppose Emily will be able to start two months after her confinement. They tell me that babies do very well at sea."

During this time, in spite of his threat, he continued to live with Mr. Wharton in Manchester Square, and went every day into the city, — whether to make arrangements and receive instructions as to Guatemala, or to carry on his old business, neither Emily nor her father knew. He never at this time spoke about his affairs to either of them, but daily referred to her future expatriation as a thing that was certain. At last there came up the actual question, — whether she were to go or not. Her father told her that though she was doubtless bound by law to obey her husband, in such a matter as this she might defy the law. "I do not think that he can actually force you on board the ship," her father said.

"But if he tells me that I must go?"

"Stay here with me," said the father. "Stay here with your baby. I'll fight it out for you. I'll so manage that you shall have all the world on your side."

Emily at that moment came to no decision, but on the following day she discussed the matter with Lopez himself. "Of course you will go with me," he said, when she asked the question.

"You mean that I must, whether I wish to go or not."

"Certainly you must. Good G——! where is a wife's place? Am I to go out without my child, and without you, while you are enjoying all the comforts of your father's wealth at home? That is not my idea of life."

"Ferdinand, I have been thinking about it very much. I must beg you to allow me to remain. I ask it of you as if I were asking my life."

"Your father has put you up to this."

"No; — not to this."

"To what then?"

"My father thinks that I should refuse to go."

"He does, does he?"

"But I shall not refuse. I shall go if you insist upon it. There shall be no contest between us about that."

"Well; I should hope not."

"But I do implore you to spare me."

"That is very selfish, Emily."

"Yes," —she said, "yes. I cannot contradict that. But so is the man selfish who prays the judge to spare his life."

"But you do not think of me. I must go."

"I shall not make you happier, Ferdinand."

"Do you think that it is a fine thing for a man to live in such a country as that all alone?"

"I think he would be better so than with a wife he does not—love."

"Who says I do not love you?"

"Or with one who does—not—love him." This she said very slowly, very softly, but looking up into his eyes as she said it.

"Do you tell me that to my face?"

"Yes;—what good can I do now by lying? You have not been to me as I thought you would be."

"And so, because you have built up some castle in the air that has fallen to pieces, you tell your husband to his face that you do not love him, and that you prefer not to live with him. Is that your idea of duty?"

"Why have you been so cruel?"

"Cruel! What have I done? Tell me what cruelty. Have I beat you? Have you been starved? Have I not asked and implored your assistance,—only to be refused? The fact is that your father and you have found out that I am not a rich man, and you want to be rid of me. Is that true or false?"

"It is not true that I want to be rid of you because you are poor."

"I do not mean to be rid of you. You will have to settle down and do your work as my wife in whatever place it may suit me to live. Your father is a rich man, but you shall not have the advantage of his wealth unless it comes to you, as it ought to come, through my hands. If your father would give me the fortune which ought to be yours there need be no going abroad. He cannot bear to part with his money, and therefore we must go. Now you know all about it." She was then turning to leave him, when he asked her a direct question. "Am I to understand that you intend to resist my right to take you with me?"

"If you bid me go,—I shall go."

"It will be better, as you will save both trouble and exposure."

Of course she told her father what had taken place, but he could only shake his head, and sit groaning over his misery in his chambers. He had explained to her what he was willing to do on her behalf, but she declined his aid. He could not tell her that she was wrong. She was the man's wife, and out of that terrible destiny she could not now escape. The only question with him was whether it would not be best to buy the man,—give him a sum of money to go, and to go alone. Could he have been quit of the man even for £20,000, he would willingly have paid the money. But the man would either not go, or would come back as soon as he had got the money. His own life, as he passed it now, with this man in the house with him, was horrible to him. For Lopez, though he had more than once threatened that he would carry his wife to another home, had taken no steps towards getting that other home ready for her.

During all this time Mr. Wharton had not seen his son. Everett had gone abroad just as his father returned to London from Brighton, and was still on the continent. He received his allowance punctually, and that was the only intercourse which took place between them. But Emily had written to him, not telling him much of her troubles,—only saying that she believed that her husband would take her to Central America early in the spring, and begging him to come home before she went.

Just before Christmas her baby was born, but the poor child did not live a couple of days. She herself at the time was so worn with care, so thin and wan and wretched, that looking in the glass she hardly knew her own face. "Ferdinand," she said to him, "I know he will not live. The Doctor says so."

"Nothing thrives that I have to do with," he answered gloomily.

"Will you not look at him?"

"Well; yes. I have looked at him, have I not? I wish to God that where he is going I could go with him."

"I wish I was;—I wish I was going," said the poor mother. Then the father went out, and before he had returned to the house the child was dead. "Oh, Ferdinand, speak one kind word to me now," she said.

"What kind word can I speak when you have told me that you do not love me? Do you think that I can forget that because—because he has gone?"

"A woman's love may always be won back again by kindness."

"Psha! How am I to kiss and make pretty speeches with my mind harassed as it is now?" But he did touch her brow with his lips before he went away.

The infant was buried, and then there was not much show of mourning in the house. The poor mother would sit gloomily alone day after day, telling herself that it was perhaps better that she should have been robbed of her treasure than have gone forth with him into the wide, unknown, harsh world with such a father as she had given him. Then she would look at all the preparations she had made,—the happy work of her fingers when her thoughts of their future use were her sweetest consolation,—and weep till she would herself feel that there never could be an end to her tears.

The second week in January had come and yet nothing further had been settled as to this Guatemala project. Lopez talked about it as though it was certain, and even told his wife that as they would move so soon it would not be now worth while for him to take other lodgings for her. But when she asked as to her own preparations,—the wardrobe necessary for the long voyage and her general outfit,—he told her that three weeks or a fortnight would be enough for all, and that he would give her sufficient notice. "Upon my word he is very kind to honour my poor house as he does," said Mr. Wharton.

"Papa, we will go at once if you wish it," said his daughter.

"Nay, Emily; do not turn upon me. I cannot but be sensible to the insult of his daily presence; but even that is better than losing you."

Then there occurred a ludicrous incident,—or combination of incidents,—which, in spite of their absurdity, drove Mr. Wharton almost frantic. First there came to him the bill from Messrs. Stewam and Sugarscraps for the dinner. At this time he kept nothing back from his daughter. "Look at that!" he said. The bill was absolutely made out in his name.

"It is a mistake, papa."

"Not at all. The dinner was given in my house, and I must pay for it. I would sooner do so than that he should pay it,—even if he had the means." So he paid Messrs. Stewam and Sugarscraps £25 9s. 6d., begging them as he did so never to send another dinner into his house, and observing that he was in the habit of entertaining his friends at less than three guineas a head. "But Château Yquem and Côte d'Or!" said Mr. Sugarscraps. "Château fiddlesticks!" said Mr. Wharton, walking out of the house with his receipt.

Then came the bill for the brougham,—for the brougham from the very day of their return to town after their wedding trip. This he showed to Lopez. Indeed the bill had been made out to Lopez and sent to Mr. Wharton with an apologetic note. "I didn't tell him to send it," said Lopez.

"But will you pay it?"

"I certainly shall not ask you to pay it." But Mr. Wharton at last did pay it, and he also paid the rent of the rooms in the Belgrave Mansions, and between £30 and £40 for dresses which Emily had got at Lewes and Allenby's under her husband's orders in the first days of their married life in London.

"Oh, papa, I wish I had not gone there," she said.

"My dear, anything that you may have had I do not grudge in the least. And even for him, if he would let you remain here, I would pay willingly. I would supply all his wants if he would only—go away."

Chapter L
Mr. Slide's Revenge

"Do you mean to say, my lady, that the Duke paid his electioneering bill down at Silverbridge?"

"I do mean to say so, Mr. Slide." Lady Eustace nodded her head, and Mr. Quintus Slide opened his mouth.

"Goodness gracious!" said Mrs. Leslie, who was sitting with them. They were in Lady Eustace's drawing-room, and the patriotic editor of the "People's Banner" was obtaining from a new ally information which might be useful to the country.

"But 'ow do you know, Lady Eustace? You'll pardon the persistency of my inquiries, but when you come to public information accuracy is everything. I never trust myself to mere report. I always travel up to the very fountain 'ead of truth."

"I know it," said Lizzy Eustace oracularly.

"Um—m!" The Editor as he ejaculated the sound looked at her ladyship with admiring eyes,—with eyes that were intended to flatter. But Lizzie had been looked at so often in so many ways, and was so well accustomed to admiration, that this had no effect on her at all. "'E didn't tell you himself; did 'e, now?"

"Can you tell me the truth as to trusting him with my money?"

"Yes, I can."

"Shall I be safe if I take the papers which he calls bills of sale?"

"One good turn deserves another, my lady."

"I don't want to make a secret of it, Mr. Slide. Pountney found it out. You know the Major?"

"Yes, I know Major Pountney. He was at Gatherum 'imself, and got a little bit of cold shoulder;—didn't he?"

"I dare say he did. What has that to do with it? You may be sure that Lopez applied to the Duke for his expenses at Silverbridge, and that the Duke sent him the money."

"There's no doubt about it, Mr. Slide," said Mrs. Leslie. "We got it all from Major Pountney. There was some bet between him and Pountney, and he had to show Pountney the cheque."

"Pountney saw the money," said Lady Eustace.

Mr. Slide stroked his hand over his mouth and chin as he sat thinking of the tremendous national importance of this communication. The man who had paid the money was the Prime Minister of England,—and was, moreover, Mr. Slide's enemy! "When the right 'and of fellowship has been rejected, I never forgive," Mr. Slide has been heard to say. Even Lady Eustace, who was not particular as to the appearance of people, remarked afterwards to her friend that Mr. Slide had looked like the devil as he was stroking his face. "It's very remarkable," said Mr. Slide; "very remarkable!"

"You won't tell the Major that we told you," said her Ladyship.

"Oh dear, no. I only just wanted to 'ear how it was. And as to embarking your money, my lady, with Ferdinand Lopez,—I wouldn't do it."

"Not if I get the bills of sale? It's for rum, and they say rum will go up to any price."

"Don't, Lady Eustace. I can't say any more,—but don't. I never mention names. But don't."

Then Mr. Slide went at once in search of Major Pountney, and having found the Major at his club extracted from him all that he knew about the Silverbridge payment. Pountney had really seen the Duke's cheque for £500. "There was some bet,—eh, Major?" asked Mr. Slide.

"No, there wasn't. I know who has been telling you. That's Lizzie Eustace, and just like her mischief. The way of it was this;—Lopez, who was very angry, had boasted that he would bring the Duke down on his marrow-bones. I was laughing at him as we sat at dinner one day afterwards, and he took out the cheque and showed it me. There was the Duke's own signature for £500,—'Omnium,' as plain as letters could make it." Armed with this full information, Mr. Slide felt that he had done all that the most punctilious devotion to accuracy could demand of him, and immediately shut himself up in his cage at the "People's Banner" office and went to work.

This occurred about the first week in January. The Duke was then at Matching with his wife and a very small party. The singular arrangement which had been effected by the Duchess in the early autumn had passed off without any wonderful effects. It had been done by her in pique, and the result had been apparently so absurd that it had at first frightened her.

But in the end it answered very well. The Duke took great pleasure in Lady Rosina's company, and enjoyed the comparative solitude which enabled him to work all day without interruption. His wife protested that it was just what she liked, though it must be feared that she soon became weary of it. To Lady Rosina it was of course a Paradise on earth. In September, Phineas Finn and his wife came to them, and in October there were other relaxations and other business. The Prime Minister and his wife visited their Sovereign, and he made some very useful speeches through the country on his old favourite subject of decimal coinage. At Christmas, for a fortnight, they went to Gatherum Castle and entertained the neighbourhood,—the nobility and squirearchy dining there on one day, and the tenants and other farmers on another. All this went very smoothly, and the Duke did not become outrageously unhappy because the "People's Banner" made sundry severe remarks on the absence of Cabinet Councils through the autumn.

After Christmas they returned to Matching, and had some of their old friends with them. There was the Duke of St. Bungay and the Duchess, and Phineas Finn and his wife, and Lord and Lady Cantrip, Barrington Erle, and one or two others. But at this period there came a great trouble. One morning as the Duke sat in his own room after breakfast he read an article in the "People's Banner," of which the following sentences were a part. "We wish to know by whom were paid the expenses incurred by Mr. Ferdinand Lopez during the late contest at Silverbridge. It may be that they were paid by that gentleman himself,—in which case we shall have nothing further to say, not caring at the present moment to inquire whether those expenses were or were not excessive. It may be that they were paid by subscription among his political friends,—and if so, again we shall be satisfied. Or it is possible that funds were supplied by a new political club of which we have lately heard much, and with the action of such a body we of course have nothing to do. If an assurance can be given to us by Mr. Lopez or his friends that such was the case we shall be satisfied.

"But a report has reached us, and we may say more than a report, which makes it our duty to ask this question. Were those expenses paid out of the private pocket of the present Prime Minister? If so, we maintain that we have discovered a blot in that nobleman's character which it is our duty to the public to expose. We will go farther and say that if it be so,—if these expenses were paid out of the private pocket of the Duke of Omnium, it is not fit that that nobleman should any longer hold the high office which he now fills.

"We know that a peer should not interfere in elections for the House of Commons. We certainly know that a Minister of the Crown should not attempt to purchase parliamentary support. We happen to know also the almost more than public manner,—are we not justified in saying the ostentation?—with which at the last election the Duke repudiated all that influence with the borough which his predecessors, and we believe he himself, had so long exercised. He came forward telling us that he, at least, meant to have clean hands;—that he would not do as his forefathers had done;—that he would not even do as he himself had done in former years. What are we to think of the Duke of Omnium as a Minister of this country, if, after such assurances, he has out of his own pocket paid the electioneering expenses of a candidate at Silverbridge?" There was much more in the article, but the passages quoted will suffice to give the reader a sufficient idea of the accusation made, and which the Duke read in the retirement of his own chamber.

He read it twice before he allowed himself to think of the matter. The statement made was at any rate true to the letter. He had paid the man's electioneering expenses. That he had done so from the purest motives he knew and the reader knows;—but he could not even explain those motives without exposing his wife. Since the cheque was sent he had never spoken of the occurrence to any human being,—but he had thought of it very often. At the time his private Secretary, with much hesitation, almost with trepidation, had counselled him not to send the money. The Duke was a man with whom it was very easy to work, whose courtesy to all dependent on him was almost exaggerated, who never found fault, and was anxious as far as possible to do everything for himself. The comfort of those around him was always matter of interest to him. Everything he held, he held as it were in trust for the enjoyment of others. But he was a man whom it was very difficult to advise. He did not like advice. He was so thin-skinned that any counsel offered to him took the form of criticism. When cautioned what shoes he should wear,—as had been done by Lady Rosina, or what wine or what horses he should buy, as was done by his butler and coachman, he was thankful, taking no pride to himself for knowledge as to shoes, wine, or horses. But as to his own conduct, private or public, as to any question of politics, as to his opinions and resolutions, he was jealous of interference. Mr. Warburton therefore had almost trembled when asking the Duke whether he was quite sure about sending the money to Lopez. "Quite sure," the Duke had answered, having at that time made up his mind. Mr. Warburton had not dared to express a further doubt, and the money had been sent. But from the moment of sending it doubts had repeated themselves in the Prime Minister's mind.

Now he sat with the newspaper in his hand thinking of it. Of course it was open to him to take no notice of the matter,—to go on as though he had not seen the article, and to let the thing die if it would die. But he knew Mr. Quintus Slide and his paper well enough to be sure that it would not die. The charge would be repeated in the "People's Banner" till it was copied into other papers; and then the further question would be asked,—why had the Prime Minister allowed such an accusation to remain unanswered? But if he did notice it, what notice should he take of it? It was true. And surely he had a right to do what he liked with his own money so long as he disobeyed no law. He had bribed no one. He had spent his money with no corrupt purpose. His sense of honour had taught him to think that the man had received injury through his wife's imprudence, and that he therefore was responsible as far as the pecuniary loss was concerned. He was not ashamed of the thing he had done;—but yet he was ashamed that it should be discussed in public.

Why had he allowed himself to be put into a position in which he was subject to such grievous annoyance? Since he had held his office he had not had a happy day, nor,—so he told himself,—had he received from it any slightest gratification, nor could he buoy himself up with the idea that he was doing good service for his country. After a while he walked into the next room and showed the paper to Mr. Warburton. "Perhaps you were right," he said, "when you told me not to send that money."

"It will matter nothing," said the private Secretary when he had read it,—thinking, however, that it might matter much, but wishing to spare the Duke.

"I was obliged to repay the man as the Duchess had—had encouraged him. The Duchess had not quite—quite understood my wishes." Mr. Warburton knew the whole history now, having discussed it all with the Duchess more than once.

"I think your Grace should take no notice of the article."

No notice was taken of it, but three days afterwards there appeared a short paragraph in large type,—beginning with a question. "Does the Duke of Omnium intend to answer the question asked by us last Friday? Is it true that he paid the expenses of Mr. Lopez when that gentleman stood for Silverbridge? The Duke may be assured that the question shall be repeated till it is answered." This the Duke also saw and took to his private Secretary.

"I would do nothing at any rate till it be noticed in some other paper," said the private Secretary. "The 'People's Banner' is known to be scandalous."

"Of course it is scandalous. And, moreover, I know the motives and the malice of the wretched man who is the editor. But the paper is read, and the foul charge if repeated will become known, and the allegation made is true. I did pay the man's election expenses;—and, moreover, to tell the truth openly as I do not scruple to do to you, I am not prepared to state publicly the reason why I did so. And nothing but that reason could justify me."

"Then I think your Grace should state it."

"I cannot do so."

"The Duke of St. Bungay is here. Would it not be well to tell the whole affair to him?"

"I will think of it. I do not know why I should have troubled you."

"Oh, my lord!"

"Except that there is always some comfort in speaking even of one's trouble. I will think about it. In the meantime you need perhaps not mention it again."

"Who? I? Oh, certainly not."

"I did not mean to others,—but to myself. I will turn it in my mind and speak of it when I have decided anything." And he did think about it,—thinking of it so much that he could hardly get the matter out of his mind day or night. To his wife he did not allude to it at all. Why trouble her with it? She had caused the evil, and he had cautioned her as to the future. She could not help him out of the difficulty she had created. He continued to turn the matter over in his thoughts till he so magnified it, and built it up into such proportions, that he again began to think that he must resign. It was, he thought, true that a man should not remain in office as Prime Minister who in such a matter could not clear his own conduct.

Then there was a third attack in the "People's Banner," and after that the matter was noticed in the "Evening Pulpit." This notice the Duke of St. Bungay saw and mentioned to Mr. Warburton. "Has the Duke spoken to you of some allegations made in the press as to the expenses of the late election at Silverbridge?" The old Duke was at this time, and had been for some months, in a state of nervous anxiety about his friend. He had almost admitted to himself that he had been wrong in recommending a politician so weakly organised to take the office of Prime Minister. He had expected the man to be more manly,—had perhaps expected him to be less conscientiously scrupulous. But now, as the thing had been done, it must be maintained. Who else was there to take the office? Mr. Gresham would not. To keep Mr. Daubeny out was the very essence of the Duke of St. Bungay's life,—the turning-point of his political creed, the one grand duty the idea of which was always present to him. And he had, moreover, a most true and most affectionate regard for the man whom he now supported, appreciating the sweetness of his character,—believing still in the Minister's patriotism, intelligence, devotion, and honesty; though he was forced to own to himself that the strength of a man's heart was wanting.

"Yes," said Warburton; "he did mention it."

"Does it trouble him?"

"Perhaps you had better speak to him about it." Both the old Duke and the private Secretary were as fearful and nervous about the Prime Minister as a mother is for a weakly child. They could hardly tell their opinions to each other, but they understood one another, and between them they coddled their Prime Minister. They were specially nervous as to what might be done by the Prime Minister's wife, nervous as to what was done by every one who came in contact with him. It had been once suggested by the private Secretary that Lady Rosina should be sent for, as she had a soothing effect upon the Prime Minister's spirit.

"Has it irritated him?" asked the Duke.

"Well;—yes, it has;—a little, you know. I think your Grace had better speak to him;—and not perhaps mention my name." The Duke of St. Bungay nodded his head, and said that he would speak to the great man and would not mention any one's name.

And he did speak. "Has any one said anything to you about it?" asked the Prime Minister.

"I saw it in the 'Evening Pulpit' myself. I have not heard it mentioned anywhere."

"I did pay the man's expenses."

"You did!"

"Yes,—when the election was over, and, as far as I can remember, some time after it was over. He wrote to me saying that he had incurred such and such expenses, and asking me to repay him. I sent him a cheque for the amount."

"But why?"

"I was bound in honour to do it."

"But why?"

There was a short pause before this second question was answered. "The man had been induced to stand by representations made to him from my house. He had been, I fear, promised certain support which certainly was not given him when the time came."

"You had not promised it?"

"No;—not I."

"Was it the Duchess?"

"Upon the whole, my friend, I think I would rather not discuss it further, even with you. It is right that you should know that I did pay the money,— and also why I paid it. It may also be necessary that we should consider whether there may be any further probable result from my doing so. But the money has been paid, by me myself,—and was paid for the reason I have stated."

"A question might be asked in the House."

"If so, it must be answered as I have answered you. I certainly shall not shirk any responsibility that may be attached to me."

"You would not like Warburton to write a line to the newspaper?"

"What;—to the 'People's Banner!'"

"It began there, did it? No, not to the 'People's Banner,' but to the 'Evening Pulpit.' He could say, you know, that the money was paid by you, and that the payment had been made because your agents had misapprehended your instructions."

"It would not be true," said the Prime Minister, slowly.

"As far as I can understand that was what occurred," said the other Duke.

"My instructions were not misapprehended. They were disobeyed. I think that perhaps we had better say no more about it."

"Do not think that I wish to press you," said the old man, tenderly; "but I fear that something ought to be done;—I mean for your own comfort."

"My comfort!" said the Prime Minister. "That has vanished long ago;— and my peace of mind, and my happiness."

"There has been nothing done which cannot be explained with perfect truth. There has been no impropriety."

"I do not know."

"The money was paid simply from an over-nice sense of honour."

"It cannot be explained. I cannot explain it even to you, and how then can I do it to all the gaping fools of the country who are ready to trample upon a man simply because he is in some way conspicuous among them?"

After that the old Duke again spoke to Mr. Warburton, but Mr. Warburton was very loyal to his chief. "Could one do anything by speaking to the Duchess?" said the old Duke.

"I think not."

"I suppose it was her Grace who did it all."

"I cannot say. My own impression is that he had better wait till the Houses meet, and then, if any question is asked, let it be answered. He himself would do it in the House of Lords, or Mr. Finn or Barrington Erle, in our House. It would surely be enough to explain that his Grace had been made to believe that the man had received encouragement at Silverbridge from his own agents, which he himself had not intended should be given, and that therefore he had thought it right to pay the money. After such an explanation what more could any one say?"

"You might do it yourself."

"I never speak."

"But in such a case as that you might do so; and then there would be no necessity for him to talk to another person on the matter."

So the affair was left for the present, though the allusions to it in the "People's Banner" were still continued. Nor did any other of the Prime Minister's colleagues dare to speak to him on the subject. Barrington Erle and Phineas Finn talked of it among themselves, but they did not mention it even to the Duchess. She would have gone to her husband at once; and they were too careful of him to risk such a proceeding. It certainly was the case that among them they coddled the Prime Minister.

Chapter LI
Coddling the Prime Minister

Parliament was to meet on the 12th of February, and it was of course necessary that there should be a Cabinet Council before that time. The Prime Minister, about the end of the third week in January, was prepared to name a day for this, and did so, most unwillingly. But he was then ill, and talked both to his friend the old Duke and his private Secretary of having the meeting held without him. "Impossible!" said the old Duke.

"If I could not go it would have to be possible."

"We could all come here if it were necessary."

"Bring fourteen or fifteen ministers out of town because a poor creature such as I am is ill!" But in truth the Duke of St. Bungay hardly believed in this illness. The Prime Minister was unhappy rather than ill.

By this time everybody in the House,—and almost everybody in the country who read the newspapers,—had heard of Mr. Lopez and his election expenses,—except the Duchess. No one had yet dared to tell her. She saw the newspapers daily, but probably did not read them very attentively. Nevertheless she knew that something was wrong. Mr. Warburton hovered about the Prime Minister more tenderly than usual; the Duke of St. Bungay was more concerned; the world around her was more mysterious, and her husband more wretched. "What is it that's going on?" she said one day to Phineas Finn.

"Everything,—in the same dull way as usual."

"If you don't tell me, I'll never speak to you again. I know there is something wrong."

"The Duke, I'm afraid, is not quite well."

"What makes him ill? I know well when he's ill and when he's well. He's troubled by something."

"I think he is, Duchess. But as he has not spoken to me I am loath to make guesses. If there be anything, I can only guess at it."

Then she questioned Mrs. Finn, and got an answer which, if not satisfactory, was at any rate explanatory. "I think he is uneasy about that Silverbridge affair."

"What Silverbridge affair?"

"You know that he paid the expenses which that man Lopez says that he incurred."

"Yes;—I know that."

"And you know that that other man Slide has found it out, and published it all in the 'People's Banner'?"

"No!"

"Yes, indeed. And a whole army of accusations has been brought against him. I have never liked to tell you, and yet I do not think that you should be left in the dark."

"Everybody deceives me," said the Duchess angrily.

"Nay;—there has been no deceit."

"Everybody keeps things from me. I think you will kill me among you. It was my doing. Why do they attack him? I will write to the papers. I encouraged the man after Plantagenet had determined that he should not be assisted,—and, because I had done so, he paid the man his beggarly money. What is there to hurt him in that? Let me bear it. My back is broad enough."

"The Duke is very sensitive."

"I hate people to be sensitive. It makes them cowards. A man when he is afraid of being blamed, dares not at last even show himself, and has to be wrapped up in lamb's wool."

"Of course men are differently organised."

"Yes;—but the worst of it is, that when they suffer from this weakness, which you call sensitiveness, they think that they are made of finer material than other people. Men shouldn't be made of Sèvres china, but of good stone earthenware. However, I don't want to abuse him, poor fellow."

"I don't think you ought."

"I know what that means. You do want to abuse me. So they've been bullying him about the money he paid to that man Lopez. How did anybody know anything about it?"

"Lopez must have told of it," said Mrs. Finn.

"The worst, my dear, of trying to know a great many people is, that you are sure to get hold of some that are very bad. Now that man is very bad. Yet they say he has married a nice wife."

"That's often the case, Duchess."

"And the contrary;—isn't it, my dear? But I shall have it out with Plantagenet. If I have to write letters to all the newspapers myself, I'll put it right." She certainly coddled her husband less than the others; and, indeed, in her heart of hearts disapproved altogether of the coddling system. But she was wont at this particular time to be somewhat tender to him because she was aware that she herself had been imprudent. Since he had discovered her interference at Silverbridge, and had made her understand its pernicious results, she had been,—not, perhaps, shamefaced, for that word describes a condition to which hardly any series of misfortunes could have reduced the Duchess of Omnium,—but inclined to quiescence by feelings of penitence. She was less disposed than heretofore to attack him with what the world of yesterday calls "chaff," or with what the world of to-day calls "cheek." She would not admit to herself that she was cowed;—but the greatness of the game and the high interest attached to her husband's position did in some degree dismay her. Nevertheless she executed her purpose of "having it out with Plantagenet." "I have just heard," she said, having knocked at the door of his own room, and having found him alone,—"I have just heard, for the first time, that there is a row about the money you paid to Mr. Lopez."

"Who told you?"

"Nobody told me,—in the usual sense of the word. I presumed that something was the matter, and then I got it out from Marie. Why had you not told me?"

"Why should I tell you?"

"But why not? If anything troubled me I should tell you. That is, if it troubled me much."

"You take it for granted that this does trouble me much." He was smiling as he said this, but the smile passed very quickly from his face. "I will not, however, deceive you. It does trouble me."

"I knew very well that something was wrong."

"I have not complained."

"One can see as much as that without words. What is it that you fear? What can the man do to you? What matter is it to you if such a one as that pours out his malice on you? Let it run off like the rain from the housetops. You are too big even to be stung by such a reptile as that." He looked into her face, admiring the energy with which she spoke to him. "As for answering him," she continued to say, "that may or may not be proper. If it should be done, there are people to do it. But I am speaking of your own inner self. You have a shield against your equals, and a sword to attack them with if necessary. Have you no armour of proof against such a creature as that? Have you nothing inside you to make you feel that he is too contemptible to be regarded?"

"Nothing," he said.

"Oh, Plantagenet!"

"Cora, there are different natures which have each their own excellencies and their own defects. I will not admit that I am a coward, believing as I do that I could dare to face necessary danger. But I cannot endure to have my character impugned,—even by Mr. Slide and Mr. Lopez."

"What matter,—if you are in the right? Why blench if your conscience accuses you of no fault? I would not blench even if it did. What;—is a man to be put in the front of everything, and then to be judged as though he could give all his time to the picking of his steps?"

"Just so! And he must pick them more warily than another."

"I do not believe it. You see all this with jaundiced eyes. I read somewhere the other day that the great ships have always little worms attached to them, but that the great ships swim on and know nothing of the worms."

"The worms conquer at last."

"They shouldn't conquer me! After all, what is it that they say about the money? That you ought not to have paid it?"

"I begin to think that I was wrong to pay it."

"You certainly were not wrong. I had led the man on. I had been mistaken. I had thought that he was a gentleman. Having led him on at first, before you had spoken to me, I did not like to go back from my word. I did go to the man at Silverbridge who sells the pots, and no doubt the man, when thus encouraged, told it all to Lopez. When Lopez went to the town he did suppose that he would have what the people call the Castle interest."

"And I had done so much to prevent it!"

"What's the use of going back to that now, unless you want me to put my neck down to be trodden on? I am confessing my own sins as fast as I can."

"God knows I would not have you trodden on."

"I am willing,—if it be necessary. Then came the question;—as I had done this evil, how was it to be rectified? Any man with a particle of spirit would have taken his rubs and said nothing about it. But as this man asked for the money, it was right that he should have it. If it is all made public he won't get very well out of it."

"What does that matter to me?"

"Nor shall I;—only luckily I do not mind it."

"But I mind it for you."

"You must throw me to the whale. Let somebody say in so many words that the Duchess did so and so. It was very wicked no doubt; but they can't kill me,—nor yet dismiss me. And I won't resign. In point of fact I shan't be a penny the worse for it."

"But I should resign."

"If all the Ministers in England were to give up as soon as their wives do foolish things, that question about the Queen's Government would become very difficult."

"They may do foolish things, dear; and yet—"

"And yet what?"

"And yet not interfere in politics."

"That's all you know about it, Plantagenet. Doesn't everybody know that Mrs. Daubeny got Dr. MacFuzlem made a bishop, and that Mrs. Gresham got her husband to make that hazy speech about women's rights, so that nobody should know which way he meant to go? There are others just as bad as me, only I don't think they get blown up so much. You do now as I ask you."

"I couldn't do it, Cora. Though the stain were but a little spot, and the thing to be avoided political destruction, I could not ride out of the punishment by fixing that stain on my wife. I will not have your name mentioned. A man's wife should be talked about by no one."

"That's high-foluting, Plantagenet."

"Glencora, in these matters you must allow me to judge for myself, and I will judge. I will never say that I didn't do it;—but that it was my wife who did."

"Adam said so,—because he chose to tell the truth."

"And Adam has been despised ever since,—not because he ate the apple, but because he imputed the eating of it to a woman. I will not do it. We have had enough of this now." Then she turned to go away,—but he called her back. "Kiss me, dear," he said. Then she stooped over him and kissed him. "Do not think I am angry with you because the thing vexes me. I am dreaming always of some day when we may go away together with the children, and rest in some pretty spot, and live as other people live."

"It would be very stupid," she muttered to herself as she left the room.

He did go up to town for the Cabinet meeting. Whatever may have been done at that august assembly there was certainly no resignation, or the world would have heard it. It is probable, too, that nothing was said about these newspaper articles. Things if left to themselves will generally die at last. The old Duke and Phineas Finn and Barrington Erle were all of opinion that the best plan for the present was to do nothing. "Has anything been settled?" the Duchess asked Phineas when he came back.

"Oh yes;—the Queen's Speech. But there isn't very much in it."

"But about the payment of this money?"

"I haven't heard a word about it," said Phineas.

"You're just as bad as all the rest, Mr. Finn, with your pretended secrecy. A girl with her first sweetheart isn't half so fussy as a young Cabinet Minister."

"The Cabinet Ministers get used to it sooner, I think," said Phineas Finn.

Parliament had already met before Mr. Slide had quite determined in what way he would carry on the war. He could indeed go on writing pernicious articles about the Prime Minister *ad infinitum*,—from year's end to year's end. It was an occupation in which he took delight, and for which he imagined himself to be peculiarly well suited. But readers will become tired even of abuse if it be not varied. And the very continuation of such attacks would seem to imply that they were not much heeded. Other papers had indeed taken the matter up,—but they had taken it up only to drop it. The subject had not been their own. The little discovery had been due not to their acumen, and did not therefore bear with them the highest interest. It had almost seemed as though nothing would come of it;—for Mr. Slide in his wildest ambition could have hardly imagined the vexation and hesitation, the nervousness and serious discussions which his words had occasioned among the great people at Matching. But certainly the thing must not be allowed to pass away as a matter of no moment. Mr. Slide had almost worked his mind up to real horror as he thought of it. What! A prime minister, a peer, a great duke,—put a man forward as a candidate for a borough, and, when the man was beaten, pay his expenses! Was this to be done,—to be done and found out and then nothing come of it in these days of purity, when a private member of Parliament, some mere nobody, loses his seat because he has given away a few bushels of coals or a score or two of rabbits! Mr. Slide's energetic love of public virtue was scandalised as he thought of the probability of such a catastrophe. To his thinking, public virtue consisted in carping at men high placed, in abusing ministers and judges and bishops—and especially in finding out something for which they might be abused. His own public virtue was in this matter very great, for it was he who had ferreted out the secret. For his intelligence and energy in that matter the country owed him much. But the country would pay him nothing, would give him none of the credit he desired, would rob him of this special opportunity of declaring a dozen times that the "People's Banner" was the surest guardian of the people's liberty,—unless he could succeed in forcing the matter further into public notice. "How terrible is the apathy of the people at large," said Mr. Slide to himself, "when they cannot be wakened by such a revelation as this!"

Mr. Slide knew very well what ought to be the next step. Proper notice should be given and a question should be asked in Parliament. Some gentleman should declare that he had noticed such and such statements in the public press, and that he thought it right to ask whether such and such payments had been made by the Prime Minister. In his meditations Mr. Slide went so far as to arrange the very words which the indignant gentleman should utter, among which words was a graceful allusion to a certain public-spirited newspaper. He did even go so far as to arrange a compliment to the editor,—but in doing so he knew that he was thinking only of that which ought to be, and not of that which would be. The time had not come as yet in which the editor of a newspaper in this country received a tithe of the honour due to him. But the question in any form, with or without a compliment to the "People's Banner," would be the thing that was now desirable.

Who was to ask the question? If public spirit were really strong in the country there would be no difficulty on that point. The crime committed had been so horrible that all the great politicians of the country ought to compete for the honour of asking it. What greater service can be trusted to the hands of a great man than that of exposing the sins of the rulers of the nation? So thought Mr. Slide. But he knew that he was in advance of the people, and that the matter would not be seen in the proper light by those who ought so to see it. There might be a difficulty in getting any peer to ask the question in the House in which the Prime Minister himself sat, and even in the other House there was now but little of that acrid, indignant opposition upon which, in Mr. Slide's opinion, the safety of the nation altogether depends.

When the statement was first made in the "People's Banner," Lopez had come to Mr. Slide at once and had demanded his authority for making it. Lopez had found the statement to be most injurious to himself. He had been paid his election expenses twice over, making a clear profit of £500 by the transaction; and, though the matter had at one time troubled his conscience, he had already taught himself to regard it as one of those bygones to which a wise man seldom refers. But now Mr. Wharton would know that he had been cheated, should this statement reach him. "Who gave you authority to publish all this?" asked Lopez, who at this time had become intimate with Mr. Slide.

"Is it true, Lopez?" asked the editor.

"Whatever was done was done in private,—between me and the Duke."

"Dukes, my dear fellow, can't be private, and certainly not when they are Prime Ministers."

"But you've no right to publish these things about me."

"Is it true? If it's true I have got every right to publish it. If it's not true, I've got the right to ask the question. If you will 'ave to do with Prime Ministers you can't 'ide yourself under a bushel. Tell me this;—is it true? You might as well go 'and in 'and with me in the matter. You can't 'urt yourself. And if you oppose me,—why, I shall oppose you."

"You can't say anything of me."

"Well;—I don't know about that. I can generally 'it pretty 'ard if I feel inclined. But I don't want to 'it you. As regards you I can tell the story one way,—or the other, just as you please." Lopez, seeing it in the same light, at last agreed that the story should be told in a manner not inimical to himself. The present project of his life was to leave his troubles in England,—Sexty

Parker being the worst of them,—and get away to Guatemala. In arranging this the good word of Mr. Slide might not benefit him, but his ill word might injure him. And then, let him do what he would, the matter must be made public. Should Mr. Wharton hear of it,—as of course he would,—it must be brazened out. He could not keep it from Mr. Wharton's ears by quarrelling with Quintus Slide.

"It was true," said Lopez.

"I knew it before just as well as though I had seen it. I ain't often very wrong in these things. You asked him for the money,—and threatened him."

"I don't know about threatening him."

"'E wouldn't have sent it else."

"I told him that I had been deceived by his people in the borough, and that I had been put to expense through the misrepresentations of the Duchess. I don't think I did ask for the money. But he sent a cheque, and of course I took it."

"Of course;—of course. You couldn't give me a copy of your letter?"

"Never kept a copy." He had a copy in his breast coat-pocket at that moment, and Slide did not for a moment believe the statement made. But in such discussions one man hardly expects truth from another. Mr. Slide certainly never expected truth from any man. "He sent the cheque almost without a word," said Lopez.

"He did write a note, I suppose?"

"Just a few words."

"Could you let me 'ave that note?"

"I destroyed it at once." This was also in his breast-pocket at the time.

"Did 'e write it 'imself?"

"I think it was his private Secretary, Mr. Warburton."

"You must be sure, you know. Which was it?"

"It was Mr. Warburton."

"Was it civil?"

"Yes, it was. If it had been uncivil I should have sent it back. I'm not the man to take impudence even from a duke."

"If you'll give me those two letters, Lopez, I'll stick to you through thick and thin. By heavens I will! Think what the 'People's Banner' is. You may come to want that kind of thing some of these days." Lopez remained silent, looking into the other man's eager face. "I shouldn't publish them, you know; but it would be so much to me to have the evidence in my hands. You might do worse, you know, than make a friend of me."

"You won't publish them?"

"Certainly not. I shall only refer to them."

Then Lopez pulled a bundle of papers out of his pocket. "There they are," he said.

"Well," said Slide, when he had read them; "it is one of the rummest transactions I ever 'eard of. Why did 'e send the money? That's what I want to know. As far as the claim goes, you 'adn't a leg to stand on."

"Not legally."

"You 'adn't a leg to stand on any way. But that doesn't much matter. He sent the money, and the sending of the money was corrupt. Who shall I get to ask the question? I suppose young Fletcher wouldn't do it?"

"They're birds of a feather," said Lopez.

"Birds of a feather do fall out sometimes. Or Sir Orlando Drought? I wonder whether Sir Orlando would do it. If any man ever 'ated another, Sir Orlando Drought must 'ate the Duke of Omnium."

"I don't think he'd let himself down to that kind of thing."

"Let 'imself down! I don't see any letting down in it. But those men who have been in cabinets do stick to one another even when they are enemies. They think themselves so mighty that they oughtn't to be 'andled like other men. But I'll let 'em know that I'll 'andle 'em. A Cabinet Minister or a cowboy is the same to Quintus Slide when he has got his pen in 'is 'and."

On the next morning there came out another article in the "People's Banner," in which the writer declared that he had in his own possession the damnatory correspondence between the Prime Minister and the late candidate at Silverbridge. "The Prime Minister may deny the fact," said the article. "We do not think it probable, but it is possible. We wish to be fair and above-board in everything. And therefore we at once inform the noble Duke that the entire correspondence is in our hands." In saying this Mr. Quintus Slide thought that he had quite kept the promise which he made when he said that he would only refer to the letters.

Chapter LII
"I Can Sleep Here To-night, I Suppose?"

That scheme of going to Guatemala had been in the first instance propounded by Lopez with the object of frightening Mr. Wharton into terms. There had, indeed, been some previous thoughts on the subject,— some plan projected before his marriage; but it had been resuscitated mainly with the hope that it might be efficacious to extract money. When by degrees the son-in-law began to feel that even this would not be operative on his father-in-law's purse,—when under this threat neither Wharton nor Emily gave way,—and when, with the view of strengthening his threat, he renewed his inquiries as to Guatemala and found that there might still be an opening for him in that direction,—the threat took the shape of a true purpose, and he began to think that he would in real earnest try his fortunes in a new world. From day to day things did not go well with him, and from day to day Sexty Parker became more unendurable. It was impossible for him to keep from his partner this plan of emigration,—but he endeavoured to make Parker believe that the thing, if done at all, was not to be done till all his affairs were settled,—or in other words all his embarrassments cleared by downright money payments, and that Mr. Wharton was to make these payments on the condition that he thus expatriated himself. But Mr. Wharton had made no such promise. Though the threatened day came nearer and nearer he could not bring himself to purchase a short respite for his daughter by paying money to a scoundrel,—which payment he felt sure would be of no permanent service. During all this time Mr. Wharton was very wretched. If he could have freed his daughter from her marriage by half his fortune he would have done it without a second thought. If he could have assuredly purchased the permanent absence of her husband, he would have done it at a large price. But let him pay what he would, he could see his way to no security. From day to day he became more strongly convinced of the rascality of this man who was his son-in-law, and who was still an inmate in his own house. Of course he had accusations enough to make within his own breast against his daughter, who, when the choice was open to her, would not take the altogether fitting husband provided for her, but had declared herself to be broken-hearted for ever unless she were allowed to throw herself away upon this wretched creature. But he blamed himself almost as much as he did her. Why had he allowed himself to be so enervated by her prayers at last as to surrender everything,—as he had done? How could he presume to think that he should be allowed to escape, when he had done so little to prevent this misery?

He spoke to Emily about it,—not often indeed, but with great earnestness. "I have done it myself," she said, "and I will bear it."

"Tell him you cannot go till you know to what home you are going."

"That is for him to consider. I have begged him to let me remain, and I can say no more. If he chooses to take me, I shall go."

Then he spoke to her about money. "Of course I have money," he said. "Of course I have enough both for you and Everett. If I could do any good by giving it to him, he should have it."

"Papa," she answered, "I will never again ask you to give him a single penny. That must be altogether between you and him. He is what they call a speculator. Money is not safe with him."

"I shall have to send it you when you are in want."

"When I am—dead there will be no more to be sent. Do not look like that, papa. I know what I have done, and I must bear it. I have thrown away my life. It is just that. If baby had lived it would have been different." This was about the end of January, and then Mr. Wharton heard of the great attack made by Mr. Quintus Slide against the Prime Minister, and heard, of course, of the payment alleged to have been made to Ferdinand Lopez by the Duke on the score of the election at Silverbridge. Some persons spoke to him on the subject. One or two friends at the club asked him what he supposed to be the truth in the matter, and Mrs. Roby inquired of him on the subject. "I have asked Lopez," she said, "and I am sure from his manner that he did get the money."

"I don't know anything about it," said Mr. Wharton.

"If he did get it I think he was very clever." It was well known at this time to Mrs. Roby that the Lopez marriage had been a failure, that Lopez was not a rich man, and that Emily, as well as her father, was discontented and unhappy. She had latterly heard of the Guatemala scheme, and had of course expressed her horror. But she sympathised with Lopez rather than with his wife, thinking that if Mr. Wharton would only open his pockets wide enough things might still be right. "It was all the Duchess's fault, you know," she said to the old man.

"I know nothing about it, and when I want to know I certainly shall not come to you. The misery he has brought upon me is so great that it makes me wish that I had never seen any one who knew him."

"It was Everett who introduced him to your house."

"It was you who introduced him to Everett."

"There you are wrong,—as you so often are, Mr. Wharton. Everett met him first at the club."

"What's the use of arguing about it? It was at your house that Emily met him. It was you that did it. I wonder you can have the face to mention his name to me."

"And the man living all the time in your own house!"

Up to this time Mr. Wharton had not mentioned to a single person the fact that he had paid his son-in-law's election expenses at Silverbridge. He had given him the cheque without much consideration, with the feeling that by doing so he would in some degree benefit his daughter; and had since regretted the act, finding that no such payment from him could be of any service to Emily. But the thing had been done,—and there had been, so far, an end of it. In no subsequent discussion would Mr. Wharton have alluded to it, had not circumstances now as it were driven it back upon his mind. And since the day on which he had paid that money he had been, as he declared to himself, swindled over and over again by his son-in-law. There was the dinner in Manchester Square, and after that the brougham, and the rent, and a score of bills, some of which he had paid and some declined to pay! And yet he had said but little to the man himself of all these injuries. Of what use was it to say anything? Lopez would simply reply that he had asked him to pay nothing. "What is it all," Lopez had once said, "to the fortune I had a right to expect with your daughter?" "You had no right to expect a shilling," Wharton had said. Then Lopez had shrugged his shoulders, and there had been an end of it.

But now, if this rumour were true, there had been positive dishonesty. From whichever source the man might have got the money first, if the money had been twice got, the second payment had been fraudulently obtained. Surely if the accusation had been untrue Lopez would have come to him and declared it to be false, knowing what must otherwise be his thoughts. Lately, in the daily worry of his life, he had avoided all conversation with the man. He would not allow his mind to contemplate clearly what was coming. He entertained some irrational, undefined hope that something would at last save his daughter from the threatened banishment. It might be, if he held his own hand tight enough, that there would not be money enough even to pay for her passage out. As for her outfit, Lopez would of course order what he wanted and have the bills sent to Manchester Square. Whether or not this was being done neither he nor Emily knew. And thus matters went on without much speech between the two men. But now the old barrister thought that he was bound to speak. He therefore waited on a certain morning till Lopez had come down, having previously desired his daughter to leave the room. "Lopez," he asked, "what is this that the newspapers are saying about your expenses at Silverbridge?"

Lopez had expected the attack and had endeavoured to prepare himself for it. "I should have thought, sir, that you would not have paid much attention to such statements in a newspaper."

"When they concern myself, I do. I paid your electioneering expenses."

"You certainly subscribed £500 towards them, Mr. Wharton."

"I subscribed nothing, sir. There was no question of a subscription,—by which you intend to imply contribution from various sources; You told me that the contest cost you £500 and that sum I handed to you, with the full understanding on your part, as well as on mine, that I was paying for the whole. Was that so?"

"Have it your own way, sir."

"If you are not more precise, I shall think that you have defrauded me."

"Defrauded you!"

"Yes, sir;—defrauded me, or the Duke of Omnium. The money is gone, and it matters little which. But if that be so I shall know that either from him or from me you have raised money under false pretences."

"Of course, Mr. Wharton, from you I must bear whatever you may choose to say."

"Is it true that you have applied to the Duke of Omnium for money on account of your expenses at Silverbridge, and is it true that he has paid you money on that score?"

"Mr. Wharton, as I said just now, I am bound to hear and to bear from you anything that you may choose to say. Your connection with my wife and your age alike restrain my resentment. But I am not bound to answer your questions when they are accompanied by such language as you have chosen to use, and I refuse to answer any further questions on this subject."

"Of course I know that you have taken the money from the Duke."

"Then why do you ask me?"

"And of course I know that you are as well aware as I am of the nature of the transaction. That you can brazen it out without a blush only proves to me that you have got beyond the reach of shame!"

"Very well, sir."

"And you have no further explanation to make?"

"What do you expect me to say? Without knowing any of the facts of the case,—except the one, that you contributed £500 to my election expenses,— you take upon yourself to tell me that I am a shameless, fraudulent swindler. And then you ask for a further explanation! In such a position is it likely that I shall explain anything;—that I can be in a humour to be explanatory? Just turn it all over in your mind, and ask yourself the question."

"I have turned it over in my own mind, and I have asked myself the question, and I do not think it probable that you should wish to explain anything. I shall take steps to let the Duke know that I as your father-in-law had paid the full sum which you had stated that you had spent at Silverbridge."

"Much the Duke will care about that."

"And after what has passed I am obliged to say that the sooner you leave this house the better I shall be pleased."

"Very well, sir. Of course I shall take my wife with me."

"That must be as she pleases."

"No, Mr. Wharton. That must be as I please. She belongs to me,—not to you or to herself. Under your influence she has forgotten much of what belongs to the duty of a wife, but I do not think that she will so far have forgotten herself as to give me more trouble than to bid her come with me when I desire it."

"Let that be as it may, I must request that you, sir, will absent yourself. I will not entertain as my guest a man who has acted as you have done in this matter,—even though he be my son-in-law."

"I can sleep here to-night, I suppose?"

"Or to-morrow if it suits you. As for Emily, she can remain here, if you will allow her to do so."

"That will not suit me," said Lopez.

"In that case, as far as I am concerned, I shall do whatever she may ask me to do. Good morning."

Mr. Wharton left the room, but did not leave the house. Before he did so he would see his daughter; and, thinking it probable that Lopez would also choose to see his wife, he prepared to wait in his own room. But, in about ten minutes, Lopez started from the hall door in a cab, and did so without going upstairs. Mr. Wharton had reason to believe that his son-in-law was almost destitute of money for immediate purposes. Whatever he might have would at any rate be serviceable to him before he started. Any home for Emily must be expensive; and no home in their present circumstances could be so reputable for her as one under her father's roof. He therefore almost hoped that she might still be left with him till that horrid day should come,—if it ever did come,—in which she would be taken away from him for ever. "Of course, papa, I shall go if he bids me," she said, when he told her all that he thought right to tell her of that morning's interview.

"I hardly know how to advise you," said the father, meaning in truth to bring himself round to the giving of some advice adverse to her husband's will.

"I want no advice, papa."

"Want no advice! I never knew a woman who wanted it more."

"No, papa. I am bound to do as he tells me. I know what I have done. When some poor wretch has got himself into perpetual prison by his misdeeds, no advice can serve him then. So it is with me."

"You can at any rate escape from your prison."

"No;—no. I have a feeling of pride which tells me that as I chose to become the wife of my husband,—as I insisted on it in opposition to all my friends,—as I would judge for myself,—I am bound to put up with my choice. If this had come upon me through the authority of others, if I had been constrained to marry him, I think I could have reconciled myself to deserting him. But I did it myself, and I will abide by it. When he bids me go, I shall go." Poor Mr. Wharton went to his chambers, and sat there the whole day without taking a book or a paper into his hands. Could there be no rescue, no protection, no relief! He turned over in his head various plans, but in a vague and useless manner. What if the Duke were to prosecute Lopez for the fraud! What if he could induce Lopez to abandon his wife,—pledging himself by some deed not to return to her,—for, say, twenty or even thirty thousand pounds! What if he himself were to carry his daughter away to the continent, half forcing and half persuading her to make the journey! Surely there might be some means found by which the man might be frightened into compliance. But there he sat,—and did nothing. And in the evening he ate a solitary mutton chop at The Jolly Blackbird, because he could not bear to face even his club, and then returned to his chambers,—to the great disgust of the old woman who had them in charge at nights. And at about midnight he crept away to his own house, a wretched old man.

Lopez when he left Manchester Square did not go in search of a new home for himself and his wife, nor during the whole of the day did he trouble himself on that subject. He spent most of the day at the rooms in Coleman Street of the San Juan Mining Association, of which Mr. Mills Happerton had once been Chairman. There was now another Chairman and other Directors; but Mr. Mills Happerton's influence had so far remained with the Company as to enable Lopez to become well known in the Company's offices, and acknowledged as a claimant for the office of resident Manager at San Juan in Guatemala. Now the present project was this,—that Lopez was to start on behalf of the Company early in May, that the Company was to pay his own personal expenses out to Guatemala, and that they should allow him while there a salary of £1000 a year for managing the affairs of the mine. As far as this offer went, the thing was true enough. It was true that Lopez had absolutely secured the place. But he had done so subject to the burden of one very serious stipulation. He was to become proprietor of 50 shares in the mine, and to pay up £100 each on those shares. It was considered that the man who was to get £1000 a year in Guatemala for managing the affair, should at any rate assist the affair, and show his confidence in the affair to an extent as great as that. Of course the holder of these 50 shares would be as fully entitled as any other shareholder to that 20 per cent. which those who promoted the mine promised as the immediate result of the speculation.

At first Lopez had hoped that he might be enabled to defer the actual payment of the £5000 till after he had sailed. When once out in Guatemala as manager, as manager he would doubtless remain. But by degrees he found that the payment must actually be made in advance. Now there was nobody to whom he could apply but Mr. Wharton. He was, indeed, forced to declare at the office that the money was to come from Mr. Wharton, and had given some excellent but fictitious reason why Mr. Wharton would not pay the money till February.

And in spite of all that had come and gone he still did hope that if the need to go were actually there he might even yet get the money from Mr. Wharton. Surely Mr. Wharton would sooner pay such a sum than be troubled at home with such a son-in-law. Should the worst come to the worst, of course he could raise the money by consenting to leave his wife at home. But this was not part of his plan, if he could avoid it. £5000 would be a very low price at which to sell his wife, and all that he might get from his connection with her. As long as he kept her with him he was in possession at any rate of all that Mr. Wharton would do for her. He had not therefore as yet made his final application to his father-in-law for the money, having found it possible to postpone the payment till the middle of February. His quarrel with Mr. Wharton this morning he regarded as having little or no effect upon his circumstances. Mr. Wharton would not give him the money because he loved him, nor yet from personal respect, nor from any sense of duty as to what he might owe to a son-in-law. It would be simply given as the price by which his absence might be purchased, and his absence would not be the less desirable because of this morning's quarrel.

But, even yet, he was not quite resolved as to going to Guatemala. Sexty Parker had been sucked nearly dry, and was in truth at this moment so violent with indignation and fear and remorse that Lopez did not dare to show himself in Little Tankard Yard; but still there were, even yet, certain hopes in that direction from which great results might come. If a certain new spirit which had just been concocted from the bark of trees in Central Africa, and which was called Bios, could only be made to go up in the market, everything might be satisfactorily arranged. The hoardings of London were already telling the public that if it wished to get drunk without any of the usual troubles of intoxication it must drink Bios. The public no doubt does read the literature of the hoardings, but then it reads so slowly! This Bios had hardly been twelve months on the boards as yet! But they were now increasing the size of the letters in the advertisements and the jocundity of the pictures,—and the thing might be done. There was, too, another hope,— another hope of instant moneys by which Guatemala might be staved off, as to which further explanation shall be given in a further chapter.

"I suppose I shall find Dixon a decent sort of a fellow?" said Lopez to the Secretary of the Association in Coleman Street.

"Rough, you know."

"But honest?"

"Oh, yes;—he's all that."

"If he's honest, and what I call loyal, I don't care a straw for anything else. One doesn't expect West-end manners in Guatemala. But I shall have a deal to do with him,—and I hate a fellow that you can't depend on."

"Mr. Happerton used to think a great deal of Dixon."

"That's all right," said Lopez. Mr. Dixon was the underground manager out at the San Juan mine, and was perhaps as anxious for a loyal and honest colleague as was Mr. Lopez. If so, Mr. Dixon was very much in the way to be disappointed.

Lopez stayed at the office all the day studying the affairs of the San Juan mine, and then went to the Progress for his dinner. Hitherto he had taken no steps whatever as to getting lodgings for himself or for his wife.

Chapter LIII
Mr. Hartlepod

When the time came at which Lopez should have left Manchester Square he was still there. Mr. Wharton, in discussing the matter with his daughter,—when wishing to persuade her that she might remain in his house even in opposition to her husband,—had not told her that he had actually desired Lopez to leave it. He had then felt sure that the man would go and would take his wife with him, but he did not even yet know the obduracy and the cleverness and the impregnability of his son-in-law. When the time came, when he saw his daughter in the morning after the notice had been given, he could not bring himself even yet to say to her that he had issued an order for his banishment. Days went by and Lopez was still there, and the old barrister said no further word on the subject. The two men never met;—or met simply in the hall or passages. Wharton himself studiously avoided such meetings, thus denying himself the commonest uses of his own house. At last Emily told him that her husband had fixed the day for her departure. The next Indian mail-packet by which they would leave England would start from Southampton on the 2nd of April, and she was to be ready to go on that day. "How is it to be till then?" the father asked in a low, uncertain voice.

"I suppose I may remain with you."

"And your husband?"

"He will be here too,—I suppose."

"Such a misery,—such a destruction of everything no man ever heard of before!" said Mr. Wharton. To this she made no reply, but continued working at some necessary preparation for her final departure. "Emily," he said, "I will make any sacrifice to prevent it. What can be done? Short of injuring Everett's interests I will do anything."

"I do not know," she said.

"You must understand something of his affairs."

"Nothing whatever. He has told me nothing of them. In earlier days,— soon after our marriage,—he bade me get money from you."

"When you wrote to me for money from Italy?"

"And after that. I have refused to do anything;—to say a word. I told him that it must be between you and him. What else could I say? And now he tells me nothing."

"I cannot think that he should want you to go with him." Then there was again a pause. "Is it because he loves you?"

"Not that, papa."

"Why then should he burden himself with a companion? His money, whatever he has, would go further without such impediment."

"Perhaps he thinks, papa, that while I am with him he has a hold upon you."

"He shall have a stronger hold by leaving you. What is he to gain? If I could only know his price."

"Ask him, papa."

"I do not even know how I am to speak to him again."

Then again there was a pause. "Papa," she said after a while, "I have done it myself. Let me go. You will still have Everett. And it may be that after a time I shall come back to you. He will not kill me, and it may be that I shall not die."

"By God!" said Mr. Wharton, rising from his chair suddenly, "if there were money to be made by it, I believe that he would murder you without scruple." Thus it was that within eighteen months of her marriage the father spoke to his daughter of her husband.

"What am I to take with me?" she said to her husband a few days later.

"You had better ask your father."

"Why should I ask him, Ferdinand? How should he know?"

"And how should I?"

"I should have thought that you would interest yourself about it."

"Upon my word I have enough to interest me just at present, without thinking of your finery. I suppose you mean what clothes you should have?"

"I was not thinking of myself only."

"You need think of nothing else. Ask him what he pleases to allow you to spend, and then I will tell you what to get."

"I will never ask him for anything, Ferdinand."

"Then you may go without anything. You might as well do it at once, for you will have to do it sooner or later. Or, if you please, go to his tradesmen and say nothing to him about it. They will give you credit. You see how it is, my dear. He has cheated me in a most rascally manner. He has allowed me to marry his daughter, and because I did not make a bargain with him as another man would have done, he denies me the fortune I had a right to expect with you. You know that the Israelites despoiled the Egyptians, and it was taken as a merit on their part. Your father is an Egyptian to me, and I will despoil him. You can tell him that I say so if you please."

And so the days went on till the first week of February had passed, and Parliament had met. Both Lopez and his wife were still living in Manchester Square. Not another word had been said as to that notice to quit, nor an allusion made to it. It was supposed to be a settled thing that Lopez was to start with his wife for Guatemala in the first week in April. Mr. Wharton had himself felt that difficulty as to his daughter's outfit, and had told her that she might get whatever it pleased her on his credit. "For yourself, my dear."

"Papa, I will get nothing till he bids me."

"But you can't go across the world without anything. What are you to do in such a place as that unless you have the things you want?"

"What do poor people do who have to go? What should I do if you had cast me off because of my disobedience?"

"But I have not cast you off."

"Tell him that you will give him so much, and then, if he bids me, I will spend it."

"Let it be so. I will tell him."

Upon that Mr. Wharton did speak to his son-in-law;—coming upon him suddenly one morning in the dining-room. "Emily will want an outfit if she is to go to this place."

"Like other people she wants many things that she cannot get."

"I will tell my tradesmen to furnish her with what she wants, up to,—well,—suppose I say £200. I have spoken to her and she wants your sanction."

"My sanction for spending your money? She can have that very quickly."

"You can tell her so;—or I will do so."

Upon that Mr. Wharton was going, but Lopez stopped him. It was now essential that the money for the shares in the San Juan mine should be paid up, and his father-in-law's pocket was still the source from which the enterprising son-in-law hoped to procure it. Lopez had fully made up his mind to demand it, and thought that the time had now come. And he was resolved that he would not ask it as a favour on bended knee. He was beginning to feel his own power, and trusted that he might prevail by other means than begging. "Mr. Wharton," he said, "you and I have not been very good friends lately."

"No, indeed."

"There was a time,—a very short time,—during which I thought that we might hit it off together, and I did my best. You do not, I fancy, like men of my class."

"Well;—well! You had better go on if there be anything to say."

"I have much to say, and I will go on. You are a rich man, and I am your son-in-law." Mr. Wharton put his left hand up to his forehead, brushing the few hairs back from his head, but he said nothing. "Had I received from you during the last most vital year that assistance which I think I had a right to expect, I also might have been a rich man now. It is no good going back to that." Then he paused, but still Mr. Wharton said nothing. "Now you know what has come to me and to your daughter. We are to be expatriated."

"Is that my fault?"

"I think it is, but I mean to say nothing further of that. This Company which is sending me out, and which will probably be the most thriving thing of the kind which has come up within these twenty years, is to pay me a salary of £1000 a year as resident manager at San Juan."

"So I understand."

"The salary alone would be a beggarly thing. Guatemala, I take it, is not the cheapest country in the world in which a man can live. But I am to go out as the owner of fifty shares on which £100 each must be paid up, and I am entitled to draw another £1000 a year as dividend on the profit of those shares."

"That will be twenty per cent."

"Exactly."

"And will double your salary."

"Just so. But there is one little ceremony to be perfected before I can be allowed to enter upon so halcyon a state of existence. The £100 a share must be paid up." Mr. Wharton simply stared at him. "I must have the £5000 to invest in the undertaking before I can start."

"Well!"

"Now I have not got £5000 myself, nor any part of it. You do not wish, I suppose, to see either me or your daughter starve. And as for me, I hardly flatter myself when I say that you are very anxious to be rid of me. £5000 is not very much for me to ask of you, as I regard it."

"Such consummate impudence I never met in my life before!"

"Nor perhaps so much unprevaricating downright truth. At any rate such is the condition of my affairs. If I am to go the money must be paid this week. I have, perhaps foolishly, put off mentioning the matter till I was sure that I could not raise the sum elsewhere. Though I feel my claim on you to be good, Mr. Wharton, it is not pleasant to me to make it."

"You are asking me for £5000 down!"

"Certainly I am."

"What security am I to have?"

"Security?"

"Yes;—that if I pay it I shall not be troubled again by the meanest scoundrel that it has ever been my misfortune to meet. How am I to know that you will not come back to-morrow? How am I to know that you will go at all? Do you think it probable that I will give you £5000 on your own simple word?"

"Then the scoundrel will stay in England,—and will generally find it convenient to live in Manchester Square."

"I'll be d——d if he does. Look here, sir. Between you and me there can be a bargain, and nothing but a bargain. I will pay the £5000,—on certain conditions."

"I didn't doubt at all that you would pay it."

"I will go with you to the office of this Company, and will pay for the shares if I can receive assurance there that the matter is as you say, and that the shares will not be placed in your power before you have reached Guatemala."

"You can come to-day, sir, and receive all that assurance."

"And I must have a written undertaking from you,—a document which my daughter can show if it be necessary,—that you will never claim her society again or trouble her with any application."

"You mistake me, Mr. Wharton. My wife goes with me to Guatemala."

"Then I will not pay one penny. Why should I? What is your presence or absence to me except as it concerns her? Do you think that I care for your threats of remaining here? The police will set that right."

"Wherever I go, my wife goes."

"We'll see to that too. If you want the money, you must leave her. Good morning."

Mr. Wharton as he went to his chambers thought the matter over. He was certainly willing to risk the £5000 demanded if he could rid himself and his daughter of this terrible incubus, even if it were only for a time. If Lopez would but once go to Guatemala, leaving his wife behind him, it would be comparatively easy to keep them apart should he ever return. The difficulty now was not in him but in her. The man's conduct had been so outrageous, so bare-faced, so cruel, that the lawyer did not doubt but that he could turn the husband out of his house, and keep the wife, even now, were it not that she was determined to obey the man whom she, in opposition to all her friends, had taken as her master. "I have done it myself, and I will bear it," was all the answer she would make when her father strove to persuade her to separate herself from her husband. "You have got Everett," she would say. "When a girl is married she is divided from her family;—and I am divided." But she would willingly stay if Lopez would bid her stay. It now seemed that he could not go without the £5000; and, when the pressure came upon him, surely he would go and leave his wife.

In the course of that day Mr. Wharton went to the offices of the San Juan mine and asked to see the Director. He was shown up into a half-furnished room, two stories high, in Coleman Street, where he found two clerks sitting upon stools;—and when he asked for the Director was shown into the back room in which sat the Secretary. The Secretary was a dark, plump little man with a greasy face, who had the gift of assuming an air of great importance as he twisted his chair round to face visitors who came to inquire about the San Juan Mining Company. His name was Hartlepod; and if the San Juan mine "turned out trumps," as he intended that it should, Mr. Hartlepod meant to be a great man in the City. To Mr. Hartlepod Mr. Wharton, with considerable embarrassment, explained as much of the joint history of himself and Lopez as he found to be absolutely necessary. "He has only left the office about half-an-hour," said Mr. Hartlepod.

"Of course you understand that he is my son-in-law."

"He has mentioned your name to us, Mr. Wharton, before now."

"And he is going out to Guatemala?"

"Oh yes;—he's going out. Has he not told you as much himself?"

"Certainly, sir. And he has told me that he is desirous of buying certain shares in the Company before he starts."

"Probably, Mr. Wharton."

"Indeed, I believe he cannot go unless he buys them."

"That may be so, Mr. Wharton. No doubt he has told you all that himself."

"The fact is, Mr. Hartlepod, I am willing, under certain stipulations, to advance him the money." Mr. Hartlepod bowed. "I need not trouble you with private affairs between myself and my son-in-law." Again the Secretary bowed. "But it seems to be for his interest that he should go."

"A very great opening indeed, Mr. Wharton. I don't see how a man is to have a better opening. A fine salary! His expenses out paid! One of the very best things that has come up for many years! And as for the capital he is to embark in the affair, he is as safe to get 20 per cent. on it,—as safe,—as safe as the Bank of England."

"He'll have the shares?"

"Oh yes;—the scrip will be handed to him at once."

"And,—and—"

"If you mean about the mine, Mr. Wharton, you may take my word that it's all real. It's not one of those sham things that melt away like snow and leave the shareholders nowhere. There's the prospectus, Mr. Wharton. Perhaps you have not seen that before. Take it away and cast your eye over it at your leisure." Mr. Wharton put the somewhat lengthy pamphlet into his pocket. "Look at the list of Directors. We've three members of Parliament, a baronet, and one or two City names that are as good—as good as the Bank of England. If that prospectus won't make a man confident I don't know what will. Why, Mr. Wharton, you don't think that your son-in-law would get those fifty shares at par unless he was going out as our general local manager. The shares ain't to be had. It's a large concern as far as capital goes. You'll see if you look. About a quarter of a million paid up. But it's all in a box as one may say. It's among ourselves. The shares ain't in the market. Of course it's not for me to say what should be done between you and your son-in-law. Lopez is a friend of mine, and a man I esteem, and all that. Nevertheless I shouldn't think of advising you to do this or that,—or not to do it. But when you talk of safety, Mr. Wharton,—why, Mr. Wharton, I don't scruple to tell you as a man who knows what these things are, that this is an opportunity that doesn't come in a man's way perhaps twice in his life."

Mr. Wharton found that he had nothing more to say, and went back to Lincoln's Inn. He knew very well that Mr. Hartlepod's assurances were not worth much. Mr. Hartlepod himself and his belongings, the clerks in his office, the look of the rooms, and the very nature of the praises which he had sung, all of them inspired anything but confidence. Mr. Wharton was a man of the world; and, though he knew nothing of City ways, was quite aware that no man in his senses would lay out £5000 on the mere word of Mr. Hartlepod. But still he was inclined to make the payment. If only he could secure the absence of Lopez,—if he could be sure that Lopez would in truth go to Guatemala, and if also he could induce the man to go without his wife, he would risk the money. The money would, of course, be thrown away,—but he would throw it away. Lopez no doubt had declared that he would not go without his wife, even though the money were paid for him. But the money was an alluring sum! As the pressure upon the man became greater, Mr. Wharton thought he would probably consent to leave his wife behind him.

In his emergency the barrister went to his attorney and told him everything. The two lawyers were closeted together for an hour, and Mr. Wharton's last words to his old friend were as follows:—"I will risk the money, Walker, or rather I will consent absolutely to throw it away,—as it will be thrown away,—if it can be managed that he shall in truth go to this place without his wife."

Chapter LIV
Lizzie

It cannot be supposed that Ferdinand Lopez at this time was a very happy man. He had, at any rate, once loved his wife, and would have loved her still could he have trained her to think as he thought, to share his wishes, and "to put herself into the same boat with him," —as he was wont to describe the unison and sympathy which he required from her. To give him his due, he did not know that he was a villain. When he was exhorting her to "get round her father" he was not aware that he was giving her lessons which must shock a well-conditioned girl. He did not understand that everything that she had discovered of his moral disposition since her marriage was of a nature to disgust her. And, not understanding all this, he conceived that he was grievously wronged by her in that she adhered to her father rather than to him. This made him unhappy, and doubly disappointed him. He had neither got the wife that he had expected nor the fortune. But he still thought that the fortune must come if he would only hold on to the wife which he had got.

And then everything had gone badly with him since his marriage. He was apt, when thinking over his affairs, to attribute all this to the fears and hesitation and parsimony of Sexty Parker. None of his late ventures with Sexty Parker had been successful. And now Sexty was in a bad condition, very violent, drinking hard, declaring himself to be a ruined man, and swearing that if this and that were not done he would have bitter revenge. Sexty still believed in the wealth of his partner's father-in-law, and still had some hope of salvation from that source. Lopez would declare to him, and up to this very time persevered in protesting, that salvation was to be found in Bios. If Sexty would only risk two or three thousand pounds more upon Bios,—or his credit to that amount, failing the immediate money,—things might still be right. "Bios be d——," said Sexty, uttering a string of heavy imprecations. On that morning he had been trusting to native produce rather than to the new African spirit. But now as the Guatemala scheme really took form and loomed on Lopez's eyesight as a thing that might be real, he endeavoured to keep out of Sexty's way. But in vain; Sexty too had heard of Guatemala, and in his misery hunted Lopez about the city. "By G——, I believe you're afraid to come to Little Tankard Yard," he said one day, having caught his victim under the equestrian statue in front of the Exchange.

"What is the good of my coming when you will do nothing when I am there?"

"I'll tell you what it is, Lopez,—you're not going out of the country about this mining business, if I know it."

"Who said I was?"

"I'll put a spoke in your wheel there, my man. I'll give a written account of all the dealings between us to the Directors. By G——, they shall know their man."

"You're an ass, Sexty, and always were. Look here. If I can carry on as though I were going to this place, I can draw £5000 from old Wharton. He has already offered it. He has treated me with a stinginess that I never knew equalled. Had he done what I had a right to expect, you and I would have been rich men now. But at last I have got a hold upon him up to £5000. As you and I stand, pretty nearly the whole of that will go to you. But don't you spoil it all by making an ass of yourself."

Sexty, who was three parts drunk, looked up into his face for a few seconds, and then made his reply. "I'm d——d if I believe a word of it." Upon this Lopez affected to laugh, and then made his escape.

All this, as I have said, did not tend to make his life happy. Though he had impudence enough, and callousness of conscience enough, to get his bills paid by Mr. Wharton as often as he could, he was not quite easy in his mind while doing so. His ambition had never been high, but it had soared higher than that. He had had great hopes. He had lived with some high people. He had dined with lords and ladies. He had been the guest of a Duchess. He had married the daughter of a gentleman. He had nearly been a member of Parliament. He still belonged to what he considered to be a first-rate club. From a great altitude he looked down upon Sexty Parker and men of Sexty's class, because of his social successes, and because he knew how to talk and to look like a gentleman. It was unpleasant to him, therefore, to be driven to the life he was now living. And the idea of going out to Guatemala and burying himself in a mine in Central America was not to him a happy idea. In spite of all that he had done he had still some hope that he might avoid that banishment. He had spoken the truth to Sexty Parker in saying that he intended to get the £5000 from Mr. Wharton without that terrible personal sacrifice, though he had hardly spoken the truth when he assured his friend that the greater portion of that money would go to him. There were many schemes fluctuating through his brain, and all accompanied by many doubts. If he could get Mr. Wharton's money by giving up his wife, should he consent to give her up? In either case should he stay or should he go? Should he run one further great chance with Bios,—and if so, by whose assistance? And if he should at last decide that he would do so by the aid of a certain friend that was yet left to him, should he throw himself at that friend's feet, the friend being a lady, and propose to desert his wife and begin the world again with her? For the lady in question was a lady in possession, as he believed, of very large means. Or should he cut his throat and have done at once with all his troubles, acknowledging to himself that his career had been a failure, and that, therefore, it might be brought with advantage to an end? "After all," said he to himself, "that may be the best way of winding up a bankrupt concern."

Our old friend Lady Eustace, in these days, lived in a very small house in a very small street bordering upon May Fair; but the street, though very small, and having disagreeable relations with a mews, still had an air of fashion about it. And with her lived the widow, Mrs. Leslie, who had introduced her to Mrs. Dick Roby, and through Mrs. Roby to Ferdinand Lopez. Lady Eustace was in the enjoyment of a handsome income, as I hope that some of my readers may remember,—and this income, during the last year or two, she had learned to foster, if not with much discretion, at any rate with great zeal. During her short life she had had many aspirations. Love, poetry, sport, religion, fashion, Bohemianism had all been tried; but in each crisis there had been a certain care for wealth which had saved her from the folly of squandering what she had won by her early energies in the pursuit of her then prevailing passion. She had given her money to no lover, had not lost it on race-courses, or in building churches;—nor even had she materially damaged her resources by servants and equipages. At the present time she was still young, and still pretty,—though her hair and complexion took rather more time than in the days when she won Sir Florian Eustace. She still liked a lover,—or perhaps two,—though she had thoroughly convinced herself that a lover may be bought too dear. She could still ride a horse, though hunting regularly was too expensive for her. She could talk religion if she could find herself close to a well-got-up clergyman,—being quite indifferent as to the denomination of the religion. But perhaps a wild dash for a time into fast vulgarity was what in her heart of hearts she liked best,—only that it was so difficult to enjoy that pleasure without risk of losing everything. And then, together with these passions, and perhaps above them all, there had lately sprung up in the heart of Lady Eustace a desire to multiply her means by successful speculation. This was the friend with whom Lopez had lately become intimate, and by whose aid he hoped to extricate himself from some of his difficulties.

Poor as he was he had contrived to bribe Mrs. Leslie by handsome presents out of Bond Street;—for, as he still lived in Manchester Square, and was the undoubted son-in-law of Mr. Wharton, his credit was not altogether gone. In the giving of these gifts no purport was, of course, named, but Mrs. Leslie was probably aware that her good word with her friend was expected. "I only know what I used to hear from Mrs. Roby," Mrs. Leslie said to her friend. "He was mixed up with Hunkey's people, who roll in money; Old Wharton wouldn't have given him his daughter if he had not been doing well."

"It's very hard to be sure," said Lizzie Eustace.

"He looks like a man who'd know how to feather his own nest," said Mrs. Leslie. "Don't you think he's very handsome?"

"I don't know that he's likely to do the better for that."

"Well; no; but there are men of whom you are sure, when you look at them, that they'll be successful. I don't suppose he was anything to begin with, but see where he is now!"

"I believe you are in love with him, my dear," said Lizzie Eustace.

"Not exactly. I don't know that he has given me any provocation. But I don't see why a woman shouldn't be in love with him if she likes. He is a deal nicer than those fair-haired men who haven't got a word to say to you, and yet look as though you ought to jump down their mouths;—like that fellow you were trying to talk to last night;—that Mr. Fletcher. He could just jerk out three words at a time, and yet he was proud as Lucifer. I like a man who if he likes me is neither ashamed nor afraid to say so."

"There is a romance there, you know. Mr. Fletcher was in love with Emily Wharton, and she threw him over for Lopez. They say he has not held up his head since."

"She was quite right," said Mrs. Leslie. "But she is one of those stiff-necked creatures who are set up with pride though they have nothing to be proud of. I suppose she had a lot of money. Lopez would never have taken her without."

When, therefore, Lopez called one day at the little house in the little street he was not an unwelcome visitor. Mrs. Leslie was in the drawing-room, but soon left it after his arrival. He had of late been often there, and when he at once introduced the subject on which he was himself intent it was not unexpected. "Seven thousand five hundred pounds!" said Lizzie, after listening to the proposition which he had come to make. "That is a very large sum of money!"

"Yes;—it's a large sum of money. It's a large affair. I'm in it to rather more than that, I believe."

"How are you to get people to drink it?" she asked after a pause.

"By telling them that they ought to drink it. Advertise it. It has become a certainty now that if you will only advertise sufficiently you may make a fortune by selling anything. Only the interest on the money expended increases in so large a ratio in accordance with the magnitude of the operation! If you spend a few hundreds in advertising you throw them away. A hundred thousand pounds well laid out makes a certainty of anything."

"What am I to get to show for my money;—I mean immediately, you know?"

"Registered shares in the Company."

"The Bios Company?"

"No;—we did propose to call ourselves Parker and Co., limited. I think we shall change the name. They will probably use my name. Lopez and Co., limited."

"But it's all for Bios?"

"Oh yes;—all for Bios."

"And it's to come from Central Africa?"

"It will be rectified in London, you know. Some English spirit will perhaps be mixed. But I must not tell you the secrets of the trade till you join us. That Bios is distilled from the bark of the Duffer-tree is a certainty."

"Have you drank any?"

"I've tasted it."

"Is it nice?"

"Very nice;—rather sweet, you know, and will be the better for mixing."

"Gin?" suggested her ladyship.

"Perhaps so,—or whisky. I think I may say that you can't do very much better with your money. You know I would not say this to you were it not true. In such a matter I treat you just as if,—as if you were my sister."

"I know how good you are,—but seven thousand five hundred! I couldn't raise so much as that just at present."

"There are to be six shares," said Lopez, "making £45,000 capital. Would you consent to take a share jointly with me? That would be three thousand seven hundred and fifty."

"But you have a share already," said Lizzie suspiciously.

"I should then divide that with Mr. Parker. We intend to register at any rate as many as nine partners. Would you object to hold it with me?" Lopez, as he asked the question, looked at her as though he were offering her half his heart.

"No," said Lizzie, slowly, "I don't suppose I should object to that."

"I should be doubly eager about the affair if I were in partnership with you."

"It's such a venture."

"Nothing venture nothing have."

"But I've got something as it is, Mr. Lopez, and I don't want to lose it all."

"There's no chance of that if you join us."

"You think Bios is so sure!"

"Quite safe," said Lopez.

"You must give me a little more time to think about it," said Lady Eustace at last, panting with anxiety, struggling with herself, anxious for the excitement which would come to her from dealing in Bios, but still fearing to risk her money.

This had taken place immediately after Mr. Wharton's offer of the £5000, in making which he had stipulated that Emily should be left at home. Then a few days went by, and Lopez was pressed for his money at the office of the San Juan mine. Did he or did he not mean to take up the mining shares allotted to him? If he did mean to do so, he must do it at once. He swore by all his gods that of course he meant to take them up. Had not Mr. Wharton himself been at the office saying that he intended to pay for them? Was not that sufficient guarantee? They knew well enough that Mr. Wharton was a man to whom the raising of £5000 could be a matter of no difficulty. But they did not know, never could know, how impossible it was to get anything done by Mr. Wharton. But Mr. Wharton had promised to pay for the shares, and when money was concerned his word would surely suffice. Mr. Hartlepod, backed by two of the Directors, said that if the thing was to go on at all, the money must really be paid at once. But the conference was ended by allowing the new local manager another fortnight in which to complete the arrangement.

Lopez allowed four days to pass by, during each of which he was closeted for a time with Lady Eustace, and then made an attempt to get at Mr. Wharton through his wife. "Your father has said that he will pay the money for me," said Lopez.

"If he has said so he certainly will do it."

"But he has promised it on the condition that you should remain at home. Do you wish to desert your husband?" To this she made no immediate answer. "Are you already anxious to be rid of me?"

"I should prefer to remain at home," she said in a very low voice.

"Then you do wish to desert your husband?"

"What is the use of all this, Ferdinand? You do not love me. You did not marry me because I loved you."

"By heaven I did;—for that and that only."

"And how have you treated me?"

"What have I done to you?"

"But I do not mean to make accusations, Ferdinand. I should only add to our miseries by that. We should be happier apart."

"Not I. Nor is that my idea of marriage. Tell your father that you wish to go with me, and then he will let us have the money."

"I will tell him no lie, Ferdinand. If you bid me go, I will go. Where you find a home I must find one too if it be your pleasure to take me. But I will not ask my father to give you money because it is my pleasure to go. Were I to say so he would not believe me."

"It is you who have told him to give it me only on the condition of your staying."

"I have told him nothing. He knows that I do not wish to go. He cannot but know that. But he knows that I mean to go if you require it."

"And you will do nothing for me?"

"Nothing,—in regard to my father." He raised his fist with the thought of striking her, and she saw the motion. But his arm fell again to his side. He had not quite come to that yet. "Surely you will have the charity to tell me whether I am to go, if it be fixed," she said.

"Have I not told you so twenty times?"

"Then it is fixed."

"Yes;—it is fixed. Your father will tell you about your things. He has promised you some beggarly sum,—about as much as a tallow-chandler would give his daughter."

"Whatever he does for me will be sufficient for me. I am not afraid of my father, Ferdinand."

"You shall be afraid of me before I have done with you," said he, leaving the room.

Then as he sat at his club, dining there alone, there came across his mind ideas of what the world would be like to him if he could leave his wife at home and take Lizzie Eustace with him to Guatemala. Guatemala was very distant, and it would matter little there whether the woman he brought with him was his wife or no. It was clear enough to him that his wife desired no more of his company. What were the conventions of the world to him? This other woman had money at her own command. He could not make it his own because he could not marry her, but he fancied that it might be possible to bring her so far under his control as to make the money almost as good as his own. Mr. Wharton's money was very hard to reach, and would be as hard to reach,—perhaps harder,—when Mr. Wharton was dead, as now, during his life. He had said a good deal to the lady since the interview of which a report has been given. She had declared herself to be afraid of Bios. She did not in the least doubt that great things might be ultimately done with Bios, but she did not quite see the way with her small capital,—

thus humbly did she speak of her wealth,—to be one of those who should take the initiative in the matter. Bios evidently required a great deal of advertisement, and Lizzie Eustace had a short-sighted objection to expend what money she had saved on the hoardings of London. Then he opened to her the glories of Guatemala, not contenting himself with describing the certainty of the 20 per cent., but enlarging on the luxurious happiness of life in a country so golden, so green, so gorgeous, and so grand. It had been the very apple of the eye of the old Spaniards. In Guatemala, he said, Cortez and Pizarro had met and embraced. They might have done so for anything Lizzie Eustace knew to the contrary. And here our hero took advantage of his name. Don Diego di Lopez had been the first to raise the banner of freedom in Guatemala when the kings of Spain became tyrants to their American subjects. All is fair in love and war, and Lizzie amidst the hard business of her life still loved a dash of romance. Yes, he was about to change the scene and try his fortune in that golden, green, and gorgeous country. "You will take your wife of course," Lady Eustace had said. Then Lopez had smiled, and shrugging his shoulders had left the room.

It was certainly the fact that she could not eat him. Other men before Lopez have had to pick up what courage they could in their attacks upon women by remembering that fact. She had flirted with him in a very pleasant way, mixing up her prettiness and her percentages in a manner that was peculiar to herself. He did not know her, and he knew that he did not know her;—but still there was the chance. She had thrown his wife more than once in his face, after the fashion of women when they are wooed by married men since the days of Cleopatra downwards. But he had taken that simply as encouragement. He had already let her know that his wife was a vixen who troubled his life. Lizzie had given him her sympathy, and had almost given him a tear. "But I am not a man to be broken-hearted because I have made a mistake," said Lopez. "Marriage vows are very well, but they shall never bind me to misery." "Marriage vows are not very well. They may be very ill," Lizzie had replied, remembering certain passages in her own life.

There was no doubt about her money, and certainly she could not eat him. The fortnight allowed him by the San Juan Company had nearly gone by when he called at the little house in the little street, resolved to push his fortune in that direction without fear and without hesitation. Mrs. Leslie again took her departure, leaving them together, and Lizzie allowed her friend to go, although the last words that Lopez had spoken had been, as he thought, a fair prelude to the words he intended to speak to-day. "And what do you think of it?" he said, taking both her hands in his.

"Think of what?"

"Of our Spanish venture."

"Have you given up Bios, my friend?"

"No; certainly not," said Lopez, seating himself beside her. "I have not taken the other half share, but I have kept my old venture in the scheme. I believe in Bios, you know."

"Ah;—it is so nice to believe."

"But I believe more firmly in the country to which I am going."

"You are going then?"

"Yes, my friend;—I am going. The allurements are too strong to be resisted. Think of that climate and of this." He probably had not heard of the mosquitoes of Central America when he so spoke. "Remember that an income which gives you comfort here will there produce for you every luxury which wealth can purchase. It is to be a king there, or to be but very common among commoners here."

"And yet England is a dear old country."

"Have you found it so? Think of the wrongs which you have endured;—of the injuries which you have suffered."

"Yes, indeed." For Lizzie Eustace had gone through hard days in her time.

"I certainly will fly from such a country to those golden shores on which man may be free and unshackled."

"And your wife?"

"Oh, Lizzie!" It was the first time that he had called her Lizzie, and she was apparently neither shocked nor abashed. Perhaps he thought too much of this, not knowing how many men had called her Lizzie in her time. "Do not you at least understand that a man or a woman may undergo that tie, and yet be justified in disregarding it altogether?"

"Oh, yes;—if there has been bigamy, or divorce, or anything of that kind." Now Lizzie had convicted her second husband of bigamy, and had freed herself after that fashion.

"To h—— with their prurient laws," said Lopez, rising suddenly from his chair. "I will neither appeal to them nor will I obey them. And I expect from you as little subservience as I myself am prepared to pay. Lizzie Eustace, will you go with me, to that land of the sun,

> Where the rage of the vulture, the love of the turtle,
> Now melt into sorrow, now madden to crime?

Will you dare to escape with me from the cold conventionalities, from the miserable thraldom of this country bound in swaddling cloths? Lizzie Eustace, if you will say the word, I will take you to that land of glorious happiness."

But Lizzie Eustace had £4000 a year and a balance at her banker's. "Mr. Lopez," she said.

"What answer have you to make me?"

"Mr. Lopez, I think you must be a fool."

He did at last succeed in getting himself into the street, and at any rate she had not eaten him.

Chapter LV
Mrs. Parker's Sorrows

The end of February had come, and as far as Mrs. Lopez knew she was to start for Guatemala in a month's time. And yet there was so much of indecision in her husband's manner, and apparently so little done by him in regard to personal preparation, that she could hardly bring herself to feel certain that she would have to make the journey. From day to day her father would ask her whether she had made her intended purchases, and she would tell him that she had still postponed the work. Then he would say no more, for he himself was hesitating, doubtful what he would do, and still thinking that when at last the time should come, he would buy his daughter's release at any price that might be demanded. Mr. Walker, the attorney, had as yet been able to manage nothing. He had seen Lopez more than once, and had also seen Mr. Hartlepod. Mr. Hartlepod had simply told him that he would be very happy to register the shares on behalf of Lopez as soon as the money was paid. Lopez had been almost insolent in his bearing. "Did Mr. Wharton think," he asked, "that he was going to sell his wife for £5000?" "I think you'll have to raise your offer," Mr. Walker had said to Mr. Wharton. That was all very well. Mr. Wharton was willing enough to raise his offer. He would have doubled his offer could he thereby have secured the annihilation of Lopez. "I will raise it if he will go without his wife, and give her a written assurance that he will never trouble her again." But the arrangement was one which Mr. Walker found it very difficult to carry out. So things went on till the end of February had come.

And during all this time Lopez was still resident in Mr. Wharton's house. "Papa," she said to him one day, "this is the cruellest thing of all. Why don't you tell him that he must go?"

"Because he would take you with him."

"It would be better so. I could come to see you."

"I did tell him to go,—in my passion. I repented of it instantly, because I should have lost you. But what did my telling matter to him? He was very indignant, and yet he is still here."

"You told him to go?"

"Yes;—but I am glad that he did not obey me. There must be an end to this soon, I suppose."

"I do not know, papa."

"Do you think that he will not go?"

"I feel that I know nothing, papa. You must not let him stay here always, you know."

"And what will become of you when he goes?"

"I must go with him. Why should you be sacrificed also? I will tell him that he must leave the house. I am not afraid of him, papa."

"Not yet, my dear;—not yet. We will see."

At this time Lopez declared his purpose one day of dining at the Progress, and Mr. Wharton took advantage of the occasion to remain at home with his daughter. Everett was now expected, and there was a probability that he might come on this evening. Mr. Wharton therefore returned from his chambers early; but when he reached the house he was told that there was a woman in the dining-room with Mrs. Lopez. The servant did not know what woman. She had asked to see Mrs. Lopez, and Mrs. Lopez had gone down to her.

The woman in the dining-room was Mrs. Parker. She had called at the house at about half-past five, and Emily had at once come down when summoned by tidings that a "lady" wanted to see her. Servants have a way of announcing a woman as a lady, which clearly expresses their own opinion that the person in question is not a lady. So it had been on the present occasion, but Mrs. Lopez had at once gone to her visitor. "Oh, Mrs. Parker, I am so glad to see you. I hope you are well."

"Indeed, then, Mrs. Lopez, I am very far from well. No poor woman, who is the mother of five children, was ever farther from being well than I am."

"Is anything wrong?"

"Wrong, ma'am! Everything is wrong. When is Mr. Lopez going to pay my husband all the money he has took from him?"

"Has he taken money?"

"Taken! he has taken everything. He has shorn my husband as bare as a board. We're ruined, Mrs. Lopez, and it's your husband has done it. When we were at Dovercourt, I told you how it was going to be. His business has left him, and now there is nothing. What are we to do?" The woman was seated on a chair, leaning forward with her two hands on her knees. The day was wet, the streets were half mud and half snow, and the poor woman, who had made her way through the slush, was soiled and wet. "I look to you to tell me what me and my children is to do. He's your husband, Mrs. Lopez."

"Yes, Mrs. Parker; he is my husband."

"Why couldn't he let Sexty alone? Why should the like of him be taking the bread out of my children's mouths? What had we ever done to him? You're rich."

"Indeed I am not, Mrs. Parker."

"Yes, you are. You're living here in a grand house, and your father's made of money. You'll know nothing of want, let the worst come to the worst. What are we to do, Mrs. Lopez? I'm the wife of that poor creature, and you're the wife of the man that has ruined him. What are we to do, Mrs. Lopez?"

"I do not understand my husband's business, Mrs. Parker."

"You're one with him, ain't you? If anybody had ever come to me and said my husband had robbed him, I'd never have stopped till I knew the truth of it. If any woman had ever said to me that Parker had taken the bread out of her children's mouths, do you think that I'd sit as you are sitting? I tell you that Lopez has robbed us,—has robbed us, and taken everything."

"What can I say, Mrs. Parker;—what can I do?"

"Where is he?"

"He is not here. He is dining at his club."

"Where is that? I will go there and shame him before them all. Don't you feel no shame? Because you've got things comfortable here, I suppose it's all nothing to you. You don't care, though my children were starving in the gutter,—as they will do."

"If you knew me, Mrs. Parker, you wouldn't speak to me like that."

"Know you! Of course I know you. You're a lady, and your father's a rich man, and your husband thinks no end of himself. And we're poor people, so it don't matter whether we're robbed and ruined or not. That's about it."

"If I had anything, I'd give you all that I had."

"And he's taken to drinking that hard that he's never rightly sober from morning to night." As she told this story of her husband's disgrace, the poor woman burst into tears. "Who's to trust him with business now? He's that broken-hearted that he don't know which way to turn, — only to the bottle. And Lopez has done it all, — done it all! I haven't got a father, ma'am, who has got a house over his head for me and my babies. Only think if you was turned out into the street with your babby, as I am like to be."

"I have no baby," said the wretched woman through her tears and sobs.

"Haven't you, Mrs. Lopez? Oh dear!" exclaimed the soft-hearted woman, reduced at once to pity. "How was it then?"

"He died, Mrs. Parker, — just a few days after he was born."

"Did he now? Well, well. We all have our troubles, I suppose."

"I have mine, I know," said Emily, "and very, very heavy they are. I cannot tell you what I have to suffer."

"Isn't he good to you?"

"I cannot talk about it, Mrs. Parker. What you tell me about yourself has added greatly to my sorrows. My husband is talking of going away, — to live out of England."

"Yes, at a place they call — I forget what they call it, but I heard it."

"Guatemala, — in America."

"I know. Sexty told me. He has no business to go anywhere, while he owes Sexty such a lot of money. He has taken everything, and now he's going to Kattymaly!" At this moment Mr. Wharton knocked at the door and entered the room. As he did so Mrs. Parker got up and curtseyed.

"This is my father, Mrs. Parker," said Emily. "Papa, this is Mrs. Parker. She is the wife of Mr. Parker, who was Ferdinand's partner. She has come here with bad news."

"Very bad news indeed, sir," said Mrs. Parker, curtseying again. Mr. Wharton frowned, not as being angry with the woman, but feeling that some further horror was to be told him of his son-in-law. "I can't help coming, sir," continued Mrs. Parker. "Where am I to go if I don't come? Mr. Lopez, sir, has ruined us root and branch,—root and branch."

"That at any rate is not my fault," said Mr. Wharton.

"But she is his wife, sir. Where am I to go if not to where he lives? Am I to put up with everything gone, and my poor husband in the right way to go to Bedlam, and not to say a word about it to the grand relations of him who did it all?"

"He is a bad man," said Mr. Wharton. "I cannot make him otherwise."

"Will he do nothing for us?"

"I will tell you all I know about him." Then Mr. Wharton did tell her all that he knew, as to the appointment at Guatemala and the amount of salary which was to be attached to it. "Whether he will do anything for you, I cannot say;—I should think not, unless he be forced. I should advise you to go to the offices of the Company in Coleman Street and try to make some terms there. But I fear,—I fear it will be all useless."

"Then we may starve."

"It is not her fault," said Mr. Wharton, pointing to his daughter. "She has had no hand in it. She knows less of it all than you do."

"It is my fault," said Emily, bursting out into self-reproach,—"my fault that I married him."

"Whether married or single he would have preyed upon Mr. Parker to the same extent."

"Like enough," said the poor wife. "He'd prey upon anybody as he could get a-hold of. And so, Mr. Wharton, you think that you can do nothing for me."

"If your want be immediate I can relieve it," said the barrister. Mrs. Parker did not like the idea of accepting direct charity, but, nevertheless, on going away did take the five sovereigns which Mr. Wharton offered to her.

After such an interview as that the dinner between the father and the daughter was not very happy. She was eaten up by remorse. Gradually she had learned how frightful was the thing she had done in giving herself to a man of whom she had known nothing. And it was not only that she had degraded herself by loving such a man, but that she had been persistent in clinging to him though her father and all his friends had told her of the danger which she was running. And now it seemed that she had destroyed her father as well as herself! All that she could do was to be persistent in her prayer that he would let her go. "I have done it," she said that night, "and I could bear it better, if you would let me bear it alone." But he only kissed her, and sobbed over her, and held her close to his heart with his clinging arms,—in a manner in which he had never held her in their old happy days.

He took himself to his own rooms before Lopez returned, but she of course had to bear her husband's presence. As she had declared to her father more than once, she was not afraid of him. Even though he should strike her,—though he should kill her,—she would not be afraid of him. He had already done worse to her than anything that could follow. "Mrs. Parker has been here to-day," she said to him that night.

"And what had Mrs. Parker to say?"

"That you had ruined her husband."

"Exactly. When a man speculates and doesn't win of course he throws the blame on some one else. And when he is too much of a cur to come himself, he sends his wife."

"She says you owe him money."

"What business have you to listen to what she says? If she comes again, do not see her. Do you understand me?"

"Yes, I understand. She saw papa also. If you owe him money, should it not be paid?"

"My dearest love, everybody who owes anything to anybody should always pay it. That is so self-evident that one would almost suppose that it might be understood without being enunciated. But the virtue of paying your debts is incompatible with an absence of money. Now, if you please, we will not say anything more about Mrs. Parker. She is not at any rate a fit companion for you."

"It was you who introduced me to her."

"Hold your tongue about her,—and let that be an end of it. I little knew what a world of torment I was preparing for myself when I allowed you to come and live in your father's house."

Chapter LVI
What the Duchess Thought of Her Husband

When the Session began it was understood in the political world that a very strong opposition was to be organised against the Government under the guidance of Sir Orlando Drought, and that the great sin to be imputed to the Cabinet was an utter indifference to the safety and honour of Great Britain, as manifested by their neglect of the navy. All the world knew that Sir Orlando had deserted the Coalition because he was not allowed to build new ships, and of course Sir Orlando would make the most of his grievance. With him was joined Mr. Boffin, the patriotic Conservative who had never listened to the voice of the seducer, and the staunch remainder of the old Tory party. And with them the more violent of the Radicals were prepared to act, not desirous, indeed, that new ships should be built, or that a Conservative Government should be established,—or, indeed, that anything should be done,—but animated by intense disgust that so mild a politician as the Duke of Omnium should be Prime Minister. The fight began at once, Sir Orlando objecting violently to certain passages in the Queen's Speech. It was all very well to say that the country was at present at peace with all the world; but how was peace to be maintained without a fleet? Then Sir Orlando paid a great many compliments to the Duke, and ended his speech by declaring him to be the most absolutely fainéant minister that had disgraced the country since the days of the Duke of Newcastle. Mr. Monk defended the Coalition, and assured the House that the navy was not only the most powerful navy existing, but that it was the most powerful that ever had existed in the possession of this or any other country, and was probably in absolute efficiency superior to the combined navies of all the world. The House was not shocked by statements so absolutely at variance with each other, coming from two gentlemen who had lately been members of the same Government, and who must be supposed to know what they were talking about, but seemed to think that upon the whole Sir Orlando had done his duty. For though there was complete confidence in the navy as a navy, and though a very small minority would have voted for any considerably increased expense, still it was well that there should be an opposition. And how can there be an opposition without some subject for grumbling,—some matter on which a minister may be attacked? No one really thought that the Prussians and French combined would invade our shores and devastate our fields, and plunder London, and carry our daughters away into captivity. The state of the funds showed very plainly that there was no such fear. But a good cry is a very good thing,—and it is always well to rub up the officials of the Admiralty by a little wholesome abuse. Sir Orlando was thought to have done his business well. Of course he did not risk a division upon the address. Had he done so he would have been "nowhere." But, as it was, he was proud of his achievement.

The ministers generally would have been indifferent to the very hard words that were said of them, knowing what they were worth, and feeling aware that a ministry which had everything too easy must lose its interest in the country, had it not been that their chief was very sore on the subject. The old Duke's work at this time consisted almost altogether in nursing the younger Duke. It did sometimes occur to his elder Grace that it might be well to let his brother retire, and that a Prime Minister, malgré lui, could not be a successful Prime Minister, or a useful one. But if the Duke of Omnium went the Coalition must go too, and the Coalition had been the offspring of the old statesman. The country was thriving under the Coalition, and there was no real reason why it should not last for the next ten years. He continued, therefore, his system of coddling, and was ready at any moment, or at every moment, to pour, if not comfort, at any rate consolation into the ears of his unhappy friend. In the present emergency, it was the falsehood and general baseness of Sir Orlando which nearly broke the heart of the Prime Minister. "How is one to live," he said, "if one has to do with men of that kind?"

"But you haven't to do with him any longer," said the Duke of St. Bungay.

"When I see a man who is supposed to have earned the name of a statesman, and been high in the councils of his sovereign, induced by personal jealousy to do as he is doing, it makes me feel that an honest man should not place himself where he may have to deal with such persons."

"According to that the honest men are to desert their country in order that the dishonest men may have everything their own way." Our Duke could not answer this, and therefore for the moment he yielded. But he was unhappy, saturnine, and generally silent except when closeted with his ancient mentor. And he knew that he was saturnine and silent, and that it behoved him as a leader of men to be genial and communicative,—listening to counsel even if he did not follow it, and at any rate appearing to have confidence in his colleagues.

During this time Mr. Slide was not inactive, and in his heart of hearts the Prime Minister was more afraid of Mr. Slide's attacks than of those made upon him by Sir Orlando Drought. Now that Parliament was sitting, and the minds of men were stirred to political feeling by the renewed energy of the House, a great deal was being said in many quarters about the last Silverbridge election. The papers had taken the matter up generally, some accusing the Prime Minister and some defending. But the defence was almost as unpalatable to him as the accusation. It was admitted on all sides that the Duke, both as a peer and as a Prime Minister, should have abstained from any interference whatever in the election. And it was also admitted on all sides that he had not so abstained,—if there was any truth at all in the allegation that he had paid money for Mr. Lopez. But it was pleaded on his behalf that the Dukes of Omnium had always interfered at Silverbridge, and that no Reform Bill had ever had any effect in reducing their influence in that borough. Frequent allusion was made to the cautious Dod who, year after year, had reported that the Duke of Omnium exercised considerable influence in the borough. And then the friendly newspapers went on to explain that the Duke had in this instance stayed his hand, and that the money, if paid at all, had been paid because the candidate who was to have been his nominee had been thrown over, when the Duke at the last moment made up his mind that he would abandon the privilege which had hitherto been always exercised by the head of his family, and which had been exercised more than once or twice in his own favour. But Mr. Slide, day after day, repeated his question, "We want to know whether the Prime Minister did or did not pay the election expenses of Mr. Lopez at the last Silverbridge election, and if so, why he paid them. We shall continue to ask this question till it has been answered, and when asking it we again say that the actual correspondence on the subject between the Duke and Mr. Lopez is in our own hands." And then, after a while, allusions were made to the Duchess;—for Mr. Slide had learned all the facts of the case from Lopez himself. When Mr. Slide found how hard it was "to draw his badger," as he expressed himself concerning his own operations, he at last openly alluded to the Duchess, running the risk of any punishment that might fall upon him by action for libel or by severe reprehension from his colleagues of the Press. "We have as yet," he said, "received no answers to the questions which we have felt ourselves called upon to ask in reference to the conduct of the Prime Minister at the Silverbridge election. We are of opinion that all interference by peers with the constituencies of the country should be put down by the strong hand of the law as thoroughly and unmercifully as we are putting down ordinary bribery. But when the offending peer is also the Prime Minister of this great country, it becomes doubly the duty of those who watch over the public safety,"—Mr. Slide was always speaking of himself as watching over the public safety,—"to animadvert upon his crime till it has been assoiled, or at any rate repented. From what we now hear we have reason to believe that the crime itself is acknowledged. Had the payment on behalf of Mr. Lopez not been made,—as it certainly was made, or the letters in our hand would be impudent forgeries,—the charge would long since have been denied. Silence in such a matter amounts to confession. But we understand that the Duke intends to escape under the plea that he has a second self, powerful as he is to exercise the baneful influence which his territorial wealth unfortunately gives him, but for the actions of which second self he, as a Peer of Parliament and as Prime Minister, is not responsible. In other words we are informed that the privilege belonging to the Palliser family at Silverbridge was exercised, not by the Duke himself, but by the Duchess;—and that the Duke paid the money when he found that the Duchess had promised more than she could perform. We should hardly have thought that even a man so notoriously weak as the Duke of Omnium would have endeavoured to ride out of responsibility by throwing the blame upon his wife; but he will certainly find that the attempt, if made, will fail.

"Against the Duchess herself we wish to say not a word. She is known as exercising a wide if not a discriminate hospitality. We believe her to be a kind-hearted, bustling, ambitious lady, to whom any little faults may easily be forgiven on account of her good-nature and generosity. But we cannot accept her indiscretion as an excuse for a most unconstitutional act performed by the Prime Minister of this country."

Latterly the Duchess had taken in her own copy of the "People's Banner." Since she had found that those around her were endeavouring to keep from her what was being said of her husband in regard to the borough, she had been determined to see it all. She therefore read the article from which two or three paragraphs have just been given,—and having read it she handed it to her friend Mrs. Finn. "I wonder that you trouble yourself with such trash," her friend said to her.

"That is all very well, my dear, from you; but we poor wretches who are the slaves of the people have to regard what is said of us in the 'People's Banner.'"

"It would be much better for you to neglect it."

"Just as authors are told not to read the criticisms;—but I never would believe any author who told me that he didn't read what was said about him. I wonder when the man found out that I was good-natured. He wouldn't find me good-natured if I could get hold of him."

"You are not going to allow it to torment you!"

"For my own sake, not a moment. I fancy that if I might be permitted to have my own way I could answer him very easily. Indeed with these dregs of the newspapers, these gutter-slanderers, if one would be open and say all the truth aloud, what would one have to fear? After all, what is it that I did? I disobeyed my husband because I thought that he was too scrupulous. Let me say as much, out loud to the public,—saying also that I am sorry for it, as I am,—and who would be against me? Who would have a word to say after that? I should be the most popular woman in England for a month,— and, as regards Plantagenet, Mr. Slide and his articles would all sink into silence. But even though he were to continue this from day to day for a twelvemonth it would not hurt me,—but that I know how it scorches him. This mention of my name will make it more intolerable to him than ever. I doubt that you know him even yet."

"I thought that I did."

"Though in manner he is as dry as a stick, though all his pursuits are opposite to the very idea of romance, though he passes his days and nights in thinking how he may take a halfpenny in the pound off the taxes of the people without robbing the revenue, there is a dash of chivalry about him worthy of the old poets. To him a woman, particularly his own woman, is a thing so fine and so precious that the winds of heaven should hardly be allowed to blow upon her. He cannot bear to think that people should even talk of his wife. And yet, Heaven knows, poor fellow, I have given people occasion enough to talk of me. And he has a much higher chivalry than that of the old poets. They, or their heroes, watched their women because they did not want to have trouble about them,—shut them up in castles, kept them in ignorance, and held them as far as they could out of harm's way."

"I hardly think they succeeded," said Mrs. Finn.

"But in pure selfishness they tried all they could. But he is too proud to watch. If you and I were hatching treason against him in the dark, and chance had brought him there, he would stop his ears with his fingers. He is all trust, even when he knows that he is being deceived. He is honour complete from head to foot. Ah, it was before you knew me when I tried him the hardest. I never could quite tell you that story, and I won't try it now; but he behaved like a god. I could never tell him what I felt,—but I felt it."

"You ought to love him."

"I do;—but what's the use of it? He is a god, but I am not a goddess;—and then, though he is a god, he is a dry, silent, uncongenial and uncomfortable god. It would have suited me much better to have married a sinner. But then the sinner that I would have married was so irredeemable a scapegrace."

"I do not believe in a woman marrying a bad man in the hope of making him good."

"Especially not when the woman is naturally inclined to evil herself. It will half kill him when he reads all this about me. He has read it already, and it has already half killed him. For myself I do not mind it in the least, but for his sake I mind it much. It will rob him of his only possible answer to the accusation. The very thing which this wretch in the newspaper says he will say, and that he will be disgraced by saying, is the very thing that he ought to say. And there would be no disgrace in it,—beyond what I might well bear for my little fault, and which I could bear so easily."

"Shall you speak to him about it?"

"No; I dare not. In this matter it has gone beyond speaking. I suppose he does talk it over with the old Duke; but he will say nothing to me about it,—unless he were to tell me that he had resigned, and that we were to start off and live in Minorca for the next ten years. I was so proud when they made him Prime Minister; but I think that I am beginning to regret it now." Then there was a pause, and the Duchess went on with her newspapers; but she soon resumed her discourse. Her heart was full, and out of a full heart the mouth speaks. "They should have made me Prime Minister, and have let him be Chancellor of the Exchequer. I begin to see the ways of Government now. I could have done all the dirty work. I could have given away garters and ribbons, and made my bargains while giving them. I could select sleek, easy bishops who wouldn't be troublesome. I could give pensions or withhold them, and make the stupid men peers. I could have the big noblemen at my feet, praying to be Lieutenants of Counties. I could dole out secretaryships and lordships, and never a one without getting something in return. I could brazen out a job and let the 'People's Banners' and the Slides make their worst of it. And I think I could make myself popular with my party, and do the high-flowing patriotic talk for the benefit of the Provinces. A man at a regular office has to work. That's what Plantagenet is fit for. He wants always to be doing something that shall be really useful, and a man has to toil at that and really to know things. But a Prime Minister should never go beyond generalities about commerce, agriculture, peace, and general philanthropy. Of course he should have the gift of the gab, and that Plantagenet hasn't got. He never wants to say anything unless he has got something to say. I could do a Mansion House dinner to a marvel!"

"I don't doubt that you could speak at all times, Lady Glen."

"Oh, I do so wish that I had the opportunity," said the Duchess.

Of course the Duke had read the article in the privacy of his own room, and of course the article had nearly maddened him with anger and grief. As the Duchess had said, the article had taken from him the very ground on which his friends had told him that he could stand. He had never consented, and never would consent, to lay the blame publicly on his wife; but he had begun to think that he must take notice of the charge made against him, and deputize some one to explain for him in the House of Commons that the injury had been done at Silverbridge by the indiscretion of an agent who had not fulfilled his employer's intentions, and that the Duke had thought it right afterwards to pay the money in consequence of this indiscretion. He had not agreed to this, but he had brought himself to think that he must agree to it. But now, of course, the question would follow:—Who was the indiscreet agent? Was the Duchess the person for whose indiscretion he had had to pay £500 to Mr. Lopez? And in this matter did he not find himself in accord even with Mr. Slide? "We should hardly have thought that even a man so notoriously weak as the Duke of Omnium would have endeavoured to ride out of responsibility by throwing the blame upon his wife." He read and reread these words till he knew them by heart. For a few moments it seemed to him to be an evil in the Constitution that the Prime Minister should not have the power of instantly crucifying so foul a slanderer;—and yet it was the very truth of the words that crushed him. He was weak,—he told himself;—notoriously weak, it must be; and it would be most mean in him to ride out of responsibility by throwing blame upon his wife. But what else was he to do? There seemed to him to be but one course,—to get up in the House of Lords and declare that he paid the money because he had thought it right to do so under circumstances which he could not explain, and to declare that it was not his intention to say another word on the subject, or to have another word said on his behalf.

There was a Cabinet Council held that day, but no one ventured to speak to the Prime Minister as to the accusation. Though he considered himself to be weak, his colleagues were all more or less afraid of him. There was a certain silent dignity about the man which saved him from the evils, as it also debarred him from the advantages, of familiarity. He had spoken on the subject to Mr. Monk and to Phineas Finn, and, as the reader knows, very often to his old mentor. He had also mentioned it to his friend Lord Cantrip, who was not in the Cabinet. Coming away from the Cabinet he took Mr. Monk's arm, and led him away to his own room in the Treasury Chambers. "Have you happened to see an article in the 'People's Banner' this morning?" he asked.

"I never see the 'People's Banner,'" said Mr. Monk.

"There it is;—just look at that." Whereupon Mr. Monk read the article. "You understand what people call constitutional practice as well as any one I know. As I told you before, I did pay that man's expenses. Did I do anything unconstitutional?"

"That would depend, Duke, upon the circumstances. If you were to back a man up by your wealth in an expensive contest, I think it would be unconstitutional. If you set yourself to work in that way, and cared not what you spent, you might materially influence the elections, and buy parliamentary support for yourself."

"But in this case the payment was made after the man had failed, and certainly had not been promised either by me or by any one on my behalf."

"I think it was unfortunate," said Mr. Monk.

"Certainly, certainly; but I am not asking as to that," said the Duke impatiently. "The man had been injured by indiscreet persons acting on my behalf and in opposition to my wishes." He said not a word about the Duchess; but Mr. Monk no doubt knew that her Grace had been at any rate one of the indiscreet persons. "He applied to me for the money, alleging that he had been injured by my agents. That being so,—presuming that my story be correct,—did I act unconstitutionally?"

"I think not," said Mr. Monk, "and I think that the circumstances, when explained, will bear you harmless."

"Thank you; thank you. I did not want to trouble you about that just at present."

Chapter LVII
The Explanation

Mr. Monk had been altogether unable to decipher the Duke's purpose in the question he had asked. About an hour afterwards they walked down to the Houses together, Mr. Monk having been kept at his office. "I hope I was not a little short with you just now," said the Duke.

"I did not find it out," said Mr. Monk, smiling.

"You read what was in the papers, and you may imagine that it is of a nature to irritate a man. I knew that no one could answer my question so correctly as you, and therefore I was a little eager to keep directly to the question. It occurred to me afterwards that I had been—perhaps uncourteous."

"Not at all, Duke."

"If I was, your goodness will excuse an irritated man. If a question were asked about this in the House of Commons, who would be the best man to answer it? Would you do it?"

Mr. Monk considered awhile. "I think," he said, "that Mr. Finn would do it with a better grace. Of course I will do it if you wish it. But he has tact in such matters, and it is known that his wife is much regarded by her Grace."

"I will not have the Duchess's name mentioned," said the Duke, turning short upon his companion.

"I did not allude to that, but I thought that the intimacy which existed might make it pleasant to you to employ Mr. Finn as the exponent of your wishes."

"I have the greatest confidence in Mr. Finn, certainly, and am on most friendly personal terms with him. It shall be so, if I decide on answering any question in your House on a matter so purely personal to myself."

"I would suggest that you should have the question asked in a friendly way. Get some independent member, such as Mr. Beverley or Sir James

Deering, to ask it. The matter would then be brought forward in no carping spirit, and you would be enabled, through Mr. Finn, to set the matter at rest. You have probably spoken to the Duke about it."

"I have mentioned it to him."

"Is not that what he would recommend?"

The old Duke had recommended that the entire truth should be told, and that the Duchess's operations should be made public. Here was our poor Prime Minister's great difficulty. He and his Mentor were at variance. His Mentor was advising that the real naked truth should be told, whereas Telemachus was intent upon keeping the name of the actual culprit in the background. "I will think it all over," said the Prime Minister as the two parted company at Palace Yard.

That evening he spoke to Lord Cantrip on the subject. Though the matter was so odious to him, he could not keep his mind from it for a moment. Had Lord Cantrip seen the article in the "People's Banner"? Lord Cantrip, like Mr. Monk, declared that the paper in question did not constitute part of his usual morning's recreation. "I won't ask you to read it," said the Duke;— "but it contains a very bitter attack upon me,—the bitterest that has yet been made. I suppose I ought to notice the matter?"

"If I were you," said Lord Cantrip, "I should put myself into the hands of the Duke of St. Bungay, and do exactly what he advises. There is no man in England knows so well as he does what should be done in such a case as this." The Prime Minister frowned and said nothing. "My dear Duke," continued Lord Cantrip, "I can give you no other advice. Who is there that has your personal interest and your honour at heart so entirely as his Grace;—and what man can be a more sagacious or more experienced adviser?"

"I was thinking that you might ask a question about it in our House."

"I?"

"You would do it for me in a manner that—that would be free from all offence."

"If I did it at all, I should certainly strive to do that. But it has never occurred to me that you would make such a suggestion. Would you give me a few moments to think about it?" "I couldn't do it," Lord Cantrip said afterwards. "By taking such a step, even at your request, I should certainly express the opinion that the matter was one on which Parliament was entitled to expect that you should make an explanation. But my own opinion is that Parliament has no business to meddle in the matter. I do not think that every action of a minister's life should be made matter of inquiry because a newspaper may choose to make allusions to it. At any rate, if any word is said about it, it should, I think, be said in the other House."

"The Duke of St. Bungay thinks that something should be said."

"I could not myself consent even to appear to desire information on a matter so entirely personal to yourself." The Duke bowed, and smiled with a cold, glittering, uncomfortable smile which would sometimes cross his face when he was not pleased, and no more was then said upon the subject.

Attempts were made to have the question asked in a far different spirit by some hostile member of the House of Commons. Sir Orlando Drought was sounded, and he for a while did give ear to the suggestion. But, as he came to have the matter full before him, he could not do it. The Duke had spurned his advice as a minister, and had refused to sanction a measure which he, as the head of a branch of the Government, had proposed. The Duke had so offended him that he conceived himself bound to regard the Duke as his enemy. But he knew,—and he could not escape from the knowledge,—that England did not contain a more honourable man than the Duke. He was delighted that the Duke should be vexed, and thwarted, and called ill names in the matter. To be gratified at this discomfiture of his enemy was in the nature of parliamentary opposition. Any blow that might weaken his opponent was a blow in his favour. But this was a blow which he could not strike with his own hands. There were things in parliamentary tactics which even Sir Orlando could not do. Arthur Fletcher was also asked to undertake the task. He was the successful candidate, the man who had opposed Lopez, and who was declared in the "People's Banner" to have emancipated that borough by his noble conduct from the tyranny of the House of Palliser. And it was thought that he might like an opportunity of making himself known in the House. But he was simply indignant when the suggestion was made to him. "What is it to me," he said, "who paid the blackguard's expenses?"

This went on for some weeks after Parliament had met, and for some days even after the article in which direct allusion was made to the Duchess. The Prime Minister could not be got to consent that no notice should be taken of the matter, let the papers or the public say what they would, nor could he be induced to let the matter be handled in the manner proposed by the elder Duke. And during this time he was in such a fever that those about him felt that something must be done. Mr. Monk suggested that if everybody held his tongue,—meaning all the Duke's friends,—the thing would wear itself out. But it was apparent to those who were nearest to the minister, to Mr. Warburton, for instance, and the Duke of St. Bungay, that the man himself would be worn out first. The happy possessor of a thick skin can hardly understand how one not so blessed may be hurt by the thong of a little whip! At last the matter was arranged. At the instigation of Mr. Monk, Sir James Deering, who was really the father of the House, an independent member, but one who generally voted with the Coalition, consented to ask the question in the House of Commons. And Phineas Finn was instructed by the Duke as to the answer that was to be given. The Duke of Omnium in giving these instructions made a mystery of the matter which he by no means himself intended. But he was so sore that he could not be simple in what he said. "Mr. Finn," he said, "you must promise me this,— that the name of the Duchess shall not be mentioned."

"Certainly not by me, if you tell me that I am not to mention it."

"No one else can do so. The matter will take the form of a simple question, and though the conduct of a minister may no doubt be made the subject of debate,—and it is not improbable that my conduct may do so in this instance,—it is, I think, impossible that any member should make an allusion to my wife. The privilege or power of returning a member for the borough has undoubtedly been exercised by our family since as well as previous to both the Reform Bills. At the last election I thought it right to abandon that privilege, and notified to those about me my intention. But that which a man has the power of doing he cannot always do without the interference of those around him. There was a misconception, and among my,—my adherents,—there were some who injudiciously advised Mr. Lopez to stand on my interest. But he did not get my interest, and was beaten;—and therefore when he asked me for the money which he had spent, I paid it to him. That is all. I think the House can hardly avoid to see that my effort was made to discontinue an unconstitutional proceeding."

Sir James Deering asked the question. "He trusted," he said, "that the House would not think that the question of which he had given notice and which he was about to ask was instigated by any personal desire on his part to inquire into the conduct of the Prime Minister. He was one who believed that the Duke of Omnium was as little likely as any man in England to offend by unconstitutional practice on his own part. But a great deal had been talked and written lately about the late election at Silverbridge, and there were those who thought,—and he was one of them,—that something should be said to stop the mouths of cavillers. With this object he would ask the Right Honourable Gentleman who led the House, and who was perhaps first in standing among the noble Duke's colleagues in that House, whether the noble Duke was prepared to have any statement on the subject made."

The House was full to the very corners of the galleries. Of course it was known to everybody that the question was to be asked and to be answered. There were some who thought that the matter was so serious that the Prime Minister could not get over it. Others had heard in the clubs that Lady Glen, as the Duchess was still called, was to be made the scapegoat. Men of all classes were open-mouthed in their denunciation of the meanness of Lopez,—though no one but Mr. Wharton knew half his villainy, as he alone knew that the expenses had been paid twice over. In one corner of the reporters' gallery sat Mr. Slide, pencil in hand, prepared to revert to his old work on so momentous an occasion. It was a great day for him. He by his own unassisted energy had brought a Prime Minister to book, and had created all this turmoil. It might be his happy lot to be the means of turning that Prime Minister out of office. It was he who had watched over the nation! The Duchess had been most anxious to be present,—but had not ventured to come without asking her husband's leave, which he had most peremptorily refused to give. "I cannot understand, Glencora, how you can suggest such a thing," he had said.

"You make so much of everything," she had replied petulantly; but she had remained at home. The ladies' gallery was, however, quite full. Mrs. Finn was there, of course, anxious not only for her friend, but eager to hear how her husband would acquit himself in his task. The wives and daughters of all the ministers were there,—excepting the wife of the Prime Minister. There never had been, in the memory of them all, a matter that was so interesting to them, for it was the only matter they remembered in which a woman's conduct might probably be called in question in the House of Commons. And the seats appropriated to peers were so crammed that above a dozen grey-headed old lords were standing in the passage which divides them from the common strangers. After all it was not, in truth, much of an affair. A very little man indeed had calumniated the conduct of a minister of the Crown, till it had been thought well that the minister should defend himself. No one really believed that the Duke had committed any great offence. At the worst it was no more than indiscretion, which was noticeable only because a Prime Minister should never be indiscreet. Had the taxation of the whole country for the next year been in dispute, there would have been no such interest felt. Had the welfare of the Indian Empire occupied the House, the House would have been empty. But the hope that a certain woman's name would have to be mentioned, crammed it from the floor to the ceiling.

The reader need not be told that that name was not mentioned. Our old friend Phineas, on rising to his legs, first apologised for doing so in place of the Chancellor of the Exchequer. But perhaps the House would accept a statement from him, as the noble Duke at the head of the Government had asked him to make it. Then he made his statement. "Perhaps," he said, "no falser accusation than this had ever been brought forward against a minister of the Crown, for it specially charged his noble friend with resorting to the employment of unconstitutional practices to bolster up his parliamentary support, whereas it was known by everybody that there would have been no matter for accusation at all had not the Duke of his own motion abandoned a recognised privilege, because, in his opinion, the exercise of that privilege was opposed to the spirit of the Constitution. Had the noble Duke simply nominated a candidate, as candidates had been nominated at Silverbridge for centuries past, that candidate would have been returned with absolute certainty, and there would have been no word spoken on the subject. It was not, perhaps, for him, who had the honour of serving under his Grace, and who, as being a part of his Grace's Government, was for the time one with his Grace, to expatiate at length on the nobility of the sacrifice here made. But they all knew there at what rate was valued a seat in that House. Thank God that privilege could not now be rated at any money price. It could not be bought and sold. But this privilege which his noble friend had so magnanimously resigned from purely patriotic motives, was, he believed, still in existence, and he would ask those few who were still in the happy, or, perhaps, he had better say in the envied, position of being able to send their friends to that House, what was their estimation of the conduct of the Duke in this matter? It might be that there were one or two such present, and who now heard him,—or, perhaps, one or two who owed their seats to the exercise of such a privilege. They might marvel at the magnitude of the surrender. They might even question the sagacity of the man who could abandon so much without a price. But he hardly thought that even they would regard it as unconstitutional.

"This was what the Prime Minister had done,—acting not as Prime Minister, but as an English nobleman, in the management of his own property and privileges. And now he would come to the gist of the accusation made; in making which, the thing which the Duke had really done had been altogether ignored. When the vacancy had been declared by the acceptance of the Chiltern Hundreds by a gentleman whose absence from the House they all regretted, the Duke had signified to his agents his intention of retiring altogether from the exercise of any privilege or power in the matter. But the Duke was then, as he was also now, and would, it was to be hoped, long continue to be, Prime Minister of England. He need hardly remind gentlemen in that House that the Prime Minister was not in a position to devote his undivided time to the management of his own property, or even to the interests of the Borough of Silverbridge. That his Grace had been earnest in his instructions to his agents, the sequel fully proved; but that earnestness his agents had misinterpreted."

Then there was heard a voice in the House, "What agents?" and from another voice, "Name them." For there were present some who thought it to be shameful that the excitement of the occasion should be lowered by keeping back all allusion to the Duchess.

"I have not distinguished," said Phineas, assuming an indignant tone, "the honourable gentlemen from whom those questions have come, and therefore I have the less compunction in telling them that it is no part of my duty on this occasion to gratify a morbid and an indecent curiosity." Then there was a cry of "Order," and an appeal to the Speaker. Certain gentlemen wished to know whether indecent was parliamentary. The Speaker, with some hesitation, expressed his opinion that the word, as then used, was not open to objection from him. He thought that it was within the scope of a member's rights to charge another member with indecent curiosity. "If," said Phineas, rising again to his legs, for he had sat down for a moment, "the gentleman who called for a name will rise in his place and repeat the demand, I will recall the word indecent and substitute another,—or others. I will tell him that he is one who, regardless of the real conduct of the Prime Minister, either as a man or as a servant of the Crown, is only anxious to inflict an unmanly wound in order that he may be gratified by seeing the pain which he inflicts." Then he paused, but as no further question was asked, he continued his statement. "A candidate had been brought forward," he said, "by those interested in the Duke's affairs. A man whom he would not name, but who, he trusted, would never succeed in his ambition to occupy a seat in that House, had been brought forward, and certain tradesmen in Silverbridge had been asked to support him as the Duke's nominee. There was no doubt about it. The House perhaps could understand that the local adherents and neighbours of a man so high in rank and wealth as the Duke of Omnium would not gladly see the privileges of their lord diminished. Perhaps, too, it occurred to them that a Prime Minister could not have his eye everywhere. There would always be worthy men in boroughs who liked to exercise some second-hand authority. At any rate it was the case that this candidate was encouraged. Then the Duke had heard it, and had put his foot upon the little mutiny, and had stamped it out at once. He might perhaps here," he said, "congratulate the House on the acquisition it had received by the failure of that candidate. So far, at any rate," he thought, "it must be admitted that the Duke had been free from blame;—but now he came to the gravamen of the charge." The gravamen of the charge is so well known to the reader that the simple account which Phineas gave of it need not be repeated. The Duke had paid the money, when asked for it, because he felt that the man had been injured by incorrect representations made to him. "I need hardly pause to stigmatise the meanness of that application," said Phineas, "but I may perhaps conclude by saying that whether the last act done by the Duke in this matter was or was not indiscreet, I shall probably have the House with me when I say that it savours much more strongly of nobility than of indiscretion."

When Phineas Finn sat down no one arose to say another word on the subject. It was afterwards felt that it would only have been graceful had Sir Orlando risen and expressed his opinion that the House had heard the statement just made with perfect satisfaction. But he did not do so, and after a short pause the ordinary business of the day was recommenced. Then there was a speedy descent from the galleries, and the ladies trooped out of their cage, and the grey-headed old peers went back to their own chamber, and the members themselves quickly jostled out through the doors, and Mr. Monk was left to explain his proposed alteration in the dog tax to a thin House of seventy or eighty members.

The thing was then over, and people were astonished that so great a thing should be over with so little fuss. It really seemed that after Phineas Finn's speech there was nothing more to be said on the matter. Everybody of course knew that the Duchess had been the chief of the agents to whom he had alluded, but they had known as much as that before. It was, however, felt by everybody that the matter had been brought to an end. The game, such as it was, had been played out. Perhaps the only person who heard Mr. Finn's speech throughout, and still hoped that the spark could be again fanned into a flame, was Quintus Slide. He went out and wrote another article about the Duchess. If a man was so unable to rule his affairs at home, he was certainly unfit to be Prime Minister. But even Quintus Slide, as he wrote his article, felt that he was hoping against hope. The charge might be referred to hereafter as one that had never been satisfactorily cleared up. That game is always open to the opponents of a minister. After the lapse of a few months an old accusation can be serviceably used, whether at the time it was proved or disproved. Mr. Slide published his article, but he felt that for the present the Silverbridge election papers had better be put by among the properties of the "People's Banner," and brought out, if necessary, for further use at some future time.

"Mr. Finn," said the Duke, "I feel indebted to you for the trouble you have taken."

"It was only a pleasant duty."

"I am grateful to you for the manner in which it was performed." This was all the Duke said, and Phineas felt it to be cold. The Duke, in truth, was grateful; but gratitude with him always failed to exhibit itself readily. From the world at large Phineas Finn received great praise for the manner in which he had performed his task.

Chapter LVIII
"Quite Settled"

The abuse which was now publicly heaped on the name of Ferdinand Lopez hit the man very hard; but not so hard perhaps as his rejection by Lady Eustace. That was an episode in his life of which even he felt ashamed, and of which he was unable to shake the disgrace from his memory. He had no inner appreciation whatsoever of what was really good or what was really bad in a man's conduct. He did not know that he had done evil in applying to the Duke for the money. He had only meant to attack the Duke; and when the money had come it had been regarded as justifiable prey. And when after receiving the Duke's money, he had kept also Mr. Wharton's money, he had justified himself again by reminding himself that Mr. Wharton certainly owed him much more than that. In a sense he was what is called a gentleman. He knew how to speak, and how to look, how to use a knife and fork, how to dress himself, and how to walk. But he had not the faintest notion of the feelings of a gentleman. He had, however, a very keen conception of the evil of being generally ill spoken of. Even now, though he was making up his mind to leave England for a long term of years, he understood the disadvantage of leaving it under so heavy a cloud;—and he understood also that the cloud might possibly impede his going altogether. Even in Coleman Street they were looking black upon him, and Mr. Hartlepod went so far as to say to Lopez himself, that, "by Jove, he had put his foot in it." He had endeavoured to be courageous under his burden, and every day walked into the offices of the Mining Company, endeavouring to look as though he had committed no fault of which he had to be ashamed. But after the second day he found that nothing was said to him of the affairs of the Company, and on the fourth day Mr. Hartlepod informed him that the time allowed for paying up his shares had passed by, and that another local manager would be appointed. "The time is not over till to-morrow," said Lopez angrily. "I tell you what I am told to tell you," said Mr. Hartlepod. "You will only waste your time by coming here any more."

He had not once seen Mr. Wharton since the statement made in Parliament, although he had lived in the same house with him. Everett Wharton had come home, and they two had met;—but the meeting had been stormy. "It seems to me, Lopez, that you are a scoundrel," Everett said to him one day after having heard the whole story,—or rather many stories,—from his father. This took place not in Manchester Square, but at the club, where Everett had endeavoured to cut his brother-in-law. It need hardly be said that at this time Lopez was not popular at his club. On the next day a meeting of the whole club was to be held that the propriety of expelling him might be discussed. But he had resolved that he would not be cowed, that he would still show himself, and still defend his conduct. He did not know, however, that Everett Wharton had already made known to the Committee of the club all the facts of the double payment.

He had addressed Everett in that solicitude to which a man should never be reduced of seeking to be recognised by at any rate one acquaintance,— and now his brother-in-law had called him a scoundrel in the presence of other men. He raised his arm as though to use the cane in his hands, but he was cowed by the feeling that all there were his adversaries. "How dare you use that language to me!" he said very weakly.

"It is the language that I must use if you speak to me."

"I am your brother-in-law, and that restrains me."

"Unfortunately you are."

"And am living in your father's house."

"That, again, is a misfortune which it appears difficult to remedy. You have been told to go, and you won't go."

"Your ingratitude, sir, is marvellous! Who saved your life when you were attacked in the park, and were too drunk to take care of yourself? Who has stood your friend with your close-fisted old father when you have lost money at play that you could not pay? But you are one of those who would turn away from any benefactor in his misfortune."

"I must certainly turn away from a man who has disgraced himself as you have done," said Everett, leaving the room. Lopez threw himself into an easy-chair, and rang the bell loudly for a cup of coffee, and lit a cigar. He had not been turned out of the club as yet, and the servant at any rate was bound to attend to him.

That night he waited up for his father-in-law in Manchester Square. He would certainly go to Guatemala now,—if it were not too late. He would go though he were forced to leave his wife behind him, and thus surrender any further hope for money from Mr. Wharton beyond the sum which he would receive as the price of his banishment. It was true that the fortnight allowed to him by the Company was only at an end that day, and that, therefore, the following morning might be taken as the last day named for the payment of the money. No doubt, also, Mr. Wharton's bill at a few days' date would be accepted if that gentleman could not at the moment give a cheque for so large a sum as was required. And the appointment had been distinctly promised to him with no other stipulation than that the money required for the shares should be paid. He did not believe in Mr. Hartlepod's threat. It was impossible, he thought, that he should be treated in so infamous a manner merely because he had had his election expenses repaid him by the Duke of Omnium! He would, therefore, ask for the money, and—renounce the society of his wife.

As he made this resolve something like real love returned to his heart, and he became for a while sick with regret. He assured himself that he had loved her, and that he could love her still;—but why had she not been true to him? Why had she clung to her father instead of clinging to her husband? Why had she not learned his ways,—as a wife is bound to learn the ways of the man she marries? Why had she not helped him in his devices, fallen into his plans, been regardful of his fortunes, and made herself one with him? There had been present to him at times an idea that if he could take her away with him to that distant country to which he thought to go, and thus remove her from the upas influence of her father's roof-tree, she would then fall into his views and become his wife indeed. Then he would again be tender to her, again love her, again endeavour to make the world soft to her. But it was too late now for that. He had failed in everything as far as England was concerned, and it was chiefly by her fault that he had failed. He would consent to leave her;—but, as he thought of it in his solitude, his eyes became moist with regret.

In these days Mr. Wharton never came home till about midnight, and then passed rapidly through the hall to his own room,—and in the morning had his breakfast brought to him in the same room, so that he might not even see his son-in-law. His daughter would go to him when at breakfast, and there, together for some half-hour, they would endeavour to look forward to their future fate. But hitherto they had never been able to look forward in accord, as she still persisted in declaring that if her husband bade her to go with him,—she would go. On this night Lopez sat up in the dining-room, and as soon as he heard Mr. Wharton's key in the door, he placed himself in the hall. "I wish to speak to you to-night, sir," he said. "Would you object to come in for a few moments?" Then Mr. Wharton followed him into the room. "As we live now," continued Lopez, "I have not much opportunity of speaking to you, even on business."

"Well, sir; you can speak now,—if you have anything to say."

"The £5000 you promised me must be paid to-morrow. It is the last day."

"I promised it only on certain conditions. Had you complied with them the money would have been paid before this."

"Just so. The conditions are very hard, Mr. Wharton. It surprises me that such a one as you should think it right to separate a husband from his wife."

"I think it right, sir, to separate my daughter from such a one as you are. I thought so before, but I think so doubly now. If I can secure your absence in Guatemala by the payment of this money, and if you will give me a document that shall be prepared by Mr. Walker and signed by yourself, assuring your wife that you will not hereafter call upon her to live with you, the money shall be paid."

"All that will take time, Mr. Wharton."

"I will not pay a penny without it. I can meet you at the office in Coleman Street to-morrow, and doubtless they will accept my written assurance to pay the money as soon as those stipulations shall be complied with."

"That would disgrace me in the office, Mr. Wharton."

"And are you not disgraced there already? Can you tell me that they have not heard of your conduct in Coleman Street, or that hearing it they disregard it?" His son-in-law stood frowning at him, but did not at the moment say a word. "Nevertheless, I will meet you there if you please, at any time that you may name, and if they do not object to employ such a man as their manager, I shall not object on their behalf."

"To the last you are hard and cruel to me," said Lopez;—"but I will meet you in Coleman Street at eleven to-morrow." Then Mr. Wharton left the room, and Lopez was there alone amidst the gloom of the heavy curtains and the dark paper. A London dining-room at night is always dark, cavernous, and unlovely. The very pictures on the walls lack brightness, and the furniture is black and heavy. This room was large, but old-fashioned and very dark. Here Lopez walked up and down after Mr. Wharton had left him, trying to think how far Fate and how far he himself were responsible for his present misfortunes. No doubt he had begun the world well. His father had been little better than a travelling pedlar, but had made some money by selling jewellery, and had educated his son. Lopez could on no score impute blame to his father for what had happened to him. And, when he thought of the means at his disposal in his early youth, he felt that he had a right to boast of some success. He had worked hard, and had won his way upwards, and had almost lodged himself securely among those people with whom it had been his ambition to live. Early in life he had found himself among those who were called gentlemen and ladies. He had been able to assume their manners, and had lived with them on equal terms. When thinking of his past life he never forgot to remind himself that he had been a guest at the house of the Duke of Omnium! And yet how was it with him now? He was penniless. He was rejected by his father-in-law. He was feared, and, as he thought, detested by his wife. He was expelled from his club. He was cut by his old friends. And he had been told very plainly by the Secretary in Coleman Street that his presence there was no longer desired. What should he do with himself if Mr. Wharton's money were now refused, and if the appointment in Guatemala were denied to him? And then he thought of poor Sexty Parker and his family. He was not naturally an ill-natured man. Though he could upbraid his wife for alluding to Mrs. Parker's misery, declaring that Mrs. Parker must take the rubs of the world just as others took them, still the misfortunes which he had brought on her and on her children did add something to the weight of his own misfortunes. If he could not go to Guatemala, what should he do with himself;—where should he go? Thus he walked up and down the room for an hour. Would not a pistol or a razor give him the best solution for all his difficulties?

On the following morning he kept his appointment at the office in Coleman Street, as did Mr. Wharton also. The latter was there first by some minutes, and explained to Mr. Hartlepod that he had come there to meet his son-in-law. Mr. Hartlepod was civil, but very cold. Mr. Wharton saw at the first glance that the services of Ferdinand Lopez were no longer in request by the San Juan Mining Company; but he sat down and waited. Now that he was there, however painful the interview would be, he would go through it. At ten minutes past eleven he made up his mind that he would wait till the half-hour,—and then go, with the fixed resolution that he would never willingly spend another shilling on behalf of that wretched man. But at a quarter past eleven the wretched man came,—swaggering into the office, though it had not, hitherto, been his custom to swagger. But misfortune masters all but the great men, and upsets the best-learned lesson of even a long life. "I hope I have not kept you waiting, Mr. Wharton. Well, Hartlepod, how are you to-day? So this little affair is to be settled at last, and now these shares shall be bought and paid for." Mr. Wharton did not say a word, not even rising from his chair, or greeting his son-in-law by a word. "I dare say Mr. Wharton has already explained himself," said Lopez.

"I don't know that there is any necessity," said Mr. Hartlepod.

"Well,—I suppose it's simple enough," continued Lopez. "Mr. Wharton, I believe I am right in saying that you are ready to pay the money at once."

"Yes;—I am ready to pay the money as soon as I am assured that you are on your route to Guatemala. I will not pay a penny till I know that as a fact."

Then Mr. Hartlepod rose from his seat and spoke. "Gentlemen," he said, "the matter within the last few days has assumed a different complexion."

"As how?" exclaimed Lopez.

"The Directors have changed their mind as to sending out Mr. Lopez as their local manager. The Directors intend to appoint another gentleman. I had already acquainted Mr. Lopez with the Directors' intention."

"Then the matter is settled?" said Mr. Wharton.

"Quite settled," said Mr. Hartlepod.

As a matter of course Lopez began to fume and to be furious. What!— after all that had been done did the Directors mean to go back from their word? After he had been induced to abandon his business in his own country, was he to be thrown over in that way? If the Company intended to treat him like that, the Company would very soon hear from him. Thank God there were laws in the land. "Yesterday was the last day fixed for the payment of the money," said Mr. Hartlepod.

"It is at any rate certain that Mr. Lopez is not to go to Guatemala?" asked Mr. Wharton.

"Quite certain," said Mr. Hartlepod. Then Mr. Wharton rose from his chair and quitted the room.

"By G——, you have ruined me among you," said Lopez;—"ruined me in the most shameful manner. There is no mercy, no friendship, no kindness, no forbearance anywhere! Why am I to be treated in this manner?"

"If you have any complaint to make," said Mr. Hartlepod, "you had better write to the Directors. I have nothing to do but my duty."

"By heavens, the Directors shall hear of it!" said Lopez as he left the office.

Mr. Wharton went to his chambers and endeavoured to make up his mind what step he must now take in reference to this dreadful incubus. Of course he could turn the man out of his house, but in so doing it might well be that he would also turn out his own daughter. He believed Lopez to be utterly without means, and a man so destitute would generally be glad to be relieved from the burden of his wife's support. But this man would care nothing for his wife's comfort; nothing even, as Mr. Wharton believed, for his wife's life. He would simply use his wife as best he might as a means for obtaining money. There was nothing to be done but to buy him off, by so much money down, and by so much at stated intervals as long as he should keep away. Mr. Walker must manage it, but it was quite clear to Mr. Wharton that the Guatemala scheme was altogether at an end. In the meantime a certain sum must be offered to the man at once, on condition that he would leave the house and do so without taking his wife with him.

So far Mr. Wharton had a plan, and a plan that was at least feasible. Wretched as he was, miserable, as he thought of the fate which had befallen his daughter,—there was still a prospect of some relief. But Lopez as he walked out of the office had nothing to which he could look for comfort. He slowly made his way to Little Tankard Yard, and there he found Sexty Parker balancing himself on the back legs of his chair, with a small decanter of public-house sherry before him. "What; you here?" he said.

"Yes;—I have come to say good-bye."

"Where are you going then? You shan't start to Guatemala if I know it."

"That's all over, my boy," said Lopez, smiling.

"What is it you mean?" said Sexty, sitting square on his chair and looking very serious.

"I am not going to Guatemala or anywhere else. I thought I'd just look in to tell you that I'm just done for,—that I haven't a hope of a shilling now or hereafter. You told me the other day that I was afraid to come here. You see that as soon as anything is fixed, I come and tell you everything at once."

"What is fixed?"

"That I am ruined. That there isn't a penny to come from any source."

"Wharton has got money," said Sexty.

"And there is money in the Bank of England,—but I cannot get at it."

"What are you going to do, Lopez?"

"Ah; that's the question. What am I going to do? I can say nothing about that, but I can say, Sexty, that our affairs are at an end. I'm very sorry for it, old boy. We ought to have made fortunes, but we didn't. As far as the work went, I did my best. Good-bye, old fellow. You'll do well some of these days yet, I don't doubt. Don't teach the bairns to curse me. As for Mrs. P. I have no hope there, I know." Then he went, leaving Sexty Parker quite aghast.

Chapter LIX
"The First and the Last"

When Mr. Wharton was in Coleman Street, having his final interview with Mr. Hartlepod, there came a visitor to Mrs. Lopez in Manchester Square. Up to this date there had been great doubt with Mr. Wharton whether at last the banishment to Guatemala would become a fact. From day to day his mind had changed. It had been an infinite benefit that Lopez should go, if he could be got to go alone, but as great an evil if at last he should take his wife with him. But the father had never dared to express these doubts to her, and she had taught herself to think that absolute banishment with a man whom she certainly no longer loved, was the punishment she had to pay for the evil she had done. It was now March, and the second or third of April had been fixed for her departure. Of course, she had endeavoured from time to time to learn all that was to be learned from her husband. Sometimes he would be almost communicative to her; at other times she could get hardly a word from him. But, through it all, he gave her to believe that she would have to go. Nor did her father make any great effort to turn his mind the other way. If it must be so, of what use would be such false kindness on his part? She had therefore gone to work to make her purchases, studying that economy which must henceforth be the great duty of her life, and reminding herself as to everything she bought that it would have to be worn with tears and used in sorrow.

And then she sent a message to Arthur Fletcher. It so happened that Sir Alured Wharton was up in London at this time with his daughter Mary. Sir Alured did not come to Manchester Square. There was nothing that the old baronet could say in the midst of all this misery,—no comfort that he could give. It was well-known now to all the Whartons and all the Fletchers that this Lopez, who had married her who was to have been the pearl of the two families, had proved himself to be a scoundrel. The two old Whartons met no doubt at some club, or perhaps in Stone Buildings, and spoke some few bitter words to each other; but Sir Alured did not see the unfortunate young woman who had disgraced herself by so wretched a marriage. But Mary came, and by her a message was sent to Arthur Fletcher. "Tell him that I am going," said Emily. "Tell him not to come; but give him my love. He was always one of my kindest friends."

"Why,—why,—why did you not take him?" said Mary, moved by the excitement of the moment to suggestions which were quite at variance with the fixed propriety of her general ideas.

"Why should you speak of that?" said the other. "I never speak of him,—never think of him. But, if you see him, tell him what I say." Arthur Fletcher was of course in the Square on the following day,—on that very day on which Mr. Wharton learned that, whatever might be his daughter's fate, she would not, at any rate, be taken to Guatemala. They two had never met since the day on which they had been brought together for a moment at the Duchess's party at Richmond. It had of course been understood by both of them that they were not to be allowed to see each other. Her husband had made a pretext of an act of friendship on his part to establish a quarrel, and both of them had been bound by that quarrel. When a husband declares that his wife shall not know a man, that edict must be obeyed,—or, if disobeyed, must be subverted by intrigue. In this case there had been no inclination to intrigue on either side. The order had been obeyed, and as far as the wife was concerned, had been only a small part of the terrible punishment which had come upon her as the result of her marriage. But now, when Arthur Fletcher sent up his name, she did not hesitate as to seeing him. No doubt she had thought it probable that she might see him when she gave her message to her cousin.

"I could not let you go without coming to you," he said.

"It is very good of you. Yes;—I suppose we are going. Guatemala sounds a long way off, Arthur, does it not? But they tell me it is a beautiful country." She spoke with a cheerful voice, almost as though she liked the idea of her journey; but he looked at her with beseeching, anxious, sorrow-laden eyes. "After all, what is a journey of a few weeks? Why should I not be as happy in Guatemala as in London? As to friends, I do not know that it will make much difference,—except papa."

"It seems to me to make a difference," said he.

"I never see anybody now,—neither your people, nor the Wharton Whartons. Indeed, I see nobody. If it were not for papa I should be glad to go. I am told that it is a charming country. I have not found Manchester Square very charming. I am inclined to think that all the world is very much alike, and that it does not matter very much where one lives,—or, perhaps, what one does. But at any rate I am going, and I am very glad to be able to say good-bye to you before I start." All this she said rapidly, in a manner unlike herself. She was forcing herself to speak so that she might save herself, if possible, from breaking down in his presence.

"Of course I came when Mary told me."

"Yes;—she was here. Sir Alured did not come. I don't wonder at that, however. And your mother was in town some time ago,—but I didn't expect her to come. Why should they come? I don't know whether you might not have better stayed away. Of course I am a Pariah now; but Pariah as I am, I shall be as good as any one else in Guatemala. You have seen Everett since he has been in town, perhaps?"

"Yes;—I have seen him."

"I hope they won't quarrel with Everett because of what I have done. I have felt that more than all,—that both papa and he have suffered because of it. Do you know, I think people are hard. They might have thrown me off without being unkind to them. It is that that has killed me, Arthur;—that they should have suffered." He sat looking at her, not knowing how to interrupt her, or what to say. There was much that he meant to say, but he did not know how to begin it, or how to frame his words. "When I am gone, perhaps, it will be all right," she continued. "When he told me that I was to go, that was my comfort. I think I have taught myself to think nothing of myself, to bear it all as a necessity, to put up with it, whatever it may be, as men bear thirst in the desert. Thank God, Arthur, I have no baby to suffer with me. Here,—here, it is still very bad. When I think of papa creeping in and out of his house, I sometimes feel that I must kill myself. But our going will put an end to all that. It is much better that we should go. I wish we might start to-morrow." Then she looked up at him, and saw that the tears were running down his face, and as she looked she heard his sobs. "Why should you cry, Arthur? He never cries,—nor do I. When baby died I cried,—but very little. Tears are vain, foolish things. It has to be borne, and there is an end of it. When one makes up one's mind to that, one does not cry. There was a poor woman here the other day whose husband he had ruined. She wept and bewailed herself till I pitied her almost more than myself;—but then she had children."

"Oh, Emily!"

"You mustn't call me by my name, because he would be angry. I have to do, you know, as he tells me. And I do so strive to do it! Through it all I have an idea that if I do my duty it will be better for me. There are things, you know, which a husband may tell you to do, but you cannot do. If he tells me to rob, I am not to rob;—am I? And now I think of it, you ought not to be here. He would be very much displeased. But it has been so pleasant once more to see an old friend."

"I care nothing for his anger," said Arthur moodily.

"Ah, but I do. I have to care for it."

"Leave him! Why don't you leave him?"

"What!"

"You cannot deceive me. You do not try to deceive me. You know that he is altogether unworthy of you."

"I will hear nothing of the kind, sir."

"How can I speak otherwise when you yourself tell me of your own misery? Is it possible that I should not know what he is? Would you have me pretend to think well of him?"

"You can hold your tongue, Arthur."

"No;—I cannot hold my tongue. Have I not held my tongue ever since you married? And if I am to speak at all, must I not speak now?"

"There is nothing to be said that can serve us at all."

"Then it shall be said without serving. When I bid you leave him, it is not that you may come to me. Though I love you better than all the world put together, I do not mean that."

"Oh, Arthur, Arthur!"

"But let your father save you. Only tell him that you will stay with him, and he will do it. Though I should never see you again, I could hope to protect you. Of course, I know,—and you know. He is—a scoundrel!"

"I will not hear it," said she, rising from her seat on the sofa with her hands up to her forehead, but still coming nearer to him as she moved.

"Does not your father say the same thing? I will advise nothing that he does not advise. I would not say a word to you that he might not hear. I do love you. I have always loved you. But do you think that I would hurt you with my love?"

"No;—no;—no!"

"No, indeed;—but I would have you feel that those who loved you of old are still anxious for your welfare. You said just now that you had been neglected."

"I spoke of papa and Everett. For myself,—of course I have separated myself from everybody."

"Never from me. You may be ten times his wife, but you cannot separate yourself from me. Getting up in the morning and going to bed at night I still tell myself that you are the one woman that I love. Stay with us, and you shall be honoured,—as that man's wife of course, but still as the dearest friend we have."

"I cannot stay," she said. "He has told me that I am to go, and I am in his hands. When you have a wife, Arthur, you will wish her to do your bidding. I hope she will do it for your sake, without the pain I have in doing his. Good-bye, dear friend."

She put her hand out and he grasped it, and stood for a moment looking at her. Then he seized her in his arms and kissed her brow and her lips. "Oh, Emily, why were you not my wife? My darling, my darling!"

She had hardly extricated herself when the door opened, and Lopez stood in the room. "Mr. Fletcher," he said, very calmly, "what is the meaning of this?"

"He has come to bid me farewell," said Emily. "When going on so long a journey one likes to see one's old friends,—perhaps for the last time." There was something of indifference to his anger in her tone, and something also of scorn.

Lopez looked from one to the other, affecting an air of great displeasure. "You know, sir," he said, "that you cannot be welcome here."

"But he has been welcome," said his wife.

"And I look upon your coming as a base act. You are here with the intention of creating discord between me and my wife."

"I am here to tell her that she has a friend to trust to if she ever wants a friend," said Fletcher.

"And you think that such trust as that would be safer than trust in her husband? I cannot turn you out of this house, sir, because it does not belong to me, but I desire you to leave at once the room which is occupied by my wife." Fletcher paused a moment to say good-bye to the poor woman, while Lopez continued with increased indignation, "If you do not go at once you will force me to desire her to retire. She shall not remain in the same room with you."

"Good-bye, Mr. Fletcher," she said, again putting out her hand.

But Lopez struck it up, not violently, so as to hurt her, but still with eager roughness. "Not in my presence," he said. "Go, sir, when I desire you."

"God bless you, my friend," said Arthur Fletcher. "I pray that I may live to see you back in the old country."

"He was—kissing you," said Lopez, as soon as the door was shut.

"He was," said Emily.

"And you tell me so to my face, with such an air as that!"

"What am I to tell you when you ask me? I did not bid him kiss me."

"But afterwards you took his part as his friend."

"Why not? I should lie to you if I pretended that I was angry with him for what he did."

"Perhaps you will tell me that you love him."

"Of course I love him. There are different kinds of love, Ferdinand. There is that which a woman gives to a man when she would fain mate with him. It is the sweetest love of all, if it would only last. And there is another love,—which is not given, but which is won, perhaps through long years, by old friends. I have none older than Arthur Fletcher, and none who are dearer to me."

"And you think it right that he should take you in his arms and kiss you?"

"On such an occasion I could not blame him."

"You were ready enough to receive it, perhaps."

"Well; I was. He has loved me well, and I shall never see him again. He is very dear to me, and I was parting from him for ever. It was the first and the last, and I did not grudge it to him. You must remember, Ferdinand, that you are taking me across the world from all my friends."

"Psha," he said, "that is all over. You are not going anywhere that I know of,—unless it be out into the streets when your father shuts his door on you." And so saying he left the room without another word.

Chapter LX
The Tenway Junction

And thus the knowledge was conveyed to Mrs. Lopez that her fate in life was not to carry her to Guatemala. At the very moment in which she had been summoned to meet Arthur Fletcher she had been busy with her needle preparing that almost endless collection of garments necessary for a journey of many days at sea. And now she was informed, by a chance expression, by a word aside, as it were, that the journey was not to be made. "That is all over," he had said,—and then had left her, telling her nothing further. Of course she stayed her needle. Whether the last word had been true or false, she could not work again, at any rate till it had been contradicted. If it were so, what was to be her fate? One thing was certain to her;—that she could not remain under her father's roof. It was impossible that an arrangement so utterly distasteful as the present one, both to her father and to herself, should be continued. But where then should they live,—and of what nature would her life be if she should be separated from her father?

That evening she saw her father, and he corroborated her husband's statement. "It is all over now," he said,—"that scheme of his of going to superintend the mines. The mines don't want him, and won't have him. I can't say that I wonder at it."

"What are we to do, papa?"

"Ah;—that I cannot say. I suppose he will condescend still to honour me with his company. I do not know why he should wish to go to Guatemala or elsewhere. He has everything here that he can want."

"You know, papa, that that is impossible."

"I cannot say what with him is possible or impossible. He is bound by none of the ordinary rules of mankind."

That evening Lopez returned to his dinner in Manchester Square, which was still regularly served for him and his wife, though the servants who attended upon him did so under silent and oft-repeated protest. He said not a word more as to Arthur Fletcher, nor did he seek any ground of quarrel with his wife. But that her continued melancholy and dejection made anything like good-humour impossible, even on his part, he would have been good-humoured. When they were alone she asked him as to their future destiny. "Papa tells me you are not going," she began by saying.

"Did I not tell you so this morning?"

"Yes;—you said so. But I did not know you were earnest. Is it all over?"

"All over,—I suppose."

"I should have thought that you would have told me with more—more seriousness."

"I don't know what you would have. I was serious enough. The fact is, that your father has delayed so long the payment of the promised money that the thing has fallen through of necessity. I do not know that I can blame the Company."

Then there was a pause. "And now," she said, "what do you mean to do?"

"Upon my word I cannot say. I am quite as much in the dark as you can be."

"That is nonsense, Ferdinand."

"Thank you! Let it be nonsense if you will. It seems to me that there is a great deal of nonsense going on in the world; but very little of it as true as what I say now."

"But it is your duty to know. Of course you cannot stay here."

"Nor you, I suppose,—without me."

"I am not speaking of myself. If you choose, I can remain here."

"And—just throw me overboard altogether."

"If you provide another home for me, I will go to it. However poor it may be I will go to it, if you bid me. But for you,—of course you cannot stay here."

"Has your father told you to say so to me?"

"No;—but I can say so without his telling me. You are banishing him from his own house. He has put up with it while he thought that you were going to this foreign country; but there must be an end of that now. You must have some scheme of life?"

"Upon my soul I have none."

"You must have some intentions for the future?"

"None in the least. I have had intentions, and they have failed;—from want of that support which I had a right to expect. I have struggled and I have failed, and now I have got no intentions. What are yours?"

"It is not my duty to have any purpose, as what I do must depend on your commands." Then again there was a silence, during which he lit a cigar, although he was sitting in the drawing-room. This was a profanation of the room on which even he had never ventured before, but at the present moment she was unable to notice it by any words. "I must tell papa," she said after a while, "what our plans are."

"You can tell him what you please. I have literally nothing to say to him. If he will settle an adequate income on us, payable of course to me, I will go and live elsewhere. If he turns me into the street without provision, he must turn you too. That is all that I have got to say. It will come better from you than from me. I am sorry, of course, that things have gone wrong with me. When I found myself the son-in-law of a very rich man I thought that I might spread my wings a bit. But my rich father-in-law threw me over, and now I am helpless. You are not very cheerful, my dear, and I think I'll go down to the club."

He went out of the house and did go down to the Progress. The committee which was to be held with the view of judging whether he was or was not a proper person to remain a member of that assemblage had not yet been held, and there was nothing to impede his entrance to the club, or the execution of the command which he gave for tea and buttered toast. But no one spoke to him; nor, though he affected a look of comfort, did he find himself much at his ease. Among the members of the club there was a much divided opinion whether he should be expelled or not. There was a strong party who declared that his conduct socially, morally, and politically, had been so bad that nothing short of expulsion would meet the case. But there were others who said that no act had been proved against him which the club ought to notice. He had, no doubt, shown himself to be a blackguard, a man without a spark of honour or honesty. But then,—as they said who thought his position in the club to be unassailable,—what had the club to do with that? "If you turn out all the blackguards and all the dishonourable men, where will the club be?" was a question asked with a great deal of vigour by one middle-aged gentleman who was supposed to know the club-world very thoroughly. He had committed no offence which the law could recognise and punish, nor had he sinned against the club rules. "He is not required to be a man of honour by any regulation of which I am aware," said the middle-aged gentleman. The general opinion seemed to be that he should be asked to go, and that, if he declined, no one should speak to him. This penalty was already inflicted on him, for on the evening in question no one did speak to him.

He drank his tea and ate his toast and read a magazine, striving to look as comfortable and as much at his ease as men at their clubs generally are. He was not a bad actor, and those who saw him and made reports as to his conduct on the following day declared that he had apparently been quite indifferent to the disagreeable incidents of his position. But his indifference had been mere acting. His careless manner with his wife had been all assumed. Selfish as he was, void as he was of all principle, utterly unmanly and even unconscious of the worth of manliness, still he was alive to the opinions of others. He thought that the world was wrong to condemn him,— that the world did not understand the facts of his case, and that the world generally would have done as he had done in similar circumstances. He did not know that there was such a quality as honesty, nor did he understand what the word meant. But he did know that some men, an unfortunate class, became subject to evil report from others who were more successful, and he was aware that he had become one of those unfortunates. Nor could he see any remedy for his position. It was all blank and black before him. It may be doubted whether he got much instruction or amusement from the pages of the magazine which he turned.

At about twelve o'clock he left the club and took his way homewards. But he did not go straight home. It was a nasty cold March night, with a catching wind, and occasional short showers of something between snow and rain,—as disagreeable a night for a gentleman to walk in as one could well conceive. But he went round by Trafalgar Square, and along the Strand, and up some dirty streets by the small theatres, and so on to Holborn and by Bloomsbury Square up to Tottenham Court Road, then through some unused street into Portland Place, along the Marylebone Road, and back to Manchester Square by Baker Street. He had more than doubled the distance,—apparently without any object. He had been spoken to frequently by unfortunates of both sexes, but had answered a word to no one. He had trudged on and on with his umbrella over his head, but almost unconscious of the cold and wet. And yet he was a man sedulously attentive to his own personal comfort and health, who had at any rate shown this virtue in his mode of living, that he had never subjected himself to danger by imprudence. But now the working of his mind kept him warm, and, if not dry, at least indifferent to the damp. He had thrown aside with affected nonchalance those questions which his wife had asked him, but still it was necessary that he should answer them. He did not suppose that he could continue to live in Manchester Square in his present condition. Nor, if it was necessary that he should wander forth into the world, could he force his wife to wander with him. If he would consent to leave her, his father-in-law would probably give him something,—some allowance on which he might exist. But then of what sort would be his life?

He did not fail to remind himself over and over again that he had nearly succeeded. He had been the guest of the Prime Minister, and had been the nominee chosen by a Duchess to represent her husband's borough in Parliament. He had been intimate with Mills Happerton who was fast becoming a millionaire. He had married much above himself in every way. He had achieved a certain popularity and was conscious of intellect. But at the present moment two or three sovereigns in his pocket were the extent of his worldly wealth and his character was utterly ruined. He regarded his fate as does a card-player who day after day holds sixes and sevens when other men have the aces and kings. Fate was against him. He saw no reason why he should not have had the aces and kings continually, especially as fate had given him perhaps more than his share of them at first. He had, however, lost rubber after rubber,—not paying his stakes for some of the last rubbers lost,—till the players would play with him no longer. The misfortune might have happened to any man;—but it had happened to him. There was no beginning again. A possible small allowance and some very retired and solitary life, in which there would be no show of honour, no flattery coming to him, was all that was left to him.

He let himself in at the house, and found his wife still awake. "I am wet to the skin," he said. "I made up my mind to walk, and I would do it;—but I am a fool for my pains." She made him some feeble answer, affecting to be half asleep, and merely turned in her bed. "I must be out early in the morning. Mind you make them dry my things. They never do anything for my telling."

"You don't want them dried to-night?"

"Not to-night, of course;—but after I am gone to-morrow. They'll leave them there without putting a hand to them, if you don't speak. I must be off before breakfast to-morrow."

"Where are you going? Do you want anything packed?"

"No; nothing. I shall be back to dinner. But I must go down to Birmingham, to see a friend of Happerton's on business. I will breakfast at the station. As you said to-day, something must be done. If it's to sweep a crossing, I must sweep it."

As she lay awake while he slept, she thought that those last words were the best she had heard him speak since they were married. There seemed to be some indication of a purpose in them. If he would only sweep a crossing as a man should sweep it, she would stand by him, and at any rate do her duty to him, in spite of all that had happened. Alas! she was not old enough to have learned that a dishonest man cannot begin even to sweep a crossing honestly till he have in very truth repented of his former dishonesty. The lazy man may become lazy no longer, but there must have been first a process through his mind whereby laziness has become odious to him. And that process can hardly be the immediate result of misfortune arising from misconduct. Had Lopez found his crossing at Birmingham he would hardly have swept it well.

Early on the following morning he was up, and before he left his room he kissed his wife. "Good-bye, old girl," he said; "don't be down-hearted."

"If you have anything before you to do, I will not be down-hearted," she said.

"I shall have something to do before night, I think. Tell your father, when you see him, that I will not trouble him here much longer. But tell him, also, that I have no thanks to give him for his hospitality."

"I will not tell him that, Ferdinand."

"He shall know it, though. But I do not mean to be cross to you. Good-bye, love." Then he stooped over her and kissed her again;—and so he took his leave of her.

It was raining hard, and when he got into the street he looked about for a cab, but there was none to be found. In Baker Street he got an omnibus which took him down to the underground railway, and by that he went to Gower Street. Through the rain he walked up to the Euston Station, and there he ordered breakfast. Could he have a mutton chop and some tea? And he was very particular that the mutton chop should be well cooked. He was a good-looking man, of fashionable appearance, and the young lady who attended him noticed him and was courteous to him. He condescended even to have a little light conversation with her, and, on the whole, he seemed to enjoy his breakfast. "Upon my word, I should like to breakfast here every day of my life," he said. The young lady assured him that, as far as she could see, there was no objection to such an arrangement. "Only it's a bore, you know, coming out in the rain when there are no cabs," he said. Then there were various little jokes between them, till the young lady was quite impressed with the gentleman's pleasant affability.

After a while he went back into the hall and took a first-class return ticket, not for Birmingham, but for the Tenway Junction. It is quite unnecessary to describe the Tenway Junction, as everybody knows it. From this spot, some six or seven miles distant from London, lines diverge east, west, and north, north-east, and north-west, round the metropolis in every direction, and with direct communication with every other line in and out of London. It is a marvellous place, quite unintelligible to the uninitiated, and yet daily used by thousands who only know that when they get there, they are to do what some one tells them. The space occupied by the convergent rails seems to be sufficient for a large farm. And these rails always run one into another with sloping points, and cross passages, and mysterious meandering sidings, till it seems to the thoughtful stranger to be impossible that the best trained engine should know its own line. Here and there and around there is ever a wilderness of waggons, some loaded, some empty, some smoking with close-packed oxen, and others furlongs in length black with coals, which look as though they had been stranded there by chance, and were never destined to get again into the right path of traffic. Not a minute passes without a train going here or there, some rushing by without noticing Tenway in the least, crashing through like flashes of substantial lightning, and others stopping, disgorging and taking up passengers by the hundreds. Men and women,—especially the men, for the women knowing their ignorance are generally willing to trust to the pundits of the place,— look doubtful, uneasy, and bewildered. But they all do get properly placed and unplaced, so that the spectator at last acknowledges that over all this apparent chaos there is presiding a great genius of order. From dusky morn to dark night, and indeed almost throughout the night, the air is loaded with a succession of shrieks. The theory goes that each separate shriek,—if there can be any separation where the sound is so nearly continuous,—is a separate notice to separate ears of the coming or going of a separate train. The stranger, as he speculates on these pandemoniac noises, is able to realise the idea that were they discontinued the excitement necessary for the minds of the pundits might be lowered, and that activity might be lessened, and evil results might follow. But he cannot bring himself to credit that theory of individual notices.

At Tenway Junction there are half-a-dozen long platforms, on which men and women and luggage are crowded. On one of these for a while Ferdinand Lopez walked backwards and forwards as though waiting for the coming of some especial train. The crowd is ever so great that a man might be supposed to walk there from morning to night without exciting special notice. But the pundits are very clever, and have much experience in men and women. A well-taught pundit, who has exercised authority for a year or two at such a station as that of Tenway, will know within a minute of the appearance of each stranger what is his purpose there,— whether he be going or has just come, whether he is himself on the way or waiting for others, whether he should be treated with civility or with some curt command,—so that if his purport be honest all necessary assistance may be rendered him. As Lopez was walking up and down, with smiling face and leisurely pace, now reading an advertisement and now watching the contortions of some amazed passenger, a certain pundit asked him his business. He was waiting, he said, for a train from Liverpool, intending, when his friend arrived, to go with him to Dulwich by a train which went round the west of London. It was all feasible, and the pundit told him that the stopping train from Liverpool was due there in six minutes, but that the express from the north would pass first. Lopez thanked the pundit and gave him sixpence,—which made the pundit suspicious. A pundit hopes to be paid when he handles luggage, but has no such expectation when he merely gives information.

The pundit still had his eye on our friend when the shriek and the whirr of the express from the north was heard. Lopez walked quickly up towards the edge of the platform, when the pundit followed him, telling him that this was not his train. Lopez then ran a few yards along the platform, not noticing the man, reaching a spot that was unoccupied;—and there he stood fixed. And as he stood the express flashed by. "I am fond of seeing them pass like that," said Lopez to the man who had followed him.

"But you shouldn't do it, sir," said the suspicious pundit. "No one isn't allowed to stand near like that. The very hair of it might take you off your legs when you're not used to it."

"All right, old fellow," said Lopez, retreating. The next train was the Liverpool train; and it seemed that our friend's friend had not come, for when the Liverpool passengers had cleared themselves off, he was still walking up and down the platform. "He'll come by the next," said Lopez to the pundit, who now followed him about and kept an eye on him.

"There ain't another from Liverpool stopping here till the 2.20," said the pundit. "You had better come again if you mean to meet him by that."

"He has come on part of the way, and will reach this by some other train," said Lopez.

"There ain't nothing he can come by," said the pundit. "Gentlemen can't wait here all day, sir. The horders is against waiting on the platform."

"All right," said Lopez, moving away as though to make his exit through the station.

Now Tenway Junction is so big a place, and so scattered, that it is impossible that all the pundits should by any combined activity maintain to the letter that order of which our special pundit had spoken. Lopez, departing from the platform which he had hitherto occupied, was soon to be seen on another, walking up and down, and again waiting. But the old pundit had had his eye upon him, and had followed him round. At that moment there came a shriek louder than all the other shrieks, and the morning express down from Euston to Inverness was seen coming round the curve at a thousand miles an hour. Lopez turned round and looked at it, and again walked towards the edge of the platform. But now it was not exactly the edge that he neared, but a descent to a pathway,—an inclined plane leading down to the level of the rails, and made there for certain purposes of traffic. As he did so the pundit called to him, and then made a rush at him,—for our friend's back was turned to the coming train. But Lopez heeded not the call, and the rush was too late. With quick, but still with gentle and apparently unhurried steps, he walked down before the flying engine—and in a moment had been knocked into bloody atoms.

Chapter LXI
The Widow and Her Friends

The catastrophe described in the last chapter had taken place during the first week in March. By the end of that month old Mr. Wharton had probably reconciled himself to the tragedy, although in fact it had affected him very deeply. In the first days after the news had reached him he seemed to be bowed to the ground. Stone Buildings were neglected, and the Eldon saw nothing of him. Indeed, he barely left the house from which he had been so long banished by the presence of his son-in-law. It seemed to Everett, who now came to live with him and his sister, as though his father were overcome by the horror of the affair. But after awhile he recovered himself, and appeared one morning in court with his wig and gown, and argued a case,—which was now unusual with him,—as though to show the world that a dreadful episode in his life was passed, and should be thought of no more. At this period, three or four weeks after the occurrence,—he rarely spoke to his daughter about Lopez; but to Everett the man's name would be often on his tongue. "I do not know that there could have been any other deliverance," he said to his son one day. "I thought it would have killed me when I first heard it, and it nearly killed her. But, at any rate, now there is peace."

But the widow seemed to feel it more as time went on. At first she was stunned, and for a while absolutely senseless. It was not till two days after the occurrence that the fact became known to her,—nor known as a certainty to her father and brother. It seemed as though the man had been careful to carry with him no record of identity, the nature of which would permit it to outlive the crash of the train. No card was found, no scrap of paper with his name; and it was discovered at last that when he left the house on the fatal morning he had been careful to dress himself in shirt and socks, with handkerchief and collar that had been newly purchased for his proposed journey and which bore no mark. The fragments of his body set identity at defiance, and even his watch had been crumpled into ashes. Of course the fact became certain with no great delay. The man himself was missing, and was accurately described both by the young lady from the refreshment room, and by the suspicious pundit who had actually seen the thing done. There was first belief that it was so, which was not communicated to Emily,—and then certainty.

There was an inquest held of course,—well, we will say on the body,—and, singularly enough, great difference of opinion as to the manner, though of course none as to the immediate cause of the death. Had it been accidental, or premeditated? The pundit, who in the performance of his duties on the Tenway platforms was so efficient and valuable, gave half-a-dozen opinions in half-a-dozen minutes when subjected to the questions of the Coroner. In his own mind he had not the least doubt in the world as to what had happened. But he was made to believe that he was not to speak his own mind. The gentleman, he said, certainly might have walked down by accident. The gentleman's back was turned, and it was possible that the gentleman did not hear the train. He was quite certain the gentleman knew of the train; but yet he could not say. The gentleman walked down before the train o' purpose; but perhaps he didn't mean to do himself an injury. There was a deal of this, till the Coroner, putting all his wrath into his brow, told the man that he was a disgrace to the service, and expressed a hope that the Company would no longer employ a man so evidently unfit for his position. But the man was in truth a conscientious and useful railway pundit, with a large family, and evident capabilities for his business. At last a verdict was given,—that the man's name was Ferdinand Lopez, that he had been crushed by an express train on the London and North Western Line, and that there was no evidence to show how his presence on the line had been occasioned. Of course Mr. Wharton had employed counsel, and of course the counsel's object had been to avoid a verdict of felo de se. Appended to the verdict was a recommendation from the jury that the Railway Company should be advised to signalise their express trains more clearly at the Tenway Junction Station.

When these tidings were told to the widow she had already given way to many fears. Lopez had gone, purporting,—as he said,—to be back to dinner. He had not come then, nor on the following morning; nor had he written. Then she remembered all that he had done and said;—how he had kissed her, and left a parting malediction for her father. She did not at first imagine that he had destroyed himself, but that he had gone away, intending to vanish as other men before now have vanished. As she thought of this something almost like love came back upon her heart. Of course he was bad. Even in her sorrow, even when alarmed as to his fate, she could not deny that. But her oath to him had not been to love him only while he was good. She had made herself a part of him, and was she not bound to be true to him, whether good or bad? She implored her father and she implored her brother to be ceaseless in their endeavours to trace him,—sometimes seeming almost to fear that in this respect she could not fully trust them. Then she discerned from their manner a doubt as to her husband's fate. "Oh, papa, if you think anything, tell me what you think," she said late on the evening of the second day. He was then nearly sure that the man who had been killed at Tenway was Ferdinand Lopez;—but he was not quite sure, and he would not tell her. But on the following morning, somewhat before noon, having himself gone out early to Euston Square, he came back to his own house,—and then he told her all. For the first hour she did not shed a tear or lose her consciousness of the horror of the thing;—but sat still and silent, gazing at nothing, casting back her mind over the history of her life, and the misery which she had brought on all who belonged to her. Then at last she gave way, fell into tears, hysteric sobbings, convulsions so violent as for a time to take the appearance of epileptic fits, and was at last exhausted and, happily for herself, unconscious.

After that she was ill for many weeks,—so ill that at times both her father and her brother thought that she would die. When the first month or six weeks had passed by she would often speak of her husband, especially to her father, and always speaking of him as though she had brought him to his untimely fate. Nor could she endure at this time that her father should say a word against him, even when she obliged the old man to speak of one whose conduct had been so infamous. It had all been her doing! Had she not married him there would have been no misfortune! She did not say that he had been noble, true, or honest,—but she asserted that all the evils which had come upon him had been produced by herself. "My dear," her father said to her one evening, "it is a matter which we cannot forget, but on which it is well that we should be silent."

"I shall always know what that silence means," she replied.

"It will never mean condemnation of you by me," said he.

"But I have destroyed your life,—and his. I know I ought not to have married him, because you bade me not. And I know that I should have been gentler with him, and more obedient, when I was his wife. I sometimes wish that I were a Catholic, and that I could go into a convent, and bury it all amidst sackcloths and ashes."

"That would not bury it," said her father.

"But I should at least be buried. If I were out of sight, you might forget it all."

She once stirred Everett up to speak more plainly than her father ever dared to do, and then also she herself used language that was very plain. "My darling," said her brother once, when she had been trying to make out that her husband had been more sinned against than sinning,—"he was a bad man. It is better that the truth should be told."

"And who is a good man?" she said, raising herself in her bed and looking him full in the face with her deep-sunken eyes. "If there be any truth in our religion, are we not all bad? Who is to tell the shades of difference in badness? He was not a drunkard, or a gambler. Through it all he was true to his wife." She, poor creature, was of course ignorant of that little scene in the little street near May Fair, in which Lopez had offered to carry Lizzie Eustace away with him to Guatemala. "He was industrious. His ideas about money were not the same as yours or papa's. How was he worse than others? It happened that his faults were distasteful to you—and so, perhaps, were his virtues."

"His faults, such as they were, brought all these miseries."

"He would have been successful now if he had never seen me. But why should we talk of it? We shall never agree. And you, Everett, can never understand all that has passed through my mind during the last two years."

There were two or three persons who attempted to see her at this period, but she avoided them all. First came Mrs. Roby, who, as her nearest neighbour, as her aunt, and as an aunt who had been so nearly allied to her, had almost a right to demand admittance. But she would not see Mrs. Roby. She sent down word to say that she was too ill. And when Mrs. Roby wrote to her, she got her father to answer the notes. "You had better let it drop," the old man said at last to his sister-in-law. "Of course she remembers that it was you who brought them together."

"But I didn't bring them together, Mr. Wharton. How often am I to tell you so? It was Everett who brought Mr. Lopez here."

"The marriage was made up in your house, and it has destroyed me and my child. I will not quarrel with my wife's sister if I can help it, but at present you had better keep apart." Then he had left her abruptly, and Mrs. Roby had not dared either to write or to call again.

At this time Arthur Fletcher saw both Everett and Mr. Wharton frequently, but he did not go to the Square, contenting himself with asking whether he might be allowed to do so. "Not yet, Arthur," said the old man. "I am sure she thinks of you as one of her best friends, but she could not see you yet."

"She would have nothing to fear," said Arthur. "We knew each other when we were children, and I should be now only as I was then."

"Not yet, Arthur;—not yet," said the barrister.

Then there came a letter, or rather two letters, from Mary Wharton;— one to Mr. Wharton and the other to Emily. To tell the truth as to these letters, they contained the combined wisdom and tenderness of Wharton Hall and Longbarns. As soon as the fate of Lopez had been ascertained and thoroughly discussed in Herefordshire, there went forth an edict that Emily had suffered punishment sufficient and was to be forgiven. Old Mrs. Fletcher did not come to this at once,—having some deep-seated feeling which she did not dare to express even to her son, though she muttered it to her daughter-in-law, that Arthur would be disgraced for ever were he to marry the widow of such a man as Ferdinand Lopez. But when this question of receiving Emily back into family favour was mooted in the Longbarns Parliament no one alluded to the possibility of such a marriage. There was the fact that she whom they had all loved had been freed by a great tragedy from the husband whom they had all condemned,—and also the knowledge that the poor victim had suffered greatly during the period of her married life. Mrs. Fletcher had frowned, and shaken her head, and made a little speech about the duties of women, and the necessarily fatal consequences when those duties are neglected. There were present there, with the old lady, John Fletcher and his wife, Sir Alured and Lady Wharton, and Mary Wharton. Arthur was not in the county, nor could the discussion have been held in his presence. "I can only say," said John, getting up and looking away from his mother, "that she shall always find a home at Longbarns when she chooses to come here, and I hope Sir Alured will say the same as to Wharton Hall." After all, John Fletcher was king in these parts, and Mrs. Fletcher, with many noddings and some sobbing, had to give way to King John. The end of all this was that Mary Wharton wrote her letters. In that to Mr. Wharton she asked whether it would not be better that her cousin should change the scene and come at once into the country. Let her come and stay a month at Wharton, and then go on to Longbarns. She might be sure that there would be no company in either house. In June the Fletchers would go up to town for a week, and then Emily might return to Wharton Hall. It was a long letter, and Mary gave many reasons why the poor sufferer would be better in the country than in town. The letter to Emily herself was shorter but full of affection. "Do, do, do come. You know how we all love you. Let it be as it used to be. You always liked the country. I will devote myself to try and comfort you." But Emily could not as yet submit to receive devotion even from her cousin Mary. Through it all, and under it all,—though she would ever defend her husband because he was dead,— she knew that she had disgraced the Whartons and brought a load of sorrow upon the Fletchers, and she was too proud to be forgiven so quickly.

Then she received another tender of affection from a quarter whence she certainly did not expect it. The Duchess of Omnium wrote to her. The Duchess, though she had lately been considerably restrained by the condition of the Duke's mind, and by the effects of her own political and social mistakes, still from time to time made renewed efforts to keep together the Coalition by giving dinners, balls, and garden parties, and by binding to herself the gratitude and worship of young parliamentary aspirants. In carrying out her plans, she had lately showered her courtesies upon Arthur Fletcher, who had been made welcome even by the Duke as the sitting member for Silverbridge. With Arthur she had of course discussed the conduct of Lopez as to the election bills, and had been very loud in condemning him. And from Arthur also she had heard something of the sorrows of Emily Lopez. Arthur had been very desirous that the Duchess, who had received them both at her house, should distinguish between the husband and the wife. Then had come the tragedy, to which the notoriety of the man's conduct of course gave additional interest. It was believed that Lopez had destroyed himself because of the disgrace which had fallen upon him from the Silverbridge affair. And for much of that Silverbridge affair the Duchess herself was responsible. She waited till a couple of months had gone by, and then, in the beginning of May, sent to the widow what was intended to be, and indeed was, a very kind note. The Duchess had heard the sad story with the greatest grief. She hoped that Mrs. Lopez would permit her to avail herself of a short acquaintance to express her sincere sympathy. She would not venture to call as yet, but hoped that before long she might be allowed to come to Manchester Square.

This note touched the poor woman to whom it was written, not because she herself was solicitous to be acquainted with the Duchess of Omnium, but because the application seemed to her to contain something like an acquittal, or at any rate a pardon, of her husband. His sin in that measure of the Silverbridge election,—a sin which her father had been loud in denouncing before the wretch had destroyed himself,—had been especially against the Duke of Omnium. And now the Duchess came forward to say that it should be forgiven and forgotten. When she showed the letter to her father, and asked him what she should say in answer to it, he only shook his head. "It is meant for kindness, papa."

"Yes;—I think it is. There are people who have no right to be kind to me. If a man stopped me in the street and offered me half-a-crown it might be kindness;—but I don't want the man's half-crown."

"I don't think it is the same, papa. There is a reason here."

"Perhaps so, my dear; but I do not see the reason."

She became very red, but even to him she would not explain her ideas. "I think I shall answer it."

"Certainly answer it. Your compliments to the Duchess and thank her for her kind inquiries."

"But she says she will come here."

"I should not notice that."

"Very well, papa. If you think so, of course I will not. Perhaps it would be an inconvenience, if she were really to come." On the next day she did write a note, not quite so cold as that which her father proposed, but still saying nothing as to the offered visit. She felt, she said, very grateful for the Duchess's kind remembrance of her. The Duchess would perhaps understand that at present her sorrow overwhelmed her.

And there was one other tender of kindness which was more surprising than even that from the Duchess. The reader may perhaps remember that Ferdinand Lopez and Lady Eustace had not parted when they last saw each other on the pleasantest terms. He had been very affectionate, but when he had proposed to devote his whole life to her and to carry her off to Guatemala she had simply told him that he was—a fool. Then he had escaped from her house and had never again seen Lizzie Eustace. She had not thought very much about it. Had he returned to her the next day with some more tempting proposition for making money she would have listened to him,— and had he begged her pardon for what had taken place on the former day she would have merely laughed. She was not more offended than she would have been had he asked her for half her fortune instead of her person and her honour. But, as it was, he had escaped and had never again shown himself in the little street near May Fair. Then she had the tidings of his death, first seeing the account in a very sensational article from the pen of Mr. Quintus Slide himself. She was immediately filled with an intense interest which was infinitely increased by the fact that the man had but a few days before declared himself to be her lover. It was bringing her almost as near to the event as though she had seen it! She was, perhaps, entitled to think that she had caused it! Nay;—in one sense she had caused it, for he certainly would not have destroyed himself had she consented to go with him to Guatemala or elsewhere. And she knew his wife. An uninteresting, dowdy creature she had called her. But, nevertheless, they had been in company together more than once. So she presented her compliments, and expressed her sorrow, and hoped that she might be allowed to call. There had been no one for whom she had felt more sincere respect and esteem than for her late friend Mr. Ferdinand Lopez. To this note there was sent an answer written by Mr. Wharton himself.

Madam,

My daughter is too ill to see even her own friends.

I am, Madam,
Your obedient servant,

Abel Wharton.

After this, life went on in a very quiet way at Manchester Square for many weeks. Gradually Mrs. Lopez recovered her capability of attending to the duties of life. Gradually she became again able to interest herself in her brother's pursuits and in her father's comforts, and the house returned to its old form as it had been before these terrible two years, in which the happiness of the Wharton and Fletcher families had been marred, and scotched, and almost destroyed for ever by the interference of Ferdinand Lopez. But Mrs. Lopez never for a moment forgot that she had done the mischief,—and that the black enduring cloud had been created solely by her own perversity and self-will. Though she would still defend her late husband if any attack were made upon his memory, not the less did she feel that hers had been the fault, though the punishment had come upon them all.

Chapter LXII
Phineas Finn Has a Book to Read

The sensation created by the man's death was by no means confined to Manchester Square, but was very general in the metropolis, and, indeed, throughout the country. As the catastrophe became the subject of general conversation, many people learned that the Silverbridge affair had not, in truth, had much to do with it. The man had killed himself, as many other men have done before him, because he had run through his money and had no chance left of redeeming himself. But to the world at large, the disgrace brought upon him by the explanation given in Parliament was the apparent cause of his self-immolation, and there were not wanting those who felt and expressed a sympathy for a man who could feel so acutely the effect of his own wrong-doing. No doubt he had done wrong in asking the Duke for the money. But the request, though wrong, might almost be justified. There could be no doubt, these apologists said, that he had been ill-treated between the Duke and the Duchess. No doubt Phineas Finn, who was now described by some opponents as the Duke's creature, had been able to make out a story in the Duke's favour. But all the world knew what was the worth and what was the truth of ministerial explanations! The Coalition was very strong; and even the question in the House, which should have been hostile, had been asked in a friendly spirit. In this way there came to be a party who spoke and wrote of Ferdinand Lopez as though he had been a martyr.

Of course Mr. Quintus Slide was in the front rank of these accusers. He may be said to have led the little army which made this matter a pretext for a special attack upon the Ministry. Mr. Slide was especially hostile to the Prime Minister, but he was not less hotly the enemy of Phineas Finn. Against Phineas Finn he had old grudges, which, however, age had never cooled. He could, therefore, write with a most powerful pen when discussing the death of that unfortunate man, the late candidate for Silverbridge, crushing his two foes in the single grasp of his journalistic fist. Phineas had certainly said some hard things against Lopez, though he had not mentioned the man's name. He had congratulated the House that it had not been contaminated by the presence of so base a creature, and he had said that he would not pause to stigmatise the meanness of the application for money which Lopez had made. Had Lopez continued to live and to endure "the slings and arrows of outrageous fortune," no one would have ventured to say that these words would have inflicted too severe a punishment. But death wipes out many faults, and a self-inflicted death caused by remorse will, in the minds of many, wash a blackamoor almost white. Thus it came to pass that some heavy weapons were hurled at Phineas Finn, but none so heavy as those hurled by Quintus Slide. Should not this Irish knight, who was so ready with his lance in the defence of the Prime Minister, asked Mr. Slide, have remembered the past events of his own rather peculiar life? Had not he, too, been poor, and driven in his poverty to rather questionable straits? Had not he been abject in his petition for office,—and in what degree were such petitions less disgraceful than a request for money which had been hopelessly expended on an impossible object, attempted at the instance of the great Cr[oe]sus who, when asked to pay it, had at once acknowledged the necessity of doing so? Could not Mr. Finn remember that he himself had stood in danger of his life before a British jury, and that, though he had been, no doubt properly, acquitted of the crime imputed to him, circumstances had come out against him during the trial which, if not as criminal, were at any rate almost as disgraceful? Could he not have had some mercy on a broken political adventurer who, in his aspirations for public life, had shown none of that greed by which Mr. Phineas Finn had been characterised in all the relations of life? As for the Prime Minister, "We," as Mr. Quintus Slide always described himself,—"We do not wish to add to the agony which the fate of Mr. Lopez must have brought upon him. He has hounded that poor man to his death in revenge for the trifling sum of money which he was called on to pay for him. It may be that the first blame lay not with the Prime Minister himself, but with the Prime Minister's wife. With that we have nothing to do. The whole thing lies in a nutshell. The bare mention of the name of her Grace the Duchess in Parliament would have saved the Duke, at any rate as effectually as he has been saved by the services of his man-of-all-work, Phineas Finn, and would have saved him without driving poor Ferdinand Lopez to insanity. But rather than do this he allowed his servant to make statements about mysterious agents, which we are justified in stigmatizing as untrue, and to throw the whole blame where but least of the blame was due. We all know the result. It was found in those gory shreds and tatters of a poor human being with which the Tenway Railway Station was bespattered."

Of course such an article had considerable effect. It was apparent at once that there was ample room for an action for libel against the newspaper, on the part of Phineas Finn if not on that of the Duke. But it was equally apparent that Mr. Quintus Slide must have been very well aware of this when he wrote the article. Such an action, even if successful, may bring with it to the man punished more of good than of evil. Any pecuniary penalty might be more than recouped by the largeness of the advertisement which such an action would produce. Mr. Slide no doubt calculated that he would carry with him a great body of public feeling by the mere fact that he had attacked a Prime Minister and a Duke. If he could only get all the publicans in London to take his paper because of his patriotic and bold conduct, the fortune of the paper would be made. There is no better trade than that of martyrdom, if the would-be martyr knows how far he may judiciously go, and in what direction. All this Mr. Quintus Slide was supposed to have considered very well.

And Phineas Finn knew that his enemy had also considered the nature of the matters which he would have been able to drag into Court if there should be a trial. Allusions, very strong allusions, had been made to former periods of Mr. Finn's life. And though there was but little, if anything, in the past circumstances of which he was ashamed,—but little, if anything, which he thought would subject him personally to the odium of good men, could they be made accurately known in all their details,—it would, he was well aware, be impossible that such accuracy should be achieved. And the story if told inaccurately would not suit him. And then, there was a reason against any public proceeding much stronger even than this. Whether the telling of the story would or would not suit him, it certainly would not suit others. As has been before remarked, there are former chronicles respecting Phineas Finn, and in them may be found adequate cause for this conviction on his part. To no outsider was this history known better than to Mr. Quintus Slide, and therefore Mr. Quintus Slide could dare almost to defy the law.

But not the less on this account were there many who told Phineas that he ought to bring the action. Among these none were more eager than his old friend Lord Chiltern, the Master of the Brake hounds, a man who really loved Phineas, who also loved the abstract idea of justice, and who could not endure the thought that a miscreant should go unpunished. Hunting was over for the season in the Brake country, and Lord Chiltern rushed up to London, having this object among others of a very pressing nature on his mind. His saddler had to be seen,—and threatened,—on a certain matter touching the horses' backs. A draught of hounds were being sent down to a friend in Scotland. And there was a Committee of Masters to sit on a moot question concerning a neutral covert in the XXX country, of which Committee he was one. But the desire to punish Slide was almost as strong in his indignant mind as those other matters referring more especially to the profession of his life. "Phineas," he said, "you are bound to do it. If you will allow a fellow like that to say such things of you, why, by heaven, any man may say anything of anybody."

Now Phineas could hardly explain to Lord Chiltern his objection to the proposed action. A lady was closely concerned, and that lady was Lord Chiltern's sister. "I certainly shall not," said Phineas.

"And why?"

"Just because he wishes me to do it. I should be falling into the little pit that he has dug for me."

"He couldn't hurt you. What have you got to be afraid of? Ruat c[oe]lum."

"There are certain angels, Chiltern, living up in that heaven which you wish me to pull about our ears, as to whom, if all their heart and all their wishes and all their doings could be known, nothing but praise could be spoken; but who would still be dragged with soiled wings through the dirt if this man were empowered to bring witness after witness into court. My wife would be named. For aught I know, your wife."

"By G——, he'd find himself wrong there."

"Leave a chimney-sweep alone when you see him, Chiltern. Should he run against you, then remember that it is one of the necessary penalties of clean linen that it is apt to be soiled."

"I'm d——d if I'd let him off."

"Yes you would, old fellow. When you come to see clearly what you would gain and what you would lose, you would not meddle with him."

His wife was at first inclined to think that an action should be taken, but she was more easily convinced than Lord Chiltern. "I had not thought," she said, "of poor Lady Laura. But is it not horrible that a man should be able to go on like that, and that there should be no punishment?" In answer to this he only shrugged his shoulders.

But the greatest pressure came upon him from another source. He did not in truth suffer much himself from what was said in the "People's Banner." He had become used to the "People's Banner" and had found out that in no relation of life was he less pleasantly situated because of the maledictions heaped upon him in the columns of that newspaper. His position in public life did not seem to be weakened by them. His personal friends did not fall off because of them. Those who loved him did not love him less. It had not been so with him always, but now, at last, he was hardened against Mr. Quintus Slide. But the poor Duke was by no means equally strong. This attack upon him, this denunciation of his cruelty, this assurance that he had caused the death of Ferdinand Lopez, was very grievous to him. It was not that he really felt himself to be guilty of the man's blood, but that any one should say that he was guilty. It was of no use to point out to him that other newspapers had sufficiently vindicated his conduct in that respect, that it was already publicly known that Lopez had received payment for those election expenses from Mr. Wharton before the application had been made to him, and that therefore the man's dishonesty was patent to all the world. It was equally futile to explain to him that the man's last act had been in no degree caused by what had been said in Parliament, but had been the result of his continued failures in life and final absolute ruin. He fretted and fumed and was very wretched,—and at last expressed his opinion that legal steps should be taken to punish the "People's Banner." Now it had been already acknowledged, on the dictum of no less a man than Sir Gregory Grogram, the Attorney-General, that the action for libel, if taken at all, must be taken, not on the part of the Prime Minister, but on that of Phineas Finn. Sir Timothy Beeswax had indeed doubted, but it had come to be understood by all the members of the Coalition that Sir Timothy Beeswax always did doubt whatever was said by Sir Gregory Grogram. "The Duke thinks that something should be done," said Mr. Warburton, the Duke's private Secretary, to Phineas Finn.

"Not by me, I hope," said Phineas.

"Nobody else can do it. That is to say it must be done in your name. Of course it would be a Government matter, as far as expense goes, and all that."

"I am sorry the Duke should think so."

"I don't see that it could hurt you."

"I am sorry the Duke should think so," repeated Phineas,—"because nothing can be done in my name. I have made up my mind about it. I think the Duke is wrong in wishing it, and I believe that were any action taken, we should only be playing into the hands of that wretched fellow, Quintus Slide. I have long been conversant with Mr. Quintus Slide, and have quite made up my mind that I will never play upon his pipe. And you may tell the Duke that there are other reasons. The man has referred to my past life, and in seeking to justify those remarks he would be enabled to drag before the public circumstances and stories, and perhaps persons, in a manner that I personally should disregard, but which, for the sake of others, I am bound to prevent. You will explain all this to the Duke?"

"I am afraid you will find the Duke very urgent."

"I must then express my great sorrow that I cannot oblige the Duke. I trust I need hardly say that the Duke has no colleague more devoted to his interest than I am. Were he to wish me to change my office, or to abandon it, or to undertake any political duty within the compass of my small powers, he would find me ready to obey his behests. But in this matter others are concerned, and I cannot make my judgment subordinate to his." The private Secretary looked very serious, and simply said that he would do his best to explain these objections to his Grace.

That the Duke would take his refusal in bad part Phineas felt nearly certain. He had been a little surprised at the coldness of the Minister's manner to him after the statement he had made in the house, and had mentioned the matter to his wife. "You hardly know him," she had said, "as well as I do."

"Certainly not. You ought to know him very intimately, and I have had but little personal friendship with him. But it was a moment in which the man might, for the moment, have been cordial."

"It was not a moment for his cordiality. The Duchess says that if you want to get a really genial smile from him you must talk to him about cork soles. I know exactly what she means. He loves to be simple, but he does not know how to show people that he likes it. Lady Rosina found him out by accident."

"Don't suppose that I am in the least aggrieved," he had said. And now he spoke again to his wife in the same spirit. "Warburton clearly thinks that he will be offended, and Warburton, I suppose, knows his mind."

"I don't see why he should. I have been reading it longer, and I still find it very difficult. Lady Glen has been at the work for the last fifteen years, and sometimes owns that there are passages she has not mastered yet. I fancy Mr. Warburton is afraid of him, and is a little given to fancy that everybody should bow down to him. Now if there is anything certain about the Duke it is this,—that he doesn't want any one to bow down to him. He hates all bowing down."

"I don't think he loves those who oppose him."

"It is not the opposition he hates, but the cause in the man's mind which may produce it. When Sir Orlando opposed him, and he thought that Sir Orlando's opposition was founded on jealousy, then he despised Sir Orlando. But had he believed in Sir Orlando's belief in the new ships, he would have been capable of pressing Sir Orlando to his bosom, although he might have been forced to oppose Sir Orlando's ships in the Cabinet."

"He is a Sir Bayard to you," said Phineas, laughing.

"Rather a Don Quixote, whom I take to have been the better man of the two. I'll tell you what he is, Phineas, and how he is better than all the real knights of whom I have ever read in story. He is a man altogether without guile, and entirely devoted to his country. Do not quarrel with him, if you can help it."

Phineas had not the slightest desire to quarrel with his chief; but he did think it to be not improbable that his chief would quarrel with him. It was notorious to him as a member of the Cabinet,—as a colleague living with other colleagues by whom the Prime Minister was coddled, and especially as the husband of his wife, who lived almost continually with the Prime Minister's wife,—that the Duke was cut to the quick by the accusation that he had hounded Ferdinand Lopez to his death. The Prime Minister had defended himself in the House against the first charge by means of Phineas Finn, and now required Phineas to defend him from the second charge in another way. This he was obliged to refuse to do. And then the Minister's private Secretary looked very grave, and left him with the impression that the Duke would be much annoyed, if not offended. And already there had grown up an idea that the Duke would have on the list of his colleagues none who were personally disagreeable to himself. Though he was by no means a strong Minister in regard to political measures, or the proper dominion of his party, still men were afraid of him. It was not that he would call upon them to resign, but that, if aggrieved, he would resign himself. Sir Orlando Drought had rebelled and had tried a fall with the Prime Minister,—and had greatly failed. Phineas determined that if frowned upon he would resign, but that he certainly would bring no action for libel against the "People's Banner."

A week passed after he had seen Warburton before he by chance found himself alone with the Prime Minister. This occurred at the house in Carlton Gardens, at which he was a frequent visitor,—and could hardly have ceased to be so without being noticed, as his wife spent half her time there. It was evident to him then that the occasion was sought for by the Duke. "Mr. Finn," said the Duke, "I wanted to have a word or two with you."

"Certainly," said Phineas, arresting his steps.

"Warburton spoke to you about that—that newspaper."

"Yes, Duke. He seemed to think that there should be an action for libel."

"I thought so too. It was very bad, you know."

"Yes;—it was bad. I have known the 'People's Banner' for some time, and it is always bad."

"No doubt;—no doubt. It is bad, very bad. Is it not sad that there should be such dishonesty, and that nothing can be done to stop it? Warburton says that you won't hear of an action in your name."

"There are reasons, Duke."

"No doubt;—no doubt. Well;—there's an end of it. I own I think the man should be punished. I am not often vindictive, but I think that he should be punished. However, I suppose it cannot be."

"I don't see the way."

"So be it. So be it. It must be entirely for you to judge. Are you not longing to get into the country, Mr. Finn?"

"Hardly yet," said Phineas, surprised. "It's only June, and we have two months more of it. What is the use of longing yet?"

"Two months more!" said the Duke. "Two months certainly. But even two months will come to an end. We go down to Matching quietly,—very quietly,—when the time does come. You must promise that you'll come with us. Eh? I make a point of it, Mr. Finn."

Phineas did promise, and thought that he had succeeded in mastering one of the difficult passages in that book.

Chapter LXIII
The Duchess and Her Friend

But the Duke, though he was by far too magnanimous to be angry with Phineas Finn because Phineas would not fall into his views respecting the proposed action, was not the less tormented and goaded by what the newspaper said. The assertion that he had hounded Ferdinand Lopez to his death, that by his defence of himself he had brought the man's blood on his head, was made and repeated till those around him did not dare to mention the name of Lopez in his hearing. Even his wife was restrained and became fearful, and in her heart of hearts began almost to wish for that retirement to which he had occasionally alluded as a distant Elysium which he should never be allowed to reach. He was beginning to have the worn look of an old man. His scanty hair was turning grey, and his long thin cheeks longer and thinner. Of what he did when sitting alone in his chamber, either at home or at the Treasury Chamber, she knew less and less from day to day, and she began to think that much of his sorrow arose from the fact that among them they would allow him to do nothing. There was no special subject now which stirred him to eagerness and brought upon herself explanations which were tedious and unintelligible to her, but evidently delightful to him. There were no quints or semi-tenths now, no aspirations for decimal perfection, no delightfully fatiguing hours spent in the manipulation of the multiplication table. And she could not but observe that the old Duke now spoke to her much less frequently of her husband's political position than had been his habit. Through the first year and a half of the present ministerial arrangement he had been constant in his advice to her, and had always, even when things were difficult, been cheery and full of hope. He still came frequently to the house, but did not often see her. And when he did see her he seemed to avoid all allusion either to the political successes or the political reverses of the Coalition. And even her other special allies seemed to labour under unusual restraint with her. Barrington Erle seldom told her any news. Mr. Rattler never had a word for her. Warburton, who had ever been discreet, became almost petrified by discretion. And even Phineas Finn had grown to be solemn, silent, and uncommunicative. "Have you heard who is the new Prime Minister?" she said to Mrs. Finn one day.

"Has there been a change?"

"I suppose so. Everything has become so quiet that I cannot imagine that Plantagenet is still in office. Do you know what anybody is doing?"

"The world is going on very smoothly, I take it."

"I hate smoothness. It always means treachery and danger. I feel sure that there will be a great blow up before long. I smell it in the air. Don't you tremble for your husband?"

"Why should I? He likes being in office because it gives him something to do; but he would never be an idle man. As long as he has a seat in Parliament, I shall be contented."

"To have been Prime Minister is something after all, and they can't rob him of that," said the Duchess, recurring again to her own husband. "I half fancy sometimes that the charm of the thing is growing upon him."

"Upon the Duke?"

"Yes. He is always talking of the delight he will have in giving it up. He is always Cincinnatus, going back to his peaches and his ploughs. But I fear he is beginning to feel that the salt would be gone out of his life if he ceased to be the first man in the kingdom. He has never said so, but there is a nervousness about him when I suggest to him the name of this or that man as his successor which alarms me. And I think he is becoming a tyrant with his own men. He spoke the other day of Lord Drummond almost as though he meant to have him whipped. It isn't what one expected from him;—is it?"

"The weight of the load on his mind makes him irritable."

"Either that, or having no load. If he had really much to do he wouldn't surely have time to think so much of that poor wretch who destroyed himself. Such sensitiveness is simply a disease. One can never punish any fault in the world if the sinner can revenge himself upon us by rushing into eternity. Sometimes I see him shiver and shudder, and then I know that he is thinking of Lopez."

"I can understand all that, Lady Glen."

"It isn't as it should be, though you can understand it. I'll bet you a guinea that Sir Timothy Beeswax has to go out before the beginning of next Session."

"I've no objection. But why Sir Timothy?"

"He mentioned Lopez' name the other day before Plantagenet. I heard him. Plantagenet pulled that long face of his, looking as though he meant to impose silence on the whole world for the next six weeks. But Sir Timothy is brass itself, a sounding cymbal of brass that nothing can silence. He went on to declare with that loud voice of his that the death of Lopez was a good riddance of bad rubbish. Plantagenet turned away and left the room and shut himself up. He didn't declare to himself that he'd dismiss Sir Timothy, because that's not the way of his mind. But you'll see that Sir Timothy will have to go."

"That, at any rate, will be a good riddance of bad rubbish," said Mrs. Finn, who did not love Sir Timothy Beeswax.

Soon after that the Duchess made up her mind that she would interrogate the Duke of St. Bungay as to the present state of affairs. It was then the end of June, and nearly one of those long and tedious months had gone by of which the Duke spoke so feelingly when he asked Phineas Finn to come down to Matching. Hope had been expressed in more than one quarter that this would be a short Session. Such hopes are much more common in June than in July, and, though rarely verified, serve to keep up the drooping spirits of languid senators. "I suppose we shall be early out of town, Duke," she said one day.

"I think so. I don't see what there is to keep us. It often happens that ministers are a great deal better in the country than in London, and I fancy it will be so this year."

"You never think of the poor girls who haven't got their husbands yet."

"They should make better use of their time. Besides, they can get their husbands in the country."

"It's quite true that they never get to the end of their labours. They are not like you members of Parliament who can shut up your portfolios and go and shoot grouse. They have to keep at their work spring and summer, autumn and winter,—year after year! How they must hate the men they persecute!"

"I don't think we can put off going for their sake."

"Men are always selfish, I know. What do you think of Plantagenet lately?" The question was put very abruptly, without a moment's notice, and there was no avoiding it.

"Think of him!"

"Yes;—what do you think of his condition;—of his happiness, his health, his capacity of endurance? Will he be able to go on much longer? Now, my dear Duke, don't stare at me like that. You know, and I know, that you haven't spoken a word to me for the last two months. And you know, and I know, how many things there are of which we are both thinking in common. You haven't quarrelled with Plantagenet?"

"Quarrelled with him! Good heavens, no."

"Of course I know you still call him your noble colleague, and your noble friend, and make one of the same team with him and all that. But it used to be so much more than that."

"It is still more than that;—very much more."

"It was you who made him Prime Minister."

"No, no, no;—and again no. He made himself Prime Minister by obtaining the confidence of the House of Commons. There is no other possible way in which a man can become Prime Minister in this country."

"If I were not very serious at this moment, Duke, I should make an allusion to the—Marines." No other human being could have said this to the Duke of St. Bungay, except the young woman whom he had petted all his life as Lady Glencora. "But I am very serious," she continued, "and I may say not very happy. Of course the big wigs of a party have to settle among themselves who shall be their leader, and when this party was formed they settled, at your advice, that Plantagenet should be the man."

"My dear Lady Glen, I cannot allow that to pass without contradiction."

"Do not suppose that I am finding fault, or even that I am ungrateful. No one rejoiced as I rejoiced. No one still feels so much pride in it as I feel. I would have given ten years of my life to make him Prime Minister, and now I would give five to keep him so. It is like it was to be king, when men struggled among themselves who should be king. Whatever he may be, I am ambitious. I love to think that other men should look to him as being above them, and that something of this should come down upon me as his wife. I do not know whether it was not the happiest moment of my life when he told me that the Queen had sent for him."

"It was not so with him."

"No, Duke,—no! He and I are very different. He only wants to be useful. At any rate, that was all he did want."

"He is still the same."

"A man cannot always be carrying a huge load up a hill without having his back bent."

"I don't know that the load need be so heavy, Duchess."

"Ah, but what is the load? It is not going to the Treasury Chambers at eleven or twelve in the morning, and sitting four or five times a week in the House of Lords till seven or eight o'clock. He was never ill when he would remain in the House of Commons till two in the morning, and not have a decent dinner above twice in the week. The load I speak of isn't work."

"What is it then?" said the Duke, who in truth understood it all nearly as well as the Duchess herself.

"It is hard to explain, but it is very heavy."

"Responsibility, my dear, will always be heavy."

"But it is hardly that;—certainly not that alone. It is the feeling that so many people blame him for so many things, and the doubt in his own mind whether he may not deserve it. And then he becomes fretful, and conscious that such fretfulness is beneath him and injurious to his honour. He condemns men in his mind, and condemns himself for condescending to condemn them. He spends one quarter of an hour in thinking that as he is Prime Minister he will be Prime Minister down to his fingers' ends, and the next in resolving that he never ought to have been Prime Minister at all." Here something like a frown passed across the old man's brow, which was, however, no indication, of anger. "Dear Duke," she said, "you must not be angry with me. Who is there to whom I can speak but you?"

"Angry, my dear! No, indeed!"

"Because you looked as though you would scold me." At this he smiled. "And of course all this tells upon his health."

"Do you think he is ill?"

"He never says so. There is no special illness. But he is thin and wan and careworn. He does not eat and he does not sleep. Of course I watch him."

"Does his doctor see him?"

"Never. When I asked him once to say a word to Sir James Thorax,—for he was getting hoarse, you know,—he only shook his head and turned on his heels. When he was in the other House, and speaking every night, he would see Thorax constantly, and do just what he was told. He used to like opening his mouth and having Sir James to look down it. But now he won't let any one touch him."

"What would you have me do, Lady Glen?"

"I don't know."

"Do you think that he is so far out of health that he ought to give it up?"

"I don't say that. I don't dare to say it. I don't dare to recommend anything. No consideration of health would tell with him at all. If he were to die to-morrow as the penalty of doing something useful to-night, he wouldn't think twice about it. If you wanted to make him stay where he is, the way to do it would be to tell him that his health was failing him. I don't know that he does want to give up now."

"The autumn months will do everything for him;—only let him be quiet."

"You are coming to Matching, Duke?"

"I suppose so,—if you ask me,—for a week or two."

"You must come. I am quite nervous if you desert us. I think he becomes more estranged every day from all the others. I know you won't do a mischief by repeating what I say."

"I hope not."

"He seems to me to turn his nose up at everybody. He used to like Mr. Monk; but he envies Mr. Monk, because Mr. Monk is Chancellor of the Exchequer. I asked him whether we shouldn't have Lord Drummond at Matching, and he told me angrily that I might ask all the Government if I liked."

"Drummond contradicted him the other day."

"I knew there was something. He has got to be like a bear with a sore head, Duke. You should have seen his face the other day, when Mr. Rattler made some suggestion to him about the proper way of dividing farms."

"I don't think he ever liked Rattler."

"What of that? Don't I have to smile upon men whom I hate like poison;—and women too, which is worse? Do you think that I love old Lady Ramsden, or Mrs. MacPherson? He used to be so fond of Lord Cantrip."

"I think he likes Lord Cantrip," said the Duke.

"He asked his lordship to do something, and Lord Cantrip declined."

"I know all about that," said the Duke.

"And now he looks gloomy at Lord Cantrip. His friends won't stand that kind of thing, you know, for ever."

"He is always courteous to Finn," said the Duke.

"Yes;—just now he is on good terms with Mr. Finn. He would never be harsh to Mr. Finn, because he knows that Mrs. Finn is the one really intimate female friend whom I have in the world. After all, Duke, besides Plantagenet and the children, there are only two persons in the world whom I really love. There are only you and she. She will never desert me;—and you must not desert me either." Then he put his hand behind her waist, and stooped over her and kissed her brow, and swore to her that he would never desert her.

But what was he to do? He knew, without being told by the Duchess, that his colleague and chief was becoming, from day to day, more difficult to manage. He had been right enough in laying it down as a general rule that Prime Ministers are selected for that position by the general confidence of the House of Commons;—but he was aware at the same time that it had hardly been so in the present instance. There had come to be a dead-lock in affairs, during which neither of the two old and well-recognised leaders of parties could command a sufficient following for the carrying on of the Government. With unusual patience these two gentlemen had now for the greater part of three Sessions sat by, offering but little opposition to the Coalition, but of course biding their time. They, too, called themselves,—perhaps thought themselves,—Cincinnatuses. But their ploughs and peaches did not suffice to them, and they longed again to be in every mouth, and to have, if not their deeds, then even their omissions blazoned in every paragraph. The palate accustomed to Cayenne pepper can hardly be gratified by simple salt. When that dead-lock had come, politicians who were really anxious for the country had been forced to look about for a Premier,—and in the search the old Duke had been the foremost. The Duchess had hardly said more than the truth when she declared that her husband's promotion had been effected by their old friend. But it is sometimes easier to make than to unmake. Perhaps the time had now in truth come, in which it would be better for the country that the usual state of things should again exist. Perhaps,—nay, the Duke now thought that he saw that it was so,—Mr. Gresham might again have a Liberal majority at his back if the Duke of Omnium could find some graceful mode of retiring. But who was to tell all this to the Duke of Omnium? There was only one man in all England to whom such a task was possible, and that was the old Duke himself,—who during the last two years had been constantly urgent with his friend not to retire! How often since he had taken office had the conscientious and timid Minister begged of his friend permission to abandon his high office! But that permission had always been refused, and now, for the last three months, the request had not been repeated. The Duchess probably was right in saying that her husband "didn't want to give it up now."

But he, the Duke of St. Bungay, had brought his friend into the trouble, and it was certainly his duty to extricate him from it. The admonition might come in the rude shape of repeated minorities in the House of Commons. Hitherto the number of votes at the command of the Ministry had not been very much impaired. A few always fall off as time goes on. Aristides becomes too just, and the mind of man is greedy of novelty. Sir Orlando, also, had taken with him a few, and it may be that two or three had told themselves that there could not be all that smoke raised by the "People's Banner" without some fire below it. But there was a good working majority,—very much at Mr. Monk's command,—and Mr. Monk was moved by none of that feeling of rebellion which had urged Sir Orlando on to his destruction. It was difficult to find a cause for resignation. And yet the Duke of St. Bungay, who had watched the House of Commons closely for nearly half a century, was aware that the Coalition which he had created had done its work, and was almost convinced that it would not be permitted to remain very much longer in power. He had seen symptoms of impatience in Mr. Daubeny, and Mr. Gresham had snorted once or twice, as though eager for the battle.

Chapter LXIV
The New K.G.

Early in June had died the Marquis of Mount Fidgett. In all England there was no older family than that of the Fichy Fidgetts, whose baronial castle of Fichy Fellows is still kept up, the glory of archaeologists and the charm of tourists. Some people declare it to be the most perfect castle residence in the country. It is admitted to have been completed in the time of Edward VI, and is thought to have been commenced in the days of Edward I. It has always belonged to the Fichy Fidgett family, who with a persistence that is becoming rarer every day, has clung to every acre that it ever owned, and has added acre to acre in every age. The consequence has been that the existing Marquis of Mount Fidgett has always been possessed of great territorial influence, and has been flattered, cajoled, and revered by one Prime Minister after another. Now the late Marquis had been, as was the custom with the Fichy Fidgetts, a man of pleasure. If the truth may be spoken openly, it should be admitted that he had been a man of sin. The duty of keeping together the family property he had performed with a perfect zeal. It had always been acknowledged on behalf of the existing Marquis, that in whatever manner he might spend his money, however base might be the gullies into which his wealth descended, he never spent more than he had to spend. Perhaps there was but little praise in this, as he could hardly have got beyond his enormous income unless he had thrown it away on race-courses and roulette tables. But it had long been remarked of the Mount Fidgett marquises that they were too wise to gamble. The family had not been an honour to the country, but had nevertheless been honoured by the country. The man who had just died had perhaps been as selfish and as sensual a brute as had ever disgraced humanity;—but nevertheless he had been a Knight of the Garter. He had been possessed of considerable parliamentary interest, and the Prime Minister of the day had not dared not to make him a Knight of the Garter. All the Marquises of Mount Fidgett had for many years past been Knights of the Garter. On the last occasion a good deal had been said about it. A feeling had even then begun to prevail that the highest personal honour in the gift of the Crown should not be bestowed upon a man whose whole life was a disgrace, and who did indeed seem to deserve every punishment which human or divine wrath could inflict. He had a large family, but they were all illegitimate. Wives generally he liked, but of his own wife he very soon broke the heart. Of all the companies with which he consorted he was the admitted king, but his subjects could do no man any honour. The Castle of Fichy Fellows was visited by the world at large, but no man or woman with a character to lose went into any house really inhabited by the Marquis. And yet he had become a Knight of the Garter, and was therefore, presumably, one of those noble Englishmen to whom the majesty of the day was willing to confide the honour, and glory, and safety of the Crown. There were many who disliked this. That a base reprobate should become a Marquis and a peer of Parliament was in accordance with the constitution of the country. Marquises and peers are not as a rule reprobates, and the misfortune was one which could not be avoided. He might have ill-used his own wife and other wives' husbands without special remark, had he not been made a Knight of the Garter. The Minister of the day, however, had known the value of the man's support, and, being thick-skinned, had lived through the reproaches uttered without much damage to himself. Now the wicked Marquis was dead, and it was the privilege and the duty of the Duke of Omnium to select another Knight.

There was a good deal said about it at the time. There was a rumour, — no doubt a false rumour, — that the Crown insisted in this instance on dictating a choice to the Duke of Omnium. But even were it so, the Duke could not have been very much aggrieved, as the choice dictated was supposed to be that of himself. The late Duke had been a Knight, and when he had died, it was thought that his successor would succeed also to the ribbon. The new Duke had been at that time in the Cabinet, and had remained there, but had accepted an office inferior in rank to that which he had formerly filled. The whole history of these things has been written, and may be read by the curious. The Duchess, newly a duchess then and very keen in reference to her husband's rank, had instigated him to demand the ribbon as his right. This he had not only declined to do, but had gone out of the way to say that he thought it should be bestowed elsewhere. It had been bestowed elsewhere, and there had been a very general feeling that he had been passed over because his easy temperament in such matters had been seen and utilised. Now, whether the Crown interfered or not, — a matter on which no one short of a writer of newspaper articles dares to make a suggestion till time shall have made mellow the doings of sovereigns and their ministers, — the suggestion was made. The Duke of St. Bungay ventured to say to his friend that no other selection was possible.

"Recommend her Majesty to give it to myself!" said the Prime Minister.

"You will find it to be her Majesty's wish. It has been very common. Sir Robert Walpole had it."

"I am not Sir Robert Walpole." The Duke named other examples of Prime Ministers who had been gartered by themselves. But our Prime Minister declared it to be out of the question. No honour of that description should be conferred upon him as long as he held his present position. The old Duke was much in earnest, and there was a great deal said on the subject,—but at last it became clear, not only to him, but to the members of the Cabinet generally, and then to the outside world, that the Prime Minister would not consent to accept the vacant honour.

For nearly a month after this the question subsided. A Minister is not bound to bestow a Garter the day after it becomes vacant. There are other Knights to guard the throne, and one may be spared for a short interval. But during that interval many eyes were turned towards the stall in St. George's Chapel. A good thing should be given away like a clap of thunder if envy, hatred, and malice are to be avoided. A broad blue ribbon across the chest is of all decorations the most becoming, or, at any rate, the most desired. And there was, I fear, an impression on the minds of some men that the Duke in such matters was weak and might be persuaded. Then there came to him an application in the form of a letter from the new Marquis of Mount Fidgett,—a man whom he had never seen, and of whom he had never heard. The new Marquis had hitherto resided in Italy, and men only knew of him that he was odious to his uncle. But he had inherited all the Fichy Fidgett estates, and was now possessed of immense wealth and great honour. He ventured, he said, to represent to the Prime Minister that for generations past the Marquises of Mount Fidgett had been honoured by the Garter. His political status in the country was exactly that enjoyed by his late uncle; but he intended that his political career should be very different. He was quite prepared to support the Coalition. "What is he that he should expect to be made a Knight of the Garter?" said our Duke to the old Duke.

"He is the Marquis of Mount Fidgett, and next to yourself, perhaps, the richest peer of Great Britain."

"Have riches anything to do with it?"

"Something certainly. You would not name a pauper peer."

"Yes;—if he was a man whose career had been highly honourable to the country. Such a man, of course, could not be a pauper, but I do not think his want of wealth should stand in the way of his being honoured by the Garter."

"Wealth, rank, and territorial influence have been generally thought to have something to do with it."

"And character nothing!"

"My dear Duke, I have not said so."

"Something very much like it, my friend, if you advocate the claim of the Marquis of Mount Fidgett. Did you approve of the selection of the late Marquis?"

"I was in the Cabinet at the time, and will therefore say nothing against it. But I have never heard anything against this man's character."

"Nor in favour of it. To my thinking he has as much claim, and no more, as that man who just opened the door. He was never seen in the Lower House."

"Surely that cannot signify."

"You think, then, that he should have it?"

"You know what I think," said the elder statesman thoughtfully. "In my opinion there is no doubt that you would best consult the honour of the country by allowing her Majesty to bestow this act of grace upon a subject who has deserved so well from her Majesty as yourself."

"It is quite impossible."

"It seems to me," said the Duke, not appearing to notice the refusal of his friend, "that in this peculiar position you should allow yourself to be persuaded to lay aside your own feeling. No man of high character is desirous of securing to himself decorations which he may bestow upon others."

"Just so."

"But here the decoration bestowed upon the chief whom we all follow, would confer a wider honour upon many than it could do if given to any one else."

"The same may be said of any Prime Minister."

"Not so. A commoner, without high permanent rank or large fortune, is not lowered in the world's esteem by not being of the Order. You will permit me to say—that a Duke of Omnium has not reached that position which he ought to enjoy unless he be a Knight of the Garter." It must be borne in mind that the old Duke, who used this argument, had himself worn the ribbon for the last thirty years. "But if—"

"Well;—well."

"But if you are,—I must call it obstinate."

"I am obstinate in that respect."

"Then," said the Duke of St. Bungay, "I should recommend her Majesty to give it to the Marquis."

"Never," said the Prime Minister, with very unaccustomed energy. "I will never sanction the payment of such a price for services which should never be bought or sold."

"It would give no offence."

"That is not enough, my friend. Here is a man of whom I only know that he has bought a great many marble statues. He has done nothing for his country, and nothing for his sovereign."

"If you are determined to look to what you call desert alone, I would name Lord Drummond." The Prime Minister frowned and looked unhappy. It was quite true that Lord Drummond had contradicted him, and that he had felt the injury grievously. "Lord Drummond has been very true to us."

"Yes;—true to us! What is that?"

"He is in every respect a man of character, and well looked upon in the country. There would be some enmity and a good deal of envy—which might be avoided by either of the courses I have proposed; but those courses you will not take. I take it for granted that you are anxious to secure the support of those who generally act with Lord Drummond."

"I don't know that I am." The old Duke shrugged his shoulders. "What I mean is, that I do not think that we ought to pay an increased price for their support. His lordship is very well as the Head of an Office; but he is not nearly so great a man as my friend Lord Cantrip."

"Cantrip would not join us. There is no evil in politics so great as that of seeming to buy the men who will not come without buying. These rewards are fairly given for political support."

"I had not, in truth, thought of Lord Cantrip."

"He does not expect it any more than my butler."

"I only named him as having a claim stronger than any that Lord Drummond can put forward. I have a man in my mind to whom I think such an honour is fairly due. What do you say to Lord Earlybird?" The old Duke opened his mouth and lifted up his hands in unaffected surprise.

The Earl of Earlybird was an old man of a very peculiar character. He had never opened his mouth in the House of Lords and had never sat in the House of Commons. The political world knew him not at all. He had a house in town, but very rarely lived there. Early Park, in the parish of Bird, had been his residence since he first came to the title forty years ago, and had been the scene of all his labours. He was a nobleman possessed of a moderate fortune, and, as men said of him, of a moderate intellect. He had married early in life and was blessed with a large family. But he had certainly not been an idle man. For nearly half a century he had devoted himself to the improvement of the labouring classes, especially in reference to their abodes and education, and had gradually, without any desire on his own part, worked himself up into public notice. He was not an eloquent man, but he would take the chair at meeting after meeting, and sit with admirable patience for long hours to hear the eloquence of others. He was a man very simple in his tastes, and had brought up his family to follow his habits. He had therefore been able to do munificent things with moderate means, and in the long course of years had failed in hiding his munificence from the public. Lord Earlybird, till after middle life, had not been much considered, but gradually there had grown up a feeling that there were not very many better men in the country. He was a fat, bald-headed old man, who was always pulling his spectacles on and off, nearly blind, very awkward, and altogether indifferent to appearance. Probably he had no more idea of the Garter in his own mind than he had of a Cardinal's hat. But he had grown into fame, and had not escaped the notice of the Prime Minister.

"Do you know anything against Lord Earlybird?" asked the Prime Minister.

"Certainly nothing against him, Duke."

"Nor anything in his favour?"

"I know him very well,—I think I may say intimately. There isn't a better man breathing."

"An honour to the peerage!" said the Prime Minister.

"An honour to humanity rather," said the other, "as being of all men the least selfish and most philanthropical."

"What more can be said of a man?"

"But according to my view he is not the sort of person whom one would wish to see made a Knight of the Garter. If he had the ribbon he would never wear it."

"The honour surely does not consist in its outward sign. I am entitled to wear some kind of coronet, but I do not walk about with it on my head. He is a man of a great heart and of many virtues. Surely the country, and her Majesty on behalf of the country, should delight to honour such a man."

"I really doubt whether you look at the matter in the right light," said the ancient statesman, who was in truth frightened at what was being proposed. "You must not be angry with me if I speak plainly."

"My friend, I do not think that it is within your power to make me angry."

"Well then,—I will get you for a moment to listen to my view on the matter. There are certain great prizes in the gift of the Crown and of the Ministers of the Crown,—the greatest of which are now traditionally at the disposal of the Prime Minister. These are always given to party friends. I may perhaps agree with you that party support should not be looked to alone. Let us acknowledge that character and services should be taken into account. But the very theory of our Government will be overset by a reversal of the rule which I have attempted to describe. You will offend all your own friends, and only incur the ridicule of your opponents. It is no doubt desirable that the high seats of the country should be filled by men of both parties. I would not wish to see every Lord-Lieutenant of a county a Whig." In his enthusiasm the old Duke went back to his old phraseology. "But I know that my opponents when their turn comes will appoint their friends to the Lieutenancies, and that so the balance will be maintained. If you or I appoint their friends, they won't appoint ours. Lord Earlybird's proxy has been in the hands of the Conservative Leader of the House of Lords ever since he succeeded his father." Then the old man paused, but his friend waited to listen whether the lecture were finished before he spoke, and the Duke of St. Bungay continued. "And, moreover, though Lord Earlybird is a very good man,—so much so that many of us may well envy him,—he is not just the man fitted for this destination. A Knight of the Garter should be a man prone to show himself, a public man, one whose work in the country has brought him face to face with his fellows. There is an aptness, a propriety, a fitness in these things which one can understand perhaps better than explain."

"Those fitnesses and aptnesses change, I think, from day to day. There was a time when a knight should be a fighting man."

"That has gone by."

"And the aptnesses and fitnesses in accordance with which the sovereign of the day was induced to grace with the Garter such a man as the late Marquis of Mount Fidgett have, I hope, gone by. You will admit that?"

"There is no such man proposed."

"And other fitnesses and aptnesses will go by, till the time will come when the man to be selected as Lieutenant of a county will be the man whose selection will be most beneficial to the county, and Knights of the Garter will be chosen for their real virtues."

"I think you are Quixotic. A Prime Minister is of all men bound to follow the traditions of his country, or, when he leaves them, to leave them with very gradual steps."

"And if he break that law and throw over all that thraldom;—what then?"

"He will lose the confidence which has made him what he is."

"It is well that I know the penalty. It is hardly heavy enough to enforce strict obedience. As for the matter in dispute, it had better stand over yet for a few days." When the Prime Minister said this the old Duke knew very well that he intended to have his own way.

And so it was. A week passed by, and then the younger Duke wrote to the elder Duke saying that he had given to the matter all the consideration in his power, and that he had at last resolved to recommend her Majesty to bestow the ribbon on Lord Earlybird. He would not, however, take any step for a few days so that his friend might have an opportunity of making further remonstrance if he pleased. No further remonstrance was made, and Lord Earlybird, much to his own amazement, was nominated to the vacant Garter.

The appointment was one certainly not popular with any of the Prime Minister's friends. With some, such as Lord Drummond, it indicated a determination on the part of the Duke to declare his freedom from all those bonds which had hitherto been binding on the Heads of Government. Had the Duke selected himself, certainly no offence would have been given. Had the Marquis of Mount Fidgett been the happy man, excuses would have been made. But it was unpardonable to Lord Drummond that he should have been passed over and that the Garter should have been given to Lord Earlybird. To the poor old Duke the offence was of a different nature. He had intended to use a very strong word when he told his friend that his proposed conduct would be Quixotic. The Duke of Omnium would surely know that the Duke of St. Bungay could not support a Quixotic Prime Minister. And yet the younger Duke, the Telemachus of the last two years,—after hearing that word,—had rebelled against his Mentor, and had obstinately adhered to his Quixotism! The greed of power had fallen upon the man,—so said the dear old Duke to himself,—and the man's fall was certain. Alas, alas; had he been allowed to go before the poison had entered his veins, how much less would have been his suffering!

Chapter LXV
"There Must Be Time"

At the end of the third week in July, when the Session was still sitting, and when no day had been absolutely as yet fixed for the escape of members, Mr. Wharton received a letter from his friend Arthur Fletcher which certainly surprised him very much, and which left him for a day or two unable to decide what answer ought to be given. It will be remembered that Ferdinand Lopez destroyed himself in March, now three months since. The act had been more than a nine days' wonder, having been kept in the memory of many men by the sedulous efforts of Quintus Slide, and by the fact that the name of so great a man as the Prime Minister was concerned in the matter. But gradually the feeling about Ferdinand Lopez had died away, and his fate, though it had outlived the nominal nine days, had sunk into general oblivion before the end of the ninth week. The Prime Minister had not forgotten the man, nor had Quintus Slide. The name was still common in the columns of the "People's Banner," and was never mentioned without being read by the unfortunate Duke. But others had ceased to talk of Ferdinand Lopez.

To the mind, however, of Arthur Fletcher the fact of the man's death was always present. A dreadful incubus had come upon his life, blighting all his prospects, obscuring all his sun by a great cloud, covering up all his hopes, and changing for him all his outlook into the world. It was not only that Emily Wharton should not have become his wife, but that the woman whom he loved with so perfect a love should have been sacrificed to so vile a creature as this man. He never blamed her,—but looked upon his fate as Fate. Then on a sudden he heard that the incubus was removed. The man who had made him and her wretched had by a sudden stroke been taken away and annihilated. There was nothing now between him and her,—but a memory. He could certainly forgive, if she could forget.

Of course he had felt at the first moment that time must pass by. He had become certain that her mad love for the man had perished. He had been made sure that she had repented her own deed in sackcloth and ashes. It had been acknowledged to him by her father that she had been anxious to be separated from her husband, if her husband would consent to such a separation. And then, remembering as he did his last interview with her, having in his mind as he did every circumstance of that caress which he had given her,—down to the very quiver of the fingers he had pressed,—he could not but flatter himself that at last he had touched her heart. But there must be time! The conventions of the world operate on all hearts, especially on the female heart, and teach that new vows, too quickly given, are disgraceful. The world has seemed to decide that a widow should take two years before she can bestow herself on a second man without a touch of scandal. But the two years is to include everything, the courtship of the second as well as the burial of the first,—and not only the courtship, but the preparation of the dresses and the wedding itself. And then this case was different from all others. Of course there must be time, but surely not here a full period of two years! Why should the life of two young persons be so wasted, if it were the case that they loved each other? There was horror here, remorse, pity, perhaps pardon; but there was no love,—none of that love which is always for a time increased in its fervour by the loss of the loved object; none of that passionate devotion which must at first make the very idea of another man's love intolerable. There had been a great escape,—an escape which could not but be inwardly acknowledged, however little prone the tongue might be to confess it. Of course there must be time;—but how much time? He argued it in his mind daily, and at each daily argument the time considered by him to be appropriate was shortened. Three months had passed and he had not yet seen her. He had resolved that he would not even attempt to see her till her father should consent. But surely a period had passed sufficient to justify him in applying for that permission. And then he bethought himself that it would be best in applying for that permission to tell everything to Mr. Wharton. He well knew that he would be telling no secret. Mr. Wharton knew the state of his feelings as well as he knew it himself. If ever there was a case in which time might be abridged, this was one; and therefore he wrote his letter,—as follows:—

3, —— Court, Temple, 24th July, 187—.

My dear Mr. Wharton,

It is a matter of great regret to me that we should see so little of each other,—and especially of regret that I should never now see Emily.

I may as well rush into the matter at once. Of course this letter will not be shown to her, and therefore I may write as I would speak if I were with you. The wretched man whom she married is gone, and my love for her is the same as it was before she had ever seen him, and as it has always been from that day to this. I could not address you or even think of her as yet, did I not know that that marriage had been unfortunate. But it has not altered her to me in the least. It has been a dreadful trouble to us all,—to her, to you, to me, and to all connected with us. But it is over, and I think that it should be looked back upon as a black chasm which we have bridged and got over, and to which we need never cast back our eyes.

I have no right to think that, though she might some day love another man, she would, therefore, love me; but I think that I have a right to try, and I know that I should have your good-will. It is a question of time, but if I let time go by, some one else may slip in. Who can tell? I would not be thought to press indecently, but I do feel that here the ordinary rules which govern men and women are not to be followed. He made her unhappy almost from the first day. She had made a mistake which you and she and all acknowledged. She has been punished; and so have I,— very severely I can assure you. Wouldn't it be a good thing to bring all this to an end as soon as possible,—if it can be brought to an end in the way I want?

Pray tell me what you think. I would propose that you should ask her to see me, and then say just as much as you please. Of course I should not press her at first. You might ask me to dinner, and all that kind of thing, and so she would get used to me. It is not as though we had not been very, very old friends. But I know you will do the best. I have put off writing to you till I sometimes think that I shall go mad over it if I sit still any longer.

Your affectionate friend,

Arthur Fletcher.

When Mr. Wharton got this letter he was very much puzzled. Could he have had his wish, he too would have left the chasm behind him as proposed by his young friend, and have never cast an eye back upon the frightful abyss. He would willingly have allowed the whole Lopez incident to be passed over as an episode in their lives, which, if it could not be forgotten, should at any rate never be mentioned. They had all been severely punished, as Fletcher had said, and if the matter could end there he would be well content to bear on his own shoulders all that remained of that punishment, and to let everything begin again. But he knew very well it could not be so with her. Even yet it was impossible to induce Emily to think of her husband without regret. It had been only too manifest during the last year of their married life that she had felt horror rather than love towards him. When there had been a question of his leaving her behind, should he go to Central America, she had always expressed herself more than willing to comply with such an arrangement. She would go with him should he order her to do so, but would infinitely sooner remain in England. And then, too, she had spoken of him while alive with disdain and disgust, and had submitted to hear her father describe him as infamous. Her life had been one long misery, under which she had seemed gradually to be perishing. Now she was relieved, and her health was re-established. A certain amount of unjoyous cheerfulness was returning to her. It was impossible to doubt that she must have known that a great burden had fallen from her back. And yet she would never allow his name to be mentioned without giving some outward sign of affection for his memory. If he was bad, so were others bad. There were many worse than he. Such were the excuses she made for her late husband. Old Mr. Wharton, who really thought that in all his experience he had never known any one worse than his son-in-law, would sometimes become testy, and at last resolved that he would altogether hold his tongue. But he could hardly hold his tongue now.

He, no doubt, had already formed his hopes in regard to Arthur Fletcher. He had trusted that the man whom he had taught himself some years since to regard as his wished-for son-in-law, might be constant and strong enough in his love to forget all that was past, and to be still willing to redeem his daughter from misery. But as days had crept on since the scene at the Tenway Junction, he had become aware that time must do much before such relief would be accepted. It was, however, still possible that the presence of the man might do something. Hitherto, since the deed had been done, no stranger had dined in Manchester Square. She herself had seen no visitor. She had hardly left the house except to go to church, and then had been enveloped in the deepest crape. Once or twice she had allowed herself to be driven out in a carriage, and, when she had done so, her father had always accompanied her. No widow, since the seclusion of widows was first ordained, had been more strict in maintaining the restraints of widowhood as enjoined. How then could he bid her receive a new lover,—or how suggest to her that a lover was possible? And yet he did not like to answer Arthur Fletcher without naming some period for the present mourning,— some time at which he might at least show himself in Manchester Square.

"I have had a letter from Arthur Fletcher," he said to his daughter a day or two after he had received it. He was sitting after dinner, and Everett was also in the room.

"Is he in Herefordshire?" she asked.

"No;—he is up in town, attending to the House of Commons, I suppose. He had something to say to me, and as we are not in the way of meeting he wrote. He wants to come and see you."

"Not yet, papa."

"He talked of coming and dining here."

"Oh yes; pray let him come."

"You would not mind that?"

"I would dine early and be out of the way. I should be so glad if you would have somebody sometimes. I shouldn't think then that I was such a—such a restraint to you."

But this was not what Mr. Wharton desired. "I shouldn't like that, my dear. Of course he would know that you were in the house."

"Upon my word, I think you might meet an old friend like that," said Everett.

She looked at her brother, and then at her father, and burst into tears. "Of course you shall not be pressed if it would be irksome to you," said her father.

"It is the first plunge that hurts," said Everett. "If you could once bring yourself to do it, you would find afterwards that you were more comfortable."

"Papa," she said slowly, "I know what it means. His goodness I shall always remember. You may tell him I say so. But I cannot meet him yet." Then they pressed her no further. Of course she had understood. Her father could not even ask her to say a word which might give comfort to Arthur as to some long distant time.

He went down to the House of Commons the next day, and saw his young friend there. Then they walked up and down Westminster Hall for nearly an hour, talking over the matter with the most absolute freedom. "It cannot be for the benefit of any one," said Arthur Fletcher, "that she should immolate herself like an Indian widow,—and for the sake of such a man as that! Of course I have no right to dictate to you,—hardly, perhaps, to give an opinion."

"Yes, yes, yes."

"It does seem to me, then, that you ought to force her out of that kind of thing. Why should she not go down to Herefordshire?"

"In time, Arthur,—in time."

"But people's lives are running away."

"My dear fellow, if you were to see her you would know how vain it would be to try to hurry her. There must be time."

Chapter LXVI
The End of the Session

The Duke of St. Bungay had been very much disappointed. He had contradicted with a repetition of noes the assertion of the Duchess that he had been the Warwick who had placed the Prime Minister's crown on the head of the Duke of Omnium, but no doubt he felt in his heart that he had done so much towards it that his advice respecting the vacant Garter, when given with so much weight, should have been followed. He was an old man, and had known the secrets of Cabinet Councils when his younger friend was a little boy. He had given advice to Lord John, and had been one of the first to congratulate Sir Robert Peel when that statesman became a free-trader. He had sat in conclave with THE Duke, and had listened to the bold Liberalism of old Earl Grey, both in the Lower and the Upper House. He had been always great in council, never giving his advice unasked, nor throwing his pearls before swine, and cautious at all times to avoid excesses on this side or on that. He had never allowed himself a hobby horse of his own to ride, had never been ambitious, had never sought to be the ostensible leader of men. But he did now think that when, with all his experience, he spoke very much in earnest, some attention should be paid to what he said. When he had described a certain line of conduct as Quixotic he had been very much in earnest. He did not usually indulge in strong language, and Quixotic, when applied to the conduct of a Prime Minister, was, to his ideas, very strong. The thing described as Quixotic had now been done, and the Duke of St. Bungay was a disappointed man.

For an hour or two he thought that he must gently secede from all private councils with the Prime Minister. To resign, or to put impediments in the way of his own chief, did not belong to his character. That line of strategy had come into fashion since he had learnt his political rudiments, and was very odious to him. But in all party compacts there must be inner parties, peculiar bonds, and confidences stricter, stronger, and also sweeter than those which bind together the twenty or thirty gentlemen who form a Government. From those closer ties which had hitherto bound him to the Duke of Omnium he thought, for a while, that he must divorce himself.

Surely on such a subject as the nomination of a Knight of the Garter his advice might have been taken,—if only because it had come from him! And so he kept himself apart for a day or two, and even in the House of Lords ceased to whisper kindly, cheerful words into the ears of his next neighbour.

But various remembrances crowded in upon him by degrees, compelling him to moderate and at last to abandon his purpose. Among these the first was the memory of the kiss which he had given the Duchess. The woman had told him that she loved him, that he was one of the very few whom she did love,—and the word had gone straight into his old heart. She had bade him not to desert her; and he had not only given her his promise, but he had converted that promise to a sacred pledge by a kiss. He had known well why she had exacted the promise. The turmoil in her husband's mind, the agony which he sometimes endured when people spoke ill of him, the aversion which he had at first genuinely felt to an office for which he hardly thought himself fit, and now the gradual love of power created by the exercise of power, had all been seen by her, and had created that solicitude which had induced her to ask for the promise. The old Duke had known them both well, but had hardly as yet given the Duchess credit for so true a devotion to her husband. It now seemed to him that though she had failed to love the man, she had given her entire heart to the Prime Minister. He sympathised with her altogether, and, at any rate could not go back from his promise.

And then he remembered, too, that if this man did anything amiss in the high office which he had been made to fill, he who had induced him to fill it was responsible. What right had he, the Duke of St. Bungay, to be angry because his friend was not all-wise at all points? Let the Droughts and the Drummonds and the Beeswaxes quarrel among themselves or with their colleagues. He belonged to a different school, in the teachings of which there was less perhaps of excitement and more of long-suffering;— but surely, also, more of nobility. He was, at any rate, too old to change, and he would therefore be true to his friend through evil and through good. Having thought this all out he again whispered some cheery word to the Prime Minister, as they sat listening to the denunciations of Lord Fawn, a Liberal lord, much used to business, but who had not been received into the Coalition. The first whisper and the second whisper the Prime Minister received very coldly. He had fully appreciated the discontinuance of the whispers, and was aware of the cause. He had made a selection on his own unassisted judgment in opposition to his old friend's advice, and this was the result. Let it be so! All his friends were turning away from him and he would have to stand alone. If so, he would stand alone till the pendulum of the House of Commons had told him that it was time for him to retire. But gradually the determined good-humour of the old man prevailed. "He has a wonderful gift of saying nothing with second-rate dignity," whispered the repentant friend, speaking of Lord Fawn.

"A very honest man," said the Prime Minister in return.

"A sort of bastard honesty,—by precept out of stupidity. There is no real conviction in it, begotten by thought." This little bit of criticism, harsh as it was, had the effect, and the Prime Minister became less miserable than he had been.

But Lord Drummond forgave nothing. He still held his office, but more than once he was seen in private conference with both Sir Orlando and Mr. Boffin. He did not attempt to conceal his anger. Lord Earlybird! An old woman! One whom no other man in England would have thought of making a Knight of the Garter! It was not, he said, personal disappointment in himself. There were half-a-dozen peers whom he would willingly have seen so graced without the slightest chagrin. But this must have been done simply to show the Duke's power, and to let the world understand that he owed nothing and would pay nothing to his supporters. It was almost a disgrace, said Lord Drummond, to belong to a Government the Head of which could so commit himself! The Session was nearly at an end, and Lord Drummond thought that no step could be conveniently taken now. But it was quite clear to him that this state of things could not be continued. It was observed that Lord Drummond and the Prime Minister never spoke to each other in the House, and that the Secretary of State for the Colonies,— that being the office which he held,—never rose in his place after Lord Earlybird's nomination, unless to say a word or two as to his own peculiar duties. It was very soon known to all the world that there was war to the knife between Lord Drummond and the Prime Minister.

And, strange to say, there seemed to be some feeling of general discontent on this very trifling subject. When Aristides has been much too just the oyster-shells become numerous. It was said that the Duke had been guilty of pretentious love of virtue in taking Lord Earlybird out of his own path of life and forcing him to write K.G. after his name. There came out an article, of course in the "People's Banner," headed, "Our Prime Minister's Good Works," in which poor Lord Earlybird was ridiculed in a very unbecoming manner, and in which it was asserted that the thing was done as a counterpoise to the iniquity displayed in "hounding Ferdinand Lopez to his death." Whenever Ferdinand Lopez was mentioned he had always been hounded. And then the article went on to declare that either the Prime Minister had quarrelled with all his colleagues, or else that all his colleagues had quarrelled with the Prime Minister. Mr. Slide did not care which it might be, but, whichever it might be, the poor country had to suffer when such a state of things was permitted. It was notorious that neither the Duke of St. Bungay nor Lord Drummond would now even speak to their own chief, so thoroughly were they disgusted with his conduct. Indeed it seemed that the only ally the Prime Minister had in his own Cabinet was the Irish adventurer, Mr. Phineas Finn. Lord Earlybird never read a word of all this, and was altogether undisturbed as he sat in his chair in Exeter Hall,—or just at this time of the year more frequently in the provinces. But the Duke of Omnium read it all. After what had passed he did not dare to show it to his brother Duke. He did not dare to tell his friend that it was said in the newspapers that they did not speak to each other. But every word from Mr. Slide's pen settled on his own memory, and added to his torments. It came to be a fixed idea in the Duke's mind that Mr. Slide was a gadfly sent to the earth for the express purpose of worrying him.

And as a matter of course the Prime Minister in his own mind blamed himself for what he had done. It is the chief torment of a person constituted as he was that strong as may be the determination to do a thing, fixed as may be the conviction that that thing ought to be done, no sooner has it been perfected than the objections of others, which before had been inefficacious, become suddenly endowed with truth and force. He did not like being told by Mr. Slide that he ought not to have set his Cabinet against him, but when he had in fact done so, then he believed what Mr. Slide told him. As soon almost as the irrevocable letter had been winged on its way to Lord Earlybird, he saw the absurdity of sending it. Who was he that he should venture to set aside all the traditions of office? A Pitt or a Peel or a Palmerston might have done so, because they had been abnormally strong. They had been Prime Ministers by the work of their own hands, holding their powers against the whole world. But he,—he told himself daily that he was only there by sufferance, because at the moment no one else could be found to take it. In such a condition should he not have been bound by the traditions of office, bound by the advice of one so experienced and so true as the Duke of St. Bungay? And for whom had he broken through these traditions and thrown away this advice? For a man who had no power whatever to help him or any other Minister of the Crown;—for one whose every pursuit in life was at variance with the acquisition of such honours as that now thrust upon him!

He could see his own obstinacy, and could even hate the pretentious love of virtue which he had himself displayed.

"Have you seen Lord Earlybird with his ribbon?" his wife said to him.

"I do not know Lord Earlybird by sight," he replied angrily.

"Nor any one else either. But he would have come and shown himself to you, if he had had a spark of gratitude in his composition. As far as I can learn you have sacrificed the Ministry for his sake."

"I did my duty as best I knew how to do it," said the Duke, almost with ferocity, "and it little becomes you to taunt me with any deficiency."

"Plantagenet!"

"I am driven," he said, "almost beyond myself, and it kills me when you take part against me."

"Take part against you! Surely there was very little in what I said." And yet, as she spoke, she repented bitterly that she had at the moment allowed herself to relapse into the sort of badinage which had been usual with her before she had understood the extent of his sufferings. "If I trouble you by what I say, I will certainly hold my tongue."

"Don't repeat to me what that man says in the newspaper."

"You shouldn't regard the man, Plantagenet. You shouldn't allow the paper to come into your hands."

"Am I to be afraid of seeing what men say of me? Never! But you need not repeat it, at any rate if it be false." She had not seen the article in question or she certainly would not have repeated the accusation which it contained. "I have quarrelled with no colleague. If such a one as Lord Drummond chooses to think himself injured, am I to stoop to him? Nothing strikes me so much in all this as the ill-nature of the world at large. When they used to bait a bear tied to a stake, every one around would cheer the dogs and help to torment the helpless animal. It is much the same now, only they have a man instead of a bear for their pleasure."

"I will never help the dogs again," she said, coming up to him and clinging within the embrace of his arm.

He knew that he had been Quixotic, and he would sit in his chair repeating the word to himself aloud, till he himself began to fear that he would do it in company. But the thing had been done and could not be undone. He had had the bestowal of one Garter, and he had given it to Lord

Earlybird! It was,—he told himself, but not correctly,—the only thing that he had done on his own undivided responsibility since he had been Prime Minister.

The last days of July had passed, and it had been at last decided that the Session should close on the 11th of August. Now the 11th of August was thought to be a great deal too near the 12th to allow of such an arrangement being considered satisfactory. A great many members were very angry at the arrangement. It had been said all through June and into July that it was to be an early Session, and yet things had been so mismanaged that when the end came everything could not be finished without keeping members of Parliament in town up to the 11th of August! In the memory of present legislators there had never been anything so awkward. The fault, if there was a fault, was attributable to Mr. Monk. In all probability the delay was unavoidable. A minister cannot control long-winded gentlemen, and when gentlemen are very long-winded there must be delay. No doubt a strong minister can exercise some control, and it is certain that long-winded gentlemen find an unusual scope for their breath when the reigning dynasty is weak. In that way Mr. Monk and the Duke may have been responsible, but they were blamed as though they, for their own special amusement, detained gentlemen in town. Indeed the gentlemen were not detained. They grumbled and growled and then fled,—but their grumblings and growlings were heard even after their departure.

"Well;—what do you think of it all?" the Duke said one day to Mr. Monk, at the Treasury, affecting an air of cheery good-humour.

"I think," said Mr. Monk, "that the country is very prosperous. I don't know that I ever remember trade to have been more evenly satisfactory."

"Ah, yes. That's very well for the country, and ought, I suppose, to satisfy us."

"It satisfies me," said Mr. Monk.

"And me, in a way. But if you were walking about in a very tight pair of boots, in an agony with your feet, would you be able just then to relish the news that agricultural wages in that parish had gone up sixpence a week?"

"I'd take my boots off, and then try," said Mr. Monk.

"That's just what I'm thinking of doing. If I had my boots off all that prosperity would be so pleasant to me! But you see you can't take your boots off in company. And it may be that you have a walk before you, and that no boots will be worse for your feet even than tight ones."

"We'll have our boots off soon, Duke," said Mr. Monk, speaking of the recess.

"And when shall we be quit of them altogether? Joking apart, they have to be worn if the country requires it."

"Certainly, Duke."

"And it may be that you and I think that upon the whole they may be worn with advantage. What does the country say to that?"

"The country has never said the reverse. We have not had a majority against us this Session on any Government question."

"But we have had narrowing majorities. What will the House do as to the Lords' amendments on the Bankruptcy Bill?" There was a Bill that had gone down from the House of Commons, but had not originated with the Government. It had, however, been fostered by Ministers in the House of Lords, and had been sent back with certain amendments for which the Lord Chancellor had made himself responsible. It was therefore now almost a Government measure. The manipulation of this measure had been one of the causes of the prolonged sitting of the Houses.

"Grogram says they will take the amendments."

"And if they don't?"

"Why then," said Mr. Monk, "the Lords must take our rejection."

"And we shall have been beaten," said the Duke.

"Undoubtedly."

"And beaten simply because the House desires to beat us. I am told that Sir Timothy Beeswax intends to speak and vote against the amendments."

"What,—Sir Timothy on one side, and Sir Gregory on the other?"

"So Lord Ramsden tells me," said the Duke. "If it be so, what are we to do?"

"Certainly not go out in August," said Mr. Monk.

When the time came for the consideration of the Lords' amendments in the House of Commons,—and it did not come till the 8th of August,—the matter was exactly as the Duke had said. Sir Gregory Grogram, with a great deal of earnestness, supported the Lords' amendment,—as he was in honour bound to do. The amendment had come from his chief, the Lord Chancellor, and had indeed been discussed with Sir Gregory before it had been proposed. He was very much in earnest;—but it was evident from Sir Gregory's earnestness that he expected a violent opposition. Immediately after him rose Sir Timothy. Now Sir Timothy was a pretentious man, who assumed to be not only an advocate but a lawyer. And he assumed also to be a political magnate. He went into the matter at great length. He began by saying that it was not a party question. The Bill, which he had had the honour of supporting before it went from their own House, had been a private Bill. As such it had received a general support from the Government. It had been materially altered in the other House under the auspices of his noble friend on the woolsack, but from those alterations he was obliged to dissent. Then he said some very heavy things against the Lord Chancellor, and increased in acerbity as he described what he called the altered mind of his honourable and learned friend the Attorney-General. He then made some very uncomplimentary allusions to the Prime Minister, whom he accused of being more than ordinarily reserved with his subordinates. The speech was manifestly arranged and delivered with the express view of damaging the Coalition, of which at the time he himself made a part. Men observed that things were very much altered when such a course as that was taken in the House of Commons. But that was the course taken on this occasion by Sir Timothy Beeswax, and was so far taken with success that the Lords' amendments were rejected and the Government was beaten in a thin House, by a large majority,—composed partly of its own men. "What am I to do?" asked the Prime Minister of the old Duke.

The old Duke's answer was exactly the same as that given by Mr. Monk. "We cannot resign in August." And then he went on. "We must wait and see how things go at the beginning of next Session. The chief question is whether Sir Timothy should not be asked to resign."

Then the Session was at an end, and they who had been staunch to the last got out of town as quick as the trains could carry them.

Chapter LXVII
Mrs. Lopez Prepares to Move

The Duchess of Omnium was not the most discreet woman in the world. That was admitted by her best friends, and was the great sin alleged against her by her worst enemies. In her desire to say sharp things, she would say the sharp thing in the wrong place, and in her wish to be good-natured she was apt to run into offences. Just as she was about to leave town, which did not take place for some days after Parliament had risen, she made an indiscreet proposition to her husband. "Should you mind my asking Mrs. Lopez down to Matching? We shall only be a very small party."

Now the very name of Lopez was terrible to the Duke's ears. Anything which recalled the wretch and that wretched tragedy to the Duke's mind gave him a stab. The Duchess ought to have felt that any communication between her husband and even the man's widow was to be avoided rather than sought. "Quite out of the question!" said the Duke, drawing himself up.

"Why out of the question?"

"There are a thousand reasons. I could not have it."

"Then I will say nothing more about it. But there is a romance there,—something quite touching."

"You don't mean that she has—a lover?"

"Well;—yes."

"And she lost her husband only the other day,—lost him in so terrible a manner! If that is so, certainly I do not wish to see her again."

"Ah, that is because you don't know the story."

"I don't wish to know it."

"The man who now wants to marry her knew her long before she had seen Lopez, and had offered to her ever so many times. He is a fine fellow, and you know him."

"I had rather not hear any more about it," said the Duke, walking away.

There was an end to the Duchess's scheme of getting Emily down to Matching,—a scheme which could hardly have been successful even had the Duke not objected to it. But yet the Duchess would not abandon her project of befriending the widow. She had injured Lopez. She had liked what she had seen of Mrs. Lopez. And she was now endeavouring to take Arthur Fletcher by the hand. She called therefore at Manchester Square on the day before she started for Matching, and left a card and a note. This was on the 15th of August, when London was as empty as it ever is. The streets at the West End were deserted. The houses were shut up. The very sweepers of the crossings seemed to have gone out of town. The public offices were manned by one or two unfortunates each, who consoled themselves by reading novels at their desks. Half the cab-drivers had gone apparently to the seaside,—or to bed. The shops were still open, but all the respectable shopkeepers were either in Switzerland or at their marine villas. The travelling world had divided itself into Cookites and Hookites;—those who escaped trouble under the auspices of Mr. Cook, and those who boldly combated the extortions of foreign innkeepers and the anti-Anglican tendencies of foreign railway officials "on their own hooks." The Duchess of Omnium was nevertheless in town, and the Duke might still be seen going in at the back entrance of the Treasury Chambers every day at eleven o'clock. Mr. Warburton thought it very hard, for he, too, could shoot grouse; but he would have perished rather than have spoken a word.

The Duchess did not ask to see Mrs. Lopez, but left her card and a note. She had not liked, she said, to leave town without calling, though she would not seek to be admitted. She hoped that Mrs. Lopez was recovering her health, and trusted that on her return to town she might be allowed to renew her acquaintance. The note was very simple, and could not be taken as other than friendly. If she had been simply Mrs. Palliser, and her husband had been a junior clerk in the Treasury, such a visit would have been a courtesy; and it was not less so because it was made by the Duchess of Omnium and by the wife of the Prime Minister. But yet among all the poor widow's acquaintances she was the only one who had ventured to call since Lopez had destroyed himself. Mrs. Roby had been told not to come. Lady Eustace had been sternly rejected. Even old Mrs. Fletcher when she had been up in town had, after a very solemn meeting with Mr. Wharton, contented herself with sending her love. It had come to pass that the idea of being immured was growing to be natural to Emily herself. The longer that it was continued the more did it seem to be impossible to her that she should break from her seclusion. But yet she was gratified by the note from the Duchess.

"She means to be civil, papa."

"Oh yes;—but there are people whose civility I don't want."

"Certainly. I did not want the civility of that horrid Lady Eustace. But I can understand this. She thinks that she did Ferdinand an injury."

"When you begin, my dear,—and I hope it will be soon,—to get back to the world, you will find it more comfortable, I think, to find yourself among your own people."

"I don't want to go back," she said, sobbing bitterly.

"But I want you to go back. All who know you want you to go back. Only don't begin at that end."

"You don't suppose, papa, that I wish to go to the Duchess?"

"I wish you to go somewhere. It can't be good for you to remain here. Indeed I shall think it wicked, or at any rate weak, if you continue to seclude yourself."

"Where shall I go?" she said, imploringly.

"To Wharton. I certainly think you ought to go there first."

"If you would go, papa, and leave me here,—just this once. Next year I will go,—if they ask me."

"When I may be dead, for aught that any of us know."

"Do not say that, papa. Of course any one may die."

"I certainly shall not go without you. You may take that as certain. Is it likely that I should leave you alone in August and September in this great gloomy house? If you stay, I shall stay." Now this meant a great deal more than it had meant in former years. Since Lopez had died Mr. Wharton had not once dined at the Eldon. He came home regularly at six o'clock, sat with his daughter an hour before dinner, and then remained with her all the evening. It seemed as though he were determined to force her out of her solitude by her natural consideration for him. She would implore him to go to his club and have his rubber, but he would never give way. No;—he didn't care for the Eldon, and disliked whist. So he said. Till at last he spoke more plainly. "You are dull enough here all day, and I will not leave you in the evenings." There was a pertinacious tenderness in this which she had not expected from the antecedents of his life. When, therefore, he told her that he would not go into the country without her, she felt herself almost constrained to yield.

And she would have yielded at once but for one fear. How could she insure to herself that Arthur Fletcher should not be there? Of course he would be at Longbarns, and how could she prevent his coming over from Longbarns to Wharton? She could hardly bring herself to ask the question of her father. But she felt an insuperable objection to finding herself in Arthur's presence. Of course she loved him. Of course in all the world he was of all the dearest to her. Of course if she could wipe out the past as with a wet towel, if she could put the crape off her mind as well as from her limbs, she would become his wife with the greatest joy. But the very feeling that she loved him was disgraceful to her in her own thoughts. She had allowed his caress while Lopez was still her husband,—the husband who had ill-used her and betrayed her, who had sought to drag her down to his own depth of baseness. But now she could not endure to think that that other man should even touch her. It was forbidden to her, she believed, by all the canons of womanhood even to think of love again. There ought to be nothing left for her but crape and weepers. She had done it all by her own obstinacy, and she could make no compensation either to her family, or to the world, or to her own feelings, but by drinking the cup of her misery down to the very dregs. Even to think of joy would in her be a treason. On that occasion she did not yield to her father, conquering him as she had conquered him before by the pleading of her looks rather than of her words.

But a day or two afterwards he came to her with arguments of a very different kind. He at any rate must go to Wharton immediately, in reference to a letter of vital importance which he had received from Sir Alured. The reader may perhaps remember that Sir Alured's heir,—the heir to the title and property,—was a nephew for whom he entertained no affection whatever. This Wharton had been discarded by all the Whartons as a profligate drunkard. Some years ago Sir Alured had endeavoured to reclaim the man, and had spent perhaps more money than he had been justified in doing in the endeavour, seeing that, as present occupier of the property, he was bound to provide for his own daughters, and that at his death every acre must go to this ne'er-do-well. The money had been allowed to flow like water for a twelvemonth, and had done no good whatever. There had then been no hope. The man was strong and likely to live,—and after a while married a wife, some woman that he took from the very streets. This had been his last known achievement, and from that moment not even had his name been mentioned at Wharton. Now there came the tidings of his death. It was said that he had perished in some attempt to cross some glaciers in Switzerland;—but by degrees it appeared that the glacier itself had been less dangerous than the brandy which he had swallowed whilst on his journey.

At any rate he was dead. As to that Sir Alured's letter was certain. And he was equally certain that he had left no son.

These tidings were quite as important to Mr. Wharton as to Sir Alured, — more important to Everett Wharton than to either of them, as he would inherit all after the death of those two old men. At this moment he was away yachting with a friend, and even his address was unknown. Letters for him were to be sent to Oban, and might, or might not, reach him in the course of a month. But in a man of Sir Alured's feelings, this catastrophe produced a great change. The heir to his title and property was one whom he was bound to regard with affection and almost with reverence, — if it were only possible for him to do so. With his late heir it had been impossible. But Everett Wharton he had always liked. Everett had not been quite all that his father and uncle had wished. But his faults had been exactly those which would be cured, — or would almost be made virtues, — by the possession of a title and property. Distaste for a profession and aptitude for Parliament would become a young man who was heir not only to the Wharton estates, but to half his father's money.

Sir Alured in his letter expressed a hope that Everett might be informed instantly. He would have written himself had he known Everett's address. But he did know that his elder cousin was in town, and he besought his elder cousin to come at once, — quite at once, — to Wharton. Emily, he said, would of course accompany her father on such an occasion. Then there were long letters from Mary Wharton, and even from Lady Wharton, to Emily. The Whartons must have been very much moved when Lady Wharton could be induced to write a long letter. The Whartons were very much moved. They were in a state of enthusiasm at these news, amounting almost to fury. It seemed as though they thought that every tenant and labourer on the estate, and every tenant and labourer's wife, would be in an abnormal condition and unfit for the duties of life, till they should have seen Everett as heir of the property. Lady Wharton went so far as to tell Emily which bedroom was being prepared for Everett, — a bedroom very different in honour from any by the occupation of which he had as yet been graced. And there were twenty points as to new wills and new deeds as to which the present baronet wanted the immediate advice of his cousin. There were a score of things which could now be done which were before impossible. Trees could be cut down, and buildings put up; and a little bit of land sold, and a little bit of land bought;—the doing of all which would give new life to Sir Alured. A life interest in an estate is a much pleasanter thing when the heir is a friend who can be walked about the property, than when he is an enemy who must be kept at arm's length. All these delights could now be Sir Alured's,—if the old heir would give him his counsel and the young one his assistance.

This change in affairs occasioned some flutter also in Manchester Square. It could not make much difference personally to old Mr. Wharton. He was, in fact, as old as the baronet, and did not pay much regard to his own chance of succession. But the position was one which would suit his son admirably, and he was now on good terms with his son. He had convinced himself that Lopez had done all that he could to separate them, and therefore found himself to be more bound to his son than ever. "We must go at once," he said to his daughter, speaking almost as though he had forgotten her misery for the moment.

"I suppose you and Everett ought to be there."

"Heaven knows where Everett is. I ought to be there, and I suppose that on such an occasion as this you will condescend to go with me."

"Condescend, papa;—what does that mean?"

"You know I cannot go alone. It is out of the question that I should leave you here."

"Why, papa?"

"And at such a time the family ought to come together. Of course they will take it very much amiss if you refuse. What will Lady Wharton think if you refuse after her writing such a letter as that? It is my duty to tell you that you ought to go. You cannot think that it is right to throw over every friend that you have in the world."

There was a great deal more said in which it almost seemed that the father's tenderness had been worn out. His words were much rougher and more imperious than any that he had yet spoken since his daughter had become a widow, but they were also more efficacious, and therefore probably more salutary. After twenty-four hours of this she found that she was obliged to yield, and a telegram was sent to Wharton,—by no means the first telegram that had been sent since the news had arrived,—saying that Emily would accompany her father. They were to occupy themselves for two days further in preparations for their journey.

These preparations to Emily were so sad as almost to break her heart. She had never as yet packed up her widow's weeds. She had never as yet even contemplated the necessity of coming down to dinner in them before other eyes than those of her father and brother. She had as yet made none of those struggles with which widows seek to lessen the deformity of their costume. It was incumbent on her now to get a ribbon or two less ghastly than those weepers which had, for the last five months, hung about her face and shoulders. And then how should she look if he were to be there? It was not to be expected that the Whartons should seclude themselves because of her grief. This very change in the circumstances of the property would be sure, of itself, to bring the Fletchers to Wharton,—and then how should she look at him, how answer him, if he spoke to her tenderly? It is very hard for a woman to tell a lie to a man when she loves him. She may speak the words. She may be able to assure him that he is indifferent to her. But when a woman really loves a man, as she loved this man, there is a desire to touch him which quivers at her fingers' ends, a longing to look at him which she cannot keep out of her eyes, an inclination to be near him which affects every motion of her body. She cannot refrain herself from excessive attention to his words. She has a god to worship, and she cannot control her admiration. Of all this Emily herself felt much,—but felt at the same time that she would never pardon herself if she betrayed her love by a gleam of her eye, by the tone of a word, or the movement of a finger. What,—should she be known to love again after such a mistake as hers, after such a catastrophe?

The evening before they started who should bustle into the house but Everett himself. It was then about six o'clock, and he was going to leave London by the night mail. That he should be a little given to bustle on such an occasion may perhaps be forgiven him. He had heard the news down on the Scotch coast, and had flown up to London, telegraphing as he did so backwards and forwards to Wharton. Of course he felt that the destruction of his cousin among the glaciers,—whether by brandy or ice he did not much care,—had made him for the nonce one of the important people of the world. The young man who would not so feel might be the better philosopher, but one might doubt whether he would be the better young man. He quite agreed with his father that it was his sister's duty to go to Wharton, and he was now in a position to speak with authority as to the duties of members of his family. He could not wait, even for one night, in order that he might travel with them. Sir Alured was impatient. Sir Alured wanted him in Herefordshire. Sir Alured had said that on such an occasion he, the heir, ought to be on the property with the shortest possible delay. His father smiled;—but with an approving smile. Everett therefore started by the night mail, leaving his father and sister to follow him on the morrow.

Chapter LXVIII
The Prime Minister's Political Creed

The Duke, before he went to Matching, twice reminded Phineas Finn that he was expected there in a day or two. "The Duchess says that your wife is coming to-morrow," the Duke said on the day of his departure. But Phineas could not go then. His services to his country were required among the dockyards and ships, and he postponed his visit till the end of September. Then he started for Matching, having the double pleasure before him of meeting his wife and his noble host and hostess. He found a small party there, but not so small as the Duchess had once suggested to him. "Your wife will be there, of course, Mr. Finn. She is too good to desert me in my troubles. And there will probably be Lady Rosina De Courcy. Lady Rosina is to the Duke what your wife is to me. I don't suppose there will be anybody else,—except, perhaps, Mr. Warburton." But Lady Rosina was not there. In place of Lady Rosina there were the Duke and Duchess of St. Bungay, with their daughters, two or three Palliser offshoots, with their wives, and Barrington Erle. There were, too, the Bishop of the diocese with his wife, and three or four others, coming and going, so that the party never seemed to be too small. "We asked Mr. Rattler," said the Duchess in a whisper to Phineas, "but he declined, with a string of florid compliments. When Mr. Rattler won't come to the Prime Minister's house, you may depend that something is going to happen. It is like pigs carrying straws in their mouths. Mr. Rattler is my pig." Phineas only laughed and said that he did not believe Rattler to be a better pig than any one else.

It was soon apparent to Phineas that the Duke's manner to him was entirely altered, so much so that he was compelled to acknowledge to himself that he had not hitherto read the Duke's character aright. Hitherto he had never found the Duke pleasant in conversation. Looking back he could hardly remember that he had in truth ever conversed with the Duke. The man had seemed to shut himself up as soon as he had uttered certain words which the circumstances of the moment had demanded. Whether it was arrogance or shyness Phineas had not known. His wife had said that the Duke was shy. Had he been arrogant the effect would have been the same. He was unbending, hard, and lucid only when he spoke on some detail of business, or on some point of policy. But now he smiled, and though hesitating a little at first, very soon fell into the ways of a pleasant country host. "You shoot," said the Duke. Phineas did shoot but cared very little about it. "But you hunt." Phineas was very fond of riding to hounds. "I am beginning to think," said the Duke, "that I have made a mistake in not caring for such things. When I was very young I gave them up, because it appeared that other men devoted too much time to them. One might as well not eat because some men are gluttons."

"Only that you would die if you did not eat."

"Bread, I suppose, would keep me alive, but still one eats meat without being a glutton. I very often regret the want of amusements, and particularly of those which would throw me more among my fellow-creatures. A man is alone when reading, alone when writing, alone when thinking. Even sitting in Parliament he is very much alone, though there be a crowd around him. Now a man can hardly be thoroughly useful unless he knows his fellow-men, and how is he to know them if he shuts himself up? If I had to begin again I think I would cultivate the amusements of the time."

Not long after this the Duke asked him whether he was going to join the shooting men on that morning. Phineas declared that his hands were too full of business for any amusement before lunch. "Then," said the Duke, "will you walk with me in the afternoon? There is nothing I really like so much as a walk. There are some very pretty points where the river skirts the park. And I will show you the spot on which Sir Guy de Palliser performed the feat for which the king gave him this property. It was a grand time when a man could get half-a-dozen parishes because he tickled the king's fancy."

"But suppose he didn't tickle the king's fancy?"

"Ah, then indeed, it might go otherwise with him. But I am glad to say that Sir Guy was an accomplished courtier."

The walk was taken, and the pretty bends of the river were seen; but they were looked at without much earnestness, and Sir Guy's great deed was not again mentioned. The conversation went away to other matters. Of course it was not long before the Prime Minister was deep in discussing the probabilities of the next Session. It was soon apparent to Phineas that the Duke was no longer desirous of resigning, though he spoke very freely of the probable necessity there might be for him to do so. At the present moment he was in his best humour. His feet were on his own property. He could see the prosperity around him. The spot was the one which he loved best in all the world. He liked his present companion, who was one to whom he was entitled to speak with freedom. But there was still present to him the sense of some injury from which he could not free himself. Of course he did not know that he had been haughty to Sir Orlando, to Sir Timothy, and others. But he did know that he had intended to be true, and he thought that they had been treacherous. Twelve months ago there had been a goal before him which he might attain, a winning-post which was still within his reach. There was in store for him the tranquillity of retirement which he would enjoy as soon as a sense of duty would permit him to seize it. But now the prospect of that happiness had gradually vanished from him. That retirement was no longer a winning-post for him. The poison of place and power and dignity had got into his blood. As he looked forward he feared rather than sighed for retirement. "You think it will go against us," he said.

Phineas did think so. There was hardly a man high up in the party who did not think so. When one branch of a Coalition has gradually dropped off, the other branch will hardly flourish long. And then the tints of a political Coalition are so neutral and unalluring that men will only endure them when they feel that no more pronounced colours are within their reach. "After all," said Phineas, "the innings has not been a bad one. It has been of service to the country, and has lasted longer than most men expected."

"If it has been of service to the country, that is everything. It should at least be everything. With the statesman to whom it is not everything there must be something wrong." The Duke, as he said this, was preaching to himself. He was telling himself that, though he saw the better way, he was allowing himself to walk on in that which was worse. For it was not only Phineas who could see the change,—or the old Duke, or the Duchess. It was apparent to the man himself, though he could not prevent it. "I sometimes think," he said, "that we whom chance has led to be meddlers in the game of politics sometimes give ourselves hardly time enough to think what we are about."

"A man may have to work so hard," said Phineas, "that he has no time for thinking."

"Or more probably, may be so eager in party conflict that he will hardly keep his mind cool enough for thought. It seems to me that many men,— men whom you and I know,—embrace the profession of politics not only without political convictions, but without seeing that it is proper that they should entertain them. Chance brings a young man under the guidance of this or that elder man. He has come of a Whig family, as was my case,—or from some old Tory stock; and loyalty keeps him true to the interests which have first pushed him forward into the world. There is no conviction there."

"Convictions grow."

"Yes;—the conviction that it is the man's duty to be a staunch Liberal, but not the reason why. Or a man sees his opening on this side or on that,— as is the case with the lawyers. Or he has a body of men at his back ready to support him on this side or on that, as we see with commercial men. Or perhaps he has some vague idea that aristocracy is pleasant, and he becomes a Conservative,—or that democracy is prospering, and he becomes a Liberal. You are a Liberal, Mr. Finn."

"Certainly, Duke."

"Why?"

"Well;—after what you have said I will not boast of myself. Experience, however, seems to show me that Liberalism is demanded by the country."

"So, perhaps, at certain epochs, may the Devil and all his works; but you will hardly say that you will carry the Devil's colours because the country may like the Devil. It is not sufficient, I think, to say that Liberalism is demanded. You should first know what Liberalism means, and then assure yourself that the thing itself is good. I dare say you have done so; but I see some who never make the inquiry."

"I will not claim to be better than my neighbours,—I mean my real neighbours."

"I understand; I understand," said the Duke laughing. "You prefer some good Samaritan on the opposition benches to Sir Timothy and the Pharisees. It is hard to come wounded out of the fight, and then to see him who should be your friend not only walking by on the other side, but flinging a stone at you as he goes. But I did not mean just now to allude to the details of recent misfortunes, though there is no one to whom I could do so more openly than to you. I was trying yesterday to explain to myself why I have, all my life, sat on what is called the Liberal side of the House to which I have belonged."

"Did you succeed?"

"I began life with the misfortune of a ready-made political creed. There was a seat in the House for me when I was twenty-one. Nobody took the trouble to ask me my opinions. It was a matter of course that I should be a Liberal. My uncle, whom nothing could ever induce to move in politics himself, took it for granted that I should run straight,—as he would have said. It was a tradition of the family, and was as inseparable from it as any of the titles which he had inherited. The property might be sold or squandered,—but the political creed was fixed as adamant. I don't know that I ever had a wish to rebel, but I think that I took it at first very much as a matter of course."

"A man seldom inquires very deeply at twenty-one."

"And if he does it is ten to one but he comes to a wrong conclusion. But since then I have satisfied myself that chance put me into the right course. It has been, I dare say, the same with you as with me. We both went into office early, and the anxiety to do special duties well probably deterred us both from thinking much of the great question. When a man has to be on the alert to keep Ireland quiet, or to prevent peculation in the dockyards, or to raise the revenue while he lowers the taxes, he feels himself to be saved from the necessity of investigating principles. In this way I sometimes think that ministers, or they who have been ministers and who have to watch ministers from the opposition benches, have less opportunity of becoming real politicians than the men who sit in Parliament with empty hands and with time at their own disposal. But when a man has been placed by circumstances as I am now, he does begin to think."

"And yet you have not empty hands."

"They are not so full, perhaps, as you think. At any rate I cannot content myself with a single branch of the public service as I used to do in old days. Do not suppose that I claim to have made any grand political invention, but I think that I have at least labelled my own thoughts. I suppose what we all desire is to improve the condition of the people by whom we are employed, and to advance our country, or at any rate to save it from retrogression."

"That of course."

"So much is of course. I give credit to my opponents in Parliament for that desire quite as readily as I do to my colleagues or to myself. The idea that political virtue is all on one side is both mischievous and absurd. We allow ourselves to talk in that way because indignation, scorn, and sometimes, I fear, vituperation, are the fuel with which the necessary heat of debate is maintained."

"There are some men who are very fond of poking the fire," said Phineas.

"Well; I won't name any one at present," said the Duke, "but I have seen gentlemen of your country very handy with the pokers." Phineas laughed, knowing that he had been considered by some to have been a little violent when defending the Duke. "But we put all that aside when we really think, and can give the Conservative credit for philanthropy and patriotism as readily as the Liberal. The Conservative who has had any idea of the meaning of the name which he carries, wishes, I suppose, to maintain the differences and the distances which separate the highly placed from their lower brethren. He thinks that God has divided the world as he finds it divided, and that he may best do his duty by making the inferior man happy and contented in his position, teaching him that the place which he holds is his by God's ordinance."

"And it is so."

"Hardly in the sense that I mean. But that is the great Conservative lesson. That lesson seems to me to be hardly compatible with continual improvement in the condition of the lower man. But with the Conservative all such improvement is to be based on the idea of the maintenance of those distances. I as a Duke am to be kept as far apart from the man who drives my horses as was my ancestor from the man who drove his, or who rode after him to the wars,—and that is to go on for ever. There is much to be said for such a scheme. Let the lords be, all of them, men with loving hearts, and clear intellect, and noble instincts, and it is possible that they should use their powers so beneficently as to spread happiness over the earth. It is one of the millenniums which the mind of man can conceive, and seems to be that which the Conservative mind does conceive."

"But the other men who are not lords don't want that kind of happiness."

"If such happiness were attainable it might be well to constrain men to accept it. But the lords of this world are fallible men; and though as units they ought to be and perhaps are better than those others who have fewer advantages, they are much more likely as units to go astray in opinion than the bodies of men whom they would seek to govern. We know that power does corrupt, and that we cannot trust kings to have loving hearts, and clear intellects, and noble instincts. Men as they come to think about it and to look forward, and to look back, will not believe in such a millennium as that."

"Do they believe in any millennium?"

"I think they do after a fashion, and I think that I do myself. That is my idea of Conservatism. The doctrine of Liberalism is, of course, the reverse.

The Liberal, if he have any fixed idea at all, must, I think, have conceived the idea of lessening distances,—of bringing the coachman and the duke nearer together,—nearer and nearer, till a millennium shall be reached by—"

"By equality?" asked Phineas, eagerly interrupting the Prime Minister, and showing his dissent by the tone of his voice.

"I did not use the word, which is open to many objections. In the first place the millennium, which I have perhaps rashly named, is so distant that we need not even think of it as possible. Men's intellects are at present so various that we cannot even realise the idea of equality, and here in England we have been taught to hate the word by the evil effects of those absurd attempts which have been made elsewhere to proclaim it as a fact accomplished by the scratch of a pen or by a chisel on a stone. We have been injured in that, because a good word signifying a grand idea has been driven out of the vocabulary of good men. Equality would be a heaven, if we could attain it. How can we to whom so much has been given dare to think otherwise? How can you look at the bowed back and bent legs and abject face of that poor ploughman, who winter and summer has to drag his rheumatic limbs to his work, while you go a-hunting or sit in pride of place among the foremost few of your country, and say that it all is as it ought to be? You are a Liberal because you know that it is not all as it ought to be, and because you would still march on to some nearer approach to equality; though the thing itself is so great, so glorious, so godlike,—nay, so absolutely divine,—that you have been disgusted by the very promise of it, because its perfection is unattainable. Men have asserted a mock equality till the very idea of equality stinks in men's nostrils."

The Duke in his enthusiasm had thrown off his hat, and was sitting on a wooden seat which they had reached, looking up among the clouds. His left hand was clenched, and from time to time with his right he rubbed the thin hairs on his brow. He had begun in a low voice, with a somewhat slipshod enunciation of his words, but had gradually become clear, resonant, and even eloquent. Phineas knew that there were stories told of certain bursts of words which had come from him in former days in the House of Commons. These had occasionally surprised men and induced them to declare that Planty Pall,—as he was then often called,—was a dark horse. But they had been few and far between, and Phineas had never heard them. Now he gazed at his companion in silence, wondering whether the speaker would go on with his speech. But the face changed on a sudden, and the Duke with an awkward motion snatched up his hat. "I hope you ain't cold," he said.

"Not at all," said Phineas.

"I came here because of that bend of the river. I am always very fond of that bend. We don't go over the river. That is Mr. Upjohn's property."

"The member for the county?"

"Yes; and a very good member he is too, though he doesn't support us;—an old-school Tory, but a great friend of my uncle, who after all had a good deal of the Tory about him. I wonder whether he is at home. I must remind the Duchess to ask him to dinner. You know him, of course."

"Only by just seeing him in the House."

"You'd like him very much. When in the country he always wears knee-breeches and gaiters, which I think a very comfortable dress."

"Troublesome, Duke; isn't it?"

"I never tried it, and I shouldn't dare now. Goodness, me; it's past five o'clock, and we've got two miles to get home. I haven't looked at a letter, and Warburton will think that I've thrown myself into the river because of Sir Timothy Beeswax." Then they started to go home at a fast pace.

"I shan't forget, Duke," said Phineas, "your definition of Conservatives and Liberals."

"I don't think I ventured on a definition;—only a few loose ideas which had been troubling me lately. I say, Finn!"

"Your Grace?"

"Don't you go and tell Ramsden and Drummond that I have been preaching equality, or we shall have a pretty mess. I don't know that it would serve me with my dear friend, the Duke."

"I will be discretion itself."

"Equality is a dream. But sometimes one likes to dream,—especially as there is no danger that Matching will fly from me in a dream. I doubt whether I could bear the test that has been attempted in other countries."

"That poor ploughman would hardly get his share, Duke."

"No;—that's where it is. We can only do a little and a little to bring it nearer to us;—so little that it won't touch Matching in our day. Here is her ladyship and the ponies. I don't think her ladyship would like to lose her ponies by my doctrine."

The two wives of the two men were in the pony carriage, and the little Lady Glencora, the Duchess's eldest daughter, was sitting between them. "Mr. Warburton has sent three messengers to demand your presence," said the Duchess, "and, as I live by bread, I believe that you and Mr. Finn have been amusing yourselves!"

"We have been talking politics," said the Duke.

"Of course. What other amusement was possible? But what business have you to indulge in idle talk when Mr. Warburton wants you in the library? There has come a box," she said, "big enough to contain the resignations of all the traitors of the party." This was strong language, and the Duke frowned;—but there was no one there to hear it but Phineas Finn and his wife, and they, at least, were trustworthy. The Duke suggested that he had better get back to the house as soon as possible. There might be something to be done requiring time before dinner. Mr. Warburton might, at any rate, want to smoke a tranquil cigar after his day's work. The Duchess therefore left the carriage, as did Mrs. Finn, and the Duke undertook to drive the little girl back to the house. "He'll surely go against a tree," said the Duchess. But,—as a fact,—the Duke did take himself and the child home in safety.

"And what do you think about it, Mr. Finn?" said her Grace. "I suppose you and the Duke have been settling what is to be done."

"We have certainly settled nothing."

"Then you must have disagreed."

"That we as certainly have not done. We have in truth not once been out of cloud-land."

"Ah;—then there is no hope. When once grown-up politicians get into cloud-land it is because the realities of the world have no longer any charm for them."

The big box did not contain the resignations of any of the objectionable members of the Coalition. Ministers do not often resign in September,— nor would it be expedient that they should do so. Lord Drummond and Sir Timothy were safe, at any rate, till next February, and might live without any show either of obedience or mutiny. The Duke remained in comparative quiet at Matching. There was not very much to do, except to prepare the work for the next Session. The great work of the coming year was to be the assimilation, or something very near to the assimilation, of the county suffrages with those of the boroughs. The measure was one which had now been promised by statesmen for the last two years,—promised at first with that half promise which would mean nothing, were it not that such promises always lead to more defined assurances. The Duke of St. Bungay, Lord Drummond, and other Ministers had wished to stave it off. Mr. Monk was eager for its adoption, and was of course supported by Phineas Finn. The Prime Minister had at first been inclined to be led by the old Duke. There was no doubt to him but that the measure was desirable and would come, but there might well be a question as to the time at which it should be made to come. The old Duke knew that the measure would come,—but believing it to be wholly undesirable, thought that he was doing good work in postponing it from year to year. But Mr. Monk had become urgent, and the old Duke had admitted the necessity. There must surely have been a shade of melancholy on that old man's mind as, year after year, he assisted in pulling down institutions which he in truth regarded as the safeguards of the nation;—but which he knew that, as a Liberal, he was bound to assist in destroying! It must have occurred to him, from time to time, that it would be well for him to depart and be at peace before everything was gone.

When he went from Matching Mr. Monk took his place, and Phineas Finn, who had gone up to London for a while, returned; and then the three between them, with assistance from Mr. Warburton and others, worked out the proposed scheme of the new county franchise, with the new divisions and the new constituencies. But it could hardly have been hearty work, as they all of them felt that whatever might be their first proposition they would be beat upon it in a House of Commons which thought that this Aristides had been long enough at the Treasury.

Chapter LXIX
Mrs. Parker's Fate

Lopez had now been dead more than five months, and not a word had been heard by his widow of Mrs. Parker and her children. Her own sorrows had been so great that she had hardly thought of those of the poor woman who had come to her but a few days before her husband's death, telling her of ruin caused by her husband's treachery. But late on the evening before her departure for Herefordshire,—very shortly after Everett had left the house,—there was a ring at the door, and a poorly-clad female asked to see Mrs. Lopez. The poorly-clad female was Sexty Parker's wife. The servant, who did not remember her, would not leave her alone in the hall, having an eye to the coats and umbrellas, but called up one of the maids to carry the message. The poor woman understood the insult and resented it in her heart. But Mrs. Lopez recognised the name in a moment, and went down to her in the parlour, leaving Mr. Wharton upstairs. Mrs. Parker, smarting from her present grievance, had bent her mind on complaining at once of the treatment she had received from the servant, but the sight of the widow's weeds quelled her. Emily had never been much given to fine clothes, either as a girl or as a married woman; but it had always been her husband's pleasure that she should be well dressed,—though he had never carried his trouble so far as to pay the bills; and Mrs. Parker's remembrance of her friend at Dovercourt had been that of a fine lady in bright apparel. Now a black shade,—something almost like a dark ghost,—glided into the room, and Mrs. Parker forgot her recent injury. Emily came forward and offered her hand, and was the first to speak. "I have had a great sorrow since we met," she said.

"Yes, indeed, Mrs. Lopez. I don't think there is anything left in the world now except sorrow."

"I hope Mr. Parker is well. Will you not sit down, Mrs. Parker?"

"Thank you, ma'am. Indeed, then, he is not well at all. How should he be well? Everything,—everything has been taken away from him." Poor Emily groaned as she heard this. "I wouldn't say a word against them as is gone, Mrs. Lopez, if I could help it. I know it is bad to bear when him who once loved you isn't no more. And perhaps it is all the worse when things didn't go well with him, and it was, maybe, his own fault. I wouldn't do it, Mrs. Lopez, if I could help it."

"Let me hear what you have to say," said Emily, determined to suffer everything patiently.

"Well;—it is just this. He has left us that bare that there is nothing left. And that, they say, isn't the worst of all,—though what can be worse than doing that, how is a woman to think? Parker was that soft, and he had that way with him of talking, that he has talked me and mine out of the very linen on our backs."

"What do you mean by saying that that is not the worst?"

"They've come upon Sexty for a bill for four hundred and fifty,—something to do with that stuff they call Bios,—and Sexty says it isn't his name at all. But he's been in that state he don't hardly know how to swear to anything. But he's sure he didn't sign it. The bill was brought to him by Lopez, and there was words between them, and he wouldn't have nothing to do with it. How is he to go to law? And it don't make much difference neither, for they can't take much more from him than they have taken." Emily as she heard all this sat shivering, trying to repress her groans. "Only," continued Mrs. Parker, "they hadn't sold the furniture, and I was thinking they might let me stay in the house, and try to do with letting lodgings,—and now they're seizing everything along of this bill. Sexty is like a madman, swearing this and swearing that;—but what can he do, Mrs. Lopez? It's as like his hand as two peas; but he was clever at everything was—was—you know who I mean, ma'am." Then Emily covered her face with her hands and burst into violent tears. She had not determined whether she did or did not believe this last accusation made against her husband. She had had hardly time to realise the criminality of the offence imputed. But she did believe that the woman before her had been ruined by her husband's speculations. "It's very bad, ma'am; isn't it?" said Mrs. Parker, crying for company. "It's bad all round. If you had five children as hadn't bread you'd know how it is that I feel. I've got to go back by the 10.15 to-night, and when I've paid for a third-class ticket I shan't have but twopence left in the world."

This utter depth of immediate poverty, this want of bread for the morrow and the next day, Emily could relieve out of her own pocket. And, thinking of this and remembering that her purse was not with her at the moment, she started up with the idea of getting it. But it occurred to her that

that would not suffice; that her duty required more of her than that. And yet, by her own power, she could do no more. From month to month, almost from week to week, since her husband's death, her father had been called upon to satisfy claims for money which he would not resist, lest by doing so he should add to her misery. She had felt that she ought to bind herself to the strictest personal economy because of the miserable losses to which she had subjected him by her ill-starred marriage. "What would you wish me to do?" she said, resuming her seat.

"You are rich," said Mrs. Parker. Emily shook her head. "They say your papa is rich. I thought you would not like to see me in want like this."

"Indeed, indeed, it makes me very unhappy."

"Wouldn't your papa do something? It wasn't Sexty's fault nigh so much as it was his. I wouldn't say it to you if it wasn't for starving. I wouldn't say it to you if it wasn't for the children. I'd lie in the ditch and die if it was only myself, because—because I know what your feelings is. But what wouldn't you do, and what wouldn't you say, if you had five children at home as hadn't a loaf of bread among 'em?" Hereupon Emily got up and left the room, bidding her visitor wait for a few minutes. Presently the offensive butler came in, who had wronged Mrs. Parker by watching his master's coats, and brought a tray with meat and wine. Mr. Wharton, said the altered man, hoped that Mrs. Parker would take a little refreshment, and he would be down himself very soon. Mrs. Parker, knowing that strength for her journey home would be necessary to her, remembering that she would have to walk all through the city to the Bishopsgate Street station, did take some refreshment, and permitted herself to drink the glass of sherry that her late enemy had benignantly poured out for her.

Emily had been nearly half-an-hour with her father before Mr. Wharton's heavy step was heard upon the stairs. And when he reached the dining-room door he paused a moment before he ventured to turn the lock. He had not told Emily what he would do, and had hardly as yet made up his own mind. As every fresh call was made upon him, his hatred for the memory of the man who had stepped in and disturbed his whole life, and turned all the mellow satisfaction of his evening into storm and gloom, was of course increased. The scoundrel's name was so odious to him that he could hardly keep himself from shuddering visibly before his daughter even when the servants called her by it. But yet he had determined that he would devote himself to save her from further suffering. It had been her fault, no doubt. But she was expiating it in very sackcloth and ashes, and he would add nothing to the burden on her back. He would pay, and pay, and pay, merely remembering that what he paid must be deducted from her share of his property. He had never intended to make what is called an elder son of Everett, and now there was less necessity than ever that he should do so, as Everett had become an elder son in another direction. He could satisfy almost any demand that might be made without material injury to himself. But these demands, one after another, scalded him by their frequency, and by the baseness of the man who had occasioned them. His daughter had now repeated to him with sobbings and wailings the whole story as it had been told to her by the woman downstairs. "Papa," she had said, "I don't know how to tell you or how not." Then he had encouraged her, and had listened without saying a word. He had endeavoured not even to shrink as the charge of forgery was repeated to him by his own child,—the widow of the guilty man. He endeavoured not to remember at the moment that she had claimed this wretch as the chosen one of her maiden heart, in opposition to all his wishes. It hardly occurred to him to disbelieve the accusation. It was so probable! What was there to hinder the man from forgery, if he could only make it believed that his victim had signed the bill when intoxicated? He heard it all;—kissed his daughter, and then went down to the dining-room.

Mrs. Parker, when she saw him, got up, and curtsied low, and then sat down again. Old Wharton looked at her from under his bushy eyebrows before he spoke, and then sat opposite to her. "Madam," he said, "this is a very sad story that I have heard." Mrs. Parker again rose, again curtsied, and put her handkerchief to her face. "It is of no use talking any more about it here."

"No, sir," said Mrs. Parker.

"I and my daughter leave town early to-morrow morning."

"Indeed, sir. Mrs. Lopez didn't tell me."

"My clerk will be in London, at No. 12, Stone Buildings, Lincoln's Inn, till I come back. Do you think you can find the place? I have written it there."

"Yes, sir, I can find it," said Mrs. Parker, just raising herself from her chair at every word she spoke.

"I have written his name, you see. Mr. Crumpy."

"Yes, sir."

"If you will permit me, I will give you two sovereigns now."

"Thank you, sir."

"And if you can make it convenient to call on Mr. Crumpy every Thursday morning about twelve, he will pay you two sovereigns a week till I come back to town. Then I will see about it."

"God Almighty bless you, sir!"

"And as to the furniture, I will write to my attorney, Mr. Walker. You need not trouble yourself by going to him."

"No, sir."

"If necessary, he will send to you, and he will see what can be done. Good night, Mrs. Parker." Then he walked across the room with two sovereigns which he dropped in her hand. Mrs. Parker, with many sobs, bade him farewell, and Mr. Wharton stood in the hall immovable till the front door had been closed behind her. "I have settled it," he said to Emily. "I'll tell you to-morrow, or some day. Don't worry yourself now, but go to bed." She looked wistfully,—so sadly, up into his face, and then did as he bade her.

But Mr. Wharton could not go to bed without further trouble. It was incumbent on him to write full particulars that very night both to Mr. Walker and to Mr. Crumpy. And the odious letters in the writing became very long;—odious because he had to confess in them over and over again that his daughter, the very apple of his eye, had been the wife of a scoundrel. To Mr. Walker he had to tell the whole story of the alleged forgery, and in doing so could not abstain from the use of hard words. "I don't suppose that it can be proved, but there is every reason to believe that it's true." And again—"I believe the man to have been as vile a scoundrel as ever was made by the love of money." Even to Mr. Crumpy he could not be reticent. "She is an object of pity," he said. "Her husband was ruined by the infamous speculations of Mr. Lopez." Then he betook himself to bed. Oh, how happy would he be to pay the two pounds weekly,—even to add to that the amount of the forged bill, if by doing so he might be saved from ever again hearing the name of Lopez.

The amount of the bill was ultimately lost by the bankers who had advanced money on it. As for Mrs. Sexty Parker, from week to week, and from month to month, and at last from year to year, she and her children,— and probably her husband also,—were supported by the weekly pension of two sovereigns which she always received on Thursday morning from the hands of Mr. Crumpy himself. In a little time the one excitement of her life was the weekly journey to Mr. Crumpy, whom she came to regard as a man appointed by Providence to supply her with 40s. on Thursday morning. As to poor Sexty Parker,—it is to be feared that he never again became a prosperous man.

"You will tell me what you did for that poor woman, papa," said Emily, leaning over her father in the train.

"I have settled it, my dear."

"You said you'd tell me."

"Crumpy will pay her two pounds a week till we know more about it." Emily pressed her father's hand and that was an end. No one ever did know any more about it, and Crumpy continued to pay the money.

Chapter LXX
At Wharton

When Mr. Wharton and his daughter reached Wharton Hall there were at any rate no Fletchers there as yet. Emily, as she was driven from the station to the house, had not dared to ask a question or even to prompt her father to do so. He would probably have told her that on such an occasion there was but little chance that she would find any visitors, and none at all that she would find Arthur Fletcher. But she was too confused and too ill at ease to think of probabilities, and to the last was in trepidation, specially lest she should meet her lover. She found, however, at Wharton Hall none but Whartons, and she found also to her great relief that this change in the heir relieved her of much of the attention which must otherwise have added to her troubles. At the first glance her dress and demeanour struck them so forcibly that they could not avoid showing their feeling. Of course they had expected to see her in black,—had expected to see her in widow's weeds. But, with her, her very face and limbs had so adapted themselves to her crape, that she looked like a monument of bereaved woe. Lady Wharton took the mourner up into her own room, and there made her a little speech. "We have all wept for you," she said, "and grieve for you still. But excessive grief is wicked, especially in the young. We will do our best to make you happy, and hope we shall succeed. All this about dear Everett ought to be a comfort to you." Emily promised that she would do her best, not, however, taking much immediate comfort from the prospects of dear Everett. Lady Wharton certainly had never in her life spoken of dear Everett while the wicked cousin was alive. Then Mary Wharton also made her little speech. "Dear Emily, I will do all that I can. Pray try to believe in me." But Everett was so much the hero of the hour, that there was not much room for general attention to any one else.

There was very much room for triumph in regard to Everett. It had already been ascertained that the Wharton who was now dead had had a child,—but that the child was a daughter. Oh,—what salvation or destruction there may be to an English gentleman in the sex of an infant! This poor baby was now little better than a beggar brat, unless the relatives who were utterly disregardful of its fate, should choose, in their charity, to make some small allowance for its maintenance. Had it by chance been a boy, Everett Wharton would have been nobody; and the child, rescued from the iniquities of his parents, would have been nursed in the best bedroom of Wharton Hall, and cherished with the warmest kisses, and would have been the centre of all the hopes of all the Whartons. But the Wharton lawyer by use of reckless telegrams had certified himself that the infant was a girl, and Everett was the hero of the day. He found himself to be possessed of a thousand graces, even in his father's eyesight. It seemed to be taken as a mark of his special good fortune that he had not clung to any business. To have been a banker immersed in the making of money, or even a lawyer attached to his circuit and his court, would have lessened his fitness, or at any rate his readiness, for the duties which he would have to perform. He would never be a very rich man, but he would have a command of ready money, and of course he would go into Parliament.

In his new position as,—not quite head of his family, but head expectant,—it seemed to him to be his duty to lecture his sister. It might be well that some one should lecture her with more severity than her father used. Undoubtedly she was succumbing to the wretchedness of her position in a manner that was repugnant to humanity generally. There is no power so useful to man as that capacity of recovering himself after a fall, which belongs especially to those who possess a healthy mind in a healthy body. It is not rare to see one,—generally a woman,—whom a sorrow gradually kills; and there are those among us, who hardly perhaps envy, but certainly admire, a spirit so delicate as to be snuffed out by a woe. But it is the weakness of the heart rather than the strength of the feeling which has in such cases most often produced the destruction. Some endurance of fibre has been wanting, which power of endurance is a noble attribute. Everett Wharton saw something of this, and being, now, the heir apparent of the family, took his sister to task. "Emily," he said, "you make us all unhappy when we look at you."

"Do I?" she said. "I am sorry for that;—but why should you look at me?"

"Because you are one of us. Of course we cannot shake you off. We would not if we could. We have all been very unhappy because,—because of what has happened. But don't you think you ought to make some sacrifice to us,—to our father, I mean, and to Sir Alured and Lady Wharton? When you go on weeping, other people have to weep too. I have an idea that people ought to be happy if it be only for the sake of their neighbours."

"What am I to do, Everett?"

"Talk to people a little, and smile sometimes. Move about quicker. Don't look when you come into a room as if you were consecrating it to tears. And, if I may venture to say so, drop something of the heaviness of your mourning."

"Do you mean that I am a hypocrite?"

"No;—I mean nothing of the kind. You know I don't. But you may exert yourself for the benefit of others without being untrue to your own memories. I am sure you know what I mean. Make a struggle and see if you cannot do something."

She did make a struggle, and she did do something. No one, not well versed in the mysteries of feminine dress, could say very accurately what it was that she had done; but every one felt that something of the weight was reduced. At first, as her brother's words came upon her ear, and as she felt the blows which they inflicted on her, she accused him in her heart of cruelty. They were very hard to bear. There was a moment in which she was almost tempted to turn upon him and tell him that he knew nothing of her sorrows. But she restrained herself, and when she was alone she acknowledged to herself that he had spoken the truth. No one has a right to go about the world as a Niobe, damping all joys with selfish tears. What did she not owe to her father, who had warned her so often against the evil she had contemplated, and had then, from the first moment after the fault was done, forgiven her the doing of it? She had at any rate learned from her misfortunes the infinite tenderness of his heart, which in the days of their unalloyed prosperity he had never felt the necessity of exposing to her. So she struggled and did do something. She pressed Lady Wharton's hand, and kissed her cousin Mary, and throwing herself into her father's arms when they were alone, whispered to him that she would try. "What you told me, Everett, was quite right," she said afterwards to her brother.

"I didn't mean to be savage," he answered with a smile.

"It was quite right, and I have thought of it, and I will do my best. I will keep it to myself if I can. It is not quite, perhaps, what you think it is, but I will keep it to myself." She fancied that they did not understand her, and perhaps she was right. It was not only that he had died and left her a young widow;—nor even that his end had been so harsh a tragedy and so foul a disgrace! It was not only that her love had been misbestowed,—not only that she had made so grievous an error in the one great act of her life which she had chosen to perform on her own judgment! Perhaps the most crushing memory of all was that which told her that she, who had through all her youth been regarded as a bright star in the family, had been the one person to bring a reproach upon the name of all these people who were so good to her. How shall a person conscious of disgrace, with a mind capable of feeling the crushing weight of personal disgrace, move and look and speak as though that disgrace had been washed away? But she made the struggle, and did not altogether fail.

As regarded Sir Alured, in spite of this poor widow's crape, he was very happy at this time, and his joy did in some degree communicate itself to the old barrister. Everett was taken round to every tenant and introduced as the heir. Mr. Wharton had already declared his purpose of abdicating any possible possession of the property. Should he outlive Sir Alured he must be the baronet; but when that sad event should take place, whether Mr. Wharton should then be alive or no, Everett should at once be the possessor of Wharton Hall. Sir Alured, under these circumstances, discussed his own death with extreme satisfaction, and insisted on having it discussed by the others. That he should have gone and left everything at the mercy of the spendthrift had been terrible to his old heart;—but now, the man coming to the property would have £60,000 with which to support and foster Wharton, with which to mend, as it were, the crevices, and stop up the holes of the estate. He seemed to be almost impatient for Everett's ownership, giving many hints as to what should be done when he himself was gone. He must surely have thought that he would return to Wharton as a spirit, and take a ghostly share in the prosperity of the farms. "You will find John Griffith a very good man," said the baronet. John Griffith had been a tenant on the estate for the last half-century, and was an older man than his landlord; but the baronet spoke of all this as though he himself were about to leave Wharton for ever in the course of the next week. "John Griffith has been a good man, and if not always quite ready with his rent, has never been much behind. You won't be hard on John Griffith?"

"I hope I mayn't have the opportunity, sir."

"Well;—well;—well; that's as may be. But I don't quite know what to say about young John. The farm has gone from father to son, and there's never been a word of a lease."

"Is there anything wrong about the young man?"

"He's a little given to poaching."

"Oh dear!"

"I've always got him off for his father's sake. They say he's going to marry Sally Jones. That may take it out of him. I do like the farms to go from father to son, Everett. It's the way that everything should go. Of course there's no right."

"Nothing of that kind, I suppose," said Everett, who was in his way a reformer, and had Radical notions with which he would not for worlds have disturbed the baronet at present.

"No;—nothing of that kind. God in his mercy forbid that a landlord in England should ever be robbed after that fashion." Sir Alured, when he was uttering this prayer, was thinking of what he had heard of an Irish Land Bill, the details of which, however, had been altogether incomprehensible to him. "But I have a feeling about it, Everett; and I hope you will share it. It is good that things should go from father to son. I never make a promise; but the tenants know what I think about it, and then the father works for the son. Why should he work for a stranger? Sally Jones is a very good young woman, and perhaps young John will do better." There was not a field or a fence that he did not show to his heir;—hardly a tree which he left without a word. "That bit of woodland coming in there,—they call it Barnton Spinnies,—doesn't belong to the estate at all." This he said in a melancholy tone.

"Doesn't it, really?"

"And it comes right in between Lane's farm and Puddock's. They've always let me have the shooting as a compliment. Not that there's ever anything in it. It's only seven acres. But I like the civility."

"Who does it belong to?"

"It belongs to Benet."

"What; Corpus Christi?"

"Yes, yes;—they've changed the name. It used to be Benet in my days. Walker says the College would certainly sell, but you'd have to pay for the land and the wood separately. I don't know that you'd get much out of it; but it's very unsightly,—on the survey map, I mean."

"We'll buy it, by all means," said Everett, who was already jingling his £60,000 in his pocket.

"I never had the money, but I think it should be bought." And Sir Alured rejoiced in the idea that when his ghost should look at the survey map, that hiatus of Barnton Spinnies would not trouble his spectral eyes.

In this way months ran on at Wharton. Our Whartons had come down in the latter half of August, and at the beginning of September Mr. Wharton returned to London. Everett, of course, remained, as he was still learning the lesson of which he was in truth becoming a little weary; and at last Emily had also been persuaded to stay in Herefordshire. Her father promised to return, not mentioning any precise time, but giving her to understand that he would come before the winter. He went, and probably found that his taste for the Eldon and for whist had returned to him. In the middle of November old Mrs. Fletcher arrived. Emily was not aware of what was being done; but, in truth, the Fletchers and Whartons combined were conspiring with the view of bringing her back to her former self. Mrs. Fletcher had not yielded without some difficulty,—for it was a part of this conspiracy that Arthur was to be allowed to marry the widow. But John had prevailed. "He'll do it any way, mother," he had said, "whether you and I like it or not. And why on earth shouldn't he do as he pleases?"

"Think what the man was, John!"

"It's more to the purpose to think what the woman is. Arthur has made up his mind, and, if I know him, he's not the man to be talked out of it." And so the old woman had given in, and had at last consented to go forward as the advanced guard of the Fletchers, and lay siege to the affections of the woman whom she had once so thoroughly discarded from her heart.

"My dear," she said, when they first met, "if there has been anything wrong between you and me, let it be among the things that are past. You always used to kiss me. Give me a kiss now." Of course Emily kissed her; and after that Mrs. Fletcher patted her and petted her, and gave her lozenges, which she declared in private to be "the sovereignest thing on earth" for debilitated nerves. And then it came out by degrees that John Fletcher and his wife and all the little Fletchers were coming to Wharton for the Christmas weeks. Everett had gone, but was also to be back for Christmas, and Mr. Wharton's visit was also postponed. It was absolutely necessary that Everett should be at Wharton for the Christmas festivities, and expedient that Everett's father should be there to see them. In this way Emily had no means of escape. Her father wrote telling her of his plans, saying that he would bring her back after Christmas. Everett's heirship had made these Christmas festivities,—which were, however, to be confined to the two families,—quite a necessity. In all this not a word was said about Arthur, nor did she dare to ask whether he was expected. The younger Mrs. Fletcher, John's wife, opened her arms to the widow in a manner that almost plainly said that she regarded Emily as her future sister-in-law. John Fletcher talked to her about Longbarns, and the children,—complete Fletcher talk,—as though she were already one of them, never, however, mentioning Arthur's name. The old lady got down a fresh supply of the lozenges from London because those she had by her might perhaps be a little stale. And then there was another sign which after a while became plain to Emily. No one in either family ever mentioned her name. It was not singular that none of them should call her Mrs. Lopez, as she was Emily to all of them. But they never so described her even in speaking to the servants. And the servants themselves, as far as was possible, avoided the odious word. The thing was to be buried, if not in oblivion, yet in some speechless grave. And it seemed that her father was joined in this attempt. When writing to her he usually made some excuse for writing also to Everett, or, in Everett's absence, to the baronet,—so that the letter for his daughter might be enclosed and addressed simply to "Emily".

She understood it all, and though she was moved to continual solitary tears by this ineffable tenderness, yet she rebelled against them. They should never cheat her back into happiness by such wiles as that! It was not fit that she should yield to them. As a woman utterly disgraced it could not become her again to laugh and be joyful, to give and take loving embraces, to sit and smile, perhaps a happy mother, at another man's hearth. For their love she was grateful. For his love she was more than grateful. How constant must be his heart, how grand his nature, how more than manly his strength of character, when he was thus true to her through all the evil she had done! Love him! Yes;—she would pray for him, worship him, fill the remainder of her days with thinking of him, hoping for him, and making his interests her own. Should he ever be married,—and she would pray that he might,—his wife, if possible, should be her friend, his children should be her darlings; and he should always be her hero. But they should not, with all their schemes, cheat her into disgracing him by marrying him.

At last her father came, and it was he who told her that Arthur was expected on the day before Christmas. "Why did you not tell me before, papa, so that I might have asked you to take me away?"

"Because I thought, my dear, that it was better that you should be constrained to meet him. You would not wish to live all your life in terror of seeing Arthur Fletcher?"

"Not all my life."

"Take the plunge and it will be over. They have all been very good to you."

"Too good, papa. I didn't want it."

"They are our oldest friends. There isn't a young man in England I think so highly of as John Fletcher. When I am gone, where are you to look for friends?"

"I'm not ungrateful, papa."

"You can't know them all, and yet keep yourself altogether separated from Arthur. Think what it would be to me never to be able to ask him to the house. He is the only one of the family that lives in London, and now it seems that Everett will spend most of his time down here. Of course it is better that you should meet him and have done with it." There was no answer to be made to this, but still she was fixed in her resolution that she would never meet him as her lover.

Then came the morning of the day on which he was to arrive, and his coming was for the first time spoken openly of at breakfast. "How is Arthur to be brought from the station?" asked old Mrs. Fletcher.

"I'm going to take the dog-cart," said Everett. "Giles will go for the luggage with the pony. He is bringing down a lot of things;—a new saddle, and a gun for me." It had all been arranged for her, this question and answer, and Emily blushed as she felt that it was so.

"We shall be so glad to see Arthur," said young Mrs. Fletcher to her.

"Of course you will."

"He has not been down since the Session was over, and he has got to be quite a speaking man now. I do so hope he'll become something some day."

"I'm sure he will," said Emily.

"Not a judge, however. I hate wigs. Perhaps he might be Lord Chancellor in time." Mrs. Fletcher was not more ignorant than some other ladies in being unaware of the Lord Chancellor's wig and exact position.

At last he came. The 9 a.m. express for Hereford,—express, at least, for the first two or three hours out of London,—brought passengers for Wharton to the nearest station at 3 p.m., and the distance was not above five miles. Before four o'clock Arthur was standing before the drawing-room fire, with a cup of tea in his hand, surrounded by Fletchers and Whartons, and being made much of as the young family member of Parliament. But Emily was not in the room. She had studied her Bradshaw, and learned the hours of the trains, and was now in her bedroom. He had looked around the moment he entered the room, but had not dared to ask for her suddenly. He had said one word about her to Everett in the cart, and that had been all. She was in the house, and he must, at any rate, see her before dinner.

Emily, in order that she might not seem to escape abruptly, had retired early to her solitude. But she, too, knew that the meeting could not be long postponed. She sat thinking of it all, and at last heard the wheels of the vehicle before the door. She paused, listening with all her ears, that she might recognise his voice, or possibly his footstep. She stood near the window, behind the curtain, with her hand pressed to her heart. She heard Everett's voice plainly as he gave some direction to the groom, but from Arthur she heard nothing. Yet she was sure that he was come. The very manner of the approach and her brother's word made her certain that there had been no disappointment. She stood thinking for a quarter of an hour, making up her mind how best they might meet. Then suddenly, with slow but certain step, she walked down into the drawing-room.

No one expected her then, or something perhaps might have been done to encourage her coming. It had been thought that she must meet him before dinner, and her absence till then was to be excused. But now she opened the door, and with much dignity of mien walked into the middle of the room. Arthur at that moment was discussing the Duke's chance for the next Session, and Sir Alured was asking with rapture whether the old Conservative party would not come in. Arthur Fletcher heard the step, turned round, and saw the woman he loved. He went at once to meet her, very quickly, and put out both his hands. She gave him hers, of course. There was no excuse for her refusal. He stood for an instant pressing them, looking eagerly into her sad face, and then he spoke. "God bless you, Emily!" he said, "God bless you!" He had thought of no words, and at the moment nothing else occurred to him to be said. The colour had covered all his face, and his heart beat so strongly that he was hardly his own master. She let him hold her two hands, perhaps for a minute, and then, bursting into tears, tore herself from him, and, hurrying out of the room, made her way again into her own chamber. "It will be better so," said old Mrs. Fletcher. "It will be better so. Do not let any one follow her."

On that day John Fletcher took her out to dinner, and Arthur did not sit near her. In the evening he came to her as she was working close to his mother, and seated himself on a low chair close to her knees. "We are all so glad to see you; are we not, mother?"

"Yes, indeed," said Mrs. Fletcher. Then, after a while, the old woman got up to make a rubber at whist with the two old men and her eldest son, leaving Arthur sitting at the widow's knee. She would willingly have escaped, but it was impossible that she should move.

"You need not be afraid of me," he said, not whispering, but in a voice which no one else could hear. "Do not seem to avoid me, and I will say nothing to trouble you. I think that you must wish that we should be friends."

"Oh, yes."

"Come out, then, to-morrow, when we are walking. In that way we shall get used to each other. You are troubled now, and I will go." Then he left her, and she felt herself to be bound to him by infinite gratitude.

A week went on and she had become used to his company. A week passed and he had spoken no word to her that a brother might not have spoken. They had walked together when no one else had been within hearing, and yet he had spared her. She had begun to think that he would spare her altogether, and she was certainly grateful. Might it not be that she had misunderstood him, and had misunderstood the meaning of them all? Might it not be that she had troubled herself with false anticipations? Surely it was so; for how could it be that such a man should wish to make such a woman his wife?

"Well, Arthur?" said his brother to him one day.

"I have nothing to say about it," said Arthur.

"You haven't changed your mind?"

"Never! Upon my word, to me, in that dress, she is more beautiful than ever."

"I wish you would make her take it off."

"I dare not ask her yet."

"You know what they say about widows generally, my boy."

"That is all very well when one talks about widows in general. It is easy to chaff about women when one hasn't got any woman in one's mind. But as it is now, having her here, loving her as I do,—by heaven! I cannot hurry her. I don't dare to speak to her after that fashion. I shall do it in time, I suppose;—but I must wait till the time comes."

Chapter LXXI
The Ladies at Longbarns Doubt

It came at last to be decided among them that when old Mr. Wharton returned to town,—and he had now been at Wharton longer than he had ever been known to remain there before,—Emily should still remain in Herefordshire, and that at some period not then fixed she should go for a month to Longbarns. There were various reasons which induced her to consent to this change of plans. In the first place she found herself to be infinitely more comfortable in the country than in town. She could go out and move about and bestir herself, whereas in Manchester Square she could only sit and mope at home. Her father had assured her that he thought that it would be better that she should be away from the reminiscences of the house in town. And then when the first week of February was past Arthur would be up in town, and she would be far away from him at Longbarns, whereas in London she would be close within his reach. Many little schemes were laid and struggles made both by herself and the others before at last their plans were settled. Mr. Wharton was to return to London in the middle of January. It was quite impossible that he could remain longer away either from Stone Buildings or from the Eldon, and then at the same time, or a day or two following, Mrs. Fletcher was to go back to Longbarns. John Fletcher and his wife and children were already gone,—and Arthur also had been at Longbarns. The two brothers and Everett had been backwards and forwards. Emily was anxious to remain at Wharton at any rate till Parliament should have met, so that she might not be at home with Arthur in his own house. But matters would not arrange themselves exactly as she wished. It was at last settled that she should go to Longbarns with Mary Wharton under the charge of John Fletcher in the first week in February. As arrangements were already in progress for the purchase of Barnton Spinnies, Sir Alured could not possibly leave his own house. Not to have walked through the wood on the first day that it became a part of the Wharton property would to him have been treason to the estate. His experience ought to have told him that there was no chance of a lawyer and a college dealing together with such rapidity; but in the present state of things he could not bear to absent himself. Orders had already been given for the cutting down of certain trees which could not have been touched had the reprobate lived, and it was indispensable that if a tree fell at Wharton he should see the fall. It thus came to pass that there was a week during which Emily would be forced to live under the roof of the Fletchers together with Arthur Fletcher.

The week came and she was absolutely received by Arthur at the door of Longbarns. She had not been at the house since it had first been intimated to the Fletchers that she was disposed to receive with favour the addresses of Ferdinand Lopez. As she remembered this it seemed to her to be an age ago since that man had induced her to believe that of all men she had ever met he was the nearest to a hero. She never spoke of him now, but of course her thoughts of him were never ending,—as also of herself in that she had allowed herself to be so deceived. She would recall to her mind with bitter inward sobbings all those lessons of iniquity which he had striven to teach her, and which had first opened her eyes to his true character,—how sedulously he had endeavoured to persuade her that it was her duty to rob her father on his behalf, how continually he had endeavoured to make her think that appearance in the world was everything, and that, being in truth poor adventurers, it behoved them to cheat the world into thinking them rich and respectable. Every hint that had been so given had been a wound to her, and those wounds were all now remembered. Though since his death she had never allowed a word to be spoken in her presence against him, she could not but hate his memory. How glorious was that other man in her eyes, as he stood there at the door welcoming her to Longbarns, fair-haired, open-eyed, with bronzed brow and cheek, and surely the honestest face that a loving woman ever loved to gaze on. During the various lessons she had learned in her married life, she had become gradually but surely aware that the face of that other man had been dishonest. She had learned the false meaning of every glance of his eyes, the subtlety of his mouth, the counterfeit man[oe]uvres of his body,—the deceit even of his dress. He had been all a lie from head to foot; and he had thrown her love aside as useless when she also would not be a liar. And here was this man,—spotless in her estimation, compounded of all good qualities, which she could now see and take at their proper value. She hated herself for the simplicity with which she had been cheated by soft words and a false demeanour into so great a sacrifice.

Life at Longbarns was very quiet during the days which she passed there before he left them. She was frequently alone with him, but he, if he still loved her, did not speak of his love. He explained it all one day to his mother. "If it is to be," said the old lady, "I don't see the use of more delay. Of course the marriage ought not to be till March twelvemonths. But if it is understood that it is to be, she might alter her dress by degrees,—and alter her manner of living. Those things should always be done by degrees. I think it had better be settled, Arthur, if it is to be settled."

"I am afraid, mother."

"Dear me! I didn't think you were the man ever to be afraid of a woman. What can she say to you?"

"Refuse me."

"Then you'd better know it at once. But I don't think she'll be fool enough for that."

"Perhaps you hardly understand her, mother."

Mrs. Fletcher shook her head with a look of considerable annoyance. "Perhaps not. But, to tell the truth, I don't like young women whom I can't understand. Young women shouldn't be mysterious. I like people of whom I can give a pretty good guess what they'll do. I'm sure I never could have guessed that she would have married that man."

"If you love me, mother, do not let that be mentioned between us again. When I said that you did not understand her, I did not mean that she was mysterious. I think that before he died, and since his death, she learned of what sort that man was. I will not say that she hates his memory, but she hates herself for what she has done."

"So she ought," said Mrs. Fletcher.

"She has not yet brought herself to think that her life should be anything but one long period of mourning, not for him, but for her own mistake. You may be quite sure that I am in earnest. It is not because I doubt of myself that I put it off. But I fear that if once she asserts to me her resolution to remain as she is, she will feel herself bound to keep her word."

"I suppose she is very much the same as other women, after all, my dear," said Mrs. Fletcher, who was almost jealous of the peculiar superiority of sentiment which her son seemed to attribute to this woman.

"Circumstances, mother, make people different," he replied.

"So you are going without having anything fixed," his elder brother said to him the day before he started.

"Yes, old fellow. It seems to be rather slack;—doesn't it?"

"I dare say you know best what you're about. But if you have set your mind on it—"

"You may take your oath on that."

"Then I don't see why one word shouldn't put it all right. There never is any place so good for that kind of thing as a country house."

"I don't think that with her it will make much difference where the house is, or what the circumstances."

"She knows what you mean as well as I do."

"I dare say she does, John. She must have a very bad idea of me if she doesn't. But she may know what I mean and not mean the same thing herself."

"How are you to know if you don't ask her?"

"You may be sure that I shall ask her as soon as I can hope that my doing so may give her more pleasure than pain. Remember, I have had all this out with her father. I have determined that I will wait till twelve months have passed since that wretched man perished."

On that afternoon before dinner he was alone with her in the library some minutes before they went up to dress for dinner. "I shall hardly see you to-morrow," he said, "as I must leave this at half-past eight. I breakfast at eight. I don't suppose any one will be down except my mother."

"I am generally as early as that. I will come down and see you start."

"I am so glad that you have been here, Emily."

"So am I. Everybody has been so good to me."

"It has been like old days,—almost."

"It will never quite be like old days again, I think. But I have been very glad to be here,—and at Wharton. I sometimes almost wish that I were never going back to London again,—only for papa."

"I like London myself."

"You! Yes, of course you like London. You have everything in life before you. You have things to do, and much to hope for. It is all beginning for you, Arthur."

"I am five years older than you are."

"What does that matter? It seems to me that age does not go by years. It is long since I have felt myself to be an old woman. But you are quite young. Everybody is proud of you, and you ought to be happy."

"I don't know," said he. "It is hard to say what makes a person happy." He almost made up his mind to speak to her then; but he had made up his mind before to put it off still for a little time, and he would not allow himself to be changed on the spur of the moment. He had thought of it much, and he had almost taught himself to think that it would be better for herself that she should not accept another man's love so soon. "I shall come and see you in town," he said.

"You must come and see papa. It seems that Everett is to be a great deal at Wharton. I had better go up to dress now, or I shall be keeping them waiting." He put out his hand to her, and wished her good-bye, excusing himself by saying that they should not be alone together again before he started.

She saw him go on the next morning,—and then she almost felt herself to be abandoned, almost deserted. It was a fine crisp winter day, dry and fresh and clear, but with the frost still on the ground. After breakfast she went out to walk by herself in the long shrubbery paths which went round the house, and here she remained for above an hour. She told herself that she was very thankful to him for not having spoken to her on a subject so unfit for her ears as love. She strengthened herself in her determination never again to listen to a man willingly on that subject. She had made herself unfit to have any dealings of that nature. It was not that she could not love. Oh, no! She knew well enough that she did love,—love with all her heart. If it were not that she were so torn to rags that she was not fit to be worn again, she could now have thrown herself into his arms with a whole heaven of joy before her. A woman, she told herself, had no right to a second chance in life, after having made such a shipwreck of herself in the first. But the danger of being seduced from her judgment by Arthur Fletcher was all over. He had been near her for the last week and had not spoken a word. He had been in the same house with her for the last ten days and had been with her as a brother might be with his sister. It was not only she who had seen the propriety of this. He also had acknowledged it, and she was—grateful to him. As she endeavoured in her solitude to express her gratitude in spoken words the tears rolled down her cheeks. She was glad, she told herself, very glad that it was so. How much trouble and pain to both of them would thus be spared! And yet her tears were bitter tears. It was better as it was;—and yet one word of love would have been very sweet. She almost thought that she would have liked to tell him that for his sake, for his dear sake, she would refuse—that which now would never be offered to her. She was quite clear as to the rectitude of her own judgment, clear as ever. And yet her heart was heavy with disappointment.

It was the end of March before she left Herefordshire for London, having spent the greater part of the time at Longbarns. The ladies at that place were moved by many doubts as to what would be the end of all this. Mrs. Fletcher the elder at last almost taught herself to believe that there would be no marriage, and having got back to that belief, was again opposed to the idea of a marriage. Anything and everything that Arthur wanted he ought to have. The old lady felt no doubt as to that. When convinced that he did want to have this widow,—this woman whose life had hitherto been so unfortunate,—she had for his sake taken the woman again by the hand, and had assisted in making her one of themselves. But how much better it would be that Arthur should think better of it! It was the maddest constancy,—this clinging to the widow of such a man as Ferdinand Lopez! If there were any doubt, then she would be prepared to do all she could to prevent the marriage. Emily had been forgiven, and the pardon bestowed must of course be continued. But she might be pardoned without being made Mrs. Arthur Fletcher. While Emily was still at Longbarns the old lady almost talked over her daughter-in-law to this way of thinking,—till John Fletcher put his foot upon it altogether. "I don't pretend to say what she may do," he said.

"Oh, John," said the mother, "to hear a man like you talk like that is absurd. She'd jump at him if he looked at her with half an eye."

"What she may do," he continued saying, without appearing to listen to his mother, "I cannot say. But that he will ask her to be his wife is as certain as that I stand here."

Chapter LXXII
"He Thinks That Our Days Are Numbered"

All the details of the new County Suffrage Bill were settled at Matching during the recess between Mr. Monk, Phineas Finn, and a very experienced gentleman from the Treasury, one Mr. Prime, who was supposed to know more about such things than any man living, and was consequently called Constitution Charlie. He was an elderly man, over sixty years of age, who remembered the first Reform Bill, and had been engaged in the doctoring of constituencies ever since. The Bill, if passed, would be mainly his Bill, and yet the world would never hear his name as connected with it. Let us hope that he was comfortable at Matching, and that he found his consolation in the smiles of the Duchess. During this time the old Duke was away, and even the Prime Minister was absent for some days. He would fain have busied himself about the Bill himself, but was hardly allowed by his colleagues to have any hand in framing it. The great points of the measure had of course been arranged in the Cabinet,—where, however, Mr. Monk's views had been adopted almost without a change. It may not perhaps be too much to assume that one or two members of the Cabinet did not quite understand the full scope of every suggested clause. The effects which clauses will produce, the dangers which may be expected from this or that change, the manner in which this or that proposition will come out in the washing, do not strike even Cabinet Ministers at a glance. A little study in a man's own cabinet, after the reading perhaps of a few leading articles, and perhaps a short conversation with an astute friend or two, will enable a statesman to be strong at a given time for, or even, if necessary, against a measure, who has listened in silence, and has perhaps given his personal assent, to the original suggestion. I doubt whether Lord Drummond, when he sat silent in the Cabinet, had realised those fears which weighed upon him so strongly afterwards, or had then foreseen that the adoption of a nearly similar franchise for the counties and boroughs must inevitably lead to the American system of numerical representation. But when time had been given him, and he and Sir Timothy had talked it all over, the mind of no man was ever clearer than that of Lord Drummond.

The Prime Minister, with the diligence which belonged to him, had mastered all the details of Mr. Monk's Bill before it was discussed in the Cabinet, and yet he found that his assistance was hardly needed in the absolute preparation. Had they allowed him he would have done it all himself. But it was assumed that he would not trouble himself with such work, and he perceived that he was not wanted. Nothing of moment was settled without a reference to him. He required that everything should be explained as it went on, down to the extension of every borough boundary; but he knew that he was not doing it himself, and that Mr. Monk and Constitution Charlie had the prize between them.

Nor did he dare to ask Mr. Monk what would be the fate of the Bill. To devote all one's time and mind and industry to a measure which one knows will fall to the ground must be sad. Work under such circumstances must be very grievous. But such is often the fate of statesmen. Whether Mr. Monk laboured under such a conviction the Prime Minister did not know, though he saw his friend and colleague almost daily. In truth no one dared to tell him exactly what he thought. Even the old Duke had become partially reticent, and taken himself off to his own woods at Long Royston. To Phineas Finn the Prime Minister would sometimes say a word, but would say even that timidly. On any abstract question, such as that which he had discussed when they had been walking together, he could talk freely enough. But on the matter of the day, those affairs which were of infinite importance to himself, and on which one would suppose he would take delight in speaking to a trusted colleague, he could not bring himself to be open. "It must be a long Bill, I suppose?" he said to Phineas one day.

"I'm afraid so, Duke. It will run, I fear, to over a hundred clauses."

"It will take you the best part of the Session to get through it?"

"If we can have the second reading early in March, we hope to send it up to you in the first week in June. That will give us ample time."

"Yes;—yes. I suppose so." But he did not dare to ask Phineas Finn whether he thought that the House of Commons would assent to the second reading. It was known at this time that the Prime Minister was painfully anxious as to the fate of the Ministry. It seemed to be but the other day that everybody connected with the Government was living in fear lest he should resign. His threats in that direction had always been made to his old friend the Duke of St. Bungay; but a great man cannot whisper his thoughts without having them carried in the air. In all the clubs it had been declared that that was the rock by which the Coalition would probably be wrecked.

The newspapers had repeated the story, and the "People's Banner" had assured the world that if it were so the Duke of Omnium would thus do for his country the only good service which it was possible that he should render it. That was at the time when Sir Orlando was mutinous and when Lopez had destroyed himself. But now no such threat came from the Duke, and the "People's Banner" was already accusing him of clinging to power with pertinacious and unconstitutional tenacity. Had not Sir Orlando deserted him? Was it not well known that Lord Drummond and Sir Timothy Beeswax were only restrained from doing so by a mistaken loyalty?

Everybody came up to town, Mr. Monk having his Bill in his pocket, and the Queen's speech was read, promising the County Suffrage Bill. The address was voted with a very few words from either side. The battle was not to be fought then. Indeed, the state of things was so abnormal that there could hardly be said to be any sides in the House. A stranger in the gallery, not knowing the condition of affairs, would have thought that no minister had for many years commanded so large a majority, as the crowd of members was always on the Government side of the House; but the opposition which Mr. Monk expected would, he knew, come from those who sat around him, behind him, and even at his very elbow. About a week after Parliament met the Bill was read for the first time, and the second reading was appointed for an early day in March.

The Duke had suggested to Mr. Monk the expedience of some further delay, giving as his reason the necessity of getting through certain routine work, should the rejection of the Bill create the confusion of a resignation. No one who knew the Duke could ever suspect him of giving a false reason. But it seemed that in this the Prime Minister was allowing himself to be harassed by fears of the future. Mr. Monk thought that any delay would be injurious and open to suspicion after what had been said and done, and was urgent in his arguments. The Duke gave way, but he did so almost sullenly, signifying his acquiescence with haughty silence. "I am sorry," said Mr. Monk, "to differ from your Grace, but my opinion in the matter is so strong that I do not dare to abstain from expressing it." The Duke bowed again and smiled. He had intended that the smile should be acquiescent, but it had been as cold as steel. He knew that he was misbehaving, but was not sufficiently master of his own manner to be gracious. He told himself on the spot,—though he was quite wrong in so telling himself,—that he had now made an enemy also of Mr. Monk, and through Mr. Monk of Phineas Finn. And now he felt that he had no friend left in whom to trust,—for the old Duke had become cold and indifferent. The old Duke, he thought, was tired of his work and anxious for rest. It was the old Duke who had brought him into this hornets' nest; had fixed upon his back the unwilling load; had compelled him to assume the place which now to lose would be a disgrace,—and the old Duke was now deserting him! He was sore all over, angry with every one, ungracious even with his private Secretary and his wife,—and especially miserable because he was thoroughly aware of his own faults. And yet, through it all, there was present to him a desire to fight on to the very last. Let his colleagues do what they might, and say what they might, he would remain Prime Minister of England as long as he was supported by a majority of the House of Commons.

"I do not know any greater step than this," Phineas said to him pleasantly one day, speaking of their new measure, "towards that millennium of which we were talking at Matching, if we can only accomplish it."

"Those moral speculations, Mr. Finn," he said, "will hardly bear the wear and tear of real life." The words of the answer, combined with the manner in which they were spoken, were stern and almost uncivil. Phineas, at any rate, had done nothing to offend him. The Duke paused, trying to find some expression by which he might correct the injury he had done; but, not finding any, passed on without further speech. Phineas shrugged his shoulders and went his way, telling himself that he had received one further injunction not to put his trust in princes.

"We shall be beaten, certainly," said Mr. Monk to Phineas, not long afterwards.

"What makes you so sure?"

"I smell it in the air. I see it in men's faces."

"And yet it's a moderate Bill. They'll have to pass something stronger before long if they throw it out now."

"It's not the Bill that they'll reject, but us. We have served our turn, and we ought to go."

"The House is tired of the Duke?"

"The Duke is so good a man that I hardly like to admit even that;—but I fear it is so. He is fretful and he makes enemies."

"I sometimes think that he is ill."

"He is ill at ease and sick at heart. He cannot hide his chagrin, and then is doubly wretched because he has betrayed it. I do not know that I ever respected and, at the same time, pitied a man more thoroughly."

"He snubbed me awfully yesterday," said Phineas, laughing.

"He cannot help himself. He snubs me at every word that he speaks, and yet I believe that he is most anxious to be civil to me. His ministry has been of great service to the country. For myself, I shall never regret having joined it. But I think that to him it has been a continual sorrow."

The system on which the Duchess had commenced her career as wife of the Prime Minister had now been completely abandoned. In the first place, she had herself become so weary of it that she had been unable to continue the exertion. She had, too, become in some degree ashamed of her failures. The names of Major Pountney and Mr. Lopez were not now pleasant to her ears, nor did she look back with satisfaction on the courtesies she had lavished on Sir Orlando or the smiles she had given to Sir Timothy Beeswax. "I've known a good many vulgar people in my time," she said one day to Mrs. Finn, "but none ever so vulgar as our ministerial supporters. You don't remember Mr. Bott, my dear. He was before your time;—one of the arithmetical men, and a great friend of Plantagenet's. He was very bad, but there have come up worse since him. Sometimes, I think, I like a little vulgarity for a change; but, upon my honour, when we get rid of all this it will be a pleasure to go back to ladies and gentlemen." This the Duchess said in her extreme bitterness.

"It seems to me that you have pretty well got rid of 'all this' already."

"But I haven't got anybody else in their place. I have almost made up my mind not to ask any one into the house for the next twelve months. I used to think that nothing would ever knock me up, but now I feel that I'm almost done for. I hardly dare open my mouth to Plantagenet. The Duke of St. Bungay has cut me. Mr. Monk looks as ominous as an owl; and your husband hasn't a word to say left. Barrington Erle hides his face and passes by when he sees me. Mr. Rattler did try to comfort me the other day by saying that everything was at sixes and sevens, and I really took it almost as a compliment to be spoken to. Don't you think Plantagenet is ill?"

"He is careworn."

"A man may be worn by care till there comes to be nothing left of him. But he never speaks of giving up now. The old Bishop of St. Austell talks of resigning, and he has already made up his mind who is to have the see. He used to consult the Duke about all these things, but I don't think he ever consults any one now. He never forgave the Duke about Lord Earlybird. Certainly, if a man wants to quarrel with all his friends, and to double the hatred of all his enemies, he had better become Prime Minister."

"Are you really sorry that such was his fate, Lady Glen?"

"Ah,—I sometimes ask myself that question, but I never get at an answer. I should have thought him a poltroon if he had declined. It is to be the greatest man in the greatest country in the world. Do ever so little and the men who write history must write about you. And no man has ever tried to be nobler than he till,—till—."

"Make no exception. If he be careworn and ill and weary, his manners cannot be the same as they were, but his purity is the same as ever."

"I don't know that it would remain so. I believe in him, Marie, more than in any man,—but I believe in none thoroughly. There is a devil creeps in upon them when their hands are strengthened. I do not know what I would have wished. Whenever I do wish, I always wish wrong. Ah, me; when I think of all those people I had down at Gatherum,—of the trouble I took, and of the glorious anticipations in which I revelled, I do feel ashamed of myself. Do you remember when I was determined that that wretch should be member for Silverbridge?"

"You haven't seen her since, Duchess?"

"No; but I mean to see her. I couldn't make her first husband member, and therefore the man who is member is to be her second husband. But I'm almost sick of schemes. Oh, dear, I wish I knew something that was really pleasant to do. I have never really enjoyed anything since I was in love, and I only liked that because it was wicked."

The Duchess was wrong in saying that the Duke of St. Bungay had cut them. The old man still remembered the kiss and still remembered the pledge. But he had found it very difficult to maintain his old relations with his friend. It was his opinion that the Coalition had done all that was wanted from it, and that now had come the time when they might retire gracefully. It is, no doubt, hard for a Prime Minister to find an excuse for going. But if the Duke of Omnium would have been content to acknowledge that he was not the man to alter the County Suffrage, an excuse might have been found that would have been injurious to no one. Mr. Monk and Mr. Gresham might have joined, and the present Prime Minister might have resigned, explaining that he had done all that he had been appointed to accomplish. He had, however, yielded at once to Mr. Monk, and now it was to be feared that the House of Commons would not accept the Bill from his hands. In such a state of things,—especially after that disagreement about Lord Earlybird,—it was difficult for the old Duke to tender his advice. He was at every Cabinet Council; he always came when his presence was required; he was invariably good-humoured;—but it seemed to him that his work was done. He could hardly volunteer to tell his chief and his colleague that he would certainly be beaten in the House of Commons, and that therefore there was little more now to be done than to arrange the circumstances of their retirement. Nevertheless, as the period for the second reading of the Bill came on, he resolved that he would discuss the matter with his friend. He owed it to himself to do so, and he also owed it to the man whom he had certainly placed in his present position. On himself politics had imposed a burden very much lighter than that which they had inflicted on his more energetic and much less practical colleague. Through his long life he had either been in office, or in such a position that men were sure that he would soon return to it. He had taken it, when it had come, willingly, and had always left it without a regret. As a man cuts in and out at a whist table, and enjoys both the game and the rest from the game, so had the Duke of St. Bungay been well pleased in either position. He was patriotic, but his patriotism did not disturb his digestion. He had been ambitious,—but moderately ambitious, and his ambition had been gratified. It never occurred to him to be unhappy because he or his party were beaten on a measure. When President of the Council, he could do his duty and enjoy London life. When in opposition, he could linger in Italy till May and devote his leisure to his trees and his bullocks. He was always esteemed, always self-satisfied, and always Duke of St. Bungay. But with our Duke it was very different. Patriotism with him was a fever, and the public service an exacting mistress. As long as this had been all he had still been happy. Not trusting much in himself, he had never aspired to great power. But now, now at last, ambition had laid hold of him,—and the feeling, not perhaps uncommon with such men, that personal dishonour would be attached to political failure. What would his future life be if he had so carried himself in his great office as to have shown himself to be unfit to resume it? Hitherto any office had sufficed him in which he might be useful;—but now he must either be Prime Minister, or a silent, obscure, and humbled man!

Dear Duke,

I will be with you to-morrow morning at 11 a.m., if you can give me half-an-hour.

Yours affectionately,

St. B.

The Prime Minister received this note one afternoon, a day or two before that appointed for the second reading, and meeting his friend within an hour in the House of Lords, confirmed the appointment. "Shall I not rather come to you?" he said. But the old Duke, who lived in St. James's Square, declared that Carlton Terrace would be in his way to Downing Street; and so the matter was settled. Exactly at eleven the two Ministers met. "I don't like troubling you," said the old man, "when I know that you have so much to think of."

"On the contrary, I have but little to think of,—and my thoughts must be very much engaged, indeed, when they shall be too full to admit of my seeing you."

"Of course we are all anxious about this Bill." The Prime Minister smiled. Anxious! Yes, indeed. His anxiety was of such a nature that it kept him awake all night, and never for a moment left his mind free by day. "And of course we must be prepared as to what shall be done either in the event of success or of failure."

"You might as well read that," said the other. "It only reached me this morning, or I should have told you of it." The letter was a communication from the Solicitor-General containing his resignation. He had now studied the County Suffrage Bill closely, and regretted to say that he could not give it a conscientious support. It was a matter of sincerest sorrow to him that relations so pleasant should be broken, but he must resign his place, unless, indeed, the clauses as to redistribution could be withdrawn. Of course he did not say this as expecting that any such concession would be made to his opinion, but merely as indicating the matter on which his objection was so strong as to over-rule all other considerations. All this he explained at great length.

"The pleasantness of the relations must have been on one side," said the veteran. "He ought to have gone long since."

"And Lord Drummond has already as good as said that unless we will abandon the same clauses, he must oppose the Bill in the Lords."

"And resign, of course."

"He meant that, I presume. Lord Ramsden has not spoken to me."

"The clauses will not stick in his throat. Nor ought they. If the lawyers have their own way about law they should be contented."

"The question is, whether in these circumstances we should postpone the second reading?" asked the Prime Minister.

"Certainly not," said the other Duke. "As to the Solicitor-General you will have no difficulty. Sir Timothy was only placed there as a concession to his party. Drummond will no doubt continue to hold his office till we see what is done in the Lower House. If the second reading be lost there,—why then his lordship can go with the rest of us."

"Rattler says we shall have a majority. He and Roby are quite agreed about it. Between them they must know," said the Prime Minister, unintentionally pleading for himself.

"They ought to know, if any men do;—but the crisis is exceptional. I suppose you think that if the second reading is lost we should resign?"

"Oh,—certainly."

"Or, after that, if the Bill be much mutilated in Committee? I don't know that I shall personally break my own heart about the Bill. The existing difference in the suffrages is rather in accordance with my prejudices. But the country desires the measure, and I suppose we cannot consent to any such material alteration as these men suggest." As he spoke he laid his hand on Sir Timothy's letter.

"Mr. Monk would not hear of it," said the Prime Minister.

"Of course not. And you and I in this measure must stick to Mr. Monk. My great, indeed my only strong desire in the matter, is to act in strict unison with you."

"You are always good and true, Duke."

"For my own part I shall not in the least regret to find in all this an opportunity of resigning. We have done our work, and if, as I believe, a majority of the House would again support either Gresham or Monk as the head of the entire Liberal party, I think that that arrangement would be for the welfare of the country."

"Why should it make any difference to you? Why should you not return to the Council?"

"I should not do so;—certainly not at once; probably never. But you,— who are in the very prime of your life—"

The Prime Minister did not smile now. He knit his brows and a dark shadow came across his face. "I don't think I could do that," he said. "Cæsar could hardly have led a legion under Pompey."

"It has been done, greatly to the service of the country, and without the slightest loss of honour or character in him who did it."

"We need hardly talk of that, Duke. You think then that we shall fail;— fail, I mean, in the House of Commons. I do not know that failure in our House should be regarded as fatal."

"In three cases we should fail. The loss of any material clause in Committee would be as bad as the loss of the Bill."

"Oh, yes."

"And then, in spite of Messrs. Rattler and Roby,—who have been wrong before and may be wrong now,—we may lose the second reading."

"And the third chance against us?"

"You would not probably try to carry on the Bill with a very small majority."

"Not with three or four."

"Nor, I think, with six or seven. It would be useless. My own belief is that we shall never carry the Bill into Committee."

"I have always known you to be right, Duke."

"I think that general opinion has set in that direction, and general opinion is generally right. Having come to that conclusion I thought it best to tell you, in order that we might have our house in order." The Duke of Omnium, who with all his haughtiness and all his reserve, was the simplest man in the world and the least apt to pretend to be that which he was not, sighed deeply when he heard this. "For my own part," continued his elder, "I feel no regret that it should be so."

"It is the first large measure that we have tried to carry."

"We did not come in to carry large measures, my friend. Look back and see how many large measures Pitt carried,—but he took the country safely through its most dangerous crisis."

"What have we done?"

"Carried on the Queen's Government prosperously for three years. Is that nothing for a minister to do? I have never been a friend of great measures, knowing that when they come fast, one after another, more is broken in the rattle than is repaired by the reform. We have done what Parliament and the country expected us to do, and to my poor judgment we have done it well."

"I do not feel much self-satisfaction, Duke. Well;—we must see it out, and if it is as you anticipate, I shall be ready. Of course I have prepared myself for it. And if, of late, my mind has been less turned to retirement than it used to be, it has only been because I have become wedded to this measure, and have wished that it should be carried under our auspices." Then the old Duke took his leave, and the Prime Minister was left alone to consider the announcement that had been made to him.

He had said that he had prepared himself, but, in so saying, he had hardly known himself. Hitherto, though he had been troubled by many doubts, he had still hoped. The report made to him by Mr. Rattler, backed as it had been by Mr. Roby's assurances, had almost sufficed to give him confidence. But Mr. Rattler and Mr. Roby combined were as nothing to the Duke of St. Bungay. The Prime Minister knew now,—he felt that he knew, that his days were numbered. The resignation of that lingering old bishop was not completed, and the person in whom he believed would not have the see. He had meditated the making of a peer or two, having hitherto been very cautious in that respect, but he would do nothing of the kind if called upon by the House of Commons to resign with an uncompleted measure. But his thoughts soon ran away from the present to the future. What was now to come of himself? How should he use his future life,—he who as yet had not passed his forty-seventh year? He regretted much having made that apparently pretentious speech about Cæsar, though he knew his old friend well enough to be sure that it would never be used against him. Who was he that he should class himself among the big ones of the world? A man may indeed measure small things by great, but the measurer should be careful to declare his own littleness when he illustrates his position by that of the topping ones of the earth. But the thing said had been true. Let the Pompey be who he might, he, the little Cæsar of the day, could never now command another legion.

He had once told Phineas Finn that he regretted that he had abstained from the ordinary amusements of English gentlemen. But he had abstained also from their ordinary occupations,—except so far as politics is one of them. He cared nothing for oxen or for furrows. In regard to his own land he hardly knew whether the farms were large or small. He had been a scholar, and after a certain fitful fashion he had maintained his scholarship, but the literature to which he had been really attached had been that of blue-books and newspapers. What was he to do with himself when called upon to resign? And he understood,—or thought that he understood,—his position too well to expect that after a while, with the usual interval, he might return to power. He had been Prime Minister, not as the leading politician on either side, not as the king of a party, but,—so he told himself,—as a stopgap. There could be nothing for him now till the insipidity of life should gradually fade away into the grave.

After a while he got up and went off to his wife's apartment, the room in which she used to prepare her triumphs and where now she contemplated her disappointments. "I have had the Duke with me," he said.

"What;—at last?"

"I do not know that he could have done any good by coming sooner."

"And what does his Grace say?"

"He thinks that our days are numbered."

"Psha!—is that all? I could have told him that ever so long ago. It was hardly necessary that he should disturb himself at last to come and tell us such well-ventilated news. There isn't a porter at one of the clubs who doesn't know it."

"Then there will be the less surprise,—and to those who are concerned perhaps the less mortification."

"Did he tell you who was to succeed you?" asked the Duchess.

"Not precisely."

"He ought to have done that, as I am sure he knows. Everybody knows except you, Plantagenet."

"If you know, you can tell me."

"Of course, I can. It will be Mr. Monk."

"With all my heart, Glencora. Mr. Monk is a very good man."

"I wonder whether he'll do anything for us. Think how destitute we shall be! What if I were to ask him for a place! Would he not give it us?"

"Will it make you unhappy, Cora?"

"What;—your going?"

"Yes;—the change altogether."

She looked him in the face for a moment before she answered, with a peculiar smile in her eyes to which he was well used,—a smile half ludicrous and half pathetic,—having in it also a dash of sarcasm. "I can dare to tell the truth," she said, "which you can't. I can be honest and straightforward. Yes, it will make me unhappy. And you?"

"Do you think that I cannot be honest too,—at any rate to you? It does fret me. I do not like to think that I shall be without work."

"Yes;—Othello's occupation will be gone,—for awhile; for awhile." Then she came up to him and put both her hands on his breast. "But yet, Othello, I shall not be all unhappy."

"Where will be your contentment?"

"In you. It was making you ill. Rough people, whom the tenderness of your nature could not well endure, trod upon you, and worried you with their teeth and wounded you everywhere. I could have turned at them again with my teeth, and given them worry for worry;—but you could not. Now you will be saved from them, and so I shall not be discontented." All this she said looking up into his face, still with that smile which was half pathetic and half ludicrous.

"Then I will be contented too," he said as he kissed her.

Chapter LXXIII
Only the Duke of Omnium

The night of the debate arrived, but before the debate was commenced Sir Timothy Beeswax got up to make a personal explanation. He thought it right to state to the House how it came to pass that he found himself bound to leave the Ministry at so important a crisis in its existence. Then an observation was made by an honourable member of the Government,— presumably in a whisper, but still loud enough to catch the sharp ears of Sir Timothy, who now sat just below the gangway. It was said afterwards that the gentleman who made the observation,—an Irish gentleman named Fitzgibbon, conspicuous rather for his loyalty to his party than his steadiness,—had purposely taken the place in which he then sat, that Sir Timothy might hear the whisper. The whisper suggested that falling houses were often left by certain animals. It was certainly a very loud whisper,— but, if gentlemen are to be allowed to whisper at all, it is almost impossible to restrain the volume of the voice. To restrain Mr. Fitzgibbon had always been found difficult. Sir Timothy, who did not lack pluck, turned at once upon his assailant, and declared that words had been used with reference to himself which the honourable member did not dare to get upon his legs and repeat. Larry Fitzgibbon, as the gentleman was called, looked him full in the face, but did not move his hat from his head or stir a limb. It was a pleasant little episode in the evening's work, and afforded satisfaction to the House generally. Then Sir Timothy went on with his explanation. The details of this measure, as soon as they were made known to him, appeared to him, he said, to be fraught with the gravest and most pernicious consequences. He was sure that the members of her Majesty's Government, who were hurrying on this measure with what he thought was indecent haste,—ministers are always either indecent in their haste or treacherous in their delay,—had not considered what they were doing, or, if they had considered, were blind as to its results. He then attempted to discuss the details of the measure, but was called to order. A personal explanation could not be allowed to give him an opportunity of anticipating the debate. He contrived, however, before he sat down, to say some very heavy things against his late chief, and especially to congratulate the Duke on the services of the honourable gentleman, the member for Mayo,—meaning thereby Mr. Laurence Fitzgibbon.

It would perhaps have been well for everybody if the measure could have been withdrawn and the Ministry could have resigned without the debate,—as everybody was convinced what would be the end of it. Let the second reading go as it might, the Bill could not be carried. There are measures which require the hopeful heartiness of a new Ministry, and the thorough-going energy of a young Parliament,—and this was one of them. The House was as fully agreed that this change was necessary, as it ever is agreed on any subject,—but still the thing could not be done. Even Mr. Monk, who was the most earnest of men, felt the general slackness of all around him. The commotion and excitement which would be caused by a change of Ministry might restore its proper tone to the House, but in its present condition it was unfit for the work. Nevertheless Mr. Monk made his speech, and put all his arguments into lucid order. He knew it was for nothing, but nevertheless it must be done. For hour after hour he went on,— for it was necessary to give every detail of his contemplated proposition. He went through it as sedulously as though he had expected to succeed, and sat down about nine o'clock in the evening. Then Sir Orlando moved the adjournment of the House till the morrow, giving as his reason for doing so the expedience of considering the details he had heard. To this no opposition was made, and the House was adjourned.

On the following day the clubs were all alive with rumours as to the coming debate. It was known that a strong party had been formed under the auspices of Sir Orlando, and that with him Sir Timothy and other politicians were in close council. It was of course necessary that they should impart to many the secrets of their conclave, so that it was known early in the afternoon that it was the intention of the Opposition not to discuss the Bill, but to move that it be read a second time that day six months. The Ministry had hardly expected this, as the Bill was undoubtedly popular both in the House and the country; and if the Opposition should be beaten in such a course, that defeat would tend greatly to strengthen the hands of the Government. But if the foe could succeed in carrying a positive veto on the second reading, it would under all the circumstances be tantamount to a vote of want of confidence. "I'm afraid they know almost more than we do as to the feeling of members," said Mr. Roby to Mr. Rattler.

"There isn't a man in the House whose feeling in the matter I don't know," said Rattler, "but I'm not quite so sure of their principles. On our own side, in our old party, there are a score of men who detest the Duke, though they would fain be true to the Government. They have voted with him through thick and thin, and he has not spoken a word to one of them since he became Prime Minister. What are you to do with such a man? How are you to act with him?"

"Lupton wrote to him the other day about something," answered the other, "I forget what, and he got a note back from Warburton as cold as ice,—an absolute slap in the face. Fancy treating a man like Lupton in that way,—one of the most popular men in the House, related to half the peerage, and a man who thinks so much of himself! I shouldn't wonder if he were to vote against us;—I shouldn't indeed."

"It has all been the old Duke's doing," said Rattler, "and no doubt it was intended for the best; but the thing has been a failure from the beginning to the end. I knew it would be so. I don't think there has been a single man who has understood what a Ministerial Coalition really means except you and I. From the very beginning all your men were averse to it in spirit."

"Look how they were treated!" said Mr. Roby. "Was it likely that they should be very staunch when Mr. Monk became Leader of the House?"

There was a Cabinet Council that day which lasted but a few minutes, and it may easily be presumed that the Ministers decided that they would all resign at once if Sir Orlando should carry his amendment. It is not unlikely that they were agreed to do the same if he should nearly carry it,— leaving probably the Prime Minister to judge what narrow majority would constitute nearness. On this occasion all the gentlemen assembled were jocund in their manner, and apparently well satisfied,—as though they saw before them an end to all their troubles. The Spartan boy did not even make a grimace when the wolf bit him beneath his frock, and these were all Spartan boys. Even the Prime Minister, who had fortified himself for the occasion, and who never wept in any company but that of his wife and his old friend, was pleasant in his manner and almost affable. "We shan't make this step towards the millennium just at present," he said to Phineas Finn as they left the room together,—referring to words which Phineas had spoken on a former occasion, and which then had not been very well taken.

"But we shall have made a step towards the step," said Phineas, "and in getting to a millennium even that is something."

"I suppose we are all too anxious," said the Duke, "to see some great effects come from our own little doings. Good-day. We shall know all about it tolerably early. Monk seems to think that it will be an attack on the Ministry and not on the Bill, and that it will be best to get a vote with as little delay as possible."

"I'll bet an even five-pound note," said Mr. Lupton at the Carlton, "that the present Ministry is out to-morrow, and another that no one names five members of the next Cabinet."

"You can help to win your first bet," said Mr. Beauchamp, a very old member, who, like many other Conservatives, had supported the Coalition.

"I shall not do that," said Lupton, "though I think I ought. I won't vote against the man in his misfortunes, though, upon my soul, I don't love him very dearly. I shall vote neither way, but I hope that Sir Orlando may succeed."

"If he do, who is to come in?" said the other. "I suppose you don't want to serve under Sir Orlando?"

"Nor certainly under the Duke of Omnium. We shall not want a Prime Minister as long as there are as good fish in the sea as have been caught out of it."

There had lately been formed a new Liberal club, established on a broader basis than the Progress, and perhaps with a greater amount of aristocratic support. This had come up since the Duke had been Prime Minister. Certain busy men had never been quite contented with the existing state of things, and had thought that the Liberal party, with such assistance as such a club could give it, would be strong enough to rule alone. That the great Liberal party should be impeded in its work and its triumph by such men as Sir Orlando Drought and Sir Timothy Beeswax was odious to the club. All the Pallisers had, from time immemorial, run straight as Liberals, and therefore the club had been unwilling to oppose the Duke personally, though he was the chief of the Coalition. And certain members of the Government, Phineas Finn, for instance, Barrington Erle, and Mr. Rattler were on the committee of the club. But the club, as a club, was not averse to a discontinuance of the present state of things. Mr. Gresham might again become Prime Minister, if he would condescend so far, or Mr. Monk. It might be possible that the great Liberal triumph contemplated by the club might not be achieved by the present House;—but the present House must go shortly, and then, with that assistance from a well-organised club, which had lately been so terribly wanting,—the lack of which had made the Coalition necessary,—no doubt the British constituencies would do their duty, and a Liberal Prime Minister, pure and simple, might reign,—almost for ever. With this great future before it, the club was very lukewarm in its support of the present Bill. "I shall go down and vote for them of course," said Mr. O'Mahony, "just for the look of the thing." In saying this Mr. O'Mahony expressed the feeling of the club, and the feeling of the Liberal party generally. There was something due to the Duke, but not enough to make it incumbent on his friends to maintain him in his position as Prime Minister.

It was a great day for Sir Orlando. At half-past four the House was full,—not from any desire to hear Sir Orlando's arguments against the Bill, but because it was felt that a good deal of personal interest would be attached to the debate. If one were asked in these days what gift should a Prime Minister ask first from the fairies, one would name the power of attracting personal friends. Eloquence, if it be too easy, may become almost a curse. Patriotism is suspected, and sometimes sinks almost to pedantry. A Jove-born intellect is hardly wanted, and clashes with the inferiorities. Industry is exacting. Honesty is unpractical. Truth is easily offended. Dignity will not bend. But the man who can be all things to all men, who has ever a kind word to speak, a pleasant joke to crack, who can forgive all sins, who is ever prepared for friend or foe but never very bitter to the latter, who forgets not men's names, and is always ready with little words,—he is the man who will be supported at a crisis such as this that was now in the course of passing. It is for him that men will struggle, and talk, and, if needs be, fight, as though the very existence of the country depended on his political security. The present man would receive no such defence;—but still the violent deposition of a Prime Minister is always a memorable occasion.

Sir Orlando made his speech, and, as had been anticipated, it had very little to do with the Bill, and was almost exclusively an attack upon his late chief. He thought, he said, that this was an occasion on which they had better come to a direct issue with as little delay as possible. If he rightly read the feeling of the House, no Bill of this magnitude coming from the present Ministry would be likely to be passed in an efficient condition. The Duke had frittered away his support in that House, and as a Minister had lost that confidence which a majority of the House had once been willing to place in him. We need not follow Sir Orlando through his speech. He alluded to his own services, and declared that he was obliged to withdraw them because the Duke would not trust him with the management of his own office. He had reason to believe that other gentlemen who had attached themselves to the Duke's Ministry had found themselves equally crippled by this passion for autocratic rule. Hereupon a loud chorus of disapprobation came from the Treasury bench, which was fully answered by opposing noises from the other side of the House. Sir Orlando declared that he need only point to the fact that the Ministry had been already shivered by the secession of various gentlemen. "Only two," said a voice. Sir Orlando was turning round to contradict the voice when he was greeted by another. "And those the weakest," said the other voice, which was indubitably that of Larry Fitzgibbon. "I will not speak of myself," said Sir Orlando pompously; "but I am authorised to tell the House that the noble lord who is now Secretary of State for the Colonies only holds his office till this crisis shall have passed."

After that there was some sparring of a very bitter kind between Sir Timothy and Phineas Finn, till at last it seemed that the debate was to degenerate into a war of man against man. Phineas, and Erle, and Laurence Fitzgibbon allowed themselves to be lashed into anger, and, as far as words went, had the best of it. But of what use could it be? Every man there had come into the House prepared to vote for or against the Duke of Omnium, — or resolved, like Mr. Lupton, not to vote at all; and it was hardly on the cards that a single vote should be turned this way or that by any violence of speaking. "Let it pass," said Mr. Monk in a whisper to Phineas. "The fire is not worth the fuel."

"I know the Duke's faults," said Phineas; "but these men know nothing of his virtues, and when I hear them abuse him I cannot stand it."

Early in the night, — before twelve o'clock, — the House divided, and even at the moment of the division no one quite knew how it would go. There would be many who would of course vote against the amendment as being simply desirous of recording their opinion in favour of the Bill generally. And there were some who thought that Sir Orlando and his followers had been too forward, and too confident of their own standing in the House, in trying so violent a mode of opposition. It would have been better, these men thought, to have insured success by a gradual and persistent opposition to the Bill itself. But they hardly knew how thoroughly men may be alienated by silence and a cold demeanour. Sir Orlando on the division was beaten, but was beaten only by nine. "He can't go on with his Bill," said Rattler in one of the lobbies of the House. "I defy him. The House wouldn't stand it, you know." "No minister," said Roby, "could carry a measure like that with a majority of nine on a vote of confidence!" The House was of course adjourned, and Mr. Monk went at once to Carlton Terrace.

"I wish it had only been three or four," said the Duke, laughing.

"Why so?"

"Because there would have been less doubt."

"Is there any at present?"

"Less possibility for doubt, I will say. You would not wish to make the attempt with such a majority?"

"I could not do it, Duke!"

"I quite agree with you. But there will be those who will say that the attempt might be made,—who will accuse us of being faint-hearted because we do not make it."

"They will be men who understand nothing of the temper of the House."

"Very likely. But still, I wish the majority had only been two or three. There is little more to be said, I suppose."

"Very little, your Grace."

"We had better meet to-morrow at two, and, if possible, I will see her Majesty in the afternoon. Good night, Mr. Monk."

"Good night, Duke."

"My reign is ended. You are a good deal an older man than I, and yet probably yours has yet to begin." Mr. Monk smiled and shook his head as he left the room, not trusting himself to discuss so large a subject at so late an hour of the night.

Without waiting a moment after his colleague's departure, the Prime Minister,—for he was still Prime Minister,—went into his wife's room, knowing that she was waiting up till she should hear the result of the division, and there he found Mrs. Finn with her. "Is it over?" asked the Duchess.

"Yes;—there has been a division. Mr. Monk has just been with me."

"Well!"

"We have beaten them, of course, as we always do," said the Duke, attempting to be pleasant. "You didn't suppose there was anything to fear?

Your husband has always bid you keep up your courage;—has he not, Mrs. Finn?"

"My husband has lost his senses, I think," she said. "He has taken to such storming and raving about his political enemies that I hardly dare to open my mouth."

"Tell me what has been done, Plantagenet," ejaculated the Duchess.

"Don't you be as unreasonable as Mrs. Finn, Cora. The House has voted against Sir Orlando's amendment by a majority of nine."

"Only nine!"

"And I shall cease to be Prime Minister to-morrow."

"You don't mean to say that it's settled?"

"Quite settled. The play has been played, and the curtain has fallen, and the lights are being put out, and the poor weary actors may go home to bed."

"But on such an amendment surely any majority would have done."

"No, my dear. I will not name a number, but nine certainly would not do."

"And it is all over?"

"My Ministry is all over, if you mean that."

"Then everything is over for me. I shall settle down in the country and build cottages, and mix draughts. You, Marie, will still be going up the tree. If Mr. Finn manages well he may come to be Prime Minister some day."

"He has hardly such ambition, Lady Glen."

"The ambition will come fast enough;—will it not, Plantagenet? Let him once begin to dream of it as possible, and the desire will soon be strong enough. How should you feel if it were so?"

"It is quite impossible," said Mrs. Finn, gravely.

"I don't see why anything is impossible. Sir Orlando will be Prime Minister now, and Sir Timothy Beeswax Lord Chancellor. After that anybody may hope to be anything. Well,—I suppose we may go to bed. Is your carriage here, my dear?"

"I hope so."

"Ring the bell, Plantagenet, for somebody to see her down. Come to lunch to-morrow because I shall have so many groans to utter. What beasts, what brutes, what ungrateful wretches men are!—worse than women when they get together in numbers enough to be bold. Why have they deserted you? What have we not done for them? Think of all the new bedroom furniture that we sent to Gatherum merely to keep the party together. There were thousands of yards of linen, and it has all been of no use. Don't you feel like Wolsey, Plantagenet?"

"Not in the least, my dear. No one will take anything away from me that is my own."

"For me, I am almost as much divorced as Catherine, and have had my head cut off as completely as Anne Bullen and the rest of them. Go away, Marie, because I am going to have a cry by myself."

The Duke himself on that night put Mrs. Finn into her carriage; and as he walked with her downstairs he asked her whether she believed the Duchess to be in earnest in her sorrow. "She so mixes up her mirth and woe together," said the Duke, "that I myself sometimes can hardly understand her."

"I think she does regret it, Duke."

"She told me but the other day that she would be contented."

"A few weeks will make her so. As for your Grace, I hope I may congratulate you."

"Oh yes;—I think so. We none of us like to be beaten when we have taken a thing in hand. There is always a little disappointment at first. But, upon the whole, it is better as it is. I hope it will not make your husband unhappy."

"Not for his own sake. He will go again into the middle of the scramble and fight on one side or the other. For my own part I think opposition the pleasantest. Good night, Duke. I am so sorry that I should have troubled you."

Then he went alone to his own room, and sat there without moving for a couple of hours. Surely it was a great thing to have been Prime Minister of England for three years,—a prize of which nothing now could rob him. He ought not to be unhappy; and yet he knew himself to be wretched and disappointed. It had never occurred to him to be proud of being a duke, or to think of his wealth otherwise than a chance incident of his life, advantageous indeed, but by no means a source of honour. And he had been aware that he had owed his first seat in Parliament to his birth, and probably also his first introduction to official life. An heir to a dukedom, if he will only work hard, may almost with certainty find himself received into one or the other regiment in Downing Street. It had not in his early days been with him as it had with his friends Mr. Monk and Phineas Finn, who had worked their way from the very ranks. But even a duke cannot become Prime Minister by favour. Surely he had done something of which he might be proud. And so he tried to console himself.

But to have done something was nothing to him,—nothing to his personal happiness,—unless there was also something left for him to do. How should it be with him now,—how for the future? Would men ever listen to him again, or allow him again to work in their behoof, as he used to do in his happy days in the House of Commons? He feared that it was all over for him, and that for the rest of his days he must simply be the Duke of Omnium.

Chapter LXXIV
"I Am Disgraced and Shamed"

Soon after the commencement of the Session Arthur Fletcher became a constant visitor in Manchester Square, dining with the old barrister almost constantly on Sundays, and not unfrequently on other days when the House and his general engagements would permit it. Between him and Emily's father there was no secret and no misunderstanding. Mr. Wharton quite understood that the young member of Parliament was earnestly purposed to marry his daughter, and Fletcher was sure of all the assistance and support which Mr. Wharton could give him. The name of Lopez was very rarely used between them. It had been tacitly agreed that there was no need that it should be mentioned. The man had come like a destroying angel between them and their fondest hopes. Neither could ever be what he would have been had that man never appeared to destroy their happiness. But the man had gone away, not without a tragedy that was appalling;— and each thought that, as regarded him, he and the tragedy might be, if not forgotten at least put aside, if only that other person in whom they were interested could be taught to seem to forget him. "It is not love," said the father, "but a feeling of shame." Arthur Fletcher shook his head, not quite agreeing with this. It was not that he feared that she loved the memory of her late husband. Such love was, he thought, impossible. But there was, he believed, something more than the feeling which her father described as shame. There was pride also;—a determination in her own bosom not to confess the fault she had made in giving herself to him whom she must now think to have been so much the least worthy of her two suitors. "Her fortune will not be what I once promised you," said the old man plaintively.

"I do not remember that I ever asked you as to her fortune," Arthur replied.

"Certainly not. If you had I should not have told you. But as I named a sum, it is right that I should explain to you that that man succeeded in lessening it by six or seven thousand pounds."

"If that were all!"

"And I have promised Sir Alured that Everett, as his heir, should have the use of a considerable portion of his share without waiting for my death. It is odd that the one of my children from whom I certainly expected the greater trouble should have fallen so entirely on his feet; and that the other—; well, let us hope for the best. Everett seems to have taken up with Wharton as though it belonged to him already. And Emily—! Well, my dear boy, let us hope that it may come right yet. You are not drinking your wine. Yes,—pass the bottle; I'll have another glass before I go upstairs."

In this way the time went by till Emily returned to town. The Ministry had just then resigned, but I think that "this great reactionary success," as it was called by the writer in the "People's Banner," affected one member of the Lower House much less than the return to London of Mrs. Lopez. Arthur Fletcher had determined that he would renew his suit as soon as a year should have expired since the tragedy which had made his love a widow,—and that year had now passed away. He had known the day well,—as had she, when she passed the morning weeping in her own room at Wharton. Now he questioned himself whether a year would suffice,—whether both in mercy to her and with the view of realizing his own hopes he should give her some longer time for recovery. But he had told himself that it should be done at the end of a year, and as he had allowed no one to talk him out of his word, so neither would he be untrue to it himself. But it became with him a deep matter of business, a question of great difficulty, how he should arrange the necessary interview,—whether he should plead his case with her at their first meeting, or whether he had better allow her to become accustomed to his presence in the house. His mother had attempted to ridicule him, because he was, as she said, afraid of a woman. He well remembered that he had never been afraid of Emily Wharton when they had been quite young,—little more than a boy and girl together. Then he had told her of his love over and over again, and had found almost a comfortable luxury in urging her to say a word, which she had never indeed said, but which probably in those days he still hoped that she would say. And occasionally he had feigned to be angry with her, and had tempted her on to little quarrels with a boyish idea that quick reconciliation would perhaps throw her into his arms. But now it seemed to him that an age had passed since those days. His love had certainly not faded. There had never been a moment when that had been on the wing. But now the azure plumage of his love had become grey as the wings of a dove, and the gorgeousness of his dreams had sobered into hopes and fears which were a constant burden to his heart. There was time enough, still time enough for happiness if she would yield;—and time enough for the dull pressure of unsatisfied aspirations should she persist in her refusal.

At last he saw her, almost by accident, and that meeting certainly was not fit for the purpose of his suit. He called at Stone Buildings the day after her arrival, and found her at her father's chambers. She had come there keeping some appointment with him, and certainly had not expected to meet her lover. He was confused and hardly able to say a word to account for his presence, but she greeted him with almost sisterly affection, saying some word of Longbarns and his family, telling him how Everett, to Sir Alured's great delight, had been sworn in as a magistrate for the County, and how at the last hunt meeting John Fletcher had been asked to take the County hounds, because old Lord Weobly at seventy-five had declared himself to be unable any longer to ride as a master of hounds ought to ride. All these things Arthur had of course heard, such news being too important to be kept long from him; but on none of these subjects had he much to say. He stuttered and stammered, and quickly went away;—not, however, before he had promised to come and dine as usual on the next Sunday, and not without observing that the anniversary of that fatal day of release had done something to lighten the sombre load of mourning which the widow had hitherto worn.

Yes;—he would dine there on the Sunday, but how would it be with him then? Mr. Wharton never went out of the house on a Sunday evening, and could hardly be expected to leave his own drawing-room for the sake of giving a lover an opportunity. No;—he must wait till that evening should have passed, and then make the occasion for himself as best he might. The Sunday came and the dinner was eaten, and after dinner there was the single bottle of port and the single bottle of claret. "How do you think she is looking?" asked the father. "She was as pale as death before we got her down into the country."

"Upon my word, sir," said he, "I've hardly looked at her. It is not a matter of looks now, as it used to be. It has got beyond that. It is not that I am indifferent to seeing a pretty face, or that I have no longer an opinion of my own about a woman's figure. But there grows up, I think, a longing which almost kills that consideration."

"To me she is as beautiful as ever," said the father proudly.

Fletcher did manage, when in the drawing-room, to talk for a while about John and the hounds, and then went away, having resolved that he would come again on the very next day. Surely she would not give an order that he should be denied admittance. She had been too calm, too even, too confident in herself for that. Yes;—he would come and tell her plainly what he had to say. He would tell it with all the solemnity of which he was capable, with a few words, and those the strongest which he could use. Should she refuse him,—as he almost knew that she would at first,—then he would tell her of her father and of the wishes of all their joint friends. "Nothing," he would say to her, "nothing but personal dislike can justify you in refusing to heal so many wounds." As he fixed on these words he failed to remember how little probable it is that a lover should ever be able to use the phrases he arranges.

On Monday he came, and asked for Mrs. Lopez, slurring over the word as best he could. The butler said his mistress was at home. Since the death of the man he had so thoroughly despised, the old servant had never called her Mrs. Lopez. Arthur was shown upstairs, and found the lady he sought,—but he found Mrs. Roby also. It may be remembered that Mrs. Roby, after the tragedy, had been refused admittance into Mr. Wharton's house. Since that there had been some correspondence, and a feeling had prevailed that the woman was not to be quarrelled with for ever. "I did not do it, papa, because of her," Emily had said with some scorn, and that scorn had procured Mrs. Roby's pardon. She was now making a morning call, and suiting her conversation to the black dress of her niece. Arthur was horrified at seeing her. Mrs. Roby had always been to him odious, not only as a personal enemy but as a vulgar woman. He, at any rate, attributed to her a great part of the evil that had been done, feeling sure that had there been no house round the corner, Emily Wharton would never have become Mrs. Lopez. As it was he was forced to shake hands with her, and forced to listen to the funereal tone in which Mrs. Roby asked him if he did not think that Mrs. Lopez looked much improved by her sojourn in Herefordshire. He shrank at the sound, and then, in order that it might not be repeated, took occasion to show that he was allowed to call his early playmate by her Christian name. Mrs. Roby, thinking that she ought to check him, remarked that Mrs. Lopez's return was a great thing for Mr. Wharton. Thereupon Arthur Fletcher seized his hat off the ground, wished them both good-bye, and hurried out of the room. "What a very odd manner he has taken up since he became a member of Parliament," said Mrs. Roby.

Emily was silent for a moment, and then with an effort,—with intense pain,—she said a word or two which she thought had better be at once spoken. "He went because he does not like to hear that name."

"Good gracious!"

"And papa does not like it. Don't say a word about it, aunt; pray don't;—but call me Emily."

"Are you going to be ashamed of your name?"

"Never mind, aunt. If you think it wrong you must stay away;—but I will not have papa wounded."

"Oh;—if Mr. Wharton wishes it;—of course." That evening Mrs. Roby told Dick Roby, her husband, what an old fool Mr. Wharton was.

The next day, quite early, Fletcher was again at the house and was again admitted upstairs. The butler, no doubt, knew well enough why he came, and also knew that the purport of his coming had at any rate the sanction of Mr. Wharton. The room was empty when he was shown into it, but she came to him very soon. "I went away yesterday rather abruptly," he said. "I hope you did not think me rude."

"Oh no."

"Your aunt was here, and I had something I wished to say but could not say very well before her."

"I knew that she had driven you away. You and Aunt Harriet were never great friends."

"Never;—but I will forgive her everything. I will forgive all the injuries that have been done me if you now will do as I ask you."

Of course she knew what it was that he was about to ask. When he had left her at Longbarns without saying a word of his love, without giving her any hint whereby she might allow herself to think that he intended to renew his suit, then she had wept because it was so. Though her resolution had been quite firm as to the duty which was incumbent on her of remaining in her desolate condition of almost nameless widowhood, yet she had been unable to refrain from bitter tears because he also had seemed to see that such was her duty. But now again, knowing that the request was coming, feeling once more confident of the constancy of his love, she was urgent with herself as to that heavy duty. She would be unwomanly, dead to all shame, almost inhuman, were she to allow herself again to indulge in love after all the havoc she had made. She had been little more than a bride when that husband, for whom she had so often been forced to blush, had been driven by the weight of his misfortunes and disgraces to destroy himself! By the marriage she had made she had overwhelmed her whole family with dishonour. She had done it with a persistency of perverse self-will which she herself could not now look back upon without wonder and horror. She, too, should have died as well as he,—only that death had not been within the compass of her powers as of his. How then could she forget it all, and wipe it away from her mind, as she would figures from a slate with a wet towel? How could it be fit that she should again be a bride with such a spectre of a husband haunting her memory? She had known that the request was to be made when he had come so quickly, and had not doubted it for a moment when he took his sudden departure. She had known it well, when just now the servant told her that Mr. Fletcher was in the drawing-room below. But she was quite certain of the answer she must make. "I should be sorry you should ask me anything I cannot do," she said in a very low voice.

"I will ask you for nothing for which I have not your father's sanction."

"The time has gone by, Arthur, in which I might well have been guided by my father. There comes a time when personal feelings must be stronger than a father's authority. Papa cannot see me with my own eyes; he cannot understand what I feel. It is simply this,—that he would have me to be other than I am. But I am what I have made myself."

"You have not heard me as yet. You will hear me?"

"Oh, yes."

"I have loved you ever since I was a boy." He paused as though he expected that she would make some answer to this; but of course there was nothing that she could say. "I have been true to you since we were together almost as children."

"It is your nature to be true."

"In this matter, at any rate, I shall never change. I never for a moment had a doubt about my love. There never has been any one else whom I have ventured to compare with you. Then came that great trouble. Emily, you must let me speak freely this once, as so much, to me at least, depends on it."

"Say what you will, Arthur. Do not wound me more than you can help."

"God knows how willingly I would heal every wound without a word if it could be done. I don't know whether you ever thought what I suffered when he came among us and robbed me,—well, I will not say robbed me of your love, because it was not mine—but took away with him that which I had been trying to win."

"I did not think a man would feel it like that."

"Why shouldn't a man feel as well as a woman? I had set my heart on having you for my wife. Can any desire be dearer to a man than that? Then he came. Well, dearest; surely I may say that he was not worthy of you."

"We were neither of us worthy," she said.

"I need not tell you that we all grieved. It seemed to us down in Herefordshire as though a black cloud had come upon us. We could not speak of you, nor yet could we be altogether silent."

"Of course you condemned me,—as an outcast."

"Did I write to you as though you were an outcast? Did I treat you when I saw you as an outcast? When I come to you to-day, is that proof that I think you to be an outcast? I have never deceived you, Emily."

"Never."

"Then you will believe me when I say that through it all not one word of reproach or contumely has ever passed my lips in regard to you. That you should have given yourself to one whom I could not think to be worthy of you was, of course, a great sorrow. Had he been a prince of men it would, of course, have been a sorrow to me. How it went with you during your married life I will not ask."

"I was unhappy. I would tell you everything if I could. I was very unhappy."

"Then came—the end." She was now weeping, with her face buried in her handkerchief. "I would spare you if I knew how, but there are some things which must be said."

"No;—no. I will bear it all—from you."

"Well! His success had not lessened my love. Though then I could have no hope,—though you were utterly removed from me,—all that could not change me. There it was,—as though my arm or my leg had been taken from me. It was bad to live without an arm or leg, but there was no help. I went on with my life and tried not to look like a whipped cur;—though John from time to time would tell me that I failed. But now;—now that it has again all changed,—what would you have me do now? It may be that after all my limb may be restored to me, that I may be again as other men are, whole, and sound, and happy;—so happy! When it may possibly be within my reach am I not to look for my happiness?" He paused, but she wept on without speaking a word. "There are those who will say that I should wait till all these signs of woe have been laid aside. But why should I wait? There has come a great blot upon your life, and is it not well that it should be covered as quickly as possible?"

"It can never be covered."

"You mean that it can never be forgotten. No doubt there are passages in our life which we cannot forget, though we bury them in the deepest silence. All this can never be driven out of your memory,—nor from mine. But it need not therefore blacken all our lives. In such a condition we should not be ruled by what the world thinks."

"Not at all. I care nothing for what the world thinks. I am below all that. It is what I think: I myself,—of myself."

"Will you think of no one else? Are any of your thoughts for me,—or for your father?"

"Oh, yes;—for my father."

"I need hardly tell you what he wishes. You must know how you can best give him back the comfort he has lost."

"But, Arthur, even for him I cannot do everything."

"There is one question to be asked," he said, rising from her feet and standing before her;—"but one; and what you do should depend entirely on the answer which you may be able truly to make to that."

This he said so solemnly that he startled her.

"What question, Arthur?"

"Do you love me?" To this question at the moment she could make no reply. "Of course I know that you did not love me when you married him."

"Love is not all of one kind."

"You know what love I mean. You did not love me then. You could not have loved me,—though, perhaps, I thought I had deserved your love. But love will change, and memory will sometimes bring back old fancies when the world has been stern and hard. When we were very young I think you loved me. Do you remember seven years ago at Longbarns, when they parted us and sent me away, because—because we were so young? They did not tell us then, but I think you knew. I know that I knew, and went nigh to swear that I would drown myself. You loved me then, Emily."

"I was a child then."

"Now you are not a child. Do you love me now,—to-day? If so, give me your hand, and let the past be buried in silence. All this has come, and gone, and has nearly made us old. But there is life before us yet, and if you are to me as I am to you it is better that our lives should be lived together." Then he stood before her with his hand stretched out.

"I cannot do it," she said.

"And why?"

"I cannot be other than the wretched thing I have made myself."

"But do you love me?"

"I cannot analyse my heart. Love you;—yes! I have always loved you. Everything about you is dear to me. I can triumph in your triumphs, rejoice at your joy, weep at your sorrows, be ever anxious that all good things may come to you;—but, Arthur, I cannot be your wife."

"Not though it would make us happy,—Fletchers and Whartons all alike?"

"Do you think I have not thought it over? Do you think that I have forgotten your first letter? Knowing your heart, as I do know it, do you imagine that I have spent a day, an hour, for months past, without asking myself what answer I should make to you if the sweet constancy of your nature should bring you again to me? I have trembled when I have heard your voice. My heart has beat at the sound of your footstep as though it would burst! Do you think I have never told myself what I had thrown away? But it is gone, and it is not now within my reach."

"It is; it is," he said, throwing himself on his knees, and twining his arms round her.

"No;—no;—no;—never. I am disgraced and shamed. I have lain among the pots till I am foul and blackened. Take your arms away. They shall not be defiled," she said as she sprang to her feet. "You shall not have the thing that he has left."

"Emily,—it is the only thing in the world that I crave."

"Be a man and conquer your love,—as I will. Get it under your feet and press it to death. Tell yourself that it is shameful and must be abandoned. That you, Arthur Fletcher, should marry the widow of that man,—the woman that he had thrust so far into the mire that she can never again be clean;—you, the chosen one, the bright star among us all;—you, whose wife should be the fairest, the purest, the tenderest of us all, a flower that has yet been hardly breathed on! While I— Arthur," she said, "I know my duty better than that. I will not seek an escape from my punishment in that way,—nor will I allow you to destroy yourself. You have my word as a woman that it shall not be so. Now I do not mind your knowing whether I love you or no." He stood silent before her, not able for the moment to go on with his prayer. "And now, go," she said. "God bless you, and give you some day a fair and happy wife. And, Arthur, do not come again to me. If you will let it be so, I shall have a delight in seeing you;—but not if you come as you have come now. And, Arthur, spare me with papa. Do not let him think that it is all my fault that I cannot do the thing which he wishes." Then she left the room before he could say another word to her.

But it was all her fault. No;—in that direction he could not spare her. It must be told to her father, though he doubted his own power of describing all that had been said. "Do not come again to me," she had said. At the moment he had been left speechless; but if there was one thing fixed in his mind, it was the determination to come again. He was sure now, not only of love that might have sufficed,—but of hot, passionate love. She had told him that her heart had beat at his footsteps, and that she had trembled as she listened to his voice;—and yet she expected that he would not come again! But there was a violence of decision about the woman which made him dread that he might still come in vain. She was so warped from herself by the conviction of her great mistake, so prone to take shame to herself for her own error, so keenly alive to the degradation to which she had been submitted, that it might yet be impossible to teach her that, though her husband had been vile and she mistaken, yet she had not been soiled by his baseness.

He went at once to the old barrister's chambers and told him the result of the meeting. "She is still a fool," said the father, not understanding at second-hand the depths of his daughter's feeling.

"No, sir,—not that. She feels herself degraded by his degradation. If it be possible we must save her from that."

"She did degrade herself."

"Not as she means it. She is not degraded in my eyes."

"Why should she not take the only means in her power of rescuing herself and rescuing us all from the evil that she did? She owes it to you, to me, and to her brother."

"I would hardly wish her to come to me in payment of such a debt."

"There is no room left," said Mr. Wharton angrily, "for soft sentimentality. Well;—she must take her bed as she makes it. It is very hard on me, I know. Considering what she used to be, it is marvellous to me that she should have so little idea left of doing her duty to others."

Arthur Fletcher found that the barrister was at the moment too angry to hear reason, or to be made to understand anything of the feelings of mixed love and admiration with which he himself was animated at the moment. He was obliged therefore to content himself with assuring the father that he did not intend to give up the pursuit of his daughter.

Chapter LXXV
The Great Wharton Alliance

When Mr. Wharton got home on that day he said not a word to Emily as to Arthur Fletcher. He had resolved to take various courses,—first to tell her roundly that she was neglecting her duty to herself and to her family, and that he would no longer take her part and be her good friend unless she would consent to marry the man whom she had confessed that she loved. But as he thought of this he became aware,—first that he could not carry out such a threat, and then that he would lack even the firmness to make it. There was something in her face, something even in her dress, something in her whole manner to himself, which softened him and reduced him to vassalage directly he saw her. Then he determined to throw himself on her compassion and to implore her to put an end to all this misery by making herself happy. But as he drew near home he found himself unable to do even this. How is a father to beseech his widowed daughter to give herself away in a second marriage? And therefore when he entered the house and found her waiting for him, he said nothing. At first she looked at him wistfully,—anxious to learn by his face whether her lover had been with him. But when he spoke not a word, simply kissing her in his usual quiet way, she became cheerful in manner and communicative. "Papa," she said, "I have had a letter from Mary."

"Well, my dear."

"Just a nice chatty letter,—full of Everett, of course."

"Everett is a great man now."

"I am sure that you are very glad that he is what he is. Will you see Mary's letter?" Mr. Wharton was not specially given to reading young ladies' correspondence, and did not know why this particular letter should be offered to him. "You don't suspect anything at Wharton, do you?" she asked.

"Suspect anything! No; I don't suspect anything." But now, having had his curiosity aroused, he took the letter which was offered to him and read it. The letter was as follows:—

Dearest Emily,—

We all hope that you had a pleasant journey up to London,
and that Mr. Wharton is quite well. Your brother Everett
came over to Longbarns the day after you started and
drove me back to Wharton in the dog-cart. It was such
a pleasant journey, though, now I remember, it rained
all the way. But Everett has always so much to say that I
didn't mind the rain. I think it will end in John taking the
hounds. He says he won't, because he does not wish to be
the slave of the whole county;—but he says it in that sort
of way that we all think he means to do it. Everett tells him
that he ought, because he is the only hunting man on this
side of the county who can afford to do it without feeling it
much; and of course what Everett says will go a long way
with him. Sarah [Sarah was John Fletcher's wife] is rather
against it. But if he makes up his mind she'll be sure to turn
round. Of course it makes us all very anxious at present to
know how it is to end, for the Master of the Hounds always
is the leading man in our part of the world. Papa went to
the bench at Ross yesterday and took Everett with him. It
was the first time that Everett had sat there. He says I am to
tell his father he has not hung anybody as yet.

They have already begun to cut down, or what they call
stubb up, Barnton Spinnies. Everett said that it is no good
keeping it as a wood, and papa agreed. So it is to go into
the home farm, and Griffiths is to pay rent for it. I don't
like having it cut down as the boys always used to get nuts
there, but Everett says it won't do to keep woods for little
boys to get nuts.

Mary Stocking has been very ill since you went, and I'm
afraid she won't last long. When they get to be so very
bad with rheumatism I almost think it's wrong to pray for
them, because they are in so much pain. We thought at one
time that mamma's ointment had done her good, but when
we came to inquire, we found she had swallowed it. Wasn't

it dreadful? But it didn't seem to do her any harm. Everett says that it wouldn't make any difference which she did.

Papa is beginning to be afraid that Everett is a Radical. But I'm sure he's not. He says he is as good a Conservative as there is in all Herefordshire, only that he likes to know what is to be conserved. Papa said after dinner yesterday that everything English ought to be maintained. Everett said that according to that we should have kept the Star Chamber. "Of course I would," said papa. Then they went at it, hammer and tongs. Everett had the best of it. At any rate he talked the longest. But I do hope he is not a Radical. No country gentleman ought to be a Radical. Ought he, dear?

Mrs. Fletcher says you are to get the lozenges at Squire's in Oxford Street, and be sure to ask for the Vade mecum lozenges. She is all in a flutter about the hounds. She says she hopes John will do nothing of the kind because of the expense; but we all know that she would like him to have them. The subscription is not very good, only £1500, and it would cost him ever so much a year. But everybody says that he is very rich and that he ought to do it. If you see Arthur give him our love. Of course a member of Parliament is too busy to write letters. But I don't think Arthur ever was good at writing. Everett says that men never ought to write letters. Give my love to Mr. Wharton.

I am, dearest Emily,
Your most affectionate Cousin,

Mary Wharton.

"Everett is a fool," said Mr. Wharton as soon as he had read the letter.

"Why is he a fool, papa?"

"Because he will quarrel with Sir Alured about politics before he knows where he is. What business has a young fellow like that to have an opinion either one side or the other, before his betters?"

"But Everett always had strong opinions."

"It didn't matter as long as he only talked nonsense at a club in London, but now he'll break that old man's heart."

"But, papa, don't you see anything else?"

"I see that John Fletcher is going to make an ass of himself and spend a thousand a year in keeping up a pack of hounds for other people to ride after."

"I think I see something else besides that."

"What do you see?"

"Would it annoy you if Everett were to become engaged to Mary?"

Then Mr. Wharton whistled. "To be sure she does put his name into every line of her letter. No; it wouldn't annoy me. I don't see why he shouldn't marry his second cousin if he likes. Only if he is engaged to her, I think it odd that he shouldn't write and tell us."

"I'm sure he's not engaged to her yet. She wouldn't write at all in that way if they were engaged. Everybody would be told at once, and Sir Alured would never be able to keep it a secret. Why should there be a secret? But I'm sure she is very fond of him. Mary would never write about any man in that way unless she were beginning to be attached to him."

About ten days after this there came two letters from Wharton Hall to Manchester Square, the shortest of which shall be given first. It ran as follows: —

> My dear Father, —
>
> I have proposed to my cousin Mary, and she has accepted me. Everybody here seems to like the idea. I hope it will not displease you. Of course you and Emily will come down. I will tell you when the day is fixed.
>
> Your affectionate son,
>
> Everett Wharton.

This the old man read as he sat at breakfast with his daughter opposite to him, while Emily was reading a very much longer letter from the same house. "So it's going to be just as you guessed," he said.

"I was quite sure of it, papa. Is that from Everett? Is he very happy?"

"Upon my word, I can't say whether he's happy or not. If he had got a new horse he would have written at much greater length about it. It seems, however, to be quite fixed."

"Oh, yes. This is from Mary. She is happy at any rate. I suppose men never say so much about these things as women."

"May I see Mary's letter?"

"I don't think it would be quite fair, papa. It's only a girl's rhapsody about the man she loves,—very nice and womanly, but not intended for any one but me. It does not seem that they mean to wait very long."

"Why should they wait? Is any day fixed?"

"Mary says that Everett talks about the middle of May. Of course you will go down."

"We must both go."

"You will at any rate. Don't promise for me just at present. It must make Sir Alured very happy. It is almost the same as finding himself at last with a son of his own. I suppose they will live at Wharton altogether now,—unless Everett gets into Parliament."

But the reader may see the young lady's letter, though her future father-in-law was not permitted to do so, and will perceive that there was a paragraph at the close of it which perhaps was more conducive to Emily's secrecy than her feelings as to the sacred obligations of female correspondence.

Monday, Wharton.

Dearest Emily,—

I wonder whether you will be much surprised at the news I have to tell you. You cannot be more so than I am at having to write it. It has all been so very sudden that I almost feel ashamed of myself. Everett has proposed to me, and I have accepted him. There;—now you know it all. Though you never can know how very dearly I love him and how thoroughly I admire him. I do think that he is everything that a man ought to be, and that I am the most fortunate young woman in the world. Only isn't it odd that I should always have to live all my life in the same house, and never change my name,—just like a man, or an old maid?

But I don't mind that because I do love him so dearly and because he is so good. I hope he will write to you and tell you that he likes me. He has written to Mr. Wharton, I know. I was sitting by him and his letter didn't take him a minute. But he says that long letters about such things only give trouble. I hope you won't think my letter troublesome. He is not sitting by me now but has gone over to Longbarns to help to settle about the hounds. John is going to have them after all. I wish it hadn't happened just at this time because all the gentlemen do think so much about it. Of course Everett is one of the committee.

Papa and mamma are both very, very glad of it. Of course it is nice for them as it will keep Everett and me here. If I had married anybody else,—though I am sure I never should,—she would have been very lonely. And of course papa likes to think that Everett is already one of us. I hope they never will quarrel about politics; but, as Everett says, the world does change as it goes on, and young men and old men never will think quite the same about things. Everett told papa the other day that if he could be put back a century he would be a Radical. Then there were ever so many words. But Everett always laughs, and at last papa comes round.

I can't tell you, my dear, what a fuss we are in already about it all. Everett wants to have our marriage early in May, so that we may have two months in Switzerland before London is what he calls turned loose. And papa says that there is no use in delaying, because he gets older every day. Of course that is true of everybody. So that we are all in a flutter about getting things. Mamma did talk of going up to town, but I believe they have things now quite as good at Hereford. Sarah, when she was married, had all her things from London, but they say that there has been a great change since that. I am sure that I think that you may get anything you want at Muddocks and Cramble's. But mamma says I am to have my veil from Howell and James's.

Of course you and Mr. Wharton will come. I shan't think it any marriage without. Papa and mamma talk of it as quite of course. You know how fond papa is of the bishop. I think he will marry us. I own I should like to be married by a bishop. It would make it so sweet and so solemn. Mr. Higgenbottom could of course assist;—but he is such an odd old man, with his snuff and his spectacles always tumbling off, that I shouldn't like to have no one else. I have often thought that if it were only for marrying people we ought to have a nicer rector at Wharton.

Almost all the tenants have been to wish me joy. They are very fond of Everett already, and now they feel that there will never be any very great change. I do think it is the very best thing that could be done, even if it were not that I am so thoroughly in love with him. I didn't think I should ever be able to own that I was in love with a man; but now I feel quite proud of it. I don't mind telling you because he is your brother, and I think that you will be glad of it.

He talks very often about you. Of course you know what it is that we all wish. I love Arthur Fletcher almost as much as if he were my brother. He is my sister's brother-in-law, and if he could become my husband's brother-in-law too, I should be so happy. Of course we all know that he wishes it. Write immediately to wish me joy. Perhaps you could go to Howell and James's about the veil. And promise to come to us in May. Sarah says the veil ought to cost about thirty pounds.

Dearest, dearest Emily,
I shall so soon be your most affectionate sister,

Mary Wharton.

Emily's answer was full of warm, affectionate congratulations. She had much to say in favour of Everett. She promised to use all her little skill at Howell and James's. She expressed a hope that the overtures to be made in regard to the bishop might be successful. And she made kind remarks even as to Muddocks and Cramble. But she would not promise that she herself would be at Wharton on the happy day. "Dear Mary," she said, "remember what I have suffered, and that I cannot be quite as other people are. I could not stand at your marriage in black clothes,—nor should I have the courage even if I had the will to dress myself in others." None of the Whartons had come to her wedding. There was no feeling of anger now left as to that. She was quite aware that they had done right to stay away. But the very fact that it had been right that they should stay away would make it wrong that the widow of Ferdinand Lopez should now assist at the marriage of one Wharton to another. This was all that a marriage ought to be; whereas that had been—all that a marriage ought not to be. In answer to the paragraph about Arthur Fletcher Emily Lopez had not a word to say.

Soon after this, early in April, Everett came up to town. Though his bride might be content to get her bridal clothes in Hereford, none but a London tailor could decorate him properly for such an occasion. During these last weeks Arthur Fletcher had not been seen in Manchester Square; nor had his name been mentioned there by Mr. Wharton. Of anything that may have passed between them Emily was altogether ignorant. She observed, or thought that she observed, that her father was more silent with her,—perhaps less tender than he had been since the day on which her husband had perished. His manner of life was the same. He almost always dined at home in order that she might not be alone, and made no complaint as to her conduct. But she could see that he was unhappy, and she knew the cause of his grief. "I think, papa," she said one day, "that it would be better that I should go away." This was on the day before Everett's arrival,—of which, however, he had given no notice.

"Go away! Where would you go to?"

"It does not matter. I do not make you happy."

"What do you mean? Who says that I am not happy? Why do you talk like that?"

"Do not be angry with me. Nobody says so. I can see it well enough. I know how good you are to me, but I am making your life wretched. I am a wet blanket to you, and yet I cannot help myself. If I could only go somewhere, where I could be of use."

"I don't know what you mean. This is your proper home."

"No;—it is not my home. I ought to have forfeited it. I ought to go where I could work and be of some use in the world."

"You might be of use if you chose, my dear. Your proper career is before you if you would condescend to accept it. It is not for me to persuade you, but I can see and feel the truth. Till you bring yourself to do that, your days will be blighted,—and so will mine. You have made one great mistake in life. Stop a moment. I do not speak often, but I wish you to listen to me now. Such mistakes do generally produce misery and ruin to all who are concerned. With you it chances that it may be otherwise. You can put your foot again upon the firm ground and recover everything. Of course there must be a struggle. One person has to struggle with circumstances, another with his foes, and a third with his own feelings. I can understand that there should be such a struggle with you; but it ought to be made. You ought to be brave enough and strong enough to conquer your regrets, and to begin again. In no other way can you do anything for me or for yourself. To talk of going away is childish nonsense. Whither would you go? I shall not urge you any more, but I would not have you talk to me in that way." Then he got up and left the room and the house, and went down to his club,—in order that she might think of what he had said in solitude.

And she did think of it;—but still continually with an assurance to herself that her father did not understand her feelings. The career of which he spoke was no doubt open to her, but she could not regard it as that which it was proper that she should fulfil, as he did. When she told her lover that she had lain among the pots till she was black and defiled, she expressed in the strongest language that which was her real conviction. He did not think her to have been defiled,—or at any rate thought that she might again bear the wings of a dove; but she felt it, and therefore knew herself to be unfit. She had said it all to her lover in the strongest words she could find, but she could not repeat them to her father. The next morning when he came into the parlour where she was already sitting, she looked up at him almost reproachfully. Did he think that a woman was a piece of furniture which you can mend, and revarnish, and fit out with new ornaments, and then send out for use, second-hand indeed, but for all purposes as good as new?

Then, while she was in this frame of mind, Everett came in upon her unawares, and with his almost boisterous happiness succeeded for a while in changing the current of her thoughts. He was of course now uppermost in his own thoughts. The last few months had made so much of him that he might be excused for being unable to sink himself in the presence of others. He was the heir to the baronetcy,—and to the double fortunes of the two old men. And he was going to be married in a manner as every one told him to increase the glory and stability of the family. "It's all nonsense about your not coming down," he said. She smiled and shook her head. "I can only tell you that it will give the greatest offence to every one. If you knew how much they talk about you down there I don't think you would like to hurt them."

"Of course I would not like to hurt them."

"And considering that you have no other brother—"

"Oh, Everett!"

"I think more about it, perhaps, than you do. I think you owe it me to come down. You will never probably have another chance of being present at your brother's marriage." This he said in a tone that was almost lachrymose.

"A wedding, Everett, should be merry."

"I don't know about that. It is a very serious sort of thing to my way of thinking. When Mary got your letter it nearly broke her heart. I think I have a right to expect it, and if you don't come I shall feel myself injured. I don't see what is the use of having a family if the members of it do not stick together. What would you think if I were to desert you?"

"Desert you, Everett?"

"Well, yes;—it is something of the kind. I have made my request, and you can comply with it or not as you please."

"I will go," she said very slowly. Then she left him and went to her own room to think in what description of garment she could appear at a wedding with the least violence to the conditions of her life.

"I have got her to say she'll come," he said to his father that evening. "If you leave her to me, I'll bring her round."

Soon after that,—within a day or two,—there came out a paragraph in one of the fashionable newspapers of the day, saying that an alliance had been arranged between the heir to the Wharton title and property and the daughter of the present baronet. I think that this had probably originated in the club gossip. I trust it did not spring directly from the activity or ambition of Everett himself.

Chapter LXXVI
Who Will It Be?

For the first day or two after the resignation of the Ministry the Duchess appeared to take no further notice of the matter. An ungrateful world had repudiated her and her husband, and he had foolishly assisted and given way to the repudiation. All her grand aspirations were at an end. All her triumphs were over. And worse than that, there was present to her a conviction that she never had really triumphed. There never had come the happy moment in which she had felt herself to be dominant over other women. She had toiled and struggled, she had battled and occasionally submitted; and yet there was present to her a feeling that she had stood higher in public estimation as Lady Glencora Palliser,—whose position had been all her own and had not depended on her husband,—than now she had done as Duchess of Omnium, and wife of the Prime Minister of England. She had meant to be something, she knew not what, greater than had been the wives of other Prime Ministers and other Dukes; and now she felt that in her failure she had been almost ridiculous. And the failure, she thought, had been his,—or hers,—rather than that of circumstances. If he had been less scrupulous and more persistent it might have been different,—or if she had been more discreet. Sometimes she felt her own failing so violently as to acquit him almost entirely. At other times she was almost beside herself with anger because all her losses seemed to have arisen from want of stubbornness on his part. When he had told her that he and his followers had determined to resign because they had beaten their foes by a majority only of nine, she took it into her head that he was in fault. Why should he go while his supporters were more numerous than his opponents? It was useless to bid him think it over again. Though she was far from understanding all the circumstances of the game, she did know that he could not remain after having arranged with his colleagues that he would go. So she became cross and sullen; and while he was going to Windsor and back and setting his house in order, and preparing the way for his successor,—whoever that successor might be,—she was moody and silent, dreaming over some impossible condition of things in accordance with which he might have remained Prime Minister—almost for ever.

On the Sunday after the fatal division,—the division which the Duchess would not allow to have been fatal,—she came across him somewhere in the house. She had hardly spoken to him since he had come into her room that night and told her that all was over. She had said that she was unwell and had kept out of sight; and he had been here and there, between Windsor and the Treasury Chambers, and had been glad to escape from her ill-humour. But she could not endure any longer the annoyance of having to get all her news through Mrs. Finn,—second hand, or third hand, and now found herself driven to capitulate. "Well," she said; "how is it all going to be? I suppose you do not know or you would have told me?"

"There is very little to tell."

"Mr. Monk is to be Prime Minister?" she asked.

"I did not say so. But it is not impossible."

"Has the Queen sent for him?"

"Not as yet. Her Majesty has seen both Mr. Gresham and Mr. Daubeny as well as myself. It does not seem a very easy thing to make a Ministry just at present."

"Why should not you go back?"

"I do not think that is on the cards."

"Why not? Ever so many men have done it, after going out,—and why not you? I remember Mr. Mildmay doing it twice. It is always the thing when the man who has been sent for makes a mess of it, for the old minister to have another chance."

"But what if the old minister will not take the chance?"

"Then it is the old minister's fault. Why shouldn't you take the chance as well as another? It isn't many days ago since you were quite anxious to remain in. I thought you were going to break your heart because people even talked of your going."

"I was going to break my heart, as you call it," he said, smiling, "not because people talked of my ceasing to be minister, but because the feeling of the House of Commons justified people in so saying. I hope you see the difference."

"No, I don't. And there is no difference. The people we are talking about are the members,—and they have supported you. You could go on if you chose. I'm sure Mr. Monk wouldn't leave you."

"It is just what Mr. Monk would do, and ought to do. No one is less likely than Mr. Monk to behave badly in such an emergency. The more I see of Mr. Monk, the higher I think of him."

"He has his own game to play as well as others."

"I think he has no game to play but that of his country. It is no use our discussing it, Cora."

"Of course I understand nothing, because I'm a woman."

"You understand a great deal,—but not quite all. You may at any rate understand this,—that our troubles are at an end. You were saying but the other day that the labours of being a Prime Minister's wife had been almost too many for you."

"I never said so. As long as you didn't give way no labour was too much for me. I would have done anything,—slaved morning and night,—so that we might have succeeded. I hate being beat. I'd sooner be cut in pieces."

"There is no help for it now, Cora. The Lord Mayor, you know, is only Lord Mayor for one year, and must then go back to private life."

"But men have been Prime Ministers for ten years at a time. If you have made up your mind, I suppose we may as well give up. I shall always think it your own fault." He still smiled. "I shall," she said.

"Oh, Cora!"

"I can only speak as I feel."

"I don't think you would speak as you do, if you knew how much your words hurt me. In such a matter as this I should not be justified in allowing your opinions to have weight with me. But your sympathy would be so much to me!"

"When I thought it was making you ill, I wished that you might be spared."

"My illness would be nothing, but my honour is everything. I, too, have something to bear as well as you, and if you cannot approve of what I do, at any rate be silent."

"Yes;—I can be silent." Then he slowly left her. As he went she was almost tempted to yield, and to throw herself into his arms, and to promise that she would be soft to him, and to say that she was sure that all he did was for the best. But she could not bring herself as yet to be good-humoured.

If he had only been a little stronger, a little thicker-skinned, made of clay a little coarser, a little other than he was, it might all have been so different!

Early on that Sunday afternoon she had herself driven to Mrs. Finn's house in Park Lane, instead of waiting for her friend. Latterly she had but seldom done this, finding that her presence at home was much wanted. She had been filled with, perhaps, foolish ideas of the necessity of doing something,—of adding something to the strength of her husband's position,—and had certainly been diligent in her work. But now she might run about like any other woman. "This is an honour, Duchess," said Mrs. Finn.

"Don't be sarcastic, Marie. We have nothing further to do with the bestowal of honours. Why didn't he make everybody a peer or a baronet while he was about it? Lord Finn! I don't see why he shouldn't have been Lord Finn. I'm sure he deserved it for the way in which he attacked Sir Timothy Beeswax."

"I don't think he'd like it."

"They all say so, but I suppose they do like it, or they wouldn't take it. And I'd have made Locock a knight;—Sir James Locock. He'd make a more knightly knight than Sir Timothy. When a man has power he ought to use it. It makes people respect him. Mr. Daubeny made a duke, and people think more of that than anything he did. Is Mr. Finn going to join the new ministry?"

"If you can tell me, Duchess, who is to be the new minister, I can give a guess."

"Mr. Monk."

"Then he certainly will."

"Or Mr. Daubeny."

"Then he certainly won't."

"Or Mr. Gresham."

"That I could not answer."

"Or the Duke of Omnium."

"That would depend upon his Grace, If the Duke came back, Mr. Finn's services would be at his disposal, whether in or out of office."

"Very prettily said, my dear. I never look round this room without thinking of the first time I came here. Do you remember, when I found the old man sitting there?" The old man alluded to was the late Duke.

"I am not likely to forget it, Duchess."

"How I hated you when I saw you! What a fright I thought you were! I pictured you to myself as a sort of ogre, willing to eat up everybody for the gratification of your own vanity."

"I was very vain, but there was a little pride with it."

"And now it has come to pass that I can't very well live without you. How he did love you!"

"His Grace was very good to me."

"It would have done no great harm, after all, if he had made you Duchess of Omnium."

"Very great harm to me, Lady Glen. As it is I got a friend that I loved dearly, and a husband that I love dearly too. In the other case I should have had neither. Perhaps I may say, that in that other case my life would not have been brightened by the affection of the present Duchess."

"One can't tell how it would have gone, but I well remember the state I was in then." The door was opened and Phineas Finn entered the room. "What, Mr. Finn, are you at home? I thought everybody was crowding down at the clubs, to know who is to be what. We are settled. We are quiet. We have nothing to do to disturb ourselves. But you ought to be in all the flutter of renewed expectation."

"I am waiting my destiny in calm seclusion. I hope the Duke is well?"

"As well as can be expected. He doesn't walk about his room with a poniard in his hand,—ready for himself or Sir Orlando; nor is he sitting crowned like Bacchus, drinking the health of the new Ministry with Lord Drummond and Sir Timothy. He is probably sipping a cup of coffee over a blue-book in dignified retirement. You should go and see him."

"I should be unwilling to trouble him when he is so much occupied."

"That is just what has done him all the harm in the world. Everybody presumes that he has so much to think of that nobody goes near him. Then he is left to boody over everything by himself till he becomes a sort of political hermit, or ministerial Lama, whom human eyes are not to look upon. It doesn't matter now; does it?" Visitor after visitor came in, and the Duchess chatted to them all, leaving the impression on everybody that heard her that she at least was not sorry to be relieved from the troubles attending her husband's late position.

She sat there over an hour, and as she was taking her leave she had a few words to whisper to Mrs. Finn. "When this is all over," she said, "I mean to call on that Mrs. Lopez."

"I thought you did go there."

"That was soon after the poor man had killed himself,—when she was going away. Of course I only left a card. But I shall see her now if I can. We want to get her out of her melancholy if possible. I have a sort of feeling, you know, that among us we made the train run over him."

"I don't think that."

"He got so horribly abused for what he did at Silverbridge; and I really don't see why he wasn't to have his money. It was I that made him spend it."

"He was, I fancy, a thoroughly bad man."

"But a wife doesn't always want to be made a widow even if her husband be bad. I think I owe her something, and I would pay my debt if I knew how. I shall go and see her, and if she will marry this other man we'll take her by the hand. Good-bye, dear. You'd better come to me early to-morrow, as I suppose we shall know something by eleven o'clock."

In the course of that evening the Duke of St. Bungay came to Carlton Terrace and was closeted for some time with the late Prime Minister. He had been engaged during that and the last two previous days in lending his aid to various political man[oe]uvres and ministerial attempts, from which our Duke had kept himself altogether aloof. He did not go to Windsor, but as each successive competitor journeyed thither and returned, some one either sent for the old Duke or went to seek his counsel. He was the Nestor of the occasion, and strove heartily to compose all quarrels, and so to arrange matters that a wholesome, moderately Liberal Ministry might be again installed for the good of the country and the comfort of all true Whigs. In such moments he almost ascended to the grand heights of patriotism, being always indifferent as to himself. Now he came to his late chief with a new project. Mr. Gresham would attempt to form a Ministry if the Duke of Omnium would join him.

"It is impossible," said the younger politician, folding his hands together and throwing himself back in his chair.

"Listen to me before you answer me with such certainty. There are three or four gentlemen who, after the work of the last three years, bearing in mind the manner in which our defeat has just been accomplished, feel themselves disinclined to join Mr. Gresham unless you will do so also. I may specially name Mr. Monk and Mr. Finn. I might perhaps add myself, were it not that I had hoped that in any event I might at length regard myself as exempt from further service. The old horse should be left to graze out his last days, Ne peccet ad extremum ridendus. But you can't consider yourself absolved on that score."

"There are other reasons."

"But the Queen's service should count before everything. Gresham and Cantrip with their own friends can hardly make a Ministry as things are now unless Mr. Monk will join them. I do not think that any other Chancellor of the Exchequer is at present possible."

"I will beseech Mr. Monk not to let any feeling as to me stand in his way. Why should it?"

"It is not only what you may think and he may think,—but what others will think and say. The Coalition will have done all that ought to have been expected from it if our party in it can now join Mr. Gresham."

"By all means. But I could give them no strength. They may be sure at any rate of what little I can do for them out of office."

"Mr. Gresham has made his acceptance of office,—well, I will not say strictly conditional on your joining him. That would hardly be correct. But he has expressed himself quite willing to make the attempt with your aid, and doubtful whether he can succeed without it. He suggests that you should join him as President of the Council."

"And you?"

"If I were wanted at all I should take the Privy Seal."

"Certainly not, my friend. If there were any question of my return we would reverse the offices. But I think I may say that my mind is fixed. If you wish it I will see Mr. Monk, and do all that I can to get him to go with you. But for myself,—I feel that it would be useless."

At last, at the Duke's pressing request, he agreed to take twenty-four hours before he gave his final answer to the proposition.

Chapter LXXVII
The Duchess in Manchester Square

The Duke said not a word to his wife as to this new proposition, and when she asked him what tidings their old friend had brought as to the state of affairs, he almost told a fib in his anxiety to escape from her persecution. "He is in some doubt what he means to do himself," said the Duke. The Duchess asked many questions, but got no satisfactory reply to any of them. Nor did Mrs. Finn learn anything from her husband, whom, however, she did not interrogate very closely. She would be contented to know when the proper time might come for ladies to be informed. The Duke, however, was determined to take his twenty-four hours all alone,—or at any rate not to be driven to his decision by feminine interference.

In the meantime the Duchess went to Manchester Square intent on performing certain good offices on behalf of the poor widow. It may be doubted whether she had clearly made up her mind what it was that she could do, though she was clear that some debt was due by her to Mrs. Lopez. And she knew too in what direction assistance might be serviceable, if only it could in this case be given. She had heard that the present member for Silverbridge had been the lady's lover long before Mr. Lopez had come upon the scene, and with those feminine wiles of which she was a perfect mistress she had extracted from him a confession that his mind was unaltered. She liked Arthur Fletcher,—as indeed she had for a time liked Ferdinand Lopez,—and felt that her conscience would be easier if she could assist in this good work. She built castles in the air as to the presence of the bride and bridegroom at Matching, thinking how she might thus repair the evil she had done. But her heart misgave her a little as she drew near to the house, and remembered how very slight was her acquaintance and how extremely delicate the mission on which she had come. But she was not the woman to turn back when she had once put her foot to any work; and she was driven up to the door in Manchester Square without any expressed hesitation on her own part. "Yes,—his mistress was at home," said the butler, still shrinking at the sound of the name which he hated. The Duchess was then shown upstairs, and was left alone for some minutes in the drawing-room. It was a large handsome apartment, hung round with valuable pictures, and having signs of considerable wealth. Since she had first invited Lopez to stand for Silverbridge she had heard much about him, and had wondered how he had gained possession of such a girl as Emily Wharton. And now, as she looked about, her wonder was increased. She knew enough of such people as the Whartons and the Fletchers to be aware that as a class they are more impregnable, more closely guarded by their feelings and prejudices against strangers than any other. None keep their daughters to themselves with greater care, or are less willing to see their rules of life changed or abolished. And yet this man, half foreigner half Jew,—and as it now appeared, whole pauper,—had stepped in and carried off a prize for which such a one as Arthur Fletcher was contending! The Duchess had never seen Emily but once,—so as to observe her well,—and had then thought her to be a very handsome woman. It had been at the garden party at Richmond, and Lopez had then insisted that his wife should be well dressed. It would perhaps have been impossible in the whole of that assembly to find a more beautiful woman than Mrs. Lopez then was,—or one who carried herself with a finer air. Now when she entered the room in her deep mourning it would have been difficult to recognise her. Her face was much thinner, her eyes apparently larger, and her colour faded. And there had come a settled seriousness on her face which seemed to rob her of her youth. Arthur Fletcher had declared that as he saw her now she was more beautiful than ever. But Arthur Fletcher, in looking at her, saw more than her mere features. To his eyes there was a tenderness added by her sorrow which had its own attraction for him. And he was so well versed in every line of her countenance, that he could see there the old loveliness behind the sorrow; the loveliness which would come forth again, as bright as ever, if the sorrow could be removed. But the Duchess, though she remembered the woman's beauty as she might that of any other lady, now saw nothing but a thing of woe wrapped in customary widow's weeds. "I hope," she said, "I am not intruding in coming to you; but I have been anxious to renew our acquaintance for reasons which I am sure you will understand."

Emily at the moment hardly knew how to address her august visitor. Though her father had lived all his life in what is called good society, he had not consorted much with dukes and duchesses. She herself had indeed on one occasion been for an hour or two the guest of this grand lady, but on that occasion she had hardly been called upon to talk to her. Now she doubted how to name the Duchess, and with some show of hesitation decided at last upon not naming her at all. "It is very good of you to come," she said in a faltering voice.

"I told you that I would when I wrote, you know. That is many months ago, but I have not forgotten it. You have been in the country since that, I think?"

"Yes, in Herefordshire. Herefordshire is our county."

"I know all about it," said the Duchess, smiling. She generally did contrive to learn "all about" the people whom she chose to take by the hand. "We have a Herefordshire gentleman sitting for,—I must not say our borough of Silverbridge." She was anxious to make some allusion to Arthur Fletcher; but it was difficult to travel on that Silverbridge ground, as Lopez had been her chosen candidate when she still wished to claim the borough as an appanage of the Palliser family. Emily, however, kept her countenance and did not show by any sign that her thoughts were running in that direction. "And though we don't presume to regard Mr. Fletcher," continued the Duchess, "as in any way connected with our local interests, he has always supported the Duke, and I hope has become a friend of ours. I think he is a neighbour of yours in the country."

"Oh, yes. My cousin is married to his brother."

"I knew there was something of that kind. He told me that there was some close alliance." The Duchess as she looked at the woman to whom she wanted to be kind did not as yet dare to express a wish that there might at some not very distant time be a closer alliance. She had come there intending to do so; and had still some hope that she might do it before the interview was over. But at any rate she would not do it yet. "Have I not heard," she said, "something of another marriage?"

"My brother is going to marry his cousin, Sir Alured Wharton's daughter."

"Ah;—I thought it had been one of the Fletchers. It was our member who told me, and he spoke as though they were all his very dear friends."

"They are dear friends,—very." Poor Emily still didn't know whether to call her Duchess, my Lady, or your Grace,—and yet felt the need of calling her by some special name.

"Exactly. I supposed it was so. They tell me Mr. Fletcher will become quite a favourite in the House. At this present moment nobody knows on which side anybody is going to sit to-morrow. It may be that Mr. Fletcher will become the dire enemy of all the Duke's friends."

"I hope not."

"Of course I'm speaking of political enemies. Political enemies are often the best friends in the world; and I can assure you from my own experience that political friends are often the bitterest enemies. I never hated any people so much as some of our supporters." The Duchess made a grimace, and Emily could not refrain from smiling. "Yes, indeed. There's an old saying that misfortune makes strange bedfellows, but political friendship makes stranger alliances than misfortune. Perhaps you never met Sir Timothy Beeswax."

"Never."

"Well;—don't. But, as I was saying, there is no knowing who may support whom now. If I were asked who would be Prime Minister to-morrow, I should take half-a-dozen names and shake them in a bag."

"It is not settled then?"

"Settled! No, indeed. Nothing is settled." At that moment indeed everything was settled, though the Duchess did not know it. "And so we none of us can tell how Mr. Fletcher may stand with us when things are arranged. I suppose he calls himself a Conservative?"

"Oh, yes!"

"All the Whartons, I suppose, are Conservatives,—and all the Fletchers."

"Very nearly. Papa calls himself a Tory."

"A very much better name, to my thinking. We are all Whigs, of course. A Palliser who was not a Whig would be held to have disgraced himself for ever. Are not politics odd? A few years ago I only barely knew what the word meant, and that not correctly. Lately I have been so eager about it, that there hardly seems to be anything else left worth living for. I suppose it's wrong, but a state of pugnacity seems to me the greatest bliss which we can reach here on earth."

"I shouldn't like to be always fighting."

"That's because you haven't known Sir Timothy Beeswax and two or three other gentlemen whom I could name. The day will come, I dare say, when you will care for politics."

Emily was about to answer, hardly knowing what to say, when the door was opened and Mrs. Roby came into the room. The lady was not announced, and Emily had heard no knock at the door. She was forced to go through some ceremony of introduction. "This is my aunt, Mrs. Roby," she said. "Aunt Harriet, the Duchess of Omnium." Mrs. Roby was beside herself,—not all with joy. That feeling would come afterwards as she would boast to her friends of her new acquaintance. At present there was the embarrassment of not quite knowing how to behave herself. The Duchess bowed from her seat, and smiled sweetly,—as she had learned to smile since her husband had become Prime Minister. Mrs. Roby curtsied, and then remembered that in these days only housemaids ought to curtsey.

"Anything to our Mr. Roby?" said the Duchess, continuing her smile,— "ours as he was till yesterday at least." This she said in an absurd wail of mock sorrow.

"My brother-in-law, your Grace," said Mrs. Roby, delighted.

"Oh indeed. And what does Mr. Roby think about it, I wonder? But I dare say you have found, Mrs. Roby, that when a crisis comes,—a real crisis,—the ladies are told nothing. I have."

"I don't think, your Grace, that Mr. Roby ever divulges political secrets."

"Doesn't he indeed! What a dull man your brother-in-law must be to live with,—that is as a politician! Good-bye, Mrs. Lopez. You must come and see me and let me come to you again. I hope, you know,—I hope the time may come when things may once more be bright with you." These last words she murmured almost in a whisper, as she held the hand of the woman she wished to befriend. Then she bowed to Mrs. Roby, and left the room.

"What was it she said to you?" asked Mrs. Roby.

"Nothing in particular, Aunt Harriet."

"She seems to be very friendly. What made her come?"

"She wrote some time ago to say she would call."

"But why?"

"I cannot tell you. I don't know. Don't ask me, aunt, about things that are passed. You cannot do it without wounding me."

"I don't want to wound you, Emily, but I really think that that is nonsense. She is a very nice woman;—though I don't think she ought to have said that Mr. Roby is dull. Did Mr. Wharton know that she was coming?"

"He knew that she said she would come," replied Emily very sternly, so that Mrs. Roby found herself compelled to pass on to some other subject. Mrs. Roby had heard the wish expressed that something "once more might be bright," and when she got home told her husband that she was sure that Emily Lopez was going to marry Arthur Fletcher. "And why the d—

— shouldn't she?" said Dick. "And that poor man destroying himself not much more than twelve months ago! I couldn't do it," said Mrs. Roby. "I don't mean to give you the chance," said Dick.

The Duchess when she went away suffered under a sense of failure. She had intended to bring about some crisis of female tenderness in which she might have rushed into future hopes and joyous anticipations, and with the freedom which will come from ebullitions of feeling, have told the widow that the peculiar circumstances of her position would not only justify her in marrying this other man but absolutely called upon her to do it. Unfortunately she had failed in her attempt to bring the interview to a condition in which this would have been possible, and while she was still making the attempt that odious aunt had come in. "I have been on my mission," she said to Mrs. Finn afterwards.

"Have you done any good?"

"I don't think I've done any harm. Women, you know, are so very different! There are some who would delight to have an opportunity of opening their hearts to a Duchess, and who might almost be talked into anything in an ecstasy."

"Hardly women of the best sort, Lady Glen."

"Not of the best sort. But then one doesn't come across the very best, very often. But that kind of thing does have an effect; and as I only wanted to do good, I wish she had been one of the sort for the occasion."

"Was she—offended?"

"Oh dear, no. You don't suppose I attacked her with a husband at the first word. Indeed, I didn't attack her at all. She didn't give me an opportunity. Such a Niobe you never saw."

"Was she weeping?"

"Not actual tears. But her gown, and her cap, and her strings were weeping. Her voice wept, and her hair, and her nose, and her mouth. Don't you know that look of subdued mourning? And yet they say that that man is dying for love. How beautiful it is to see that there is such a thing as constancy left in the world."

When she got home she found that her husband had just returned from the old Duke's house, where he had met Mr. Monk, Mr. Gresham, and Lord Cantrip. "It's all settled at last," he said cheerfully.

Chapter LXXVIII
The New Ministry

When the ex-Prime Minister was left by himself after the departure of his old friend his first feeling had been one of regret that he had been weak enough to doubt at all. He had long since made up his mind that after all that had passed he could not return to office as a subordinate. That feeling as to the impropriety of Cæsar descending to serve under others which he had been foolish enough to express, had been strong with him from the very commencement of his Ministry. When first asked to take the place which he had filled the reason strong against it had been the conviction that it would probably exclude him from political work during the latter half of his life. The man who has written Q.C. after his name must abandon his practice behind the bar. As he then was, although he had already been driven by the unhappy circumstance of his peerage from the House of Commons which he loved so well, there were still open to him many fields of political work. But if he should once consent to stand on the top rung of the ladder, he could not, he thought, take a lower place without degradation. Till he should have been placed quite at the top no shifting his place from this higher to that lower office would injure him in his own estimation. The exigencies of the service and not defeat would produce such changes as that. But he could not go down from being Prime Minister and serve under some other chief without acknowledging himself to have been unfit for the place he had filled. Of all that he had quite assured himself. And yet he had allowed the old Duke to talk him into a doubt!

As he sat considering the question he acknowledged that there might have been room for doubt, though in the present emergency there certainly was none. He could imagine circumstances in which the experience of an individual in some special branch of his country's service might be of such paramount importance to the country as to make it incumbent on a man to sacrifice all personal feeling. But it was not so with him. There was nothing now which he could do, which another might not do as well. That blessed task of introducing decimals into all the commercial relations of British life, which had once kept him aloft in the air, floating as upon eagle's wings, had been denied him. If ever done it must be done from the House of Commons; and the people of the country had become deaf to the charms of that great reform. Othello's occupation was, in truth, altogether gone, and there was no reason by which he could justify to himself the step down in the world which the old Duke had proposed to him.

Early on the following morning he left Carlton Terrace on foot and walked as far as Mr. Monk's house, which was close to St. James's Street. Here at eleven o'clock he found his late Chancellor of the Exchequer in that state of tedious agitation in which a man is kept who does not yet know whether he is or is not to be one of the actors in the play just about to be performed. The Duke had never before been in Mr. Monk's very humble abode, and now caused some surprise. Mr. Monk knew that he might probably be sent for, but had not expected that any of the ex-Prime Ministers of the day would come to him. People had said that not improbably he himself might be the man,—but he himself had indulged in no such dream. Office had had no great charms for him;—and if there was one man of the late Government who could lay it down without a personal regret, it was Mr. Monk. "I wish you to come with me to the Duke's house in St. James's Square," said the late Prime Minister. "I think we shall find him at home."

"Certainly. I will come this moment." Then there was not a word spoken till the two men were in the street together. "Of course I am a little anxious," said Mr. Monk. "Have you anything to tell me before we get there?"

"You of course must return to office, Mr. Monk."

"With your Grace—I certainly will do so."

"And without, if there be the need. They who are wanted should be forthcoming. But perhaps you will let me postpone what I have to say till we see the Duke. What a charming morning;—is it not? How sweet it would be down in the country." March had gone out like a lamb, and even in London the early April days were sweet,—to be followed, no doubt, by the usual nipping inclemency of May. "I never can get over the feeling," continued the Duke, "that Parliament should sit for the six winter months, instead of in summer. If we met on the first of October, how glorious it would be to get away for the early spring!"

"Nothing less strong than grouse could break up Parliament," said Mr. Monk; "and then what would the pheasants and the foxes say?"

"It is giving up almost too much to our amusements. I used to think that I should like to move for a return of the number of hunting and shooting gentlemen in both Houses. I believe it would be a small minority."

"But their sons shoot, and their daughters hunt, and all their hangers-on would be against it."

"Custom is against us, Mr. Monk; that is it. Here we are. I hope my friend will not be out, looking up young Lords of the Treasury." The Duke of St. Bungay was not in search of cadets for the Government, but was at this very moment closeted with Mr. Gresham, and Mr. Gresham's especial friend Lord Cantrip. He had been at this work so long and so constantly that his very servants had their ministerial-crisis manners and felt and enjoyed the importance of the occasion. The two newcomers were soon allowed to enter the august conclave, and the five great senators greeted each other cordially. "I hope we have not come inopportunely," said the Duke of Omnium. Mr. Gresham assured him almost with hilarity that nothing could be less inopportune;—and then the Duke was sure that Mr. Gresham was to be the new Prime Minister, whoever might join him or whoever might refuse to do so. "I told my friend here," continued our Duke, laying his hand upon the old man's arm, "that I would give him his answer to a proposition he made me within twenty-four hours. But I find that I can do so without that delay."

"I trust your Grace's answer may be favourable to us," said Mr. Gresham,—who indeed did not doubt much that it would be so, seeing that Mr. Monk had accompanied him.

"I do not think that it will be unfavourable, though I cannot do as my friend has proposed."

"Any practicable arrangement—" began Mr. Gresham, with a frown, however, on his brow.

"The most practicable arrangement, I am sure, will be for you to form your Government without hampering yourself with a beaten predecessor."

"Not beaten," said Lord Cantrip.

"Certainly not," said the other Duke.

"It is because of your success that I ask your services," said Mr. Gresham.

"I have none to give,—none that I cannot better bestow out of office than in. I must ask you, gentlemen, to believe that I am quite fixed. Coming here with my friend Mr. Monk, I did not state my purpose to him; but I begged him to accompany me, fearing lest in my absence he should feel it incumbent on himself to sail in the same boat with his late colleague."

"I should prefer to do so," said Mr. Monk.

"Of course it is not for me to say what may be Mr. Gresham's ideas; but as my friend here suggested to me that, were I to return to office, Mr. Monk would do so also, I cannot be wrong in surmising that his services are desired." Mr. Gresham bowed assent. "I shall therefore take the liberty of telling Mr. Monk that I think he is bound to give his aid in the present emergency. Were I as happily placed as he is in being the possessor of a seat in the House of Commons, I too should hope that I might do something."

The four gentlemen, with eager pressure, begged the Duke to reconsider his decision. He could take this office and do nothing in it,—there being, as we all know, offices the holders of which are not called upon for work,—or he could take that place which would require him to labour like a galley slave. Would he be Privy Seal? Would he undertake the India Board? But the Duke of Omnium was at last resolute. Of this administration he would not at any rate be a member. Whether Cæsar might or might not at some future time condescend to command a legion, he could not do so when the purple had been but that moment stripped from his shoulders. He soon afterwards left the house with a repeated request to Mr. Monk that he would not follow his late chief's example.

"I regret it greatly," said Mr. Gresham when he was gone.

"There is no man," said Lord Cantrip, "whom all who know him more thoroughly respect."

"He has been worried," said the old Duke, "and must take time to recover himself. He has but one fault,—he is a little too conscientious, a little too scrupulous." Mr. Monk, of course, did join them, making one or two stipulations as he did so. He required that his friend Phineas Finn should be included in the Government. Mr. Gresham yielded, though poor Phineas was not among the most favoured friends of that statesman. And so the Government was formed, and the crisis was again over, and the lists which all the newspapers had been publishing for the last three days were republished in an amended and nearly correct condition. The triumph of the "People's Banner," as to the omission of the Duke, was of course complete. The editor had no hesitation in declaring that he, by his own sagacity and persistency, had made certain the exclusion of that very unfit and very pressing candidate for office.

The list was filled up after the usual fashion. For a while the dilettanti politicians of the clubs, and the strong-minded women who take an interest in such things, and the writers in newspapers, had almost doubted whether, in the emergency which had been supposed to be so peculiar, any Government could be formed. There had been,—so they had said,—peculiarities so peculiar that it might be that the much-dreaded deadlock had come at last. A Coalition had been possible and, though antagonistic to British feelings generally, had carried on the Government. But what might succeed the Coalition, nobody had known. The Radicals and Liberals together would be too strong for Mr. Daubeny and Sir Orlando. Mr. Gresham had no longer a party of his own at his back, and a second Coalition would be generally spurned. In this way there had been much political excitement, and a fair amount of consequent enjoyment. But after a few days the old men had rattled into their old places,—or, generally, old men into new places,—and it was understood that Mr. Gresham would be again supported by a majority.

As we grow old it is a matter of interest to watch how the natural gaps are filled in the two ranks of parliamentary workmen by whom the Government is carried on, either in the one interest or the other. Of course there must be gaps. Some men become too old,—though that is rarely the case. A Peel may perish, or even a Palmerston must die. Some men, though long supported by interest, family connection, or the loyalty of colleagues, are weighed down at last by their own incapacity and sink into peerages. Now and again a man cannot bear the bondage of office, and flies into rebellion and independence which would have been more respectable had it not been the result of discontent. Then the gaps must be filled. Whether on this side or on that, the candidates are first looked for among the sons of Earls and Dukes,—and not unnaturally, as the sons of Earls and Dukes may be educated for such work almost from their infancy. A few rise by the slow process of acknowledged fitness,—men who probably at first have not thought of office but are chosen because they are wanted, and whose careers are grudged them, not by their opponents or rivals, but by the Browns and Joneses of the world who cannot bear to see a Smith or a Walker become something so different to themselves. These men have a great weight to carry, and cannot always shake off the burden of their origin and live among begotten statesmen as though they too had been born to the manner. But perhaps the most wonderful ministerial phenomenon,—though now almost too common to be longer called a phenomenon,—is he who rises high in power and place by having made himself thoroughly detested and also,— alas for parliamentary cowardice!—thoroughly feared. Given sufficient audacity, a thick skin, and power to bear for a few years the evil looks and cold shoulders of his comrades, and that is the man most sure to make his way to some high seat. But the skin must be thicker than that of any animal known, and the audacity must be complete. To the man who will once shrink at the idea of being looked at askance for treachery, or hated for his ill condition, the career is impossible. But let him be obdurate, and the bid will come. "Not because I want him, do I ask for him," says some groaning chief of a party,—to himself, and also sufficiently aloud for others' ears,—"but because he stings me and goads me, and will drive me to madness as a foe." Then the pachydermatous one enters into the other's heaven, probably with the resolution already formed of ousting that unhappy angel. And so it was in the present instance. When Mr. Gresham's completed list was published to the world, the world was astonished to find that Sir Timothy was to be Mr. Gresham's Attorney-General. Sir Gregory Grogram became Lord Chancellor, and the Liberal chief was content to borrow his senior law adviser from the Conservative side of the late Coalition. It could not be that Mr. Gresham was very fond of Sir Timothy;—but Sir Timothy in the late debates had shown himself to be a man of whom a minister might well be afraid.

Immediately on leaving the old Duke's house, the late Premier went home to his wife, and, finding that she was out, waited for her return. Now that he had put his own decision beyond his own power he was anxious to let her know how it was to be with them. "I think it is settled at last," he said.

"And you are coming back?"

"Certainly not that. I believe I may say that Mr. Gresham is Prime Minister."

"Then he oughtn't to be," said the Duchess crossly.

"I am sorry that I must differ from you, my dear, because I think he is the fittest man in England for the place."

"And you?"

"I am a private gentleman who will now be able to devote more of his time to his wife and children than has hitherto been possible with him."

"How very nice! Do you mean to say that you like it?"

"I am sure that I ought to like it. At the present moment I am thinking more of what you will like."

"If you ask me, Plantagenet, you know I shall tell the truth."

"Then tell the truth."

"After drinking brandy so long I hardly think that 12s. claret will agree with my stomach. You ask for the truth, and there it is,—very plainly."

"Plain enough!"

"You asked, you know."

"And I am glad to have been told, even though that which you tell me is not pleasant hearing. When a man has been drinking too much brandy, it may be well that he should be put on a course of 12s. claret."

"He won't like it; and then,—it's kill or cure."

"I don't think you're gone so far, Cora, that we need fear that the remedy will be fatal."

"I am thinking of you rather than myself. I can make myself generally disagreeable, and get excitement in that way. But what will you do? It's all very well to talk of me and the children, but you can't bring in a Bill for reforming us. You can't make us go by decimals. You can't increase our consumption by lowering our taxation. I wish you had gone back to some Board." This she said looking up into his face with an anxiety which was half real and half burlesque.

"I had made up my mind to go back to no Board,—for the present. I was thinking that we could spend some months in Italy, Cora."

"What; for the summer;—so as to be in Rome in July! After that we could utilise the winter by visiting Norway."

"We might take Norway first."

"And be eaten up by mosquitoes! I've got to be too old to like travelling."

"What do you like, dear?"

"Nothing;—except being the Prime Minister's wife; and upon my word there were times when I didn't like that very much. I don't know anything else that I'm fit for. I wonder whether Mr. Gresham would let me go to him as housekeeper? Only we should have to lend him Gatherum, or there would be no room for the display of my abilities. Is Mr. Monk in?"

"He keeps his old office."

"And Mr. Finn?"

"I believe so; but in what place I don't know."

"And who else?"

"Our old friend the Duke, and Lord Cantrip, and Mr. Wilson,—and Sir Gregory will be Lord Chancellor."

"Just the old stupid Liberal team. Put their names in a bag and shake them, and you can always get a ministry. Well, Plantagenet;—I'll go anywhere you like to take me. I'll have something for the malaria at Rome, and something for the mosquitoes in Norway, and will make the best of it. But I don't see why you should run away in the middle of the Session. I would stay and pitch into them, all round, like a true ex-minister and independent member of Parliament." Then as he was leaving her she fired a last shot. "I hope you made Sir Orlando and Sir Timothy peers before you gave up."

It was not till two days after this that she read in one of the daily papers that Sir Timothy Beeswax was to be Attorney-General, and then her patience almost deserted her. To tell the truth, her husband had not dared to mention the appointment when he first saw her after hearing it. Her explosion first fell on the head of Phineas Finn, whom she found at home with his wife, deploring the necessity which had fallen upon him of filling the fainéant office of Chancellor of the Duchy of Lancaster. "Mr. Finn," she said, "I congratulate you on your colleagues."

"Your Grace is very good. I was at any rate introduced to many of them under the Duke's auspices."

"And ought, I think, to have seen enough of them to be ashamed of them. Such a regiment to march through Coventry with!"

"I do not doubt that we shall be good enough men for any enemies we may meet."

"It cannot but be that you should conquer all the world with such a hero among you as Sir Timothy Beeswax. The idea of Sir Timothy coming back again! What do you feel about it?"

"Very indifferent, Duchess. He won't interfere much with me, as I have an Attorney-General of my own. You see I'm especially safe."

"I do believe men would do anything," said the Duchess, turning to Mrs. Finn. "Of course I mean in the way of politics! But I did not think it possible that the Duke of St. Bungay should again be in the same Government with Sir Timothy Beeswax."

Chapter LXXIX
The Wharton Wedding

It was at last settled that the Wharton marriage should take place during the second week in June. There were various reasons for the postponement. In the first place Mary Wharton, after a few preliminary inquiries, found herself forced to declare that Messrs. Muddocks and Cramble could not send her forth equipped as she ought to be equipped for such a husband in so short a time. "Perhaps they do it quicker in London," she said to Everett with a soft regret, remembering the metropolitan glories of her sister's wedding. And then Arthur Fletcher could be present during the Whitsuntide holidays; and the presence of Arthur Fletcher was essential. And it was not only his presence at the altar that was needed;—Parliament was not so exacting but that he might have given that;—but it was considered by the united families to be highly desirable that he should on this occasion remain some days in the country. Emily had promised to attend the wedding, and would of course be at Wharton for at least a week. As soon as Everett had succeeded in wresting a promise from his sister, the tidings were conveyed to Fletcher. It was a great step gained. When in London she was her own mistress; but surrounded as she would be down in Herefordshire by Fletchers and Whartons, she must be stubborn indeed if she should still refuse to be taken back into the flock, and be made once more happy by marrying the man whom she confessed that she loved with her whole heart. The letter to Arthur Fletcher containing the news was from his brother John, and was written in a very business-like fashion. "We have put off Mary's marriage a few days, so that you and she should be down here together. If you mean to go on with it, now is your time." Arthur, in answer to this, merely said he would spend the Whitsuntide holidays at Longbarns.

It is probable that Emily herself had some idea in her own mind of what was being done to entrap her. Her brother's words to her had been so strong, and the occasion of his marriage was itself so sacred to her, that she had not been able to refuse his request. But from the moment that she had made the promise, she felt that she had greatly added to her own difficulties. That she could yield to Arthur never occurred to her. She was certain of her own persistency. Whatever might be the wishes of others, the fitness of things required that Arthur Fletcher's wife should not have been the widow of Ferdinand Lopez,—and required also that the woman who had married Ferdinand Lopez should bear the results of her own folly. Though since his death she had never spoken a syllable against him,—if those passionate words be excepted which Arthur himself had drawn from her,—still she had not refrained from acknowledging the truth to herself. He had been a man disgraced,—and she as his wife, having become his wife in opposition to the wishes of all her friends, was disgraced also. Let them do what they will with her, she would not soil Arthur Fletcher's name with this infamy. Such was still her steadfast resolution; but she knew that it would be, not endangered, but increased in difficulty by this visit to Herefordshire.

And then there were other troubles. "Papa," she said, "I must get a dress for Everett's marriage."

"Why not?"

"I can't bear, after all that I have cost you, putting you to such useless expense."

"It is not useless, and such expenses as that I can surely afford without groaning. Do it handsomely and you will please me best."

Then she went forth and chose her dress,—a grey silk, light enough not to throw quite a gloom on the brightness of the day, and yet dark enough to declare that she was not as other women are. The very act of purchasing this, almost blushing at her own request as she sat at the counter in her widow's weeds, was a pain to her. But she had no one whom she could employ. On such an occasion she could not ask her aunt Harriet to act for her, as her aunt was distrusted and disliked. And then there was the fitting on of the dress,—very grievous to her, as it was the first time since the heavy black mourning came home that she had clothed herself in other garments.

The day before that fixed for the marriage she and her father went down to Herefordshire together, the conversation on the way being all in respect to Everett. Where was he to live? What was he to do? What income would he require till he should inherit the good things which destiny had in store for him? The old man seemed to feel that Providence, having been so very good to his son in killing that other heir, had put rather a heavy burden on himself. "He'll want a house of his own, of course," he said, in a somewhat lachrymose tone.

"I suppose he'll spend a good deal of his time at Wharton."

"He won't be content to live in another man's house altogether, my dear; and Sir Alured can allow him nothing. It means, of course, that I must give him a thousand a year. It seems very natural to him, I dare say, but he might have asked the question before he took a wife to himself."

"You won't be angry with him, papa!"

"It's no good being angry. No;—I'm not angry. Only it seems that everybody is uncommonly well pleased without thinking who has to pay for the piper."

On that evening, at Wharton, Emily still wore her mourning dress. No one, indeed, dared to speak to her on the subject, and Mary was even afraid lest she might appear in black on the following day. We all know in what condition is a house on the eve of a marriage,—how the bride feels that all the world is going to be changed, and that therefore everything is for the moment disjointed; and how the rest of the household, including the servants, are led to share the feeling. Everett was of course away. He was over at Longbarns with the Fletchers, and was to be brought to Wharton Church on the following morning. Old Mrs. Fletcher was at Wharton Hall,—and the bishop, whose services had been happily secured. He was formally introduced to Mrs. Lopez, the use of the name for the occasion being absolutely necessary, and with all the smiling urbanity which as a bishop he was bound to possess, he was hardly able not to be funereal as he looked at her and remembered her story. Before the evening was over Mrs. Fletcher did venture to give a hint. "We are so glad you have come, my dear."

"I could not stay away when Everett said he wished it."

"It would have been wrong; yes, my dear,—wrong. It is your duty, and the duty of us all, to subordinate our feelings to those of others. Even sorrow may be selfish." Poor Emily listened but could make no reply. "It is sometimes harder for us to be mindful of others in our grief than in our joy. You should remember, dear, that there are some who will never be light-hearted again till they see you smile."

"Do not say that, Mrs. Fletcher."

"It is quite true;—and right that you should think of it. It will be particularly necessary that you should think of it to-morrow. You will have to wear a light dress, and—"

"I have come provided," said the widow.

"Try then to make your heart as light as your frock. You will be doing it for Everett's sake, and for your father's, and for Mary's sake—and Arthur's. You will be doing it for the sake of all of us on a day that should be joyous." She could not make any promise in reply to this homily, but in her heart of hearts she acknowledged that it was true, and declared to herself that she would make the effort required of her.

On the following morning the house was of course in confusion. There was to be a breakfast after the service, and after the breakfast the bride was to be taken away in a carriage and four as far as Hereford on her route to Paris;—but before the great breakfast there was of course a subsidiary breakfast,—or how could bishop, bride, or bridesmaids have sustained the ceremony? At this meal Emily did not appear, having begged for a cup of tea in her own room. The carriages to take the party to the church, which was but the other side of the park, were ordered at eleven, and at a quarter before eleven she appeared for the first time in her grey silk dress, and without a widow's cap. Everything was very plain, but the alteration was so great that it was impossible not to look at her. Even her father had not seen the change before. Not a word was said, though old Mrs. Fletcher's thanks were implied by the graciousness of her smile. As there were four bridesmaids and four other ladies besides the bride herself, in a few minutes she became obscured by the brightness of the others;—and then they were all packed in their carriages and taken to the church. The eyes which she most dreaded did not meet hers till they were all standing round the altar. It was only then that she saw Arthur Fletcher, who was there as her brother's best man, and it was then that he took her hand and held it for half a minute as though he never meant to part with it, hidden behind the wide-spread glories of the bridesmaids' finery.

The marriage was as sweet and solemn as a kind-hearted bishop could make it, and all the ladies looked particularly well. The veil from London,—with the orange wreath, also metropolitan,—was perfect, and as for the dress, I doubt whether any woman would have known it to be provincial. Everett looked the rising baronet, every inch of him, and the old barrister smiled and seemed, at least, to be well pleased. Then came the breakfast, and the speech-making, in which Arthur Fletcher shone triumphantly. It was a very nice wedding, and Mary Wharton,—as she had been and still was,—felt herself for a moment to be a heroine. But, through it all, there was present to the hearts of most of them a feeling that much more was to be effected, if possible, than this simple and cosy marriage, and that the fate of Mary Wharton was hardly so important to them as that of Emily Lopez.

When the carriage and four was gone there came upon the household the difficulty usual on such occasions of getting through the rest of the day. The bridesmaids retired and repacked their splendours so that they might come out fresh for other second-rate needs, and with the bridesmaids went the widow. Arthur Fletcher remained at Wharton with all the other Fletchers for the night, and was prepared to renew his suit on that very day, if an opportunity were given him; but Emily did not again show herself till a few minutes before dinner, and then she came down with all the appurtenances of mourning which she usually wore. The grey silk had been put on for the marriage ceremony and for that only. "You should have kept your dress at any rate for the day," said Mrs. Fletcher. She replied that she had changed it for Everett, and that as Everett was gone there was no further need for her to wear clothes unfitted to her position. Arthur would have cared very little for the clothes could he have had his way with the woman who wore them,—could he have had his way even so far as to have found himself alone with her for half-an-hour. But no such chance was his. She retreated from the party early, and did not show herself on the following morning till after he had started for Longbarns.

All the Fletchers went back,—not, however, with any intention on the part of Arthur to abandon his immediate attempt. The distance between the houses was not so great but that he could drive himself over at any time. "I shall go now," he said to Mr. Wharton, "because I have promised John to fish with him to-morrow, but I shall come over on Monday or Tuesday, and stay till I go back to town. I hope she will at any rate let me speak to her." The father said he would do his best, but that that obstinate resumption of her weeds on her brother's very wedding day had nearly broken his heart.

When the Fletchers were back at Longbarns, the two ladies were very severe on her. "It was downright obstinacy," said the squire's wife, "and it almost makes me think it would serve her right to leave her as she is."

"It's pride," said the old lady. "She won't give way. I said ever so much to her,—but it's no use. I feel it the more because we have all gone so much out of the way to be good to her after she had made such a fool of herself. If it goes on much longer, I shall never forgive her again."

"You'll have to forgive her, mother," said her eldest son, "let her sins be what they may,—or else you'll have to quarrel with Arthur."

"I do think it's very hard," said the old lady, taking herself out of the room. And it was hard. The offence in the first instance had been very great, and the forgiveness very difficult. But Mrs. Fletcher had lived long enough to know that when sons are thoroughly respectable a widowed mother has to do their bidding.

Emily, through the whole wedding day, and the next day, and day after day, remembered Mrs. Fletcher's words. "There are some who will never be light-hearted again till they see you smile." And the old woman had named her dearest friends, and had ended by naming Arthur Fletcher. She had then acknowledged to herself that it was her duty to smile in order that others might smile also. But how is one to smile with a heavy heart? Should one smile and lie? And how long and to what good purpose can such forced contentment last? She had marred her whole life. In former days she had been proud of all her virgin glories,—proud of her intellect, proud of her beauty, proud of that obeisance which beauty, birth, and intellect combined, exact from all comers. She had been ambitious as to her future life;—had intended to be careful not to surrender herself to some empty fool;—had thought herself well qualified to pick her own steps. And this had come of it! They told her that she might still make everything right, annul the past and begin the world again as fresh as ever,—if she would only smile and study to forget! Do it for the sake of others, they said, and then it will be done for yourself also. But she could not conquer the past. The fire and water of repentance, adequate as they may be for eternity, cannot burn out or wash away the remorse of this life. They scorch and choke;—and unless it be so there is no repentance. So she told herself,—and yet it was her duty to be light-hearted that others around her might not be made miserable by her sorrow! If she could be in truth light-hearted, then would she know herself to be unfeeling and worthless.

On the third day after the marriage Arthur Fletcher came back to Wharton with the declared intention of remaining there till the end of the holidays. She could make no objection to such an arrangement, nor could she hasten her own return to London. That had been fixed before her departure and was to be made together with her father. She felt that she was being attacked with unfair weapons, and that undue advantage was taken of the sacrifice which she had made for her brother's sake. And yet,—yet how good to her they all were! How wonderful was it that after the thing she had done, after the disgrace she had brought on herself and them, after the destruction of all that pride which had once been hers, they should still wish to have her among them! As for him,—of whom she was always thinking,—of what nature must be his love, when he was willing to take to himself as his wife such a thing as she had made herself! But, thinking of this, she would only tell herself that as he would not protect himself, she was bound to be his protector. Yes;—she would protect him, though she could dream of a world of joy that might be hers if she could dare to do as he would ask her.

He caught her at last and forced her to come out with him into the grounds. He could tell his tale better as he walked by her side than sitting restlessly on a chair or moving awkwardly about the room as on such an occasion he would be sure to do. Within four walls she would have some advantage over him. She could sit still and be dignified in her stillness. But in the open air, when they would both be on their legs, she might not be so powerful with him, and he perhaps might be stronger with her. She could not refuse him when he asked her to walk with him. And why should she refuse him? Of course he must be allowed to utter his prayer,—and then she must be allowed to make her answer. "I think the marriage went off very well," he said.

"Very well. Everett ought to be a happy man."

"No doubt he will be,—when he settles down to something. Everything will come right for him. With some people things seem to go smooth; don't they? They have not hitherto gone smoothly with you and me, Emily."

"You are prosperous. You have everything before you that a man can wish, if only you will allow yourself to think so. Your profession is successful, and you are in Parliament, and everyone likes you."

"It is all nothing."

"That is the general discontent of the world."

"It is all nothing,—unless I have you too. Remember that I had said so long before I was successful, when I did not dream of Parliament; before we had heard of the name of the man who came between me and my happiness. I think I am entitled to be believed when I say so. I think I know my own mind. There are many men who would have been changed by the episode of such a marriage."

"You ought to have been changed by it,—and by its result."

"It had no such effect. Here I am, after it all, telling you as I used to tell you before, that I have to look to you for my happiness."

"You should be ashamed to confess it, Arthur."

"Never;—not to you, nor to all the world. I know what it has been. I know you are not now as you were then. You have been his wife, and are now his widow."

"That should be enough."

"But, such as you are, my happiness is in your hands. If it were not so, do you think that all my family as well as yours would join in wishing that you may become my wife? There is nothing to conceal. When you married that man you know what my mother thought of it; and what John thought of it, and his wife. They had wanted you to be my wife; and they want it now,—because they are anxious for my happiness. And your father wishes it, and your brother wishes it,—because they trust me, and think that I should be a good husband to you."

"Good!" she exclaimed, hardly knowing what she meant by repeating the word.

"After that you have no right to set yourself up to judge what may be best for my happiness. They who know how to judge are all united. Whatever you may have been, they believe that it will be good for me that you should now be my wife. After that you must talk about me no longer, unless you will talk of my wishes."

"Do you think I am not anxious for your happiness?"

"I do not know;—but I shall find out in time. That is what I have to say about myself. And as to you, is it not much the same? I know you love me. Whatever the feeling was that overcame you as to that other man,—it has gone. I cannot now stop to be tender and soft in my words. The thing to be said is too serious to me. And every friend you have wants you to marry the man you love and to put an end to the desolation which you have brought on yourself. There is not one among us all, Fletchers and Whartons, whose comfort does not more or less depend on your sacrificing the luxury of your own woe."

"Luxury!"

"Yes; luxury. No man ever had a right to say more positively to a woman that it was her duty to marry him, than I have to you. And I do say it. I say it on behalf of all of us, that it is your duty. I won't talk of my own love now, because you know it. You cannot doubt it. I won't even talk of yours, because I am sure of it. But I say that it is your duty to give up drowning us all in tears, burying us in desolation. You are one of us, and should do as all of us wish you. If, indeed, you could not love me it would be different. There! I have said what I've got to say. You are crying, and I will not take your answer now. I will come to you again to-morrow, and then you shall answer me. But, remember when you do so that the happiness of many people depends on what you say." Then he left her very suddenly and hurried back to the house by himself.

He had been very rough with her,—had not once attempted to touch her hand or even her arm, had spoken no soft word to her, speaking of his own love as a thing too certain to need further words; and he had declared himself to be so assured of her love that there was no favour for him now to ask, nothing for which he was bound to pray as a lover. All that was past. He had simply declared it to be her duty to marry him, and had told her so with much sternness. He had walked fast, compelling her to accompany him, had frowned at her, and had more than once stamped his foot upon the ground. During the whole interview she had been so near to weeping that she could hardly speak. Once or twice she had almost thought him to be cruel;—but he had forced her to acknowledge to herself that all that he had said was true and unanswerable. Had he pressed her for an answer at the moment she would not have known in what words to couch a refusal. And yet as she made her way alone back to the house she assured herself that she would have refused.

He had given her four-and-twenty hours, and at the end of that time she would be bound to give him her answer,—an answer which must then be final. And as she said this to herself she found that she was admitting a doubt. She hardly knew how not to doubt, knowing, as she did, that all whom she loved were on one side, while on the other was nothing but the stubbornness of her own convictions. But still the conviction was left to her. Over and over again she declared to herself that it was not fit, meaning thereby to assure herself that a higher duty even than that which she owed to her friends, demanded from her that she should be true to her convictions. She met him that day at dinner, but he hardly spoke to her. They sat together in the same room during the evening, but she hardly once heard his voice. It seemed to her that he avoided even looking at her. When they separated for the night he parted from her almost as though they had been strangers. Surely he was angry with her because she was stubborn,—thought evil of her because she would not do as others wished her! She lay awake during the long night thinking of it all. If it might be so! Oh;—if it might be so! If it might be done without utter ruin to her own self-respect as a woman!

In the morning she was down early,—not having anything to say, with no clear purpose as yet before her,—but still with a feeling that perhaps that morning might alter all things for her. He was the latest of the party, not coming in for prayers as did all the others, but taking his seat when the others had half finished their breakfast. As he sat down he gave a general half-uttered greeting to them all, but spoke no special word to any of them. It chanced that his seat was next to hers, but to her he did not address himself at all. Then the meal was over, and the chairs were withdrawn, and the party grouped itself about with vague, uncertain movements, as men and women do before they leave the breakfast table for the work of the day. She meditated her escape, but felt that she could not leave the room before Lady Wharton or Mrs. Fletcher,—who had remained at Wharton to keep her mother company for a while. At last they went;—but then, just as she was escaping, he put his hand upon her and reminded her of her appointment. "I shall be in the hall in a quarter of an hour," he said. "Will you meet me there?" Then she bowed her head to him and passed on.

She was there at the time named and found him standing by the hall door, waiting for her. His hat was already on his head and his back was almost turned to her. He opened the door, and, allowing her to pass out first, led the way to the shrubbery. He did not speak to her till he had closed behind her the little iron gate which separated the walk from the garden, and then he turned upon her with one word. "Well?" he said. She was silent for a moment, and then he repeated his eager question: "Well;—well?"

"I should disgrace you," she said, not firmly as before, but whispering the words.

He waited for no other assent. The form of the words told him that he had won the day. In a moment his arms were round her, and her veil was off, and his lips were pressed to hers;—and when she could see his countenance the whole form of his face was altered to her. It was bright as it used to be bright in old days, and he was smiling on her as he used to smile. "My own," he said;—"my wife—my own!" And she had no longer the power to deny him. "Not yet, Arthur; not yet," was all that she could say.

Chapter LXXX
The Last Meeting at Matching

The ex-Prime Minister did not carry out his purpose of leaving London in the middle of the season and travelling either to Italy or Norway. He was away from London at Whitsuntide longer perhaps than he might have been if still in office, and during this period regarded himself as a man from whose hands all work had been taken,—as one who had been found unfit to carry any longer a burden serviceably; but before June was over he and the Duchess were back in London, and gradually he allowed himself to open his mouth on this or that subject in the House of Lords,—not pitching into everybody all round, as his wife had recommended, but expressing an opinion now and again, generally in support of his friends, with the dignity which should belong to a retired Prime Minister. The Duchess too recovered much of her good temper,—as far at least as the outward show went. One or two who knew her, especially Mrs. Finn, were aware that her hatred and her ideas of revenge were not laid aside; but she went on from day to day anathematizing her special enemies and abstained from reproaching her husband for his pusillanimity. Then came the question as to the autumn. "Let's have everybody down at Gatherum, just as we had before," said the Duchess.

The proposition almost took away the Duke's breath. "Why do you want a crowd, like that?"

"Just to show them that we are not beaten because we are turned out."

"But, inasmuch as we were turned out, we were beaten. And what has a gathering of people at my private house to do with a political man[oe]uvre? Do you especially want to go to Gatherum?"

"I hate the place. You know I do."

"Then why should you propose to go there?" He hardly yet knew his wife well enough to understand that the suggestion had been a joke. "If you don't wish to go abroad—"

"I hate going abroad."

"Then we'll remain at Matching. You don't hate Matching."

"Ah dear! There are memories there too. But you like it."

"My books are there."

"Blue-books," said the Duchess.

"And there is plenty of room if you wish to have friends."

"I suppose we must have somebody. You can't live without your Mentor."

"You can ask whom you please," he said almost fretfully.

"Lady Rosina, of course," suggested the Duchess. Then he turned to the papers before him and wouldn't say another word. The matter ended in a party much as usual being collected at Matching about the middle of October,—Telemachus having spent the early part of the autumn with Mentor at Long Royston. There might perhaps be a dozen guests in the house, and among them of course were Phineas Finn and his wife. And Mr. Grey was there, having come back from his eastern mission,—whose unfortunate abandonment of his seat at Silverbridge had caused so many troubles,—and Mrs. Grey, who in days now long passed had been almost as necessary to Lady Glencora as was now her later friend Mrs. Finn,—and the Cantrips, and for a short time the St. Bungays. But Lady Rosina De Courcy on this occasion was not present. There were few there whom my patient readers have not seen at Matching before; but among those few was Arthur Fletcher.

"So it is to be," said the Duchess to the member for Silverbridge one morning. She had by this time become intimate with "her member," as she would sometimes call him in joke, and had concerned herself much as to his matrimonial prospects.

"Yes, Duchess; it is to be,—unless some unforeseen circumstance should arise."

"What circumstance?"

"Ladies and gentlemen sometimes do change their minds;—but in this case I do not think it likely."

"And why ain't you being married now, Mr. Fletcher?"

"We have agreed to postpone it till next year;—so that we may be quite sure of our own minds."

"I know you are laughing at me; but nevertheless I am very glad that it is settled. Pray tell her from me that I shall call again as soon as ever she is Mrs. Fletcher, though I don't think she repaid either of the last two visits I made her."

"You must make excuses for her, Duchess."

"Of course. I know. After all she is a most fortunate woman. And as for you,—I regard you as a hero among lovers."

"I'm getting used to it," she said one day to Mrs. Finn.

"Of course you'll get used to it. We get used to anything that chance sends us in a marvellously short time."

"What I mean is that I can go to bed, and sleep, and get up and eat my meals without missing the sound of the trumpets so much as I did at first. I remember hearing of people who lived in a mill, and couldn't sleep when the mill stopped. It was like that with me when our mill stopped at first. I had got myself so used to the excitement of it, that I could hardly live without it."

"You might have all the excitement still, if you pleased. You need not be dead to politics because your husband is not Prime Minister."

"No; never again,—unless he should come back. If any one had told me ten years ago that I should have taken an interest in this or that man being in the Government, I should have laughed him to scorn. It did not seem possible to me then that I should care what became of such men as Sir Timothy Beeswax and Mr. Roby. But I did get to be anxious about it when Plantagenet was shifted from one office to another."

"Of course you did. Do you think I am not anxious about Phineas?"

"But when he became Prime Minister, I gave myself up to it altogether. I shall never forget what I felt when he came to me and told me that perhaps it might be so;—but told me also that he would escape from it if it were possible. I was the Lady Macbeth of the occasion all over;—whereas he was so scrupulous, so burdened with conscience! As for me, I would have taken it by any means. Then it was that the old Duke played the part of the three witches to a nicety. Well, there hasn't been any absolute murder, and I haven't quite gone mad."

"Nor need you be afraid, though all the woods of Gatherum should come to Matching."

"God forbid! I will never see anything of Gatherum again. What annoys me most is, and always was, that he wouldn't understand what I felt about it;—how proud I was that he should be Prime Minister, how anxious that he should be great and noble in his office;—how I worked for him, and not at all for any pleasure of my own."

"I think he did feel it."

"No;—not as I did. At last he liked the power,—or rather feared the disgrace of losing it. But he had no idea of the personal grandeur of the place. He never understood that to be Prime Minister in England is as much as to be an Emperor in France, and much more than being President in America. Oh, how I did labour for him,—and how he did scold me for it with those quiet little stinging words of his! I was vulgar!"

"Is that a quiet word?"

"Yes;—as he used it;—and indiscreet, and ignorant, and stupid. I bore it all, though sometimes I was dying with vexation. Now it's all over, and here we are as humdrum as any one else. And the Beeswaxes, and the Robys, and the Droughts, and the Pountneys, and the Lopezes, have all passed over the scene! Do you remember that Pountney affair, and how he turned the poor man out of the house?"

"It served him right."

"It would have served them all right to be turned out,—only they were there for a purpose. I did like it in a way, and it makes me sad to think that the feeling can never come again. Even if they should have him back again, it would be a very lame affair to me then. I can never again rouse myself to the effort of preparing food and lodging for half the Parliament and their wives. I shall never again think that I can help to rule England by coaxing unpleasant men. It is done and gone, and can never come back again."

Not long after this the Duke took Mr. Monk, who had come down to Matching for a few days, out to the very spot on which he had sat when he indulged himself in lecturing Phineas Finn on Conservatism and Liberalism generally, and then asked the Chancellor of the Exchequer what he thought of the present state of public affairs. He himself had supported Mr. Gresham's government, and did not belong to it because he could not at present reconcile himself to filling any office. Mr. Monk did not scruple to say that in his opinion the present legitimate division of parties was preferable to the Coalition which had existed for three years. "In such an arrangement," said Mr. Monk, "there must always be a certain amount of distrust, and such a feeling is fatal to any great work."

"I think I distrusted no one till separation came,—and when it did come it was not caused by me."

"I am not blaming any one now," said the other; "but men who have been brought up with opinions altogether different, even with different instincts as to politics, who from their mother's milk have been nourished on codes of thought altogether opposed to each other, cannot work together with confidence even though they may desire the same thing. The very ideas which are sweet as honey to the one are bitter as gall to the other."

"You think, then, that we made a great mistake?"

"I will not say that," said Mr. Monk. "There was a difficulty at the time, and that difficulty was overcome. The Government was carried on, and was on the whole respected. History will give you credit for patriotism, patience, and courage. No man could have done it better than you did;—probably no other man of the day so well."

"But it was not a great part to play?" The Duke in his nervousness, as he said this, could not avoid the use of that questioning tone which requires an answer.

"Great enough to satisfy the heart of a man who has fortified himself against the evil side of ambition. After all, what is it that the Prime Minister of such a country as this should chiefly regard? Is it not the prosperity of the country? It is not often that we want great measures, or new arrangements that shall be vital to the country. Politicians now look for grievances, not because the grievances are heavy, but trusting that the honour of abolishing them may be great. It is the old story of the needy knife-grinder who, if left to himself, would have no grievance of which to complain."

"But there are grievances," said the Duke. "Look at monetary denominations. Look at our weights and measures."

"Well; yes. I will not say that everything has as yet been reduced to divine order. But when we took office three years ago we certainly did not intend to settle those difficulties."

"No, indeed," said the Duke, sadly.

"But we did do all that we meant to do. For my own part, there is only one thing in it that I regret, and one only which you should regret also till you have resolved to remedy it."

"What thing is that?"

"Your own retirement from official life. If the country is to lose your services for the long course of years during which you will probably sit in Parliament, then I shall think that the country has lost more than it has gained by the Coalition."

The Duke sat for a while silent, looking at the view, and, before answering Mr. Monk,—while arranging his answer,—once or twice in a half-absent way, called his companion's attention to the scene before him. But during this time he was going through an act of painful repentance. He was condemning himself for a word or two that had been ill-spoken by himself, and which, since the moment of its utterance, he had never ceased to remember with shame. He told himself now, after his own secret fashion, that he must do penance for these words by the humiliation of a direct contradiction of them. He must declare that Cæsar would at some future time be prepared to serve under Pompey. Then he made his answer. "Mr. Monk," he said, "I should be false if I were to deny that it pleases me to hear you say so. I have thought much of all that for the last two or three months. You may probably have seen that I am not a man endowed with that fortitude which enables many to bear vexations with an easy spirit. I am given to fretting, and I am inclined to think that a popular minister in a free country should be so constituted as to be free from that infirmity. I shall certainly never desire to be at the head of a Government again. For a few years I would prefer to remain out of office. But I will endeavour to look forward to a time when I may again perhaps be of some humble use."